J. R. Ward lives in the South with her incredibly supportive husband and her beloved golden retriever. After graduating from law school, she began working in health care in Boston and spent many years as chief of staff for one of the premier academic medical centres in the nation.

Visit her and the Black Dagger Brotherhood at www.jrward.com

LOVER
ETERNAL

J. R. WARD

piatkus

PIATKUS

First published in the United States in 2006 by New American Library,
A Division of Penguin Group (USA) Inc., New York
First published in Great Britain in 2007 by Piatkus Books
This paperback edition published in 2010 by Piatkus Books
Reprinted 2011

A CIP catalogue record for this book
is available from the British Library.

ISBN 978-0-7499-3819-2

Typeset in Garamond 3 by
Palimpsest Book Production Limited, Grangemouth, Stirlingshire
Printed in the UK by CPI Mackays, Chatham ME5 8TD

Piatkus
An imprint of
Little, Brown Book Group
100 Victoria Embankment
London EC4Y 0DY

An Hachette UK Company
www.hachette.co.uk

www.piatkus.co.uk

ACKNOWLEDGMENTS

With immense gratitude to the readers of the Black
Dagger Brotherhood.
Without you, the brothers wouldn't have a home on
the page.

Thank you so very much:
Karen Solem, Kara Cesare, Claire Zion, Kara Welsh,
Rose Hilliard.

With love to my family and friends,
and with continued reverence for my
Executive Committee:
Sue Grafton, Dr. Jessica Andersen, Betsey Vaughan.

GLOSSARY OF TERMS AND PROPER NOUNS

Black Dagger Brotherhood (pr. n.) Highly trained vampire warriors who protect their species against the Lessening Society. As a result of selective breeding within the race, brothers possess immense physical and mental strength as well as rapid healing capabilities. They are not siblings for the most part, and are inducted into the brotherhood upon nomination by the brothers. Aggressive, self-reliant, and secretive by nature, they exist apart from civilians, having little contact with members of the other classes except when they need to feed. They are the subjects of legend and the objects of reverence within the vampire world. They may be killed only by the most serious of wounds, e.g., a gunshot or stab to the heart, etc.

blood slave (n.) Male or female vampire who has been subjugated to serve the blood needs of another. The practice of keeping blood slaves has largely been discontinued, though it has not been outlawed.

the Chosen (n.) Female vampires who have been bred to serve the Scribe Virgin. They are considered members of the aristocracy, though they are spiritually rather than temporally focused. They have little or no inter-action with males, but can be mated to brothers at the Scribe Virgin's direction to propagate their class. They have the ability to prognosticate. In the past, they were used to meet the blood needs of unmated members of the brotherhood, but that practice has been abandoned by the brothers.

doggen (n.) Member of the servant class within the vampire world. *Doggen* have old, conservative traditions about service to their superiors, following a formal code of dress and behavior. They are able to go out during the day, but they age relatively quickly. Life expectancy is approximately five hundred years.

the Fade (pr. n.) Nontemporal realm where the dead reunite with their loved ones and pass eternity.

First Family (pr. n.) The king and queen of the vampires, and any children they may have.

hellren (n.) Male vampire who has been mated to a female. Males may take more than one female as a mate.

leelan (adj.) A term of endearment loosely translated as "dearest one."

Lessening Society (pr. n.) Order of slayers convened by the Omega for the purpose of eradicating the vampire species.

lesser (n.) De-souled human who as a member of the Lessening Society targets vampires for extermination. *Lessers* must be stabbed through the chest in order to be killed; otherwise they are ageless. They do not eat or drink and are impotent. Over time, their hair, skin, and irises lose pigmentation until they are blond, blush-less, and pale-eyed. They smell like baby powder. Inducted into the society by the Omega, they retain a ceramic jar thereafter into which their heart was placed after it was removed.

needing period (n.) Female vampire's time of fertility, generally lasting for two days and accompanied by intense sexual cravings. Occurs approximately five years after a female's transition and then once a decade there-after. All males respond to some degree if they are around a female in her need. It can be a dangerous time, with conflicts and fights breaking out between competing males, particularly if the female is not mated.

the Omega (pr. n.) Malevolent, mystical figure who has

targeted the vampires for extinction out of resentment directed toward the Scribe Virgin. Exists in a nontemporal realm and has extensive powers, though not the power of creation.

princeps (n.) Highest level of the vampire aristocracy, second only to members of the First Family or the Scribe Virgin's Chosen. Must be born to the title; it may not be conferred.

pyrocant (n.) Refers to a critical weakness in an individual. The weakness can be internal, such as an addiction, or external, such as a lover.

rythe (n.) Ritual manner of assuaging honor granted by one who has offended another. If accepted, the offended chooses a weapon and strikes the offender, who presents him- or herself without defenses.

the Scribe Virgin (pr. n.) Mystical force who is counselor to the king as well as the keeper of vampire archives and the dispenser of privileges. Exists in a nontemporal realm and has extensive powers. Capable of a single act of creation, which she expended to bring the vampires into existence.

shellan (n.) Female vampire who has been mated to a male. Females generally do not take more than one mate due to the highly territorial nature of bonded males.

the Tomb (pr. n.) Sacred vault of the Black Dagger Brotherhood. Used as a ceremonial site as well as a storage facility for the jars of *lessers*. Ceremonies performed there include inductions, funerals, and disciplinary actions against brothers. No one may enter except for members of the brotherhood, the Scribe Virgin, or candidates for induction.

transition (n.) Critical moment in a vampire's life when he or she transforms into an adult. Thereafter, they must drink the blood of the opposite sex to survive and are unable to withstand sunlight. Occurs generally in the mid-twenties. Some vampires do not survive their transitions, males in particular. Prior to their transitions, vampires are physically weak, sexually unaware and unresponsive, and unable to dematerialize.

vampire (n.) Member of a species separate from that of Homo sapiens. Vampires must drink the blood of the opposite sex to survive. Human blood will keep them alive, though the strength does not last long. Following their transitions, which occur in their mid-twenties, they are unable to go out into sunlight and must feed from the vein regularly. Vampires cannot "convert" humans through a bite or transfer of blood, though they are in rare cases able to breed with the other species. Vampires can dematerialize at will, though they must be able to calm themselves and concentrate to do so and may not carry anything heavy with them. They are able to strip the memories of humans, provided such memories are short term. Some vampires are able to read minds. Life expectancy is upward of a thousand years, or in some cases even longer.

wahlker (n.) An individual who has died and returned to the living from the Fade. They are accorded great respect and are revered for their travails.

ONE

"Ah, hell, V, you're *killing* me." Butch O'Neal mined through his sock drawer, looking for black silk, finding white cotton.

No, wait. He pulled out one dress sock. Not exactly a triumph.

"If I were killing you, cop, footwear'd be the last thing on your mind."

Butch glanced over at his roommate. His fellow Red Sox fan. His . . . well, one of his two best friends.

Both of whom, as it turned out, happened to be vampires.

Fresh from the shower, Vishous had a towel wrapped around his waist, his chest muscles and thick arms out on display. He was pulling on a black leather driving glove, covering up his tattooed left hand.

"Do you have to go for my dress blacks?"

V grinned, fangs flashing in the midst of his goatee. "They feel good."

"Why don't you ask Fritz to get you some?"

"He's too busy feeding your jones for clothes, man."

Okay, so maybe Butch had recently gotten in touch with his inner Versace, and who'd have thought he'd had it in him, but how hard could it be to get an extra dozen silkies in the house?

"I'll ask him for you."

"Aren't you a gentleman." V pushed back his dark hair. The tattoos at his left temple made an appearance and then were covered up again. "You need the Escalade tonight?"

"Yeah, thanks." Butch stuffed his feet into Gucci loafers, bareback.

"So you're going to see Marissa?"

Butch nodded. "I need to know. One way or the other."

And he had a feeling it was going to be *the other*.

"She's a good female."

She sure the hell was, which was probably why she wasn't returning his calls. Ex-cops who liked Scotch weren't exactly good relationship material for women, human or vampire. And the fact that he wasn't one of her kind didn't help the situation.

"Well, cop, Rhage and I'll be throwing back a few at One Eye. You come and find us when you're done—"

Banging, like someone was hitting the front door with a battering ram, brought their heads around.

V hiked up the towel. "Goddamn it, flyboy is going to have to learn how to use a doorbell."

"You try talking to him. He doesn't listen to me."

"Rhage doesn't listen to anyone." V jogged down the hall.

As the thundering dried up, Butch went over to his ever-expanding tie collection. He chose a pale-blue Brioni, popped the collar of his white button-down, and slipped the silk around his neck. As he strolled out to the living room, he could hear Rhage and V talking over 2Pac's "RU still down?"

Butch had to laugh. Man, his life had taken him to a lot of places, most of them ugly, but he'd never thought he'd end up living with six warrior vampires. Or being on the fringes of their fight to protect their dwindling, hidden species. Somehow, though, he belonged with the Black Dagger Brotherhood. And he and Vishous and Rhage were an awesome threesome.

Rhage lived in the mansion across the courtyard with the rest of the Brotherhood, but the troika hung out in the gatehouse, where V and Butch crashed. The Pit, as the place was now known, was sweet digs compared to the hovels Butch had lived in. He and V had two bedrooms, two

2

bathrooms, a galley kitchen, and a living room that was decorated in a winsome, postmodern, Frat-House-Basement style: a pair of leather couches, plasma-screen high-def TV, foosball table, gym bags everywhere.

As Butch stepped into the main room, he got a load of Rhage's ensemble for the night: Black leather trench coat fell from his shoulders to his ankles. Black wife-beater was tucked into leathers. Shitkickers topped him out at six-eight or so. In the getup, the vampire was flat-out, drop-dead gorgeous. Even to a certified hetero like Butch.

The son of a bitch actually bent the laws of physics, he was so attractive. Blond hair was cut short in the back and left longer in the front. Teal-blue eyes were the color of Bahamas seawater. And that face made Brad Pitt look like a candidate for *The Swan*.

But he was no mama's boy, in spite of being a charmer. Something dark and lethal seethed behind the flashy exterior, and you knew it the minute you saw him. He gave off the vibe of a guy who'd smile while he set the record straight with his fists, even if he was spitting his own teeth out while he took care of business.

"What's doing, Hollywood?" Butch asked.

Rhage smiled, revealing a splendid set of pearlies with those long canines. "Time to go out, cop."

"Damn, vampire, didn't you get enough last night? That redhead looked like serious stuff. And so did her sister."

"You know me. Always hungry."

Yeah, well, fortunately for Rhage, there was an endless stream of women more than happy to oblige his needs. And sweet Jesus, the guy had them. Didn't drink. Didn't smoke. But he ran through the ladies like nothing Butch had ever seen.

And it wasn't like Butch knew a lot of choirboys.

Rhage looked over at V. "Go get dressed, man. Unless you were thinking of hitting One Eye in a towel?"

"Quit clocking me, my brother."

"Then gitcha ass moving."

Vishous stood up from behind a table weighed down with enough computer equipment to give Bill Gates a hard-on. From this command center, V ran the security and monitoring systems for the Brotherhood's compound, including the main house, the underground training facility, the Tomb and their Pit, as well as the system of underground tunnels that connected the buildings. He controlled everything: the retractable steel shutters that were installed over every window; the locks on the steel doors; the temperatures in the rooms; the lights; the security cameras; the gates.

V had set up the whole kit and caboodle by himself before the Brotherhood had moved in three weeks ago. The buildings and tunnels had already been up since the early 1900s, but they'd been unused for the most part. After events in July, however, the decision was made to consolidate the Brotherhood's operations, and they'd all come here.

As V went to his bedroom, Rhage took a Tootsie Roll Pop out of his pocket, ripped off the red paper, and put the thing in his mouth. Butch could feel the guy staring. And he wasn't surprised when the brother started in on him.

"So I can't believe you're getting all dolled up for a trip to One Eye, cop. I mean, this is heavy-duty, even for you. The tie, the cuff links—those are all new, right?"

Butch smoothed the Brioni down his chest and reached for the Tom Ford jacket that matched his black slacks. He didn't want to go into the Marissa thing. Just skirting around the subject with V had been enough. Besides, what could he say?

She blew my doors off when I met her, but she's been avoiding me for the past three weeks. So instead of taking the hint, I'm heading over to beg like a desperate loser.

4

Yeah, he really wanted to trot that out in front of Mr. Perfect, even if the guy was a good buddy.

Rhage rolled the lollipop around in his mouth. "Tell me something. Why do you bother with the clothes, man? You don't do anything with your mojo. I mean, I see you turn down females at the bar all the time. You saving yourself for marriage?"

"Yup. That's right. Got myself tied in a knot until I walk down that aisle."

"Come on, I really am curious. Are you holding it for someone?" When there was only silence, the vampire laughed softly. "Do I know her?"

Butch narrowed his eyes, weighing whether the conversation would be over faster if he kept his mouth shut. Probably not. Once Rhage got started, he didn't quit until he decided he was finished. He talked the same way he killed.

Rhage shook his head ruefully. "Doesn't she want you?"

"We're going to find out tonight."

Butch checked his cash level. Sixteen years as a homicide detective hadn't lined his pockets with much to speak of. Now that he was hanging with the Brotherhood? He had so much of the green, he couldn't possibly spend it fast enough.

"You're lucky, cop."

Butch glanced over. "How you figure?"

"I've always wondered what it would be like to settle down with a female of worth."

Butch laughed. The guy was a sex god, an erotic legend in his race. V had said that stories about Rhage were passed from father to son when the time was right. The idea that he'd downshift into being someone's husband was absurd.

"Okay, Hollywood, what's the punch line? Come on, hit me with it."

Rhage winced and looked away.

Holy hell, the guy had been serious. "Whoa. Listen, I didn't mean to—"

"Nah, it's cool." The smile reappeared, but the eyes were flat. He sauntered over to the wastebasket and dropped the lollipop stick in the trash. "Now, can we get out of here? I'm tired of waiting for you boys."

Mary Luce pulled into her garage, shut off her Civic, and stared at the snow shovels hanging on pegs in front of her.

She was tired, although her day hadn't been strenuous. Answering phones and filing papers at a law office just wasn't taxing, physically or mentally. So she really shouldn't be exhausted.

But maybe that was the point. She wasn't being challenged, so she was wilting.

Could it be time to go back to the kids? After all, it was what she was trained for. What she loved. What nourished her. Working with her autistic patients and helping them find ways of communicating had brought her all kinds of rewards, personally and professionally. And the two-year hiatus had not been her choice.

Maybe she should call the center, see if they had an opening. Even if they didn't, she could volunteer until something became available.

Yes, tomorrow she would do that. There was no reason to wait.

Mary grabbed her purse and got out of the car. As the garage door trundled shut, she went around to the front of her house and picked up the mail. Flipping through bills, she paused to test the chilly October night with her nose. Her sinuses hummed. Autumn had swept out the dregs of summer a good month ago, the change of seasons ushered in on the back of a cold rush of air from Canada.

She loved the fall. And upstate New York did it proud, in her opinion.

Caldwell, New York, the town she was born and would most likely die in, was more than an hour north of Manhattan, so it was technically considered "upstate." Split in half by the Hudson River, the Caldie, as it was known by natives, was every midsize city in America. Wealthy parts, poor parts, nasty parts, normal parts. Wal-Marts and Targets and McDonald'ses. Museums and libraries. Suburban malls strangling a faded downtown. Three hospitals, two community colleges, and a bronze statue of George Washington in the park.

She tilted her head back and looked at the stars, thinking that it would never occur to her to leave. Whether that spoke of loyalty or lack of imagination, she wasn't sure.

Maybe it was her house, she thought as she headed for her front door. The converted barn was situated on the edge of an old farmhouse property, and she'd put in an offer fifteen minutes after she'd gone through it with a real estate agent. Inside, the spaces were cozy and small. It was . . . lovely.

Which was why she'd bought it four years ago, right after the death of her mother. She'd needed lovely then, as well as a complete change of scenery. Her barn was everything her childhood home had not been. Here, the pine floorboards were the color of honey, varnished clear, not stained. Her furniture was from Crate and Barrel, all fresh, nothing worn or old. The throw rugs were sisal, short-napped and trimmed with suede. And everything from the slipcovers to the drapes to the walls to the ceilings was creamy white.

Her aversion to darkness had been her interior decorator. And hey, if it's all a variation on beige, the stuff matches, right?

She put her keys and her purse down in the kitchen and grabbed the phone. She was told that *You have . . . two . . . new messages.*

"Hey, Mary, it's Bill. Listen, I'm going to take you up on your offer. If you could cover me at the hotline tonight for an hour or so that would be great. Unless I hear from you, I'll assume you're still free. Thanks again."

She deleted it with a *beep*.

"Mary, this is Dr. Della Croce's office. We'd like you to come in as a follow-up to your quarterly physical. Would you please call to schedule an appointment when you get this message? We'll accommodate you. Thanks, Mary."

Mary put the phone down.

The shaking started in her knees and worked its way up into the muscles in her thighs. When it hit her stomach, she considered running for the bathroom.

Follow-up. We'll accommodate you.

It's back, she thought. The leukemia was back.

8

TWO

"What the hell are we going to tell him? He's coming here in twenty minutes!"

Mr. O regarded his colleague's theatrics with a bored stare, thinking that if the *lesser* did any more hopping up and down, the idiot would qualify as a pogo stick.

Goddamn, but E was a fuckup. Why his sponsor had brought him into the Lessening Society in the first place was a mystery. The man had little drive. No focus. And no stomach for their new direction in the war against the vampire race.

"What are we going—"

"*We* aren't going to tell him anything," O said as he looked around the basement. Knives, razors, and hammers were scattered out of order on the cheap sideboard in the corner. There were pools of blood here and there, but not under the table, where they belonged. And mixed in with the red was a glossy black, thanks to E's flesh wounds.

"But the vampire escaped before we got any information out of him!"

"Thanks for the recap."

The two of them had just started working the male over when O went out on an assist. By the time he got back, E had lost control of the vampire, been sliced in a couple of places, and was all by his little lonesome bleeding in a corner.

That prick boss of theirs was going to be shit-wild, and even though O despised the man, he and Mr. X had one thing in common: Sloppiness was for crap.

O watched E dance around a little more, finding in the jerky movements the solution to both an immediate problem and a longer-term one. As O smiled, E, the fool, seemed relieved.

"Don't worry about a thing," O murmured. "I'll tell him we took the body out and left it for the sun in the woods. No big deal."

"You'll talk to him?"

"Sure, man. You'd better take off, though. He's going to be pissed."

E nodded and bolted for the door. "Later."

Yeah, say good-night, motherfucker, O thought as he started to clean up the basement.

The shitty little house they were working in was unremarkable from the street, sandwiched between a burned-out shell that had once been a barbecue restaurant and a condemned rooming house. This part of town, a mix of squalid residential and lowbrow commercial, was perfect for them. Around here, folks didn't go out after dark, gun pops were as common as car alarms, and nobody said nothing if someone let out a scream or two.

Also, coming and going from the site was easy. Thanks to the neighborhood hardies, all of the streetlights had been shot out and the ambient glow from other buildings was negligible. As an added benefit, the house had an exterior bulkhead entry into its basement. Carrying a fully loaded body bag in and out was no problem.

Although even if someone saw something, it would be the work of a moment to eliminate the exposure. No big surprise to the community, either. White trash had a way of finding their graves. Along with wife beating and beer sucking, dying was probably their only other core competency.

O picked up a knife and wiped E's black blood off the blade.

The basement was not big and the ceiling was low, but there was enough room for the old table they used as a workstation and the battered sideboard they kept their instruments on. Still, O didn't think it was the right facility. It was impossible to safely and securely store a vampire here, and this meant they lost an important tool of persuasion. Time wore down mental and physical faculties. If leveraged correctly, the passage of days was as powerful as anything you could break a bone with.

What O wanted was something out in the woods, something big enough so he could keep his captives over a period of time. As vampires went up in smoke with the dawn, they had to be kept protected from the sun. But if you just locked them in a room, you ran the risk of their dematerializing right out of your hands. He needed something steel to cage them . . .

Up above, the back door shut and footsteps came down the stairs.

Mr. X walked under a naked bulb.

The *Fore-lesser* was about six-four and built like a linebacker. As with all slayers who'd been in the Society for a long time, he'd paled out. His hair and skin were the color of flour, and his irises were as clear and colorless as window glass. Like O, he was dressed in standard-issue *lesser* gear: black cargo pants and a black turtleneck with weapons hidden under a leather jacket.

"So tell me, Mr. O, how goes your work?"

As if the chaos in the basement wasn't explanation enough.

"Am I in charge of this house?" O demanded.

Mr. X walked casually over to the sideboard and picked up a chisel. "In a manner of speaking, yes."

"So am I permitted to ensure that this"—he moved his hand around the disorder—"doesn't happen again?"

"What did happen?"

"The details are boring. A civilian escaped."

"Will it survive?"

"I don't know."

"Were you here when it happened?"

11

"No."

"Tell me everything." Mr. X smiled as silence stretched out. "You know, Mr. O, your loyalty could get you in trouble. Don't you want me to punish the right person?"

"I want to take care of it myself."

"I'm sure you do. Except if you don't tell me, I might have to take the cost of failure out of your hide anyway. Is that worth it?"

"If I'm allowed to do what I will with the responsible party, yeah."

Mr. X laughed. "I can only imagine what that might be."

O waited, watching the chisel's sharp head catch light as Mr. X walked around the room.

"I paired you with the wrong man, didn't I?" Mr. X murmured as he picked a set of handcuffs off the floor. He dropped them on the sideboard. "I thought Mr. E might rise to your level. He didn't. And I'm glad you came to me first before you disciplined him. We both know how much you like to work independently. And how much it pisses me off."

Mr. X looked over his shoulder, dead eyes fixed on O. "In light of all this, particularly because you approached me first, you can have Mr. E."

"I want to do it with an audience."

"Your squadron?"

"And others."

"Trying to prove yourself again?"

"Setting a higher standard."

Mr. X smiled coldly. "You are an arrogant little bastard, aren't you?"

"I'm as tall as you are."

Suddenly, O found himself unable to move his arms or legs. Mr. X had pulled this paralyzing shit before, so it wasn't entirely unexpected. But the guy still had the chisel in his hand and he was coming closer.

O fought the hold, sweat breaking out as he struggled and got nowhere.

Mr. X leaned in so their chests were touching. O felt something brush against his ass.

"Have fun, son," the man whispered into O's ear. "But do yourself a favor. Remember that however long your pants are, you're not me. I'll see you later."

The man strode out of the basement. The door upstairs opened and shut.

As soon as O could move, he reached into his back pocket.

Mr. X had given him the chisel.

Rhage stepped from the Escalade and scanned the darkness around One Eye, hoping a couple of *lessers* would jump out at them. He didn't expect to get lucky. He and Vishous had trolled for hours tonight, and they'd gotten a whole lot of nothing. Not even a sighting. It was damn eerie.

And to someone like Rhage, who depended on fighting for personal reasons, it was also frustrating as hell.

Like all things, though, the war between the Lessening Society and the vampires went in cycles, and they were currently in a downturn. Which made sense. Back in July, the Black Dagger Brotherhood had taken out the Society's local recruitment center along with about ten of their best men. Clearly, the *lessers* were reconnoitering.

Thank God, there were other ways to burn off his edge.

He looked at the sprawling nest of depravity that was the Brotherhood's current R & R hangout. One Eye was on the edge of town, so the folks inside were bikers and guys who worked construction, tough types who tended toward the redneck rather than the slick persuasion. The bar was your standard-issue watering hole. Single-story building surrounded by a collar of asphalt. Trucks, American sedans, and Harleys parked in the spots. From tiny windows, beer signs glowed red, blue, and yellow, the logos Coors and Bud Light and Michelob.

No Coronas or Heinekens for these boys.

As he shut the car door, his body was humming, his skin prickling, his thick muscles twitching. He stretched out his arms, trying to buy himself a little relief. He wasn't surprised when it made no difference. His curse was throwing its weight around, taking him into dangerous territory. If he didn't get some kind of release soon, he was going to have a serious problem. Hell, he was going to *be* a serious problem.

Thank you very much, Scribe Virgin.

Bad enough that he'd been born a live wire with too much physical power, a fuckup with a gift of strength he hadn't appreciated or harnessed. But then he'd pissed off the mystical female who lorded over their race. Man, she'd been only too happy to put down another layer of crap on the compost heap he'd been born with. Now, if he didn't blow off steam on a regular basis, he turned deadly.

Fighting and sex were the only two releases that brought him down, and he used them like a diabetic with insulin. A steady stream of both helped keep him level, but they didn't always do the trick. And when he lost it, things got nasty for everyone, himself included.

God, he was tired of being stuck inside his body, managing its demands, trying not to fall into a brutal oblivion. Sure, his stunner of a face and the strength were all fine and good. But he would have traded both to a scrawny, ugly mo'fo, if it would have gotten him some peace. Hell, he couldn't even remember what serenity was like. He couldn't even remember who he was.

The disintegration of himself had started up pretty

quick. After only a couple of years into the curse, he'd stopped hoping for any true relief and simply tried to get by without hurting anyone. That was when he'd started to die on the inside, and now, over a hundred years later, he was mostly numb, nothing more than glossy window dressing and empty charm.

On every level that counted, he'd given up trying to pretend he was anything but a menace. Because the truth was, no one was safe when he was around. And that was what really killed him, even more than the physical stuff he had to go through when the curse came out of him. He lived in fear of hurting one of his brothers. And, as of about a month ago, Butch.

Rhage walked around the SUV and looked through the windshield at the human male. God, who'd have thought he'd ever be tight with a Homo sapiens?

"We going to see you later, cop?"

Butch shrugged. "Don't know."

"Good luck, man."

"It'll be what it is."

Rhage swore softly as the Escalade took off and he and Vishous walked across the parking lot.

"Who is she, V? One of us?"

"Marissa."

"*Marissa?* As in Wrath's former *shellan*?" Rhage shook his head. "Oh, man, I need details. V, you gotta hook me."

"I don't ride him about it. And neither should you."

"Aren't you curious?"

V didn't reply as they came up to the bar's front entrance.

"Oh, right. You already know, don't you?" Rhage said. "You know what's going to happen."

V merely lifted his shoulders and reached for the door.

Rhage planted his hand on the wood, stopping him. "Hey, V, you ever dream of me? You ever see my future?"

Vishous swiveled his head around. In the neon glow of

a Coors sign, his left eye, the one with the tattoos around it, went all black. The pupil just expanded until it ate up the iris and the white part, until there was nothing but a hole.

It was like staring into infinity. Or maybe into the Fade as you died.

"Do you really want to know?" the brother said.

Rhage let his hand drop to his side. "Only one thing I care about. Am I going to live long enough to get away from my curse? You know, find a slice of calm?"

The door flew open and a drunken man lurched out like a truck with a broken axle. The guy headed for the bushes, threw up, and then lay facedown on the asphalt.

Death was one sure way to find peace, Rhage thought. And everyone died. Even vampires. Eventually.

He didn't meet his brother's eyes again. "Scratch it, V. I don't want to know."

He'd been cursed once already and still had another ninety-one years before he was free. Ninety-one years, eight months, four days until his punishment was over and the beast would no longer be a part of him. Why should he volunteer for a cosmic whammy like knowing he wouldn't live long enough to be free of the damn thing?

"Rhage."

"What?"

"I'll tell you this. Your destiny's coming for you. And she's coming soon."

Rhage laughed. "Oh, yeah? What's the female like? I prefer them—"

"She's a virgin."

A chill shot down Rhage's spine and nailed him in the ass. "You're kidding, right?"

"Look in my eye. Do you think I'm jerking you off?"

V paused for a moment and then opened the door,

releasing the smell of beer and human bodies along with the pulse of an old Guns N' Roses song.

As they went inside, Rhage muttered, "You're some freaky shit, my brother. You really are."

THREE

Pavlov had a point, Mary thought while she drove down-town. Her panic reaction to the message from Dr. Della Croce's office was a trained one, not something logical. "Further tests" could be a lot of things. Just because she associated any kind of news from a physician with catas-trophe didn't mean she could see into the future. She had no idea what, if anything, was wrong. After all, she'd been in remission for close to two years and she felt well enough. Sure, she got tired, but who didn't? Her job and volunteer work kept her busy.

First thing in the morning she'd call for the appoint-ment. For now she was just going to work the beginning of Bill's shift at the suicide hotline.

As the anxiety backed off a little, she took a deep breath. The next twenty-four hours were going to be an endurance test, with her nerves turning her body into a trampoline and her mind into a whirlpool. The trick was waiting through the panic phases and then shoring up her strength when the fear lightened up.

She parked the Civic in an open lot on Tenth Street and walked quickly toward a worn-out six-story building. This was the dingy part of town, the residue of an effort back in the seventies to professionalize a nine-square-block area of what was then a "bad neighborhood." The optimism hadn't worked, and now boarded-up office space mixed with low-rent housing.

She paused at the entrance and waved to the two cops passing by in a patrol car.

The headquarters of the Suicide Prevention Hotline were on the second floor in the front, and she glanced up at the glowing windows. Her first contact with the nonprofit had been as a caller. Three years later, she manned a phone every Thursday, Friday, and Saturday night. She also covered holidays and relieved people when they needed it.

No one knew she'd ever dialed in. No one knew she'd had leukemia. And if she had to go back to war with her blood, she was going to keep that to herself as well.

Having watched her mother die, she didn't want anyone standing over her bed weeping. She already knew the impotent rage that came when saving grace didn't heel on command. She had no interest in a replay of the theatrics while she was fighting for breath and swimming in a sea of failing organs.

Okay. Nerves were back.

Mary heard a shuffle over to the left and caught a flash of movement, as if someone had ducked out of sight behind the building. Snapping to attention, she punched a code into a lock, went inside, and climbed the stairs. When she got to the second floor, she buzzed the intercom for entrance into the hotline's offices.

As she walked past the reception desk, she waved to the executive director, Rhonda Knute, who was on the phone. Then she nodded to Nan, Stuart, and Lola, who were on deck tonight, and settled into a vacant cubicle. After making sure she had plenty of intake forms, a couple of pens, and the hotline's intervention reference book, she took a bottle of water out of her purse.

Almost immediately one of her phone lines rang, and she checked the screen for caller ID. She knew the number. And the police had told her it was a pay phone. Downtown.

It was her caller.

The phone rang a second time and she picked up, following the hotline's script. "Suicide Prevention Hotline, this is Mary. How may I help you?"

Silence. Not even breathing.

19

Dimly, she heard the hum of a car engine flare and then fade in the background. According to the police's audit of incoming calls, the person always phoned from the street and varied his location so he couldn't be traced.

"This is Mary. How may I help you?" She dropped her voice and broke protocol. "I know it's you, and I'm glad you're reaching out tonight again. But please, can't you tell me your name or what's wrong?"

She waited. The phone went dead.

"Another one of yours?" Rhonda asked, taking a sip from a mug of herbal tea.

Mary hung up. "How did you know?"

The woman nodded across her shoulder. "I heard a lot of rings out there, but no one got farther than the greeting. Then all of a sudden you were hunched over your phone."

"Yeah, well—"

"Listen, the cops got back to me today. There's nothing they can do short of assigning details to every pay phone in town, and they're not willing to go that far at this point."

"I told you. I don't feel like I'm in danger."

"You don't know that you're not."

"Come on, Rhonda, this has been going on for nine months now, right? If they were going to jump me, they would have already. And I really want to help—"

"That's another thing I'm concerned about. You clearly feel like protecting whoever the caller is. You're getting too personal."

"No, I'm not. They're calling here for a reason, and I know I can take care of them."

"Mary, stop. Listen to yourself." Rhonda pulled a chair over and lowered her voice as she sat down. "This is . . . hard for me to say. But I think you need a break."

Mary recoiled. "From what?"

"You're here too much."

"I work the same number of days as everyone else."

"But you stay here for hours after your shift is through, and you cover for people all the time. You're too involved. I know you're substituting for Bill right now, but when he comes I want you to leave. And I don't want you back here for a couple of weeks. You need some perspective. This is hard, draining work, and you have to have a proper distance from it."

"Not now, Rhonda. Please, not now. I need to be here now more than ever."

Rhonda gently squeezed Mary's tense hand. "This isn't an appropriate place for you to work out your own issues, and you know that. You're one of the best volunteers I've got, and I want you to come back. But only after you've had some time to clear your head."

"I may not have that kind of time," Mary whispered under her breath.

"What?"

Mary shook herself and forced a smile. "Nothing. Of course, you're right. I'll leave as soon as Bill comes in."

Bill arrived about an hour later, and Mary was out of the building in two minutes. When she got home, she shut her door and leaned back against the wood panels, listening to all the silence. The horrible, crushing silence.

God, she wanted to go back to the hotline's offices. She needed to hear the soft voices of the other volunteers. And the phones ringing. And the drone of the fluorescent lights in the ceiling . . .

Because with no distractions, her mind flushed up terrible images: Hospital beds. Needles. Bags of drugs hanging next to her. In an awful mental snapshot, she saw her head bald and her skin gray and her eyes sunken until she didn't look like herself, until she *wasn't* herself.

And she remembered what it felt like to cease being a person. After the doctors started treating her with chemo, she'd quickly sunk into the fragile underclass of the sick, the dying, becoming nothing more than a pitiful, scary reminder of other people's mortality, a poster child for the terminal nature of life.

Mary darted across the living room, shot through the kitchen, and threw open the slider. As she burst out into the night, fear had her gasping for breath, but the shock of frosty air slowed her lungs down.

You don't know that anything's wrong. You don't know what it is . . .

She repeated the mantra, trying to pitch a net on the thrashing panic as she headed for the pool.

The Lucite in-ground was no more than a big hot tub, and its water, thickened and slowed by the cold, looked like black oil in the moonlight. She sat down, took off her shoes and socks, and dangled her feet in the icy depths. She kept them submerged even when they numbed, wishing she had the gumption to jump in and swim down to the grate at the bottom. If she held on to the thing for long enough, she might be able to anesthetize herself completely.

She thought of her mother. And how Cissy Luce had died in her own bed in the house the two of them had always called home.

Everything about that bedroom was still so clear: The way the light had come through the lace curtains and landed on things in a snowflake pattern. Those pale-yellow walls and the off-white wall-to-wall rug. That comforter her mother had loved, the one with the little pink roses on a cream background. The smell of nutmeg and ginger from a dish of potpourri. The crucifix above the curving headboard and the big Madonna icon on the floor in the corner.

The memories burned, so Mary forced herself to see the room as it had been after everything was over, the illness, the dying, the cleaning up, the selling of the house.

She saw it right before she'd moved out. Neat. Tidy. Her mother's Catholic crutches packed away, the faint shadow left by the cross on the wall covered by a framed Andrew Wyeth print.

The tears wouldn't stay put. They came slowly, relentlessly, falling into the water. She watched them hit the surface and disappear.

When she looked up, she was not alone.

Mary leaped to her feet and stumbled back, but stopped herself, wiping her eyes. It was just a boy. A teenage boy. Dark-haired, pale-skinned. So thin he was emaciated, so beautiful he didn't look human.

"What are you doing here?" she asked, not particularly afraid. It was hard to be scared of anything that angelic. "Who are you?"

He just shook his head.

"Are you lost?" He sure looked it. And it was too cold for him to be out just in the jeans and T-shirt he was wearing. "What's your name?"

He lifted a hand to his throat and moved it back and forth while shaking his head. As if he were a foreigner and frustrated by the language barrier.

"Do you speak English?"

He nodded and then his hands started flying around. American Sign Language. He was using ASL.

Mary reached back to her old life, when she'd trained her autistic patients to use their hands to communicate.

Do you read lips or can you hear? she signed back at him.

He froze, as if her understanding him had been the last thing he'd expected.

I can hear very well. I just can't talk.

Mary stared at him for a long moment. "You are the caller."

He hesitated. Then nodded his head. *I never meant to scare you. And I don't call to annoy you. I just . . . like to know you're there. But there's nothing weird to it, honest. I swear.*

His eyes met hers steadily.

"I believe you." Except what did she do now? The hotline prohibited contact with callers.

Yeah, well, she wasn't about to kick the poor kid off her property.

"You want something to eat?"

He shook his head. *Maybe I could just sit with you awhile? I'll stay on the other side of the pool.*

As if he were used to people telling him to get away from them.

"No," she said. He nodded once and turned away. "I mean, sit down here. Next to me."

He came at her slowly, as if expecting her to change her mind. When all she did was sit down and put her feet back in the pool, he took off a pair of ratty sneakers, rolled up his baggy pants, and picked a spot about three feet from her.

God, he was so small.

He slipped his feet in the water and smiled.

It's cold, he signed.

"You want a sweater?"

He shook his head and moved his feet in circles.

"What's your name?"

John Matthew.

Mary smiled, thinking they had something in common. "Two New Testament prophets."

The nuns gave it to me.

"Nuns?"

There was a long pause, as if he were debating what to tell her.

"You were in an orphanage?" she prompted gently. She recalled that there was still one in town, run by Our Lady of Mercy.

I was born in a bathroom stall in a bus station. The janitor who found me took me to Our Lady. The nuns thought up the name.

She kept her wince to herself. "Ah, where do you live now? Were you adopted?"

He shook his head.

"Foster parents?" Please, God, let there be foster parents. Nice foster parents. Who kept him warm and fed. Good people who told him he mattered even if his parents had deserted him.

When he didn't reply, she eyed his old clothes, and the older expression on his face. He didn't look as if he'd known a lot of nice.

Finally, his hands moved. *My place is on Tenth Street.*

Which meant he was either a poacher living in a condemned building or a tenant in a rat-infested hovel. How he managed to be so clean was a miracle.

"You live around the hotline's offices, don't you? Which was how you knew I was on this evening even though it wasn't my shift."

He nodded. *My apartment is across the street. I watch you come and go, but not in a sneaky way. I guess I think of you as a friend. When I called the first time . . . you know, it was on a whim or something. You answered . . . and I liked the way your voice sounded.*

He had beautiful hands, she thought. Like a girl's. Graceful. Delicate.

"And you followed me home tonight?"

Pretty much every night. I have a bike, and you're a slow driver. I figure if I watch over you, you'll be safer. You stay so late, and that's not a good part of town for a woman to be alone in. Even if she's in a car.

Mary shook her head, thinking he was an odd one. He looked like a child, but his words were those of a man. And all things considered, she probably should be creeped out. This kid latching on to her, thinking he was some kind of protector even though it looked as if he were the one who needed to be rescued.

Tell me why you were crying just now, he signed.

His eyes were very direct, and it was eerie to have an adult male stare anchored by a child's face.

"Because I might be out of time," she blurted.

"Mary? Are you up for a visit?"

Mary looked over her right shoulder. Bella, her only neighbor, had walked across the two-acre meadow that ran between their properties and was standing on the edge of the lawn.

"Hey, Bella. Ah, come meet John."

Bella glided up to the pool. The woman had moved into the big old farmhouse a year ago and they'd taken to talking at night. At six feet tall, and with a mane of dark waves that fell to the small of her back, Bella was a total knockout. Her face was so beautiful it had taken Mary months to stop staring, and the woman's body was right off the cover of *Sports Illustrated*'s swimsuit edition.

So naturally John was looking awestruck.

Mary wondered idly what it would be like to get that reception from a man, even a prepubescent one. She'd never been beautiful, falling instead into that vast category of women who were neither bad-looking nor good-looking. And that had been before chemo had done a number on her hair and skin.

Bella leaned down with a slight smile and offered her hand to the boy. "Hi."

John reached up and touched her briefly, as if he weren't sure she was real. Funny, Mary had often felt the same way about the woman. There was something too . . . much about her. She just seemed larger than life, more vivid than the other people Mary ran into. Certainly more gorgeous.

Although Bella sure didn't act the part of the femme fatale. She was quiet and unassuming and she lived alone, apparently working as a writer. Mary never saw her in the daytime, and no one ever seemed to come or go out of the old farmhouse.

John looked at Mary, his hands moving. *Do you want me to leave?*

Then, as if anticipating her answer, he pulled his feet from the water.

She put her hand on his shoulder, trying to ignore the sharp thrust of bone just under his shirt.

"No. Stay."

Bella took off her running shoes and socks and flicked her toes over the surface of the water. "Yeah, come on, John. Stay with us."

FOUR

Rhage saw the first one he wanted tonight. She was a blond human female, all sexed-up and ready to go. Like the rest of her kind in the bar, she'd been throwing him signals: Flashing her ass. Fluffing her teased hair.

"Find something you like?" V said dryly.

Rhage nodded and crooked his finger at the female. She came when called. He liked that in a human.

He was tracking the shift of her hips when his view was blocked by another tight female body. He looked up and forced his eyes not to roll.

Caith was one of his kind, and beautiful enough with her black hair and those dark eyes. But she was a Brother chaser, always sniffing around, offering herself. He had the sense she saw them as prizes, something to brag about. And how irritating was that.

As far as he was concerned, she put the *itch* in *bitch*.

"Hey, Vishous," she said in a low, sexy voice.

"Evenin', Caith." V took a sip of his Grey Goose. "What up?"

"Wondering what you're doing."

Rhage looked around Caith's hips. Thank God the blonde wasn't put off by a little competition. She was still coming toward the table.

"You going to say hello, Rhage?" Caith prompted.

"Only if you get out of the way. You're blocking my view."

The female laughed. "Another of your cast of thousands. How lucky she is."

"You wish, Caith."

"Yes, I do." Her eyes, predatory and hot, glided over him. "Maybe you'd like to hang with Vishous and me?"

As she reached out to stroke his hair, he caught her wrist. "Don't even try it."

"How is it you'll do so many humans and deny me?"

"Just not interested."

She leaned down, talking into his ear. "You should try me sometime."

He jerked her away from him, tightening his hand on her bones.

"That's right, Rhage, squeeze harder. I like it when it hurts." He let go immediately, and she smiled while rubbing her wrist. "So are you busy, V?"

"I'm settling in right now. But maybe a little later."

"You know where to find me."

When she left, Rhage glanced over at his brother. "I don't know how you can stand her."

V tossed back his vodka, watching the female with hooded eyes. "She has her attributes."

The blonde arrived, stopping in front of Rhage and striking a little pose. He put both hands on her hips and pulled her forward so she straddled his thighs.

"Hi," she said, moving against his hold. She was busy looking him over, sizing up his clothes, eyeing the heavy gold Rolex peeking out from under his trench coat's sleeve. The calculation in her eyes was as cold as the center of his chest.

God, if he could have left he would have; he was so sick of this shit. But his body needed the release, demanded it. He could feel his drive rising and, as always, that god-awful burn left his dead heart in the dust.

"What's your name?" he asked.

"Tiffany."

"Nice to meet you, Tiffany," he said, lying.

Less than ten miles away, at Mary's pool in her backyard, she, John, and Bella were having a surprisingly jolly time.

Mary laughed out loud and looked at John. "You're not serious."

It's true. I shuttled back and forth between the theaters.

"What did he say?" Bella asked, grinning.

"He saw *The Matrix* four times the day it opened."

The woman laughed. "John, I'm sorry to break this to you, but that's pathetic."

He beamed at her, blushing a little.

"Did you get into the whole *Lord of the Rings* thing, too?" she asked.

He shook his head, signed, and looked expectantly at Mary.

"He says he likes martial arts," she translated. "Not elves."

"Can't blame him there. That whole hairy feet thing? Can't do it."

A gust of wind came up, teasing fallen leaves into the pool. As they floated by, John reached out and grabbed one.

"What's that on your wrist?" Mary asked.

John held his arm out so she could inspect the leather bracelet. There were orderly markings on it, some kind of cross between hieroglyphics and Chinese characters.

"That's gorgeous."

I made it.

"May I see?" Bella asked, leaning over. Her smile disintegrated and her eyes narrowed on John's face. "Where did you get this?"

"He says he made it."

"Where did you say you're from?"

John retracted his arm, clearly a little unnerved by Bella's sudden focus.

"He lives here," Mary said. "He was born here."

"Where are his parents?"

Mary faced her friend, wondering why Bella was so intense. "He doesn't have any."

"None?"

"He told me he grew up in the foster-care system, right, John?"

John nodded and cradled his arm against his stomach, protecting the bracelet.

"Those markings," Bella prompted. "Do you know what they mean?"

The boy shook his head and then winced and rubbed his temples. After a moment, his hands signed slowly.

"He says they don't mean anything," Mary murmured. "He just dreams of them and he likes the way they look. Bella, ease off, okay?"

The woman seemed to catch herself. "Sorry. I . . . ah, I'm really sorry."

Mary glanced at John and tried to take the pressure off him. "So what other movies do you like?"

Bella got to her feet and shoved on her running shoes. Without the socks. "Will you guys excuse me for a moment? I'll be right back."

Before Mary could say anything, the woman jogged across the meadow. When she was out of earshot, John looked up at Mary. He was still wincing.

I should go now.

"Does your head hurt?"

John pushed his knuckles into the space between his eyebrows. *I feel like I just ate ice cream really fast.*

"When did you have dinner?"

He shrugged. *I don't know.*

Poor kid was probably hypoglycemic. "Listen, why don't you come inside and eat with me? Last thing I had was take-out for lunch, and that was about eight hours ago."

His pride was obvious in the firm shake of his head. *I'm not hungry.*

"Then will you sit with me while I have a late dinner?" Maybe she could entice him to eat that way.

31

John stood up and held out his hand as if to help her to her feet. She took his small palm and leaned on him just enough so he'd feel some of her weight. Together they headed for her back door, shoes in hand, bare feet leaving wet prints on the chilly flagstone around the pool.

Bella burst into her kitchen and stalled out. She'd had no particular plan when she'd taken off. She just knew she had to do something.

John was a problem. A serious problem.

She couldn't believe she hadn't recognized him for what he was right off the bat. Then again, he hadn't gone through the change yet. And why would a vampire be hanging out in Mary's backyard?

Bella nearly laughed. She hung out in Mary's backyard. So why couldn't others like her do the same?

Putting her hands on her hips, she stared at the floor. What the hell was she going to do? When she'd searched John's conscious mind, she'd found nothing about his race, his people, his traditions. The boy didn't know a thing, had no idea who he really was or what he was going to turn into. And he honestly didn't know what those symbols meant.

She did. They spelled out TEHRROR in the Old Language. A warrior's name.

How was it possible he'd been lost to the human world? And how long did he have before his transition hit? He looked as if he was in his early twenties, which meant he had a year or two. But if she was wrong, if he was closer to twenty-five, he could be in immediate danger. If he didn't have a female vampire to help him through the change, he was going to die.

Her first thought was to call her brother. Rehvenge always knew what to do about everything. The problem was, once that male got involved in a situation, he took over completely. And he tended to scare the hell of everyone.

Havers—she could ask Havers for help. As a physician, he could tell how long the boy had before the transition. And maybe John could stay at the clinic until his future was clearer.

Yeah, except he wasn't sick. He was a pretransition male, so he was physically weak, but she'd sensed no illness in him. And Havers ran a medical facility, not some kind of rooming house.

Besides, what about that name? It was a warrior's—
Bingo.

She went out of the kitchen and into the sitting room, heading for the address book she kept on her desk. In the back, on the last page, she'd written a number that had been circulating for the last ten years or so. Rumor had it that, if you called, you could reach the Black Dagger Brotherhood. The race's warriors.

They would want to know there was a boy with one of their names left to fend for himself. Maybe they would take John in.

Her palms were sweaty as she picked up the phone, and she half expected either for the number not to go through or to have it answered by someone telling her to go to hell. Instead, all she got was an electronic voice repeating what she had dialed and then a beep.

"I . . . ah, my name is Bella. I'm looking for the Brotherhood. I need . . . help." She left her number and hung up, thinking less was more. If she was misinformed, she didn't want to leave a detailed message on some human's voice mail.

She looked out a window, seeing the meadow and the glow of Mary's house in the distance. She had no idea how long it would take for someone to get back to her, if at all. She should probably go back and find out where the kid lived. And how he knew Mary.

God, Mary. That awful disease was back. Bella had sensed its return and had been debating how to handle what she knew when Mary had mentioned she was going in for her quarterly physical. That had been a couple of days ago, and tonight Bella had planned to ask how things had gone. Maybe she could help the female in some small way.

Moving quickly, she went back to the French doors that faced the meadow. She'd find out more about John and—

The phone rang.

So soon? Couldn't be.

She reached across the counter and picked up the kitchen's extension. "Hello?"

"Bella?" The male voice was low. Commanding.

"Yes."

"You called us."

Holy Moses, it worked.

She cleared her throat. Like any civilian, she knew all about the Brotherhood: their names, their reputations, their triumphs and legends. But she'd never actually met one. And it was a little hard to believe she was talking to a warrior in her kitchen.

So get to the point, she told herself.

"I, ah, I have an issue." She explained to the male what she knew about John.

There was silence for a moment. "Tomorrow night you will bring him to us."

Oh, man. Just how would she pull that off?

"Ah, he doesn't speak. He can hear, but he needs a translator to be understood."

"Then bring one with him."

She wondered how Mary would feel about getting tangled up in their world. "The female he's using tonight is a human."

"We'll take care of her memory."

34

"How do I get to you?"

"We will send a car for you. At nine o'clock."

"My address is—"

"We know where you live."

As the phone went dead, she shivered a little.

Okay. Now she just had to get John and Mary to agree to see the Brotherhood.

When she got back to Mary's barn, John was sitting at the kitchen table while the female ate some soup. They both looked up as she approached, and she tried to be casual as she sat down. She waited a little bit before throwing the ball out.

"So, John, I know some folks who are into the martial arts." Which wasn't exactly a lie. She'd heard the brothers were good at all kinds of fighting. "And I was wondering, would you have any interest in meeting them?"

John cocked his head and moved his hands around while looking at Mary.

"He wants to know why. For training?"

"Maybe."

John signed some more.

Mary wiped her mouth. "He says that he can't afford the cost of training. And that he's too small."

"If it were free would he go?" God, what was she doing, promising things she couldn't deliver? Heaven knew what the Brotherhood would do with him. "Listen, Mary, I can take him to a place where he can meet . . . tell him it's a place where master fighters hang out. He could talk to them. Get to know them. He might like to—"

John tugged on Mary's sleeve, signed some, and then stared at Bella.

"He wants to remind you that he can hear perfectly well."

Bella looked at John. "I'm sorry."

He nodded, accepting the apology.

"Just come meet them tomorrow," she said. "What do you have to lose?"

John shrugged and made a graceful movement with his hand.

Mary smiled. "He says okay."

"And you'll have to come, too. To translate."

Mary seemed taken aback, but then stared at the boy. "What time?"

"Nine o'clock," Bella replied.

"I'm sorry, I'll be working then."

"At night. Nine o'clock at night."

FIVE

Butch walked into One Eye feeling like someone had pulled the stoppers out of a number of his internal organs. Marissa had refused to see him and, though he wasn't surprised, it still hurt like a bitch.

So it was time for some Scotch therapy.

After sidestepping a drunken bouncer, a knot of floozies, and a pair of arm wrestlers, Butch found the troika's regular table. Rhage was in the far corner behind it, up against the wall with a brunette. V was nowhere in sight, but a glass filled with Grey Goose and a knotted drink stirrer were in front of a chair.

Butch was two shots in and not feeling much better when Vishous came out from the back. His shirt was untucked and wrinkled at the bottom, and right on his heels was a black-haired woman. V waved her off when he saw Butch.

"Hey, cop," the brother said as he sat down.

Butch tipped his shot glass. "What's doing?"

"How—"

"No go."

"Aw, hell, man. I'm sorry."

"Me, too."

V's phone went off and he cocked it open. The vampire said two words, put the thing back in his pocket, and reached for his coat.

"That was Wrath. We've got to be back at the house in a half hour."

Butch thought about sitting and drinking alone. That plan had *bad idea* written all over it. "You want to poof it or ride back with me?"

"We got time to drive."

Butch tossed the Escalade's keys across the table. "Bring the car around. I'll grab Hollywood."

He got up and headed for the dark corner. Rhage's trench coat was flared out around the brunette's body. God only knew how far things had gone underneath.

"Rhage, buddy. We gotta bounce."

The vampire lifted his head, all tight lips and narrowed eyes.

Butch held his hands up. "I'm not cock-blocking for kicks and giggles. The mother ship called."

With a curse, Rhage stepped back. The brunette's clothes were disarranged and she was panting, but they hadn't gotten to showtime yet. Hollywood's leathers were all where they should be.

As Rhage retreated, the woman grabbed at him as if realizing the orgasm of her life was about to walk out the door. With a smooth movement, he passed his hand in front of her face and she froze. Then she looked down at herself as if trying to figure out how she'd come to be so aroused.

Rhage turned away with a glower, but by the time he and Butch were outside, he was shaking his head ruefully.

"Cop, listen, I'm sorry if I gave you the evil eye back there. I get a little . . . focused."

Butch clapped him on the shoulder. "No problem."

"Hey, how did your female—"

"Not a chance."

"Damn, Butch. That rots."

They piled into the Escalade and headed north, following Route 22 deeper into the countryside. They were going at quite a clip, Trick Daddy's *Thug Matrimony* thumping like a jackhammer, when V hit the brakes. In a clearing, back about a hundred yards from the road, there was something hanging from a tree.

No, someone was in the process of hanging something

from a tree. With an audience of pale-haired, black-clothed tough guys watching.

"*Lessers*," V muttered, easing off onto the shoulder.

Before they came to a full stop, Rhage exploded out of the car, running flat-out toward the group.

Vishous looked across the front seat. "Cop, you might want to stay—"

"Fuck you, V."

"You armed with one of mine?"

"No, I'm going out there naked." Butch grabbed a Glock out from under the seat, flipping off the semi's safety as he and Vishous jumped to the ground.

Butch had seen only two *lessers* before, and they freaked him out. They looked like men, they moved and talked like men, but they weren't alive. One look in their eyes and you knew the slayers were empty vessels, the soul gone somewhere else. And they stank to high heaven.

But then again, he never could stand the smell of baby powder.

Out in the clearing, the *lessers* assumed attack positions and reached into their jackets as Rhage covered the yards of meadow grass like a freight train. He fell upon the group in some kind of suicidal surge, no weapon drawn.

Jesus, the guy was nuts. At least one of those slayers had taken out a handgun.

Butch leveled the Glock and tracked the action, but couldn't get a clean shot. And then he realized he didn't need to play back-up.

Rhage handled the *lessers* by himself, all animal strength and reflexes. He was ripping some kind of martial-arts hybrid, his trench coat flaring out behind him as he kicked heads and punched torsos. He was deadly beautiful in the moonlight, his face twisted into a snarl, his big body pummeling the tar out of those *lessers*.

A holler lit off to the right and Butch wheeled around.

V had taken down a *lesser* who'd tried to run, and the brother was all over the damn thing like white on rice.

Leaving the *Fight Club* stuff to the vampires, Butch headed over to the tree. Strung up from a thick branch was the body of another *lesser*. The thing had been worked over but good.

Butch loosened the rope and lowered the body, checking over his shoulder because the smacks and grunts of fighting were suddenly louder. Three more *lessers* had joined the fray, but he wasn't worried about his boys.

He knelt down to the slayer in front of him and started going through its pockets. He was pulling out a wallet when a gun went off with an awful popping sound. Rhage hit the ground. Flat on his back.

Butch didn't think twice. He shifted into firing position and aimed at the *lesser* who was about to plow another slug into Rhage. The Glock's trigger never got pulled. From out of nowhere, there was a brilliant flash of white, like a nuke had gone off. Night turned to day as everything in the clearing was illuminated: the autumnal trees, the fighting, the flat space.

As the brilliance receded, someone came running at Butch. When he recognized V, he lowered the gun.

"Cop! Get in the fucking car!" The vampire was hauling ass, legs pumping like he was about to get served.

"What about Rhage—"

Butch didn't get the rest of the sentence out. V hit him like a piledriver, doing a grab and drag that ended only when they were both in the Escalade and the doors were shut.

Butch turned on the brother. "We're not leaving Rhage out there!"

A mighty roar split the night, and Butch slowly turned his head.

In the clearing he saw a creature. Some eight feet tall, it was built along the lines of a dragon, with teeth like

40

a T. rex and a slashing pair of front claws. The thing flickered in the moonlight, its powerful body and tail covered with iridescent purple and lime-green scales.

"What the hell is that?" Butch whispered, fumbling to make sure the door was locked.

"Rhage in a really bad mood."

The monster let loose another howl and went after the *lessers* as though they were toys. And it . . . *Good Lord*. There wasn't going to be anything left of the slayers. Not even bones.

Butch felt himself beginning to hyperventilate.

Dimly, he heard the sound of a lighter being teed off, and he glanced across the seat. V's face caught and held the flare of yellow as he lit a hand-rolled with shaky hands. When the brother exhaled, the tang of Turkish tobacco filled the air.

"Since when has he . . ." Butch turned back to the creature feature playing in the clearing. And totally lost his train of thought.

"Rhage pissed off the Scribe Virgin, so she cursed him. Gave him two hundred years of hell. Anytime he gets too worked up, presto-change-o. Pain can set it off. Anger. Physical frustration, if you feel me."

Butch cocked an eyebrow. And to think he'd gotten between that guy and a woman he wanted. Never pulling that kind of stupidity again.

As the carnage continued, Butch began to feel as if he were watching the Sci-Fi Channel with the sound on mute. Man, this kind of violence was out of even his league. In all his years as a homicide detective, he'd seen plenty of dead bodies, some of which had been hard-core gruesome. But he'd never witnessed a slaughter in live action before, and oddly, the shock of it removed the experience from reality.

Thank God.

Although he had to admit the beast was a smooth

mover. The way it spun that *lesser* up into the air and
caught the slayer with its . . .

"Does it happen often?" he asked.

"Often enough. That's why he goes for the sex. Keeps
him calm. I'll tell you this, you don't screw around with
the beast. It doesn't know who's a friend and who's lunch.
All we can do is wait around until Rhage comes back and
then take care of him."

Something bounced on the hood of the Escalade with
a bang. Oh, God, was that a head? No, a boot. Maybe
the creature didn't like the taste of rubber.

"Take care of him?" Butch murmured.

"How'd you like it if every bone in your body was
broken? He goes through a change when that thing comes
out and, as it leaves, he gets nailed again."

In short order, the clearing was empty of *lessers*. With
another deafening roar, the beast wheeled around as if
looking for more to consume. Finding no other slayers,
its eyes focused on the Escalade.

"Can it get into the car?" Butch asked.

"If it really wants to. Fortunately, it can't be very
hungry."

"Yeah, well . . . what if it's got room for Jell-o," Butch
muttered.

The beast shook its head, black mane tossing in the
moonlight. Then it howled and charged at them, running
on two legs. The pounding of its stride called thunder
and tremors out of the earth.

Butch checked the door lock one more time. Then
thought about being a pansy and maybe hitting the
floor.

The creature stopped right next to the SUV and fell
into a crouch. It was close enough so its breath fogged
Butch's window on the exhale, and, up close, the thing
was hideous. White narrowed eyes. Snarling jowls. And
the full set of fangs in its gaping mouth was right out of

a fever nightmare. Black blood ran down its chest like crude oil.

The beast lifted its muscled forelegs.

Jesus, those claws were like daggers. Made Freddie Krueger's set of fun and games look like pipe cleaners.

But Rhage was in there. Somewhere.

Butch put his hand to the window, as if he could reach the brother.

The creature cocked its head, white eyes blinking. Abruptly it heaved a great breath, and then the massive body started to shake. A high, piercing cry came out of its throat, cracking through the night. There was another flash of brilliance. And then Rhage was lying naked on the ground.

Butch threw open the car door and knelt by his friend.

Rhage shook uncontrollably on the dirt and grass, his skin clammy, his eyes squeezed shut, his mouth moving slowly. There was black blood all over his face, in his hair, down his chest. His stomach was horribly distended. And there was a small hole in his shoulder where the bullet had hit him.

Butch yanked off his jacket and put it over the vampire. Leaning down, he tried to catch the words that were being mumbled. "What was that?"

"Hurt? You . . . V?"

"Nah, we're doing good."

Rhage seemed to relax a little. "Take me home. . . . Please . . . get me home."

"Don't you worry about a thing. We're gonna take care of you."

O moved fast across the clearing, heading away from the slaughter, running low to the ground. His truck was parked down the road, about a mile away. He figured he had another three to four minutes before he got to it, and so far nothing was chasing him.

He'd taken off the instant that flash of light had ripped through the clearing, knowing damn well that nothing good came after a sparkler like that. He'd figured it was either nerve gas or the precursor to one fuck of an explosion, but then he'd heard a roar. As he'd looked over his shoulder, he'd stopped dead. Something had been doing a number on his fellow *lessers*, picking them off like flies.

A creature. From out of nowhere.

He hadn't watched for long, and, as he ran now, O glanced back once again to make sure he wasn't being followed. The path behind was still clear, and up ahead he saw the truck. When he got to it, he threw himself inside, cranked the engine over, and hit the gas.

First order of business was to separate from the scene. A massacre like that was going to attract attention, either because of what it looked and sounded like while it was happening or because of what was left when it was over. Second was to reconnoiter. Mr. X was going to be split-personality pissed at this. O's squadron of primes was gone, and the other *lessers* that he'd invited to watch E's discipline were dead, too. Six slayers in little over a half hour.

And goddamn it, he didn't know much about the monster who'd done the damage. They'd been hanging E's body in the tree when the Escalade had pulled over to the side of the road. A blond warrior had gotten out, so big, so fast, he was obviously a member of the Brotherhood. There had been another male with him, also incredibly lethal, as well as a human, although Christ only knew what that guy had been doing with the two brothers.

The fight had gone on for about eight or nine minutes. O had taken on the blond, had punched him a number of times with no measurable effect on the vampire's stamina or strength. The two of them had been deep in

44

hand-to-hand when one of the other *lessers* had fired a gun. O had ducked and rolled, nearly getting shot himself. When he'd looked up, the vampire was clutching his shoulder and falling backward.

O had lunged for him, wanting to have the kill, but, as he sprang forward, the *lesser* with the gun had tried to get at the vampire himself. The idiot had tripped on O's leg and knocked both of them to the ground. Then that light had gone off and the monster had appeared. Was it possible that the thing had come out of the blond warrior somehow? Man, what a secret weapon that would be.

O pictured the warrior, recalling every aspect of the male from his eyes to his face to the clothes he wore and the way he moved. Having a good description of the fair-haired brother was critical for use in the Society's interrogations. Specific questions posed to captives were more likely to lead to good answers.

And information on the brothers was what they were looking for. After decades of just knocking off civilians, the *lessers* were now targeting the Brotherhood specifically. Without those warriors, the vampire race would be completely vulnerable, and the slayers could finally finish their job eradicating the species.

O pulled into the parking lot of the local laser-tag place, thinking that the only good thing about the evening had been when he'd killed E slowly. Taking out his irritation on the slayer's body had been like drinking a cool beer on a hot summer day. Satisfying. Calming.

But what had happened afterward had put him right back on edge.

O flipped open his phone and hit speed dial. There was no reason to wait until he got home to make a report. Mr. X's reaction was going to be worse if he thought the news had been delayed.

"We've had a situation," he said when the call was answered.

Five minutes later he hung up, turned the truck around, and headed back to the rural part of town.

Mr. X had demanded an audience. At his private cabin in the woods.

SIX

Rhage could see only shadows, as his eyes were incapable of focusing or processing much light. He hated the loss of faculty and did his best to track the two big shapes moving around him. When hands gripped under his armpits and latched onto his ankles, he groaned.

"Easy there, Rhage, we're just gonna lift you for a sec, true?" V said.

A fireball of pain shot through his body as he was taken up off the ground and carried around to the back of the Escalade. They laid him down. Doors shut. The engine turned over with a low purr.

He was so cold his teeth knocked together, and he tried to draw whatever was across his shoulders closer. He couldn't make his hands work, but someone pulled what he assumed was a jacket more tightly around him.

"Just hang in there, big guy."

Butch. It was Butch.

Rhage struggled to speak, hating the foul taste in his mouth.

"Nah, relax, Hollywood. You're cool. V and I are going to get you home."

The car started to move, bumping up and down as if it were getting off the shoulder and onto the road. He moaned like a sissy, but he couldn't help it. His body felt as though it had been beaten all over with a baseball bat. A bat with a spike on the end.

And the bone and muscle aches were a minor problem compared to his stomach. He was praying he'd make it back to the house before he threw up in V's car, but there was no guarantee he'd hold out that long. His salivary glands were working overtime, so he had to swallow repeatedly. Which made his gag reflex fire up. Which spurred on the churning nausea. Which made him want to . . .

Trying to pull himself out of the spiral, he breathed slowly through his nose.

"How we doing there, Hollywood?"

"Promise me. Shower. First thing."

"You got it, buddy."

Rhage figured he must have passed out, because he came awake as he was being hauled from the car. He heard familiar voices. V's. Butch's. A deep growl that could only be Wrath.

He lost consciousness again. When he came back, something cold was against his back.

"Can you stand up for me?" Butch asked.

Rhage gave it a shot and was grateful when his thighs accepted his weight. And now that he was out of the car, the nausea was a little better.

His ears caught a sweet chiming noise, and a moment later a warm rush fell over his body.

"How we doing, Rhage? Too hot?" Butch's voice. Up close.

The cop was in the shower with him. And he smelled Turkish tobacco. V must be in the bathroom, too.

"Hollywood? This too hot for you?"

"No." He reached around for the soap, fumbling. "Can't see."

"Just as well. No reason for you to know what we look like naked together. Frankly, I'm traumatized enough for the both of us."

Rhage smiled a little as a washcloth scrubbed over his face, neck, chest.

God, that felt fantastic. He craned his head back, letting the soap and water wash away the remnants of the beast's doing.

Too soon the shower was off. A towel was wrapped around his hips while another one dried him off.

"There anything else we can do for you before you get horizontal?" Butch asked.

"Alka-Seltzer. Cabinet."

"V, fire up some of that shit, would you?" Butch's arm came around Rhage's waist. "Lean on me, buddy. Yeah, that's right—*whoa*. Damn, we've got to stop feeding you."

Rhage let himself be led across the marble floor and onto the carpet in the bedroom.

"All right, big guy, down you go."

Oh, yeah. Bed. Bed was good.

"And look who's here. It's Nurse Vishous."

Rhage felt his head get tilted up and then a glass was put to his lips. When he'd taken all he could, he collapsed against the pillows. He was about to pass out again when he heard Butch's hushed voice.

"At least the bullet went through him clean. But, man, he doesn't look good."

V answered quietly. "He'll be all right in a day or so. He recovers quickly from anything, but it's still tough."

"That creature was something else."

"He worries a lot about it coming out." There was the rasp of a lighter and then a fresh waft of that wonderful tobacco. "He tries not to show how afraid of it he is. Gotta keep up that glossy front and all. But he's terrified of hurting someone."

"First question he asked when he came back was whether you and I were okay."

Rhage tried to force himself to sleep. The black void was a hell of a lot better than listening to his friends pity him.

Ninety-one years, eight months, four days. And then he would be free.

Mary was desperate to get to sleep. She closed her eyes. Did the deep breathing thing. Relaxed her toes one by one. Ran through all the telephone numbers she knew. None of it worked.

She rolled over and stared at the ceiling. When her mind kicked up an image of John, she was grateful. The boy was better than so many other subjects she could dwell on.

She couldn't believe he was twenty-three, although the more she thought about him, it did seem possible. *Matrix* fixation aside, he was incredibly mature. Old, really.

When it had come time for him to go, she'd insisted on driving him back to his apartment. Bella had asked to come, too, so the three of them had gone downtown with his bike sticking out of the back of the Civic. Leaving the boy in front of that miserable apartment building had been hard. She'd almost begged him to come home with her.

But at least he'd agreed to be at Bella's tomorrow night. And maybe the martial-arts academy would open some doors for him. She had a feeling he didn't have many friends, and thought Bella was sweet to make the effort on his behalf.

With a little grin, Mary pictured the way John had looked at the other woman. Such shy admiration. And Bella handled the attention gracefully, though she was no doubt used to those kinds of stares. Probably got them all the time.

For a moment Mary indulged herself and imagined looking out at the world through Bella's flawless eyes. And walking on Bella's flawless legs. And swinging Bella's flawless hair over a shoulder.

The fantasizing was a good diversion. She decided she'd go to New York City and strut down Fifth Avenue wearing something fabulous. No, the beach. She'd head for the beach in a black bikini. Hell, maybe a black bikini with a *thong*.

Okay, this was getting a little creepy.

Still, it would have been great, just once, to have a man stare at her with total adoration. To have him be . . . *enthralled*. Yes, that was the word. She would have loved for a man to be enthralled by her.

Except it was never going to happen. That time in her life, of youth and beauty and dewy sexuality, had passed. Had never been, actually. And now she was a nothing-special thirty-one-year-old who'd led a very hard life, thanks to the cancer.

Mary groaned. Oh, this was great. She wasn't panicking, but she was knee-deep in self-pity. And the shit was like sludge, clingy and disgusting.

She clicked on the light and reached for *Vanity Fair* with grim resolve. *Dominick Dunne, take me away*, she thought.

SEVEN

After Rhage fell asleep, Butch walked with V down the hall to Wrath's private study. Usually Butch didn't hang around for Brotherhood business, but Vishous was going to report on what they'd found on the way home, and Butch was the only one who'd gotten a look at the *lesser* in the tree.

As he came through the door, he had the same reaction he always did to the Versailles decor: it just didn't fit. All the gold curlicue things on the walls and the paintings of little fat boys with wings on the ceiling and the flimsy, fancy furniture. The place looked like a hangout for those old-fashioned, powdered-wig French guys. Not a war room for a bunch of heavy-duty fighters.

But whatever. The Brotherhood had moved into the mansion because it was convenient and secure, not because they liked the way it was tricked up.

He picked a chair with spindly legs and tried to sit down without letting all of his weight go. As he settled in, he shot a nod to Tohrment, who was on the silk-covered couch across the way. The vampire took up most of the piece of furniture, his big body sprawled across the powder-blue cushions. His military-cut black hair and his thick shoulders pronounced him a hard-ass, but that navy-blue gaze of his told another story.

Underneath all the warrior tough stuff, Tohr was a really nice guy. And surprisingly empathic, considering he kicked around the undead for a living. He was the official leader of the Brotherhood since Wrath had ascended to the throne two months ago, and the only fighter who didn't live at the mansion. Tohr's *shellan*, Wellsie, was expecting their first child and not about to move in with a bunch of single guys. And who could blame her?

"So I guess you boys had some fun on the way home," Tohr said to Vishous.

"Yeah, Rhage really let loose," V replied as he poured himself a shot of vodka from the wet bar.

Phury came in next and nodded hello. Butch liked the brother a lot, even though they didn't have much in common. Well, except for their wardrobe fetish, although even there they differed. Butch's clotheshorse routine was a fresh coat of paint on a cheap house. Phury's style and masculine elegance were down to the bone. He was lethal, there was no doubt about it, but he had a metrosexual vibe to him.

The refined-gentleman impression wasn't just a result of his sharp duds, like the black cashmere sweater and fine twill slacks he was sporting right now. The brother had the most amazing head of hair Butch had ever seen. The long, thick waves of blond and red and brown were outrageously beautiful, even for a woman. And his odd yellow eyes, that shone bright as gold in the sunshine, added to his whole deal.

Why he was celibate was a total mystery.

As Phury went over to the bar and poured himself a glass of port, his limp was barely noticeable. Butch had heard that the guy's lower leg had been lost somewhere along the line. He had an artificial limb now, and evidently it didn't hinder him on the battlefield in the slightest.

Butch glanced over as someone else came into the room.

Unfortunately, Phury's twin had decided to show up on time, but at least Zsadist went to the far corner and stayed away from everyone. This was just fine with Butch, because that bastard made him jumpy.

Z's scarred face and glossy black eyes were just the tip of the iceberg for freakiness. The skull-trimmed hair, the tats around his neck and wrists, the piercings: he was a total package of menace and had the high-octane hatred to back up the impression he made. In law enforcement slang, he was a triple threat, that one. Stone cold. Mean as a snake. And unpredictable as hell.

Apparently Zsadist had been abducted from his family as an infant and sold into some kind of slavery. The hundred or so years he'd spent in captivity had sucked out anything even remotely human—er, vampire—in him. He was nothing but dark emotions trapped in a ruined skin now. And if you knew what was good for you, you stayed the hell out of his way.

From out in the hall there was the sound of heavy footfalls. The brothers got quiet, and a moment later Wrath filled the doorway.

Wrath was a huge, dark-haired, cruel-lipped nightmare of a guy. He wore black wraparound shades all the time, lots of leather, and was about the last person on the planet anyone would want to screw with.

The hard-ass also happened to be the first on Butch's list of men to have at his back. He and Wrath had forged a bond on the night Wrath had been shot getting his wife back from the *lessers*. Butch had helped out, and that was that. They were tight.

Wrath entered the room like he owned the whole world. The brother was total emperor material, which made sense, because that was what he was. The Blind King. The last purebred vampire left on the planet. The ruler of his race.

Wrath glanced in Butch's direction. "You took good care of Rhage tonight. I appreciate it."

"He'd have done the same for me."

"Yeah, he would've." Wrath went behind the desk and sat down, crossing his arms over his chest. "Here's what we got. Havers had a trauma case come in tonight. Civilian male. Beat to shit, barely conscious. Before he died, he told Havers that he'd been worked over by the *lessers*.

54

They wanted to know about the Brotherhood, where we lived, what he knew about us."

"Another one," Tohr murmured.

"Yeah. I think we're seeing a shift in the Lessening Society's strategy. The male described a place specifically set up for rough interrogation. Unfortunately, he died before he could give a location." Wrath pegged Vishous with a stare. "V, I want you to go to the civilian's family and tell them that the death will be avenged. Phury, get over to Havers's and talk to the nurse who caught most of what the male said. See if you can get a bead on where they had him and how he escaped. I'm not going to have those bastards using my civilians as scratching posts."

"They're working over their own kind, too," V interjected. "We found a *lesser* being strung up in a tree on the way home. Surrounded by his friends."

"What did they do to the guy?"

Butch spoke up. "Plenty. He wasn't breathing anymore and then some. Do they take out their own a lot?"

"No. They don't."

"Then it's a hell of a coincidence, don't you think? Civilian gets free of a torture camp tonight. *Lesser* shows up looking like a pincushion."

"I'm with you there, cop." Wrath turned to V. "You get any info off those *lessers?* Or did Rhage clean house?"

V shook his head. "Everything was gone."

"Not exactly." Butch reached into his pocket and took out the wallet he'd removed from the treed *lesser*. "I got this off the one they turned on." He riffled through and found the driver's license. "Gary Essen. Hey, he lived in my old building. Just goes to show, you never know about your neighbors."

"I'll search the apartment," Tohr said.

As Butch tossed the wallet over, the brothers got up, ready to leave.

Tohr spoke before anyone took off. "There's one other

thing. Got a phone call tonight. Civilian female found a young male out on his own. He had the name Tehrror on him. I told her to bring him to the training center tomorrow night."

"Interesting," Wrath said.

"He doesn't speak, and his translator's coming with him. It's a human, by the way." Tohr smiled and put the *lesser*'s wallet in the back pocket of his leathers. "But don't worry about it. We'll scrub her memories."

As Mr. X opened up his cabin's front door, his mood was not improved by Mr. O's affect. The *lesser* on the other side was looking steady, unflappable. Humility would have gotten him further, but any form of weakness or submission was not in the man's nature. Yet.

Mr. X motioned his subordinate in. "You know something, this confession-of-failure thing we've got going on is not working for me. And I should have known not to trust you. You mind explaining why you killed your squadron?"

Mr. O pivoted around. "Excuse me?"

"Don't try to hide behind lies, it's annoying." Mr. X shut the door.

"I didn't kill them."

"But a creature did? Please, Mr. O. You could at least be more original. Better yet, blame it on the Brotherhood. That would be more plausible."

Mr. X walked across the cabin's main room, keeping quiet for a while so his subordinate could get good and worked up. He idly checked his laptop and then glanced around his private quarters. The place was rustic, the furniture sparse, the seventy-five surrounding acres a good buffer. The toilet didn't work, but, as *lessers* didn't eat, that kind of facility was unnecessary. The shower ran just fine, however.

And until they settled on another recruitment center, this humble outpost was the society's headquarters.

"I told you exactly what I saw," Mr. O said, breaking the silence tightly. "Why would I lie?"

"The *why* is irrelevant to me." Mr. X casually opened the door to the bedroom. The hinges creaked. "You should know that I sent a squadron to the scene while you were driving out here. They reported that there was nothing left of the bodies, so I assume you stabbed them into the great unknown. And they confirmed that there had been one hell of fight, a lot of blood. I can imagine how your squadron fought against you. You must have been spectacular to win."

"If I'd killed them like that, why are my clothes mostly clean?"

"You changed before coming here. You're not stupid." Mr. X positioned himself in the bedroom's doorway. "So here's where we are, Mr. O. You are a pain in the ass, and the question I need to ask myself is whether you're worth all this aggravation. Those were Primes you killed out there. Seasoned *lessers*. Do you know how long—"

"I didn't kill them—"

Mr. X took two easy steps forward and coldcocked Mr. O in the jaw. The other man went down to the floor.

Mr. X put his boot on the side of Mr. O's face, pinning him. "Let's quit it with that, okay? What I was saying was, do you have any idea how long it takes to make a Prime? Decades, centuries. You managed to wipe out three of them in one night. Which brings you to a total of four, counting Mr. M, who you sliced without my permission. And then there were the Betas you slayed tonight, as well."

Mr. O was spitting mad, his eyes glaring up from around the Timberland's sole. Mr. X leaned into his foot until those lids were wide, no longer narrow.

"So, again, I have to ask myself, are you worth it? You're only three years into the society. You're strong, you're effective, but you're proving impossible to control. I put you with Primes because I assumed you'd fall in line with their level of excellence and temper yourself. Instead, you killed them."

Mr. X felt his blood rise and reminded himself that anger was not appropriate for a leader. Calm, levelheaded domination worked best. He took a deep breath before speaking again.

"You took out some of our best assets tonight. And it is going to stop, Mr. O. Right now."

Mr. X lifted his boot. The other *lesser* immediately sprang up from the floor.

Just as Mr. O was about to speak, an odd, discordant hum weaved through the night. He looked toward the sound.

Mr. X smiled. "Now if you don't mind, get the hell into that bedroom."

Mr. O crouched into an attack pose. "What's that?"

"It's time for a little behavior modification. A little punishment, too. So get into the bedroom."

By now the sound was so loud it was more a vibration of the air than something ears could register.

Mr. O shouted, "I told you the truth."

"Into the bedroom. The time for talking's passed." Mr. X glanced over his shoulder, in the direction of the hum. "Oh, for chrissakes."

He froze the large muscles in the other *lesser*'s body and manhandled Mr. O into the other room, shoving him down on the bed.

The front door burst wide open.

Mr. O's eyes bulged as he took in the Omega. "Oh . . . God . . . no . . ."

Mr. X tidied up the man's clothes, straightening the jacket and the shirt. For good measure, he smoothed all that dark-brown hair down and kissed Mr. O's forehead, as if he were a child.

"If you'll excuse me," Mr. X murmured, "I'm going to leave the two of you alone."

Mr. X took the back door out of the cabin. He was just getting into his car when the screams started.

EIGHT

"Ah, Bella, I think our ride is here." Mary let the curtain fall back into place. "Either that or a third-world dictator is lost in Caldwell."

John headed for the window. *Wow*, he signed. *Check out that Mercedes. Those blackened windows look bulletproof.*

The three of them left Bella's house and walked over to the sedan. A little old man, dressed in black livery, got out of the driver's side and came around to greet them. Incongruously, he was a cheery sort, all smiles. With the loose skin on his face, his long earlobes, and all those jowls, he looked like he was melting, though his radiant happiness suggested disintegration was a fine state to be in.

"I am Fritz," he said, bowing low. "Please allow me to drive you."

He opened the rear door and Bella slid inside first. John was next, and when Mary was settled back against the seat, Fritz closed the door. A second later they were on the road.

As the Mercedes glided along, Mary tried to see where they were going, except the windows were too dark. She assumed they were headed north, but who knew?

"Where is this place, Bella?" she asked.

"It's not far." But the woman didn't sound all that confident. In fact, she'd been on edge since Mary and John had shown up.

"Do you know where we're being taken?"

"Oh, sure." The woman smiled and looked at John. "We're going to meet some of the most amazing males you've ever seen."

Mary's instincts knocked around in her chest, sending all kinds of tread-carefully signals. God, she wished she'd taken her own car.

Twenty minutes later, the Mercedes slowed to a stop. Inched forward. Stopped again. This happened at regular intervals a number of times. Then Fritz put down his window and spoke into some kind of intercom. They cruised along a little farther, then came to a stop. The engine was turned off.

Mary reached for the door. It was locked.

America's Most Wanted, *here we come*, she thought. She could just imagine their pictures on the TV, victims of violent crime.

But the driver let them out immediately, still with that smile on his face. "Won't you follow me?"

As Mary got out, she looked around. They were in some kind of underground parking lot, except there were no other cars. Just two small buses, like the kind you took around an airport.

They stuck close to Fritz and went through a pair of thick metal doors that opened into a maze of fluorescent-lit corridors. Thank God the guy seemed to know where he was going. There were branches splitting off in all directions with no rational plan, as if the place had been designed to get people lost and keep them that way.

Except someone would always know where you were, she thought. Every ten yards there was a pod set into the ceiling. She'd seen them before in malls, and the hospital had them, too. Surveillance cameras.

Finally they were shown into a small room with a two-sided mirror, a metal table, and five metal chairs. A small camera was mounted in the corner opposite the door. It was exactly like a police interrogation room, or what one must be like according to the sets on *NYPD Blue*.

"You will not have to wait long," Fritz said with a little bow. As he ducked out, the door eased shut of its own volition.

Mary went over and tried the handle, surprised to find it released easily. Then again, whoever was in charge here clearly didn't have to worry about losing track of their visitors.

She looked over at Bella. "You mind telling me what this place is?"

"It's a facility."

"A facility."

"You know, for training."

Yeah, but for what kind of training? "Are these folks of yours with the government or something?"

"Oh, no. No."

John signed, *This doesn't look like a martial-arts academy.*

Yeah, no kidding.

"What did he say?" Bella asked.

"He's as curious as I am."

Mary turned back to the door, opened it, and stuck her head out into the hall. When she heard a rhythmic sound, she stepped from the room, but didn't wander.

Footsteps. No, a shuffling. *What the—*

A tall blond man dressed in a black muscle shirt and leather pants lurched around a corner. He was unsteady on his bare feet, with one hand on the wall and his eyes focused downward. He seemed to be watching the floor carefully, as if he were relying on his depth perception to balance himself.

He looked drunk or maybe sick, but . . . good lord, he was beautiful. In fact, his face was so dazzling she had to blink a couple of times. Perfectly square jaw. Full lips. High cheekbones. Broad forehead. Hair was thick and wavy, lighter in the front, darker in the back where it was cut short.

And his body was just as spectacular as his head.

62

Big-boned. Thickly muscled. No fat. His skin was golden even under the fluorescent lights.

Suddenly he looked at her. His eyes were an electric teal blue, so bright, so vivid, they were almost neon. And they stared right through her.

Mary sank back just the same and thought the lack of response wasn't a surprise. Men like him didn't notice women like her. It was a fact of nature.

She should just go back into the room. There was no sense in watching him not acknowledge her as he passed. Trouble was, the closer he got, the more mesmerized she became.

God, he really was . . . beautiful.

Rhage felt like holy hell as he weaved down the corridor. Every time the beast came out of him and his vision headed off for a little vacation, his eyes took their own sweet time in getting back to work. The body didn't want to play, either, his legs and arms hanging like heavy weights off his torso, not exactly useless, but damn close.

And his stomach was still off. The very idea of food made him nauseous.

But he'd had it with being stuck in his room. Twelve hours flat on his back was enough wasted time. He was determined to get to the training center's gym, hop on a recumbent bike, and loosen himself up a little—

He stopped, tensing. He couldn't see much, but he knew for sure he was not alone in the hall. Whoever it was stood close beside him, to his left. And it was a stranger.

He spun around and yanked the figure out of a doorway, grabbing it by the throat, forcing the body into the opposite wall. Too late he realized it was a female, and the high-pitched gasp shamed him. He quickly eased up on his grip, but he did not let go.

The slender neck under his palm was warm, soft. Her pulse was frantic, blood racing through the veins that came up from her heart. He leaned down and drew a breath through his nose. Only to jerk back.

Jesus Christ, she was a human. And she was sick, maybe dying.

"Who are you?" he demanded. "How did you get in here?"

There was no answer, just quick breathing. She was utterly terrified of him, the smell of her fear like wood smoke in his nose.

He softened his voice. "I'm not going to hurt you. But you don't belong here, and I want to know who you are."

Her throat undulated under his hand, as if she were swallowing. "My name . . . my name is Mary. I'm here with a friend."

Rhage stopped breathing. His heart skipped a beat and then slowed.

"Say that again," he whispered.

"Ah, my name is Mary Luce. I'm a friend of Bella's . . . We came here with a boy, with John Matthew. We were invited."

Rhage shivered, a balmy rush blooming out all over his skin, The musical lilt of her voice, the rhythm of her speech, the sound of her words, it all spread through him, calming him, comforting him. Chaining him sweetly.

He closed his eyes. "Say something else."

"What?" she asked, baffled.

"Talk. Talk to me. I want to hear your voice again."

She was silent, and he was about to demand that she speak when she said, "You don't look well. Do you need a doctor?"

He found himself swaying. The words didn't matter. It was her sound: low, soft, a quiet brushing in his ears. He felt as if he were being stroked on the inside of his skin.

"More," he said, twisting his palm around to the front of her neck so he could feel the vibrations in her throat better.

"Could you . . . could you please let go of me?"

"No." He brought his other arm up. She was wearing some kind of fleece, and he moved the collar aside, putting his hand on her shoulder so she couldn't get away from him. "Talk."

She started to struggle. "You're crowding me."

"I know. *Talk*."

"Oh, for God's sake, what do you want me to say?"

Even exasperated, her voice was beautiful. "Anything."

"Fine. Get your hand off my throat and let me go or I'm going to knee you where it counts."

He laughed. Then sank his lower body into her, trapping her with his thighs and hips. She stiffened against him, but he got an ample feel of her. She was built lean, though there was no doubt she was a female. Her breasts hit his chest, her hips cushioned his, her stomach was soft.

"Keep talking," he said in her ear. God, she smelled good. Clean. Fresh. Like lemon.

When she pushed against him, he leaned his full weight into her. Her breath came out in a rush.

"Please," he murmured.

Her chest moved against his as if she were inhaling. "I . . . er, I have nothing to say. Except get off of me."

He smiled, careful to keep his mouth closed. There was no sense showing off his fangs, especially if she didn't know what he was.

"So say that."

"What?"

"Nothing. Say nothing. Over and over and over again. Do it."

She bristled, the scent of fear replaced by a sharp spice, like fresh, pungent mint from a garden. She was annoyed now.

"*Say it*," he commanded, needing to feel more of what she did to him.

"*Fine*. Nothing. Nothing." Abruptly she laughed, and the sound shot right through to his spine, burning him. "Nothing, nothing. *No*-thing. No-*thing*. Noooooothing. There, is that good enough for you? Will you let me go now?"

"No."

She fought against him again, creating a delicious friction between their bodies. And he knew the moment when her anxiety and irritation turned to something hot. He smelled her arousal, a lovely sweetening in the air, and his body answered her call.

He got hard as a diamond.

"Talk to me, Mary." He moved his hips in a slow circle against her, rubbing his erection on her belly, increasing his ache and her heat.

After a moment the tension eased out of her, softening her against the thrust of his muscles and his arousal. Her hands flattened on his waist. And then slowly slid around to the small of his back, as if she were unsure why she was responding to him the way she was.

He arched against her, to show his approval and encourage her to touch more of him. When her palms moved up his spine, he growled low in his throat and dropped his head down so his ear was closer to her mouth. He wanted to give her another word to say, something like *luscious* or *whisper* or *strawberry*.

Hell, *antidisestablishmentarianism* would do it.

The effect she had on him was druglike, a tantalizing combination of sexual need and profound ease. Like he was having an orgasm and falling into a peaceful sleep at the same time. It was like nothing he'd ever felt before.

A chill shot through him, sucking the warmth out of his body.

He snapped his head back as he thought about what Vishous had said to him.

"Are you a virgin?" Rhage demanded.

The stiffness in her body returned, like cement setting solid. She shoved hard against him, moving him not one inch.

"I *beg* your pardon. What kind of question is that?"

Anxiety tightened his hand on her shoulder. "Have you ever been taken by a male? *Answer the question*."

Her lovely voice turned high, frightened. "Yes. Yes, I've had . . . a lover."

Disappointment loosened his grip. But relief was right on its heels.

All things considered, he wasn't sure he needed to meet his destiny this ten minutes.

Besides, even if she wasn't his fate, this human female was extraordinary . . . something special.

Something he had to have.

Mary took a deep breath as the hold on her throat relaxed.

Be careful what you ask for, she thought, remembering how she'd wanted a man to be enthralled by her.

God, this was so not what she'd expected the experience to be like. She was utterly overwhelmed. By the male body pressing into her. By the promise of sex seething out of him. By the lethal power he could wield if he decided to squeeze her neck again.

"Tell me where you live," the man said.

When she didn't answer, he undulated his hips, that massive erection moving, circling, pressing into her stomach.

Mary shut her eyes. And tried not to wonder what it would feel like if he were inside of her while he was doing that.

His head came down and his lips brushed the side of her neck. Nuzzled her. "Where do you live?"

She felt a soft, moist stroke. God, his tongue. Running up her throat.

"You're going to tell me eventually," he murmured. "But take your time. I'm not in a big hurry right now."

His hips left her briefly, returning as his thigh pushed between her legs and brushed against her core. The hand at the base of her neck swept down to her sternum, coming to rest between her breasts.

"Your heart is beating fast, Mary."

"Th-that's because I'm frightened."

"Fear isn't the only thing you're feeling. Why don't you check out what your hands are up to?"

Shoot. They were high on his biceps. And they were gripping him, pulling him closer. Her nails were digging into his skin.

When she let go of him, he frowned. "I like the way that feels. Don't stop."

The door opened behind them.

"Mary? Are you oka—Oh . . . my God." Bella's words trailed off.

Mary braced herself as the man twisted his torso and looked at Bella. His eyes squinted, flicked up and down, and then came back to Mary.

"Your friend's worried about you," he said softly. "You can tell her she shouldn't be."

Mary tried to get loose and wasn't surprised when he mastered the jerky movements easily.

"I have an idea," she muttered. "Why don't you let me go, and then I won't have to reassure her?"

A dry male voice cut through the hall. "Rhage, that female wasn't brought here for your pleasure, and this isn't One Eye, my brother. No sex in the hall."

Mary tried to turn her head, but the hand between her breasts slid up her throat and took her chin, stopping her. Teal-blue eyes bored into hers.

"I'm going to ignore them both. If you do the same, we can make them disappear."

"Rhage, let her go." A sharp torrent of words followed, spoken in a language she didn't understand.

While the tirade went on, the blond's brilliant gaze stayed on her, his thumb running gently back and forth along her jaw. He was lazy, affectionate, but when he replied to the other man, his voice was hard and aggressive, as powerful as his body. Another series of words came back, this time less combative. Like the other guy was trying to reason with him.

Abruptly the blond let her go and stepped back. The absence of his warm, heavy body was a curious shock.

"See you later, Mary." He brushed her cheek with his forefinger and then turned from her.

Feeling weak in the knees, she sagged against the wall as he staggered away, steadying himself by throwing his arm out to the side.

God, when he'd had her at his mercy, she'd forgotten she was ill.

"Where's the boy?" the other male voice demanded.

Mary looked to her left. The guy was big and dressed in black leather, with a military haircut and a shrewd pair of navy-blue eyes.

A soldier, she thought, somehow put at ease by him.

"The boy?" he prompted.

"John's in there," Bella replied.

"Then let's get to it."

The man opened the door and leaned against it so she and Bella had to squeeze past him. He paid no attention to them as they went by, but stared at John instead. John looked right back at him, eyes narrowed as if he were trying to place the soldier.

When they were all sitting at the table, the man nodded to Bella. "You were the one who called."

"Yes. And this is Mary Luce. And John. John Matthew."

"I'm Tohrment." He refocused on John. "How you doing, son?"

John signed, and Mary had to clear her throat before translating. "He says, 'Fine, sir. How are you?'"

"I'm all right." The man smiled a little and then glanced at Bella. "I want you to wait in the hall. I'll talk to you after I speak with him."

Bella hesitated.

"That isn't a request," he said in a level voice.

After Bella left, the guy turned his chair toward John, leaned back in it, and kicked his long legs out. "So tell me, son, where did you grow up?"

John moved his hands, and Mary said, "Here in town. First in an orphanage, then with a couple of sets of foster parents."

"You know anything about your mom or dad?"

John shook his head.

"Bella told me you had a bracelet with some designs on it. Would you show it to me?"

John pulled up his sleeve and extended his arm. The man's hand engulfed the boy's wrist.

"That's real nice, son. You make it?"

John nodded.

"And where'd you get the idea for the design?"

John extracted himself from the soldier's grip and started to sign. When he stopped, Mary said, "He dreams of the pattern."

"Yeah? Mind if I ask what your dreams are like?" The man returned to his casual pose in the chair, but his eyes were narrow.

Screw martial-arts training, Mary thought. This wasn't about some karate lessons. This was an interrogation.

As John hesitated, she wanted to grab the kid and march out, but she had a feeling the boy would fight her. He was utterly absorbed by the man, intense and intent.

70

"It's all right, son. Whatever it is, it's okay."

John lifted his hands, and Mary spoke as he signed.

"Er . . . he's in a dark place. Kneeling in front of an altar. Behind it, he sees writing on the wall, hundreds of lines of writing in black stone—John, wait, slow down. I can't translate when you go so fast." Mary concentrated on the boy's hands. "He says in the dream he keeps going over and touching a strip of writing that looks like this."

The man frowned.

When John looked down, as if embarrassed, the soldier said, "Don't you worry, son, we're cool. Is there anything else you can think of about yourself that strikes you as odd? Things that maybe make you different from other folks?"

Mary shifted in her chair, really uncomfortable with the way things were going. John was clearly going to answer any question put to him, but, for God's sake, they didn't know who this man was. And Bella, though she'd made the introduction, had been obviously uncomfortable.

Mary lifted her hands, about to sign a warning to John, when the kid unbuttoned his shirt. He opened one side, flashing a circular scar above his left pectoral.

The man leaned forward, studied the marking, and then moved back. "Where did you get that?"

The boy's hands flew around in front of him.

"He says he was born with it."

"Is there anything else?" the man asked.

John glanced over at Mary. He took a deep breath and signed, *I dream of blood. Of fangs. Of . . . biting.*

Mary felt her eyes widen before she could stop herself.

John looked at her anxiously. *Don't worry, Mary. I'm not a sicko or anything. I was terrified when the dreams first came to me, and it's not like I can control what my brain does, you know.*

71

"Yeah, I know," she said, reaching out and squeezing his hand.

"What did he say?" the man asked.

"That last part was meant for me."

She inhaled deeply. And went back to translating.

NINE

Bella leaned back against the wall in the corridor and started braiding pieces of her hair, something she did when she was nervous.

She'd heard members of the Brotherhood were almost a separate species, but she'd never thought that was true. Until now. Those two males were not just colossal on a physical scale; they radiated dominance and aggression. Hell, they made her brother look like an amateur in the hard-ass department, and Rehvenge was the toughest thing she'd ever come across.

Dear God, what had she done in bringing Mary and John here? She was a little less concerned for the boy, but what about Mary? The way that blond warrior had acted around her was flat-out trouble. You could have boiled an ocean with the kind of lust he'd thrown off, and members of the Black Dagger Brotherhood were not used to being denied. From what she'd heard, when they wanted a female, they took her.

Thankfully, they weren't known to rape, although, going by what she'd seen just now, they wouldn't have to. Those warriors' bodies were made for sex. Mating with one of them, being possessed by all that strength, would be an extraordinary experience.

Although Mary, as a human, might very well not feel that way.

Bella looked up and down the hall, restless, tense. There was no one around, and if she had to stand still any longer she was going to have a headful of cornrows. She shook out her hair, picked a random direction, and meandered. When she caught the sound of a rhythmic pounding in the distance, she followed the thumping to a pair of metal doors. She opened one side and walked through.

The gymnasium was the size of a pro-basketball court, its wooden floor varnished to a high gloss. Bright-blue mats were laid out here and there and caged fluorescent lights dangled from the high ceiling. A balcony with stadium seating jutted out on the left, and beneath the overhang a series of punching bags was strung up.

A magnificent male was beating the crap out of one of them, his back to her. Dancing on the balls of his feet, light as a breeze, he threw punch after punch, ducking, hitting, driving the heavy bag forward with his force so the thing hung at an angle.

She couldn't see his face, but he had to be attractive. His skull-trimmed hair was light brown, and he wore a skintight black turtleneck and a pair of loose black nylon workout pants. A holster crisscrossed over his broad back.

The door clicked shut behind her.

With a swipe of his arm, the male whipped a black-bladed dagger out and buried it into the bag. He ripped the thing open, sand and padding pouring down in a rush onto the mat. And then he spun around.

Bella clapped a hand over her mouth. His face was scarred, as if someone had tried to cut it in half with a knife. The thick line started at his forehead, went down the bridge of his nose, and curved over his cheek. It ended at the side of his mouth, distorting his upper lip.

Narrowed eyes, black and cold as night, took her in and then widened ever so slightly. He seemed nonplussed, his big body unmoving save for the deep breaths he took.

The male wanted her, she thought. And was unsure what to do about it.

Except just like that, the speculation and odd confusion were buried. What took their place was an icy anger that scared the hell out of her. Keeping her eyes on him, she backed into the door and pumped the release bar.

When she got nowhere, she had a feeling he was trapping her inside.

The male watched her struggle for a moment and then came after her. As he stalked across the mats, he flipped his dagger into the air and caught it by the handle. Flipped it up, snatched it back. Up and down.

"Don't know what you're doing here," he said in a low voice. "Other than fucking up my workout."

As those eyes went over her face and body, his hostility was palpable, but he was also throwing off raw heat, a kind of sexual menace she really shouldn't have been captivated by.

"I'm sorry. I didn't know . . ."

"Didn't know what, female?"

God, he was so close now. And he was so much bigger than her.

She flattened herself against the door. "I'm sorry—"

The male punched his hands into the metal on either side of her head. She eyed the knife he was holding, but then forgot all about the weapon as he leaned into her. He stopped just before their bodies touched.

Bella took a deep breath, smelling him. His scent was more like a fire in her nose than anything she could name. And she responded to it, warming, wanting.

"You're sorry," he said, tilting his head to the side and focusing on her neck. When he smiled, his fangs were long and very white. "Yeah, I bet you are."

"I am very sorry."

"So prove it."

"How?" she croaked.

"Get on your hands and knees. I'll take your apology from there."

A door on the other side of the gymnasium burst open.

"Oh, Christ . . . Let her go!" Another male, this one with a long head of hair, jogged across the vast floor. "Hands off, Z. Right now."

The scarred male leaned down to her, putting that misshapen mouth close to her ear. Something pressed into her sternum, over her heart. His fingertip.

"You just got saved, female."

He stepped around her and went out the door, just as the other male came up to her.

"Are you okay?"

Bella eyed the decimated punching bag. She couldn't seem to breathe, although whether that was from fear or something altogether sexual, she wasn't sure. Probably a combination of both.

"Yes, I think so. Who was that?"

The male opened the door and led her back to the interrogation room without answering her question. "Do yourself a favor and stay here, okay?"

Good advice, she thought, as she was left by herself.

TEN

Rhage came awake with a jolt. As he looked at the clock on his bedside table, he was psyched when he could focus his eyes and read the thing. Then pissed off when he saw what time it was.

Where the hell was Tohr? He'd promised to call as soon as he was done with the human female, but that had been more than six hours ago.

Rhage reached for the phone and dialed Tohr's cell. When he got voice mail, he cursed and hung up.

As he got out of bed, he stretched carefully. He was sore and sick to his stomach, but able to move a lot better. A quick shower and a fresh set of leathers had him feeling even more himself, and he headed for Wrath's study. Dawn was coming soon, and if Tohr wasn't answering his phone, he was probably doing a download to the king before he went home.

The room's double doors were open, and lo and behold, Tohrment was wearing a track in the Aubusson carpet, pacing while talking to Wrath.

"Just who I was looking for," Rhage drawled.

Tohr glanced over. "I was coming to your room next."

"Sure you were. What's doing, Wrath?"

The Blind King smiled. "Glad to see you're getting back to fighting form, Hollywood."

"Oh, I'm ready, all right." Rhage stared at Tohr. "You got something to tell me?"

"Not really."

"You're saying you don't know where the human lives?"

"I don't know if you need to go see her, how about that?"

77

Wrath leaned back in his chair, putting his feet up on the desk. His enormous shitkickers made the delicate thing look like a footstool.

He smiled. "One of you steakheads want to bring me up to speed?"

"Private biz," Rhage murmured. "Nothing special."

"The hell it is." Tohr turned to Wrath. "Our boy over here seems to want to get to know the kid's human translator better."

Wrath shook his head. "Oh, no, you don't, Hollywood. Lie down with some other female. God knows, there's enough of them out there for you." He nodded at Tohr. "As I was saying, I've got no objection to the boy joining the first class of trainees, provided you verify his background. And that human needs to be checked out, too. If the kid disappears all of a sudden, I don't want her causing trouble."

"I'll take care of her," Rhage said. When they both gave him a look, he shrugged. "Either you let me or I'll follow whoever does. One way or the other, I will find that female."

Tohr's brows turned his forehead into a plow field. "Will you back off, my brother? Assuming the boy comes here, there's too close a connection with that human. Just drop it."

"Sorry. I want her."

"Christ. You can be a real pain in the ass, you know that? No impulse control, but totally single-minded. Helluva combination."

"Look, one way or the other, I'm going to have her. Now do you want me to check her out while I do it or not?"

When Tohr rubbed his eyes, and Wrath cursed, Rhage knew he'd won.

"Fine," Tohr muttered. "Find out her background and her connection to the kid and then do what you will with her. But at the end of it, you strip her memories and you don't see her again. Do you hear me? You wipe yourself out of her when you're finished and you *do not* see her again."

"Deal."

Tohr flipped open his cell and punched a few buttons. "I'm text-messaging the human's number to you."

"And her friend's."

"You're going to do her, too?"

"Just give it to me, Tohr."

Bella was getting into bed for the day when the phone rang. She picked it up, hoping it wasn't her brother. She hated when he checked to make sure she was at home when night receded. Like she might be out screwing males or something.

"Hello?" she said.

"You will call Mary and you will tell her to meet me tonight for dinner."

Bella bolted upright. *The blond warrior.*

"Did you hear what I said?"

"Yes . . . but what do you want with her?" As if she didn't already know.

"Call her now. Tell her that I am a friend of yours and she'll enjoy herself. It will be better that way."

"Better than what?"

"My breaking into her house to get to her. Which is what I'll do, if I have to."

Bella closed her eyes and saw Mary against that wall, the male looming over her as he held her in place. He was coming after her for one and only one reason: to release all that sex in his body. Release it into her.

"Oh, God . . . please don't hurt her. She's not one of us. And she's ill."

"I know. I'm not going to harm her."

Bella put her head in her hand, wondering just how a

79

hard male like him would know what hurt and what didn't.

"Warrior . . . she doesn't know about our race. She's— I beg you, don't—"

"She won't remember me after it's done."

Like that was supposed to make her feel less awful? As it was, she felt like she was serving Mary up on a platter.

"You can't stop me, female. But you can make it easier on your friend. Think about it. She'll feel safer if she meets me in a public place. She won't know what I am. It will be as normal as it can be for her."

Bella hated being pushed around, hated the sense that she was betraying Mary's friendship.

"I wish I'd never brought her along," she muttered.

"I don't." There was a pause. "She has an . . . unusual way about her."

"What if she denies you?"

"She won't."

"But if she does?"

"That's her choice. She won't be forced. I swear to you."

Bella let her hand drop to her throat, tangling a finger in the Diamonds by the Yard chain she always wore.

"Where?" she said with dejection. "Where should she meet you?"

"Where do humans meet for normal dates?"

How the hell would she know? Except then she remembered Mary saying something about a colleague of hers meeting a man . . . What was the name of the place?

"TGI Friday's," she said. "There's one in Lucas Square."

"Fine. Tell her eight o'clock tonight."

"What name do I give her?"

"Tell her it's . . . Hal. Hal E. Wood."

"Warrior?"

"Yeah?"

"Please . . ."

His voice actually softened. "Don't worry, Bella. I'll treat her well."

The phone went dead.

In Mr. X's cabin deep in the woods, O slowly sat up on the bed, easing himself to the vertical. He brushed his hands across his wet cheeks.

The Omega had left only an hour ago, and O's body was still leaking out of several places, wounds and otherwise. He wasn't sure he was up to moving, but he had to get the hell away from this bedroom.

When he tried to stand his vision spun wildly, so he sat down. Through the little window across the room, he saw dawn breaking, the warm glow splintered by the boughs of pine trees. He hadn't expected the punishment to last a whole day. And had been sure at many points that he wouldn't make it through.

The Omega had taken him to places inside of himself that he'd been shocked to find he had. Places of fear and self-loathing. Of utter humiliation and degradation. And now, in the aftermath, he felt as if he had no skin, as if he were totally open and exposed, a raw laceration that just happened to be breathing.

The door opened. Mr. X's shoulders filled the frame. "How are we doing?"

O covered himself with a blanket and then opened his mouth. Nothing came out. He coughed a few times. "I . . . made it."

"I was hoping you would."

For O, it was difficult to see the man dressed in regular clothes, holding a clipboard, looking as if he were ready to start another productive workday. Compared to where O had spent the last twenty-four hours, the normalcy seemed fake and vaguely threatening.

Mr. X smiled a little. "So, you and I are going to strike

81

a deal. You get in line and stay there, and that won't happen again."

O was too exhausted to argue. The fight in him would come back—he knew it would—but right now all he wanted was soap and hot water. And some time alone.

"What do you say to me?" Mr. X demanded.

"Yes, sensei." O didn't care what he had to do, what he had to say. He just had to get away from the bed . . . the room . . . the cabin.

"There are some clothes in the closet. You good enough to drive?"

"Yeah. Yeah . . . I'm fine."

O pictured the shower at his house, all creamy tile and white grout. Clean. So very clean. And he would be, too, when he got out of it.

"I want you to do yourself a favor, Mr. O. When you go about your work, remember what all that felt like. Call it up, keep it fresh in your mind, and take it out on your subjects. I may be irritated by your initiative, but I would despise you if you went soft on me. Are we clear?"

"Yes, sensei."

Mr. X turned away, but then glanced over his shoulder. "I think I know why the Omega let you survive. As he left, he was quite complimentary. I know he'd like to see you again. Shall I tell him you'd welcome his visits?"

O made a strangled sound. He couldn't help it.

Mr. X laughed softly. "Perhaps not."

ELEVEN

Mary parked in the TGI Friday's lot. Looking around at the cars and minivans, she wondered how the hell she'd agreed to meet some man for dinner. Close as she could recall, Bella had phoned and talked her into it this morning, but damned if she could remember any of the particulars.

Then again, she wasn't retaining much. Tomorrow morning she was going to the doctor's for the follow-up, and with that hanging over her, she was in a daze. Take last night, for instance. She could have sworn she went somewhere with John and Bella, except the evening was a total black hole. Work was the same. She'd gone through the motions at the law office today, making simple mistakes and staring into space.

As she got out of the Civic, she tightened herself up mentally as best she could. She owed the poor man she was meeting an effort to be alert, but, other than that, she didn't feel any pressure. She'd made it clear to Bella this was friends only. Split the check. Nice to meet you; see you later.

Which would have been her attitude even if she hadn't been distracted by the whole Russian-roulette medical lottery hanging over her head. Aside from the fact that she might be sick again, she was way out of practice with the whole dating thing and not looking to get back in shape. Who needed the drama? Most single guys in their early thirties were still looking for fun or they would have been married already, and she was the antifun, buzz-kill type. Serious by nature, with some hard-core experience.

And she didn't look like a party, either. The unremarkable hair growing out of her head was pulled back tight and cinched in a scrunchie. The creamy Irish knit sweater she had on was baggy and warm. Her khakis were comfortable, and her flats were brown and scuffed at the toes. She probably looked like the mother she would never be.

When she walked into the restaurant, she found the hostess and was led to a booth in the back corner. As she put her purse down, she smelled green peppers and onions and looked up. A waitress whipped by with a sizzling iron plate.

The restaurant was busy, a great cacophony rising up from all the life in the place. While waiters danced around with trays of steaming food or piles of used dishes, families and couples and groups of friends laughed, talked, argued. The mad chaos struck her as more awesome than ordinary, and sitting by herself she felt utterly separate, a poser among the real people.

They all had happy futures. She had . . . more doctor's appointments to go to.

With a curse, she clipped her emotions into place, trimming off the panic and catastrophizing, leaving behind nothing but a resolve not to dwell on Dr. Della Croce tonight.

Mary thought of topiaries and smiled a little, just as a harried waitress came up to the table. The woman put down a plastic glass of water, spilling some.

"You waiting for someone?"

"Yes, I am."

"You want a drink?"

"This is fine. Thanks."

As the waitress took off, Mary sipped the water, tasted metal, and pushed the glass away. Out of the corner of her eye she caught a flurry of movement at the front door.

Holy . . . Wow.

A man had walked into the restaurant. A really, really . . . *very* fine man.

He was blond. Movie-star beautiful. And monumental in a black leather trench coat. His shoulders were as broad as the door he'd come through, his legs so long he was taller than anyone in the place. And as he strode through the knot of people at the entrance, the other men looked down or away or at their watches, as if they knew they couldn't measure up to what he had going on.

Mary frowned, feeling like she'd seen him somewhere before.

Yeah, it's called the big screen, she told herself. Maybe there was a movie being shot here in town.

The man stepped up to the hostess and ran his eyes over the woman as if trying her on for size. The redhead blinked up at him in stunned disbelief, but then clearly her estrogen receptors came to the rescue. She pulled her hair forward, as if she wanted to make sure he noticed the stuff, and then kicked out her hip as if she'd popped the thing out of joint.

Don't worry, Mary thought. *He sees you, honey.*

As the two of them started coming through the restaurant, the man surveyed every table, and Mary wondered who he was eating with.

Aha. Two booths away there was a blonde seated alone. Her fuzzy blue sweater was skintight, the angora shrink-wrap showing off a dazzling display of assets. And the woman was radiating anticipation as she watched him come through the restaurant.

Bingo. Ken and Barbie.

Well, not really Ken. As the guy walked along, there was something about him that wasn't WASPy handsome in spite of his amazing looks. Something . . . animalistic. He just didn't carry himself as other people did.

Actually, he moved like a predator, thick shoulders rolling with his gait, head turning, scanning. She had the discomforting sense that, if he wanted to, he could wipe out everyone in the place with his bare hands.

Calling on her willpower, Mary forced herself to stare into her water glass. She didn't want to be like all the other gawking fools.

Oh, hell, she had to look up again.

He'd bypassed the blonde and was standing in front of a brunette directly across the aisle. The woman was smiling broadly. Which seemed only reasonable.

"Hey," he said.

Well, what do you know. Voice was spectacular, too. A deep, resonant drawl.

"Hi, yourself."

The man's tone sharpened. "You are not Mary."

Mary tensed. *Oh, no.*

"I'll be anyone you want."

"I'm looking for Mary Luce."

Oh . . . shit.

Mary cleared her throat, wishing she were anywhere else, anyone else. "I'm . . . ah, I'm Mary."

The man turned around. As vivid, teal-blue eyes bored into her, his big body stiffened.

Mary looked down quickly, jabbing the straw into her water.

Not what you were expecting, am I? she thought.

As silence stretched out, clearly he was searching for a socially acceptable excuse to cut and run.

God, how could Bella have humiliated her like this?

Rhage stopped breathing and just took the human in. Oh, she was lovely. Nothing he'd expected, but lovely nonetheless.

Her skin was pale and smooth, like fine ivory stationery. The bones of her face were equally delicate, her jaw a graceful arch running from her ears to her chin, her cheeks high and tinted with a natural blush. Her neck was long and slender, like her hands and probably her legs. Her deep-brown hair was pulled back into a ponytail.

She wore no makeup, he couldn't detect any perfume, and the only jewelry she had on was a pair of tiny pearl earrings. Her off-white sweater was bulky and loose, and he was willing to bet her pants were also baggy.

There was absolutely nothing about her that courted notice. She wasn't anything like the females he went for. And she held his attention like a marching band.

"Hello, Mary," he said softly.

He was hoping she would look back up at him, because he hadn't been able to catch enough of her eyes. And he couldn't wait to hear her voice again. The two words she'd spoken had been so quiet and not nearly enough.

He stuck his hand out, itching to touch her. "I'm Hal."

She let his palm hang between them as she reached for her purse and started to scootch her way out of the booth.

He planted himself in her path. "Where are you going?"

"Look, it's okay. I won't tell Bella. We'll just pretend we had dinner."

Rhage closed his eyes and tuned out the background noise so he could absorb the sound of her voice. His body stirred and calmed, weaved a little.

And then he realized what she'd said.

"Why would we lie? We are going to have dinner together."

Her lips tightened, but at least she stopped trying to escape.

When he was sure she wasn't going to bolt, he sat down and tried to get his legs to fit under the table. As she looked at him, he stopped shifting his knees around.

Dear God. Her eyes didn't match the gentle lilt of her voice at all. They belonged to a warrior.

Gunmetal gray, surrounded by lashes the color of her hair, they were grave, serious, reminding him of males who

87

had fought and survived battle. They were staggeringly beautiful in their strength.

His voice vibrated. "I am *so* going to . . . have dinner with you."

Those eyes flared and then narrowed. "Have you always done charity work?"

"Excuse me?"

A waitress came over and slowly put down a glass of water in front of him. He could smell the female's lusty response to his face and his body and it annoyed him.

"Hi, I'm Amber," she said. "What can I get you to drink?"

"Water is fine. Mary, do you want anything else?"

"No, thanks."

The waitress stepped a little closer to him. "Can I tell you about our specials?"

"All right."

As the list went on and on, Rhage didn't look away from Mary. She was hiding her eyes from him, damn it.

The waitress cleared her throat. A couple of times. "You sure I can't get you a beer? Or maybe something with a little more kick? How about a shot—"

"We're fine, and you can come back later for the order. Thanks."

Amber took the hint.

When they were alone, Mary said, "Really, let's just end—"

"Have I given you any indication that I don't want to eat with you?"

She put a hand on top of the menu in front of her, tracing the picture of a plate of ribs. Abruptly she pushed the thing away. "You keep staring at me."

"Males do that." *When they find a female they want*, he added to himself.

"Yeah, well, not to me they don't. I can imagine how seriously underwhelmed you are, but I don't need you focusing on the particulars, know what I mean? And I'm really not interested in enduring an hour of you taking one for the team."

God, that voice. She was doing it to him again, his skin flaring with shivers and then settling down, loosening. He took a deep breath, trying to catch some of her natural, lemony scent.

As silence cropped up between them, he nudged her menu back at her. "Decide what you're going to order, unless you just want to sit there while I eat."

"I can leave anytime I want."

"True. But you won't."

"Oh, and why's that?" Her eyes flashed, and his body lit up like a football stadium.

"You're not going to bail because you like Bella too much to embarrass her by walking out on me. And unlike you, I will tell her you ditched me."

Mary frowned. "Blackmail?"

"Persuasion."

She slowly opened the menu and glanced at it. "You're still staring at me."

"I know."

"Would you mind looking somewhere else? The menu, that brunette across the aisle. There's a blonde two booths back, in case you haven't noticed."

"You don't ever wear perfume, do you?"

Her eyes flipped up to his. "No, I don't."

"May I?" He nodded to one of her hands.

"Excuse me?"

He couldn't very well tell her he wanted to smell her skin up close. "Considering we're having dinner and all, seems only civil to shake hands, doesn't it? And even though you shut me down the first time I tried to be polite, I'm willing to give it another shot."

When she didn't answer, he reached across the table and took her hand into his. Before she could react, he pulled her arm forward, bent down, and pressed his lips to her knuckles. He breathed in deeply.

His body's response to her scent was immediate. His erection punched at the fly of his leathers, straining, pushing. He shifted around to make some more room in his pants.

God, he couldn't wait to get her home alone.

TWELVE

Mary stopped breathing as Hal released her hand.

Maybe she was dreaming. Yeah, that had to be it. Because he was too gorgeous. Too sexy. And way too focused on her to be real.

The waitress came back, getting as close to Hal as she could without actually being in his lap. And wouldn't you know it, the woman had freshened her lip gloss. That mouth of hers looked like it had had an oil change with something called Fresh Pink. Or Curious Coral. Or something equally ridiculous.

Mary shook her head, surprised she was being so bitchy.

"What can I get you?" the waitress asked Hal.

He glanced across the table and lifted an eyebrow. Mary shook her head and started flipping through the menu.

"Okay, whadda we got here," he said, opening his own. "Let's have the Chicken Alfredo. The NY strip, rare. And a cheeseburger, also rare. Double on the fries. And some nachos. Yeah, I want the nachos with everything on them. Double that, too, will you?"

Mary could only stare as he closed the menu and waited.

The waitress looked a little awkward. "Is all that for both you and your sister?"

As if family obligation was the only reason a man like him would be out with a woman like her. *Oh, man* . . .

"No, that's for me. And she's my date, not my sister. Mary?"

"I . . . ah, I'll just have a Caesar salad, whenever his"— *feeding trough?*— "dinner comes."

The waitress took the menus and left.

"So, Mary, tell me a little about yourself."

"Why don't we just make it about you?"

"Because then I won't hear you talk."

Mary stiffened, something bubbling below the surface of her consciousness.

Talk. I want to hear your voice.

Say nothing. Over and over and over again. Do it.

She could have sworn this man had said those things to her, but she'd never met him before. God knew, she would have remembered that.

"What do you do for a living?" he prompted.

"Er . . . I'm an executive assistant."

"Where?"

"A law firm here in town."

"But you did something else, didn't you?"

She wondered how much Bella had told him. God, she hoped the woman hadn't brought up the illness. Maybe that was why he was staying.

"Mary?"

"I used to work with kids."

"Teacher?"

"Therapist."

"Head or body?"

"Both. I was a rehab specialist for autistic children."

"What got you started in it?"

"Do we have to do this?"

"Do what?"

"All the let's-pretend-to-get-to-know-you stuff."

He frowned, leaning back as the waitress put a huge plate of nachos on the table.

The woman bent down to his ear. "Shhh, don't tell anyone. I stole these from another order. They can wait, and you look very hungry."

Hal nodded, smiled, but seemed uninterested.

She had to give him credit for being polite, Mary thought. Now that he was sitting across the table from her, he didn't seem to notice any other women at all.

He offered the plate to her. When she shook her head, he popped a nacho in his mouth.

"I'm not surprised small talk annoys you," he said.

"Why's that?"

"You've been through too much."

She frowned. "What exactly did Bella tell you about me?"

"Nothing much."

"So how do you know I've been through anything?"

"It's in your eyes."

Oh, hell. He was smart, too. Talk about the total package.

"But I hate to break it to you," he said, making fast but neat work of the nachos, "I don't care if you're annoyed. I want to know what got you interested in that line of work, and you're going to tell me."

"You are arrogant."

"Surprise, surprise." He smiled tightly. "And you're avoiding my question. What got you started in it?"

The answer was her mother's struggle with muscular dystrophy. After seeing what her mom went through, helping other people find ways around their limitations had been a calling. Maybe even a way to work off some guilt at being healthy when her mother had been so compromised.

And then Mary had gotten hit with some serious compromises herself.

Funny, the first thing she'd thought of when she'd been diagnosed was that it wasn't fair. She'd watched her mother do the disease thing, had suffered right alongside. So why was the universe requiring her to know firsthand the kind of pain she'd witnessed? It was right then and there that she'd realized there was no quota on misery for people, no quantifiable threshold that, once reached, got you miraculously taken out of the distress pool.

"I never wanted to do anything else," she hedged.

"Then why did you stop?"

"My life changed."

93

Thankfully, he didn't follow up on that one. "Did you like working with handicapped kids?"

"They're not . . . they weren't handicapped."

"Sorry," he said, clearly meaning it.

The sincerity in his voice popped the lid off her reserve in a way compliments or smiles never would have.

"They're just different. They experience the world in a different way. Normal is just what's average, it's not necessarily the only way of being, or living—" She stopped, noticing he'd closed his eyes. "Am I boring you?"

His lids lifted slowly. "I love to hear you talk."

Mary swallowed a gasp. His eyes were neon, glowing, iridescent.

Those had to be contacts, she thought. People's eyes just didn't come in that teal color.

"Different doesn't bother you, does it?" he murmured.

"No."

"That's good."

For some reason, she found herself smiling at him.

"I was right," he whispered.

"About what?"

"You're lovely when you smile."

Mary looked away.

"What's the matter?"

"Please don't put on the charm. I'd rather deal with small talk."

"I'm honest, not charming. Just ask my brothers. I'm constantly putting my foot in my mouth."

There were more of him? Boy, that'd be a hell of a family Christmas card. "How many brothers do you have?"

"Five. Now. We lost one." He took a long drink of water, as if he didn't want her to see his eyes.

"I'm sorry," she said quietly.

"Thanks. It's still fresh. And I miss him like hell."

The waitress arrived with a heavy tray. When the plates were lined up in front of him and Mary's salad was down on the table, the woman lingered until Hal thanked her pointedly.

He went for the Alfredo first. He sank his fork into the tangle of fettuccine, twisted until a knot of pasta was on the tines, and carried the noodles to his mouth. He chewed thoughtfully and added some salt. He tested the strip steak next. Shook on a little pepper. Then he picked up the cheeseburger. It was halfway to his mouth when he frowned and put it back down. He used his fork and knife to take a bite.

He ate like a total gentleman. With an almost dainty air.

Abruptly, he looked at her. "What?"

"Sorry, I, ah . . ." She picked at her salad. And promptly went back to watching him eat.

"You keep staring at me and I'm going to blush," he drawled.

"I'm sorry."

"I'm not. I like your eyes on me."

Mary's body shimmered to life. And she responded with total grace by launching a crouton into her lap.

"So what are you looking at?" he asked.

She used her napkin to dab at the dressing skid on her pants. "Your table manners. They're very good."

"Food is to be savored."

She wondered what else he enjoyed like that. Slowly. Thoroughly. God, she could just imagine the kind of love life he had. He'd be amazing in bed. That big body, that golden skin, those long, tapered fingers . . .

Mary's throat went dry and she made a grab for her glass. "But do you always . . . eat so much?"

"Actually, the stomach's off. I'm taking it easy." He shook a little more salt on the fettuccine. "So you used to work with autistic children, but now you're at a law firm. What else do you do with your time? Hobbies? Interests?"

"I like to cook."

"Really? I like to eat."

She frowned, trying not to imagine him sitting at her table.

"You're irritated again."

She waved her hand around. "I'm not."

"Yeah, you are. Don't like the idea of cooking something for me, do you?"

His unfettered honesty made her think she could tell him anything and he'd respond with exactly what he thought and felt. Good or bad.

"Hal, do you have any kind of filter between your brain and your mouth?"

"Not really." He finished the Alfredo and moved the plate aside. The steak was up next. "So what about your parents?"

She took a deep breath. "My mother died about four years ago. My father was killed when I was two in a wrong-place-wrong-time kind of thing."

He paused. "That's hard. Losing both of them."

"Yes, it was."

"Both of mine are gone, too. But at least they made it to old age. Do you have sisters? Brothers?"

"No. It was just me and my mother. And now only me."

There was a long silence. "So how do you know John?"

"John . . . oh, John Matthew? Did Bella tell you about him?"

"After a fashion."

"I don't know him all that well. He just kind of came into my life recently. I think he's a special kid, a kind one, even though I get the sense things haven't been easy for him."

"You know his parents?"

"He told me he doesn't have any."

"You know where he lives?"

"I know the area of town. It's not a very good one."

"Do you want to save him, Mary?"

What an odd question, she thought.

"I don't think he needs to be saved, but I'd like to be his friend. Truthfully, I barely know him. He just showed up at my house one night."

Hal nodded, as if she'd given him an answer he'd wanted.

"How do you know Bella?" she asked.

"Don't you like your salad?"

She looked down at her plate. "I'm not hungry."

"You sure about that?"

"Yes."

As soon as he'd finished his burger and fries, he reached over for the small menu by the salt and pepper shakers.

"Is dessert more to your liking?" he asked.

"Not tonight."

"You should eat more."

"I had a big lunch."

"No, you didn't."

Mary crossed her arms over her chest. "How would you know?"

"I can sense your hunger."

She stopped breathing. God, those eyes of his were gleaming again. So blue, so bright, the color endless, like the sea. An ocean to swim in. To drown in. To die in.

"How do you know I'm . . . hungry?" she said, feeling as if the world were slipping away.

His voice dropped until it was almost a purr. "I'm right, aren't I? So why does it matter how?"

Fortunately, the waitress arrived to pick up the dishes and broke the moment. By the time Hal had ordered an apple crisp, some kind of brownie thing, and a cup of coffee, Mary felt like she was back on the planet.

"So what do you do for a living?" she asked.

"This and that."

"Acting? Modeling?"

He laughed. "No. I may be decorative, but I prefer to be useful."

"And how are you useful?"

"I guess you could say I'm a soldier."

"You're in the military?"

"Kind of."

Well, that would explain the deadly air. The physical confidence. The sharpness in his eyes.

"What branch?" Marines, she thought. Or maybe a SEAL. He was that hard.

Hal's face tightened up. "Just another soldier."

From out of nowhere, a cloud of perfume invaded Mary's nose. It was the redheaded hostess sweeping up to the table.

"Was everything okay?" As Hal looked over, you could practically hear the woman sizzle.

"Fine, thanks," he said.

"Good." She slipped something onto the table. A napkin. With a number and a name on it.

As the woman flashed her eyes and sauntered off, Mary looked down at her hands. Out of the corner of her eye, she saw her purse.

Time to go, she thought. For some reason she didn't want to watch Hal put that napkin in his pocket. Even though he had every right to do so.

"Well, this has been . . . interesting," she said. She picked up her bag and shuffled out of the booth.

"Why are you leaving?" His frown made him look like true military material, taking him very far away from the sexy male pinup stuff.

Unease flickered in her chest. "I'm tired. But, thanks, Hal. This has been . . . Well, thanks."

As she tried to get by him, he took her hand, stroking her inner wrist with his thumb. "Stay while I eat my dessert."

She looked away from his perfect face and his broad

shoulders. The brunette across the aisle was getting to her feet and eyeing him, a business card in her hand.

Mary leaned down. "I'm sure you'll find plenty of others to keep you company. In fact, one's headed your way right now. I'd say good luck with her, but she looks like a sure thing."

Mary made a beeline for the exit. The chilly air and the relative silence were a relief after the crush of people, except as she approached her car, she had the eerie sense she wasn't alone. She glanced over her shoulder.

Hal was right behind her, even though she'd left him in the restaurant. She wheeled around, heart pounding like it wanted out of her ribs.

"Jesus! What are you doing?"

"Walking you to your car."

"I . . . ah. Don't bother."

"Too late. This Civic is yours, right?"

"How did you—"

"The lights flashed as you unlocked it."

She moved away from him, but, as she backed up, Hal came forward. When she bumped against her car, she put her hands out.

"Stop."

"Don't be scared of me."

"Then don't crowd me."

She turned away from him and went for the door handle. His hand shot out, clamping on the seam between the window and the roof.

Yeah, she was going to get behind the wheel. When he let her.

"Mary?" His deep voice was right next to her head, and she jumped.

She felt the raw seduction of him and imagined his body as a cage locked around her. With a treasonous shift, her fear changed into something wanton and needy.

"Let me go," she whispered.

"Not yet."

She heard him take a deep breath, as if he were smelling her, and then her ears were flooded by a rhythmic pumping sound, as though he were purring. Her body loosened, heated, opened between her legs as if it was prepared to accept him inside.

Good God, she had to get away from him.

She grabbed onto his forearm and pushed. Which got her nowhere.

"Mary?"

"*What?*" she snapped, resentful because she was turned on when she should have been petrified. For God's sake, he was a stranger, a big, pushy stranger, and she was a woman alone with no one to miss her if she didn't make it home.

"Thank you for not bailing on me."

"You're welcome. Now how about letting me leave?"

"As soon as you let me kiss you good-night."

Mary had to open her mouth to get enough air into her lungs.

"Why?" she asked hoarsely. "Why would you want to do that?"

His hands fell onto her shoulders and turned her around. He towered over her, blocking out the glow from the restaurant, the lights in the parking lot, the stars far above.

"Just let me kiss you, Mary." His hands slid up her throat and on to the sides of her face. "Only once. Okay?"

"No, it's not okay," she whispered as he tilted her head back.

His lips descended and her mouth trembled. It had been so long since she'd been kissed. And never by a man like him.

The contact was soft, gentle. Unexpected, given the size of him.

And just as a blast of heat licked over her breasts and landed between her legs, she heard a hiss.

Hal stumbled back and looked at her strangely. With a jerky movement, his heavy arms crossed over his chest, as if he were holding on to himself.

"Hal?"

He said nothing, just stood there, staring. If she didn't know better, she'd think he was shaken.

"Hal, are you all right?"

He shook his head once.

Then he walked away, disappearing into the darkness beyond the parking lot.

THIRTEEN

Rhage materialized in the courtyard between the Pit and the mansion.

He couldn't put an exact bead on the sensation inside his skin, but it was some kind of low-level buzz in his muscles and bones, like the vibration of a tuning fork. What he did know for sure was that he'd never felt the hum before. And that it had kicked off the moment his mouth had touched Mary's.

Since anything new and different with his body was bad, he'd immediately gotten the hell away from her, and not being around the female seemed to help. Trouble was, now that the feeling was fading, his body's need for release was causing him to twitch. Which wasn't fair. After the beast came out, he usually got at least a few days off.

He checked his watch.

Damn it, he wanted to go out hunting for *lessers* to take himself down a notch or two, but since Tohr had taken over command of the Brotherhood, new rules had been laid out. After changing, Rhage was supposed to cool his jets for a couple days until he was back on all burners. With Darius's death this past summer, the number of brothers had been reduced to six, and then Wrath had ascended to the throne, so they were just five now. The race couldn't afford to lose another warrior.

The forced R & R made sense, but he hated being told what to do. And he couldn't stand not being out in the field, especially when he needed to drain off some juice.

Taking a set of keys from his coat, he went over to his souped-up GTO. The car came awake with a roar, and a minute and a half later he was out on the open road. He didn't know which direction he was headed in. Didn't care.

Mary. That kiss.

God, her mouth had been unbelievably sweet as it trembled under his, so sweet he'd wanted to part her lips with his tongue and slide inside of her. Slide and retreat and come back again for another taste. And then do the same with his body between her legs.

Except he'd had to stop. Whatever that hum was, it got him wired, so it was dangerous. The damn reaction didn't make sense, though. Mary calmed him, brought him some ease. Sure, he wanted her, and that was going to wire him out, but it shouldn't be enough to get him dangerous.

Ah, hell. Maybe he'd misinterpreted the response. Maybe that current had been sexual attraction of a more profound sort than he was used to . . . Which was typically nothing but the urge to come just so his body was less likely to flip out on him.

He thought about the females he'd had. There had been countless numbers of them, all nameless, faceless bodies he'd released into, not one of them a source of real pleasure for him. He'd touched them and kissed them only because, unless they got off too, he felt like a total user.

Shit, he felt like a user anyway. He *was* a user.

So even if he hadn't been thrown by the buzz from kissing Mary, he still would have left her in that parking lot. With her lovely voice and her warrior eyes and her trembling mouth, Mary could not be just another screw. Taking her, even if she was willing, seemed like a violation of something pure. Something better than he was.

His cell phone rang and he took it out of his pocket. As he checked caller ID, he cursed, but answered the thing anyway. "Hey, Tohr. I was going to call you."

"I just saw your car peel out of here. Are you meeting the human female now?"

"I already did."

"That was quick. She must have treated you right."

Rhage ground his teeth. For once he had no quick comeback. "I talked to her about the kid. We've got no problem there. She likes him, she feels badly for him, but if he disappeared, she wouldn't cause a problem. She only met him recently."

"Good job, Hollywood. So where you headed now?"

"Just driving."

Tohr's voice softened. "You hate not being able to fight, don't you?"

"Wouldn't you?"

"Of course, but don't worry, tomorrow night will come soon enough, and you'll be back in action. In the meantime, you could work off a little more of that sauce of yours at One Eye." Tohr chuckled. "By the way, I heard about the sisters you did two nights ago, one right after another. Man, you're amazing, you know that?"

"Yeah, Tohr, can I ask you a favor?"

"Anything, my brother."

"Could you not . . . ride me about the females?" Rhage took a deep breath. "Because the truth is, I hate it, I really do."

He meant to stop there, but suddenly the words were coming out and he couldn't shut up.

"I hate the anonymity of it. I hate the way my chest aches afterward. I hate the smells on my body and in my hair when I get home. But most of all, I hate the fact that I'm going to have to do it again because, if I don't, I could end up hurting one of you guys or some innocent bystander." He exhaled through his mouth. "And those two sisters you're so impressed with? See, here's the thing. I only pick the ones who don't give a shit who they're with, because otherwise it's not fair. Those two bar chippies checked out my watch and my roll and figured I was a pimp trophy. The fucking was about as intimate as a car accident. And tonight? You're going home to Wellsie. I'm going home alone. Just like I did yesterday. Just like I'm going to do the day after. The whoring isn't fun for me, and it's been killing me for years, so please give it a rest, dig?"

There was a long silence. "Jesus . . . I'm sorry. I didn't know. I had no idea—"

"Yeah, ah . . ." He really needed to stop this conversation. "Look, I gotta go. I gotta . . . go. Later."

"No, wait, Rhage—"

Rhage turned his phone off and pulled over to the side of the road. As he looked around, he realized he was out in the middle of nowhere, with nothing but the forest for company. He put his head down on the steering wheel.

Visions of Mary came to him. And he realized he'd neglected to scrub her memories.

Neglected? *Yeah, right.* He hadn't cleaned her out because he wanted to see her again. And he wanted her to remember him.

Oh, man . . . This was bad stuff. All the way around.

FOURTEEN

Mary flopped over in bed and pushed the covers and blankets off with her feet. Half-asleep, she splayed her legs out to try to cool down.

Damn it, had she left the thermostat on too high—

Horrible suspicion shot her into consciousness, her mind coming to attention on a wave of dread.

Low-grade fever. She had a low-grade fever.

Oh, hell . . . She knew the feel of it too well, the flush, the dry heat, the joint aches. And the clock said 4:18 A.M. Which, when she'd been sick before, was about the time her temperature liked to flare up.

Reaching overhead, she cracked open the window behind her bed. Cold air took the invitation to heart and rushed inside, cooling her, calming her. The fever broke soon afterward, a sheen of sweat announcing its retreat.

Maybe she was just coming down with a cold. People with her medical history did get normal sicknesses like the rest of the world. Really.

Except either way, rhinovirus or recurrence, there'd be no going back to sleep. She pulled a fleece on over her T-shirt and boxers and went downstairs. On her way to the kitchen, she turned on every light switch she passed until all the dark corners in the house were illuminated.

Destination: her coffeepot. There was no question that answering some office e-mail and getting ready for the break of the Columbus Day long weekend was better than lying in bed and counting the time before her doctor's appointment.

Which was in five and a half hours, by the way.

God, she hated the waiting.

She filled the Krups machine with water and went into the cupboard for the coffee can. It was nearly empty, so she took out her backup supply and the handheld can opener and—

She was not alone.

Mary leaned forward, looking out the window above the sink. With no exterior lights on she couldn't see anything, so she went around to the slider and flipped the switch next to the door.

"Good Lord!"

A massive black shape was on the other side of the glass.

Mary scrambled for the phone, but stopped when she saw the flash of blond hair.

Hal lifted his hand in greeting.

"Hey." His voice was muffled through the glass.

Mary wrapped her arms around her stomach. "What are you doing here?"

His wide shoulders shrugged. "Wanted to see you."

"Why? And why now?"

Another shrug. "Seemed like a good idea."

"Are you deranged?"

"Yes."

She almost smiled. And then reminded herself that she had no close neighbors and he was practically the size of her house.

"How did you find me?" Maybe Bella had told him where she lived.

"Can I come in? Or maybe you could come out, if you'd feel more comfortable that way?"

"Hal, it's four thirty in the morning."

"I know. But you're awake and so am I."

God, he was so big in all that black leather, and with his face mostly in shadow he was more menacing than beautiful.

And she was actually considering opening the door? Clearly she was also deranged.

"Look, Hal, I don't think it's a good idea."

He stared at her through the glass. "Maybe we can just talk this way, then?"

Mary stared at him, dumbfounded. The guy was willing to hang around, locked out of her house like a criminal, just so they could chat?

"Hal, no offense, but there are about a hundred thousand women in this zip code who would not only let you into their homes, but would take you to bed. Why don't you go find one of them and leave me alone?"

"They aren't you."

The darkness falling across his face made his eyes impossible to read. But his tone of voice was so damn sincere.

In the long pause that followed, she tried to convince herself not to let him inside.

"Mary, if I wanted to hurt you, I could do it in an instant. You could lock every door and every window and I'd still get inside. All I want is . . . to talk to you some more."

She eyed the width of his shoulders. He had a point about the breaking and entering. And she had a feeling that if she told him the best she could do was a closed door between them, he would pull up one of her lawn chairs and sit down on the terrace.

She unlatched the slider, opened it, and stepped back. "Just explain something to me."

He smiled tightly as he came in. "Shoot."

"Why aren't you with a woman who wants you?" Hal flinched. "What I mean is, those women tonight at the restaurant, they were all over you. Why aren't you having" —crazy hot sex— "er . . . fun with one of them?"

"I'd rather be here talking with you than inside one of those females."

She recoiled a little at his candor, and then realized he wasn't being crude, just bluntly honest.

Well, at least she had one thing right: when he'd walked away after that soft kiss, she'd assumed it was because he hadn't felt any heat. Evidently she'd hit the nail on the head. He wasn't here for sex, and she told herself it was good he didn't lust after her. Almost believed it, too.

"I was about to make some coffee, would you like some?"

He nodded and started wandering around the living room, taking note of her things. Against all of her white furniture and cream walls, his black clothes and heavy build were ominous, but then she looked at his face. He was wearing a silly little grin, as if he were happy just to be inside her house. Kind of like an animal who'd been chained in the yard and finally allowed indoors.

"You want to take off your coat?" she said.

He slid the leather from his shoulders and tossed it over to her sofa. The thing landed with a dull thump, crushing the cushions.

What the hell was in those pockets? she wondered.

But then she looked at his body and forgot all about the stupid coat. He was wearing a black T-shirt that showed off a powerful set of arms. His chest was wide and well defined, his stomach tight enough so she could see his six-pack even through the shirt. His legs were long, his thighs thick—

"Do you like what you see?" he asked in a low, quiet voice.

Yeah, right. She was *so* not answering that one.

She headed for the kitchen. "How strong do you like your coffee?"

Picking up the can opener, she pierced the Hills Bros lid and started cranking like there was no tomorrow. The top fell loose into the grounds and she reached inside to pick it out.

"I asked you a question," he said, right next to her ear.

She jerked and sliced her thumb open on the metal. With a groan, she brought her hand up and looked at the cut. It was deep, bleeding.

Hal cursed. "I didn't mean to startle you."

"I'll live."

She turned on the faucet, but before she could get her hand under the rush he gripped her wrist.

"Let me see." Without giving her a chance to protest, he bent down over her finger. "That's a bad one."

He put her thumb in his mouth and sucked gently.

Mary gasped. The warm, wet, pulling sensation paralyzed her. And then she felt the sweep of his tongue. When he released her, she could only stare at him.

"Oh . . . Mary," he said sadly.

She was too shocked to wonder about his change of mood. "You shouldn't have done that."

"Why?"

Because it felt so good. "How do you know I don't have HIV or something?"

His shoulders lifted. "Wouldn't matter if you did."

She paled, thinking he was positive and she'd just let him put an open cut into his mouth.

"And no, Mary, I don't have the disease."

"Then why wouldn't it—"

"I just wanted to make it better. See? No more bleeding."

She looked down at her thumb. The cut was sealed up. Partially healed. *How the hell—*

"Now are you going to answer me?" Hal said, as if deliberately cutting off the questions she was about to ask.

As she glanced up, she noticed his eyes were doing that glow thing, the teal blue taking on an otherworldly, hypnotic sheen.

"What was the question?" she murmured.

"Does my body please you?"

She tightened her lips. Man, if he got off on hearing women say he was beautiful, he was going home disappointed.

"And what would you do if it didn't?" she shot back.

"I would cover myself."

"Yeah, right."

He cocked his head to the side, as if thinking he'd read her wrong. Then he headed out to the living room where his coat was.

Good lord, he was serious.

"Hal, come back. You don't have to . . . I, ah, I like your body just fine."

He smiled as he returned to her. "I'm glad. I want to please you."

Fine, dandy, she thought. *Then lose the shirt, peel off those leather pants, and lie down on my tile. We'll take turns being on the bottom.*

Cursing herself, she went back to making the coffee. As she spooned grounds into the machine, she could feel Hal looking at her. And hear him take deep breaths, as if he were smelling her. And sensed he was . . . inching nearer all the time.

The forerunners of panic threaded through her body. He was too close. Too big. Too . . . beautiful. And the heat and lust he called out of her were too powerful.

When the pot was on, she backed away from him.

"Why don't you want me to please you?" he said.

"Stop using that word." Because when he said *please*, all she could think about was sex.

"Mary." His voice was deep, resonant. Penetrating. "I want to—"

She covered her ears. Suddenly there was way too much of him in her house. In her head.

"This was a bad idea. I think you should go."

111

She felt a big hand land lightly on her shoulder.

Mary stepped out of his reach, choking up. He was health and vitality and raw sex and a hundred other things she couldn't have. He was so totally alive, and she was . . . most likely sick again.

Mary went over to the slider and opened it. "Leave, okay? Please just leave."

"I don't want to."

"Get out. *Please.*" But he merely stared at her. "Christ, you're like a stray dog I can't get rid of. Why don't you go pester someone else?"

Hal's powerful body stiffened. For a moment it seemed like he was going to say something harsh, but then he picked up his coat. As he swung the leather around his shoulders and went for the door, he didn't look at her.

Oh, great. Now she felt awful.

"Hal. Hal, wait." She grabbed his hand. "I'm sorry. Hal—"

"Don't call me that," he snapped.

When he shrugged off her grip, she stepped in his way. And really wished she hadn't. His eyes were utterly cold. Chips of aqua-colored glass.

The words he spoke were sharp-edged. "I'm sorry I offended you. I can imagine it's a big goddamned burden to have someone want to get to know you."

"Hal—"

He pushed her aside easily. "You say that one more time and I'm going to put a fist through the wall."

He strode outside, walking into the woods that ran down the left edge of her property.

On impulse, Mary shoved her feet into a pair of running shoes, grabbed a jacket, and shot through the slider. She ran across the lawn, calling out for him. When she got to the forest's edge, she paused.

There were no branches snapping, no twigs cracking,

no sounds of a big man walking. But he'd gone in this direction. Hadn't he?

"Hal?" she called out.

It was a long while before she turned and went back inside.

FIFTEEN

"You did well tonight, Mr. O."

O stepped out of the shed behind the cabin, thinking Mr. X's approval was such bullshit. He kept the irritation to himself, though. He was barely a day out of the Omega's clutches and not really in the mood to get all worked up.

"But the male didn't tell us anything," he muttered.

"That's because he didn't know anything."

O paused. In the dim dawn, Mr. X's white face glowed like a night-light.

"Excuse me, sensei?"

"I worked him over myself before you got here. I had to be sure I could depend on you, but didn't want to waste an opportunity in the event you were no longer solid."

Which explained the male's condition. O had assumed the vampire had just fought hard when he'd been abducted.

Wasted time, wasted effort, O thought, getting out his car keys.

"You got any more tests for me?" *You prick.*

"Not right now." Mr. X checked his watch. "Your new squadron should be here soon, so put those keys away. Let's go inside."

O's revulsion at being anywhere near the cabin made him lose feeling in his feet. The damn things went totally numb on him.

But he smiled. "Lead on, sensei."

When they were indoors, he went directly to the bedroom and propped himself against the doorjamb. Even though his lungs had turned into cotton balls, he kept his cool. If he'd avoided the space, Mr. X would have thought of a reason to send him into it. The bastard knew that poking fresh wounds was the only way to determine the extent of the healing or the festering.

While slayers filed into the cabin, O took stock of them. He didn't recognize a single one, but then the longer a member was in the Society, the more anonymous he became. With hair, skin, and eye colors fading to pale, eventually a *lesser* just looked like a *lesser*.

As the other men checked him out, they glared at his dark hair. In the Society new recruits were at the bottom of the ladder, and it was unusual for one to be included in a group of seasoned men. *Yeah, well, fuck that.* O met each of them in the eye, making it clear that if they wanted to take him on he was more than happy to return the goddamned favor.

Faced with the possibility of physical confrontation, he came alive. It was like waking up after a good night's sleep, and he relished the surges of aggression, the good old need to dominate. It assured him that he was as he had always been. That the Omega hadn't taken his core away, after all.

The meeting didn't last long, and it was standard stuff. Introductions. A reminder that every morning each one of them had to check in via e-mail. There was also a refreshment of the persuasion strategy and some quotas for capture and killing.

When it was over, O was the first to head for the door. Mr. X stepped in front of him.

"You will stay."

Those pale eyes held on to his, watching, waiting to see a flash of fear.

O nodded once and spread his stance. "Sure, sensei. Whatever you like."

From over Mr. X's shoulder, O watched the others head out in the manner of strangers. No talking, eyes straight ahead, bodies not touching even casually. Clearly none of them knew one another, so they must have been called in from different districts. Which meant Mr. X was reaching down into the ranks.

As the door closed behind the last man, O's skin tingled with panic, but he held himself rock still.

Mr. X looked him up and down. Then walked over to the laptop on the kitchen table and fired the thing up. Almost as an afterthought, he said, "I'm putting you in charge of both squadrons. I want them trained in the persuasion techniques we use. I want them working as units." He looked up from the glowing screen. "And I want them to remain breathing, do you understand?"

O frowned. "Why didn't you announce this while they were here?"

"Don't tell me you need that kind of help?"

The mocking tone had O's eyes narrowing. "I can handle them just fine."

"You'd better."

"We done?"

"Never. But you can go."

O started for the door, except he knew the moment he got to it there would be something more. As he put his hand on the knob, he found himself pausing.

"There something you want to say to me?" Mr. X murmured. "I thought you were leaving."

O glanced across the room and pulled something out of his ass to justify his hesitation. "We can't use the house downtown anymore for persuasion, not since that vampire escaped. We need another facility in addition to the one behind here."

"I'm aware of that. Or did you think I was sending you out to look at land for no reason?"

So that was the plan. "The acreage I checked out yesterday wasn't right. Too much swamp, and too many roads intersect around it. Do you have any other parcels in mind?"

116

"I'll e-mail the Multiple Listings to you. And until I decide where we will build, you'll bring the captives here."

"There's not enough room in the shed for an audience."

"I'm talking about the bedroom. It's quite large. As you know."

O swallowed and kept his voice smooth. "If you want me to teach, I'll need more space than that."

"You will come here until we build. That clear enough for you, or do you want a diagram?"

Fine. He'd deal.

O opened the door.

"Mr. O, I believe you have forgotten something."

Jesus. Now he knew what people meant when they said their skin crawled.

"Yes, sensei?"

"I want you to thank me for the promotion."

"Thank you, sensei," O said with a tight jaw.

"Don't disappointment me, son."

Yeah, fuck you, daddy.

O bowed a little and left quickly. It felt good to get in his truck and drive away. Better than good. It felt like a goddamned liberation.

On the way to his house, O pulled into a CVS. It didn't take him long to find what he needed, and ten minutes later he shut his front door and deactivated his security alarm. His place was a tiny two-story in a not-so-hot residential section of town, and the location provided good cover. Most of his neighbors were elderly, and those who weren't were green-carders who worked two and three jobs. No one bothered him.

As he walked upstairs to the bedroom, the sound of his footsteps echoing up from the bare floors and bouncing off the empty walls was oddly comforting. Still, the house wasn't a home and never had been. The thing was a barrack. A mattress and a Barcalounger were all he had for furniture. Blinds hung in front of every piece of glass, blocking any view. Closets were stocked with weapons and uniforms. The kitchen was completely empty, the appliances unused since he'd moved in.

He stripped and took a gun into the bathroom along with the white plastic CVS bag. Leaning in toward the mirror, he parted his hair. His roots were showing about an eighth of an inch of pale.

The change had started about a year ago. First a few hairs, right on top, then a whole patch that spread from front to back. His temples had held out the longest, though now even they were fading.

Clairol Hydrience No. 48 Sable Cove took care of the problem, got him back to brown. He'd started with Hair Color for Men, but soon discovered that the shit for women worked better and lasted longer.

He popped open the box and didn't bother with the clear plastic gloves. Emptying the tube into the squeeze bottle, he shook the stuff up and threaded it through to his scalp in sections. He hated the chemical smell. The maintenance. The skunk stripe. But the idea of paling out repulsed him.

Why *lessers* lost their pigmentation over time was an unknown. Or at least, he'd never asked. The *whys* didn't matter to him. He just didn't want to be lost in a great anonymity with the others.

He put down the squeeze bottle and stared at himself in the mirror. He looked like a total idiot, brown grease slathered all over his head. Jesus Christ, what was he turning into?

Well, wasn't that a stupid question. The deed was long done, and it was too late for regrets.

Man, on the night of his initiation, when he'd traded a part of himself for the chance to kill for years and years and years, he'd thought he'd known what he was giving up and what he was getting in return. The deal had seemed more than fair.

And for three years, it had continued to strike him as a good one. The impotence hadn't bothered him much, because the woman he wanted was dead. The not eating and drinking had taken some getting used to, but he'd never been a big chowhound or a drunk. And he'd been eager to lose his old identity, because the police were looking for him.

The plus side had seemed tremendous. The strength had been more than he'd expected. He'd been one hell of a skull-cracker when he'd worked as a bouncer back in Sioux City. But after the Omega was through doing his thing, O had inhuman tensile power in his arms, legs, and chest, and he'd liked using it.

Another bonus was the financial freedom. The Society gave him everything he needed to do his job, covering the costs of his house, his truck, his weapons and clothes, his electronic toys. He was utterly free to hunt his prey.

Or he had been for the first couple of years. When Mr. X had taken command, that autonomy had come to an end. Now there were check-ins. Squadrons. Quotas.

Visits with the Omega.

O got in the shower and washed the crap out of his hair. As he toweled off, he went back to the mirror and peered at his face. His irises, once brown like his hair, were turning gray.

In another year or so, everything that used to be him would be gone.

He cleared his throat. "My name is David Ormond. David. Ormond. Son of Bob and Lilly. Ormond. Ormond."

God, the name sounded weird as it left his mouth. And in his head, he heard Mr. X's voice referring to him as Mr. O.

A tremendous emotion swelled in him, panic and sorrow combined. He wanted to go back. He wanted . . . to go back, to undo, to erase. The deal for his soul had only seemed good. In reality, it was a special kind of hell. He was a living, breathing, killing ghost. No longer a man, but a thing.

O dressed with trembling hands and jumped into his truck. By the time he was downtown, he was no longer thinking logically. He parked on Trade Street and started walking the alleys. It took some time before he found what he was looking for.

A whore with long, dark hair. Who, as long as she didn't flash her teeth, looked a little like his Jennifer had.

He slipped her fifty bucks and took her behind a Dumpster.

"I want you to call me David," he said.

"Sure thing." She smiled as she undid her coat and flashed her bare chest. "What do you want to call—"

He clamped a hand over her mouth and started to squeeze. He didn't stop until her eyes were popping.

"Say my name," he commanded.

O released his grip and waited. When all she did was hyperventilate, he took out his knife and pressed it into her throat.

"Say my name."

"David," she whispered.

"Tell me that you love me." When she hesitated, he pricked the skin of her neck with the tip of the blade. Her blood welled up and slid down the shiny metal. "Say it."

Her sloppy breasts, so unlike Jennifer's, pumped up and down. "I . . . I love you."

He closed his eyes. The voice was all wrong.

This just wasn't giving him what he needed.

O's anger rose to an uncontrollable level.

SIXTEEN

Rhage heaved the barbell up from his chest, teeth bared, body shaking, sweat pouring off him.

"That's ten," Butch called out.

Rhage set the load back on the stand above him, hearing the thing groan as the weights rattled and fell still.

"Add another fifty."

Butch leaned over the bar. "You got five-twenty-five on there already, my man."

"And I *need* another fifty."

Hazel eyes narrowed. "Easy, Hollywood. You want to shred your pecs, that's your business. But don't take my head off."

"Sorry." He sat up and shook out his burning arms. It was nine in the morning, and he and the cop had been in the weight room since seven. There wasn't one part of his body that wasn't on fire, but quitting was a long way off. He was shooting for the kind of physical exhaustion that went into the bone.

"Are we there yet?" he muttered.

"Let me tighten the clamps. Okay, good to go."

Rhage lay back down, hoisted the barbell off the stand, and let it rest on his chest. He marshaled his breathing before pumping the weight.

Stray. Dog.

Stray. Dog.

Stray. Dog.

He controlled the load until the last two reps, when Butch had to step in and spot.

"You finished?" Butch asked as he helped settle the bar on the stand.

Rhage sat up and panted, resting his forearms on his knees. "One more set of reps after this break."

Butch came around in front, twisting the shirt he'd taken off into a rope. Thanks to all the lifting they'd been doing, the male's chest and arm muscles were thickening up, and he hadn't been small to begin with. He couldn't pull the kind of iron Rhage did, but, for a human, the guy was a bulldozer.

"You're getting into some kind of shape, cop."

"Aw, come on, now." Butch grinned. "Don't let that shower we took go to your head."

Rhage fired a towel at the male. "Just pointing out your beer gut's gone."

"It was a Scotch pot. And I don't miss it." Butch ran a hand over his six-pack. "Now, tell me something. Why are you beating the crap out of yourself this morning?"

"You have much interest in talking about Marissa?"

The human's face tightened up. "Not particularly."

"So you can understand if I don't have a lot to say."

Butch's dark brows rose. "You've got a woman? As in, one specific woman?"

"I thought we weren't talking about females."

The cop crossed his arms and frowned. Kind of like he was assessing a blackjack hand and trying to decide whether to take another hit from the dealer.

He spoke fast and hard. "I've got it bad for Marissa. She won't see me. That's it, the whole story. Now tell me about your nightmare."

Rhage had to smile. "The idea I'm not the only one on the skids is a relief."

"That tells me nothing. I want details."

"The female threw me out of her house early this morning after doing a job on my ego."

"What kind of hatchet did she use?"

"An unflattering comparison between me and a free-agent canine."

"Ouch." Butch twisted the shirt in the other direction. "So naturally, you're dying to see her again."

"Pretty much."

"You're pathetic."

"I know."

"But I can almost beat that." The cop shook his head. "Last night, I . . . ah . . . I drove out to Marissa's brother's house. I don't even know how the Escalade got there. I mean, the last thing I need is to run into her, you feel me?"

"Let me guess. You waited around in hopes of catching a—"

"In the bushes, Rhage. I sat in the bushes. Under her bedroom window."

"Wow. That's . . ."

"Yeah. In my old life I could have arrested me for stalking. Look, maybe we should change the topic."

"Great idea. Finish the update about that civilian male who escaped from the *lessers*."

Butch leaned back against the concrete wall, crossing one arm over his chest and pulling it into a stretch. "So Phury talked with the nurse who'd treated him. The guy was pretty well gone, but he managed to tell her that they were asking questions about you brothers. Where you live. How you get around. The victim didn't give a specific address where he'd been worked over, but it has to be somewhere downtown, because that's where he was found, and God knew he couldn't have gotten far. Oh, and he kept mumbling letters. X. O. E."

"That's how *lessers* refer to themselves."

"Catchy. Very 007." Butch went to work on his other arm, his shoulder cracking. "Anyway, I peeled a wallet off the *lesser* who'd been strung up in that tree, and Tohr went over to the guy's place. It had been cleaned out, like they knew he was gone."

"Was the jar there?"

"Tohr said no."

"Then they'd definitely been by."

"What's in those things anyway?"

"The heart."

"Nasty. But better than other parts of the anatomy, considering someone told me they can't get it up." Butch dropped his arms and sucked his teeth, a little thinking noise released from his mouth. "You know, all this is starting to make sense. Remember those dead prostitutes I investigated in the back alleys this summer? The ones with the bite marks on their necks and the heroin in their blood?"

"Zsadist's girlfriends, man. It's the way he feeds. Humans only, although how he stays alive on that weak blood is a mystery."

"He said he didn't do it."

Rhage rolled his eyes. "And you think you can believe him?"

"But if we take him at his word—Hey, just humor me, Hollywood. If we believe him, then I have another explanation."

"What's that?"

"Bait. If you wanted to abduct a vampire, how do you do it? Put out food, man. Put it out, wait until one comes, drug them, and drag them wherever you want. I found darts at the scenes, like the kind you'd tranquilize an animal with."

"Jesus."

"And get this. I was listening to the police scanner this morning. Another prostitute was found dead in an alley, close to where the others were killed. I had V hack into the police server, and the online report noted that her throat had been slashed."

"You tell Wrath and Tohr all this?"

"No."

"You should."

The human shifted. "I don't know how much to get involved, you know? I mean, I don't want to stick my nose where it shouldn't be. I'm not one of you."

"But you belong with us. Or at least that's what V said."

Butch frowned. "He did?"

"Yeah. That's why we brought you here with us instead of . . . well, you know."

"Putting me in the ground?" The human cocked a half smile.

Rhage cleared his throat. "Not that any of us would have enjoyed that. Well, except for Z. Actually, no, he doesn't enjoy anything . . . The truth is, cop, you've kind of grown on—"

Tohrment's voice cut him off. "Jesus Christ, Hollywood!"

The male stalked into the weight room like a bull. And of all the Brotherhood, he was the levelheaded one. So something was on fire.

"What's up, my brother?" Rhage asked.

"Got a little message for you in the general mailbox. From that human. Mary." Tohr planted his hands on his hips, upper body jutting forward. "Why the hell does she remember you? And how does she have our number?"

"I didn't tell her how to call us."

"And you didn't scrub her memory, either. What the good goddamn are you thinking?"

"She's not going to be a problem."

"She already is. She's on our phone."

"Relax, man—"

Tohr jabbed a finger at him. "You fix her before I have to, you feel me?"

Rhage was off the bench and up in his brother's face in the blink of an eye. "No one goes near her, not unless they want to deal with me. This includes you."

Tohr's navy-blue eyes narrowed. They both knew who

was going to win if they got down to it. No one could take Rhage in hand-to-hand; it was a proven fact. And he was prepared to beat a no-touch commitment out of Tohrment if he had to. Right here, right now.

Tohr spoke in a grim tone. "I want you to take a deep breath and step off from me, Hollywood."

When Rhage didn't move, footsteps smacked across the mats and Butch's arm went around his waist.

"Why don't you cool off a little, big guy," Butch drawled. "Let's just break up this party, okay?"

Rhage allowed himself to get pulled back, but he kept his eyes on Tohr's. Tension crackled in the air.

"What's going on here?" Tohr demanded.

Rhage stepped free of Butch and paced around the weight room, winding in and out of the barbells on the floor and all the benches.

"Nothing. There's nothing going on. She doesn't know what I am and I don't know how she got the number. Maybe that civilian female gave it to her."

"Look at me, my brother. Rhage, stop where you are and look at me."

Rhage halted and shifted his eyes.

"Why didn't you scrub her? You know once their memories are long-term, you can't get them clean enough. Why didn't you do it when you had the chance?" As silence stretched out between them, Tohr shook his head. "Do *not* tell me you are getting involved with her."

"Whatever, man."

"I'll take that as a *yes*. Christ, my brother . . . what are you thinking? You know you shouldn't get tangled up with a human, and especially not with her because of the boy." Tohr's gaze sharpened. "I'm giving you an order. Again. I want you to scrub yourself from that female's memories, and I don't want you to see her anymore."

"I told you, she doesn't know what I am—"

126

"Are you trying to negotiate with me on this? You can't be that stupid."

Rhage shot his brother a nasty look. "And you really don't want me up in your grille again. This time, I won't let the cop peel me off."

"You kiss her with that mouth of yours yet? Whatcha tell her about your fangs, Hollywood?" As Rhage closed his eyes and cursed, Tohr's tone eased up. "Be real. She's a complication we don't need, and she's trouble for you because you chose her over a command from me. I'm not doing this to bust your balls, Rhage. It's safer for everybody. Safer for her. You will do this, my brother."

Safer for her.

Rhage leaned down and grabbed his ankles. He stretched his hamstrings so hard, he nearly pulled them off the backs of his legs.

Safer for Mary.

"I'll take care of it," he said finally.

"Ms. Luce? Please come with me."

Mary looked up and didn't recognize the nurse. The woman seemed really young in her loose pink uniform, was probably right out of school. And she got younger as she smiled because of the dimples.

"Ms. Luce?" She shifted the voluminous file in her arms.

Mary put her purse strap on her shoulder, got to her feet, and followed the woman out of the waiting room. They went halfway down a long, buff-colored hall and paused in front of a check-in station.

"I'm just going to weigh you and take your temperature." The nurse smiled again and got even more points for being good with the scale and the thermometer. She was quick. Friendly.

"You've lost some weight, Ms. Luce," she said, while making a note in the file. "How's your eating?"

"The same."

"We're down here on the left."

The examination rooms were all alike. Framed Monet poster and a little window with drawn blinds. Desk with pamphlets and a computer. Exam table with a piece of white paper stretched over it. Sink area with various supplies. Red biohazard container in the corner.

Mary felt like throwing up.

"Dr. Della Croce said she wanted to take your vitals." The nurse handed over a neatly folded square of fabric. "If you'll put this on, she'll be right in."

The gowns were all the same, too. Thin, soft cotton, blue with a small pink pattern. There were two sets of ties. She was never sure whether she was putting the damn things on right, whether the slit should go in the front or the back. She chose the front today.

When she was finished changing, Mary slid up onto the table and dangled her feet off the edge. It was chilly without her clothes, and she looked at them, all neatly arranged on the chair next to the desk. She would have paid good money to get back in them.

With a chime and a whistle, her cell phone went off in her purse. She dropped back down to the floor and padded over in her socks.

She didn't recognize the number as she checked caller ID and answered out of hope. "Hello?"

"Mary."

The sound of the rich male voice made her sag with relief. She'd been so sure Hal wouldn't return her call.

"Hi. Hi, Hal. Thanks for calling." She looked around for a place to sit that wasn't on the exam table. Moving her clothes to her lap, she eased into the chair. "Look, I'm really sorry about last night. I just—"

There was a knock and then the nurse poked her head in.

"Excuse me, did you release your bone scans from last July to us?"

"Yes. They should be in my record." When the nurse shut the door, Mary said, "Sorry."

"Where are you?"

"I, ah . . ." She cleared her throat. "It's not important. I just wanted you to know how bad I felt about what I said to you."

There was a long silence.

"I just panicked," she said.

"Why?"

"You make me . . . I don't know, you're just . . ." Mary fiddled with the edge of the gown. The words tumbled out. "I've got cancer, Hal. I mean, I've had it and it might be back."

"I know."

"So Bella told you." Mary waited for him to confirm it; when he didn't she took a deep breath. "I'm not using the leukemia as an excuse for the way I behaved. It's just . . . I'm in a weird place right now. My emotions are bouncing all over and having you in my house"—*being totally attracted to you*—"it triggered something and I lashed out."

"I understand."

Somehow, she felt as though he did.

But God, his silences were a killer. She began to feel like a fool for keeping him on the line.

"Anyway, that's all I wanted to say."

"I'll pick you up tonight at eight. Your house."

She gripped the phone. God, she wanted to see him so badly. "I'll be waiting for you."

From outside the door of the exam room, Dr. Della Croce's voice rose and fell in concert with the nurse's.

"And Mary?"

"Yes?"

"Wear your hair down for me."

There was a knock and the doctor came in.

"All right. I will," Mary said before hanging up. "Hey, Susan."

129

"Hi, Mary." As Dr. Della Croce crossed the shallow room, she smiled and her brown eyes crinkled at the corners. She was about fifty, with thick white hair that was squared off at her jawline.

The doctor sat down behind the desk and crossed her legs. As she took a moment to collect herself, Mary shook her head.

"I hate it when I'm right," she muttered.

"About what?"

"It's back, isn't it."

There was a slight pause. "I'm sorry, Mary."

SEVENTEEN

Mary didn't go to work. Instead she drove home, stripped, and got into bed. A quick call to the office and she had the rest of the day as well as the following week off. She was going to need the time. After the long Columbus Day weekend she was going in for a variety of tests and second opinions, and then she and Dr. Della Croce were going to meet and discuss options.

The weird thing was, Mary wasn't surprised. She'd always known in her heart that they'd browbeaten the disease into a retreat, not a surrender.

Or maybe she was just in shock and being sick felt familiar.

When she thought about what she was facing, what scared her wasn't the pain; it was the loss of time. How long until they got it back under control? How long would the next respite last? When could she get back to her life?

She refused to think there was an alternative to remission. She wasn't going to go there.

Turning over onto her side, she stared at the wall across the room and thought of her mother. She saw her mom rolling a rosary through her fingertips, murmuring words of devotion while lying in bed. The combination of the rubbing and the whispering had helped her find an ease beyond that which the morphine was able to give her. Because somehow, even in the midst of her curse, even at the apex of the pain and fear, her mother had believed in miracles.

Mary had wanted to ask her mom if she actually thought she'd be saved, and not in the metaphorical sense, but in a practical way. Had Cissy truly believed that if she said the right words and had the right objects around her that she would be cured, that she would walk again, live again?

The questions were never posed. That kind of inquiry would have been cruel, and Mary had known the answer anyway. She'd had the sense that her mother had waited for a temporal redemption right up until the very end.

But then, maybe Mary had just projected what she would have wished for. To her, saving grace meant you got to live out your life like a normal person: you were healthy and strong, and the prospect of death was just some far-off, barely acknowledged hypothetical. A debt to be paid off in a future you couldn't imagine.

Perhaps her mother had looked at it in a different way, but one thing was for sure: her outcome hadn't changed. The prayers hadn't saved her.

Mary closed her eyes, and exhaustion sucked her down. As she was swallowed whole, she was grateful for the temporary emptiness. She slept for hours, fading in and out of consciousness, flopping around on the bed.

At seven o'clock she woke up and reached for the phone, dialing the number Bella had given her to reach Hal. She hung up without leaving a message. Canceling was probably the right thing to do, because she wasn't going to be great company, but damn it, she was feeling selfish. She wanted to see him. Hal made her feel alive, and right now she was desperate for that buzz.

After a quick shower, she threw on a skirt and a turtleneck. In the full-length mirror on the bathroom door both were looser than they had been, and she thought about the scale this morning at the doctor's. She should probably eat like Hal tonight, because God knew there was no reason to diet right now. If she was facing another round of chemo, she should be packing on the pounds.

The thought froze her in place.

She drew her hands through her hair, pulling it out from

132

her scalp, letting it seep through her fingers and fall to her shoulders. So unremarkable in all its brownness, she thought. And so unimportant in the larger scheme of things.

The idea of losing it made her want to weep.

With a grim expression, she gathered the lengths together, twisted them into a knot, and clipped them into place.

She was out her front door and waiting in her driveway a few minutes later. The cold was a shock, and she realized she'd forgotten to put on a coat. She went back inside, grabbed a black wool jacket, and lost her keys in the process.

Where were her keys? Had she left her keys in the—

Yup, keys were in the door.

She shut herself out of the house, turned the lock, and pitched the metal tangle into her coat pocket.

While waiting, she thought of Hal.

Wear your hair down for me.

All right.

She freed the barrette and finger-combed the stuff as best she could. And then she fell still.

The night was so quiet, she thought. And this was why she loved living in farm country; she had no neighbors except for Bella.

Which reminded her: she'd meant to call and report in on the date, but hadn't felt up to it. Tomorrow. She would talk to Bella tomorrow. And report on two dates.

A sedan turned onto the lane about a half mile away, accelerating in a low growl she heard clearly. If it hadn't been for the two headlights, she'd have assumed a Harley was coming up her road.

As the deep-purple muscle car stopped in front of her, she thought it looked like a GTO of some sort. Glossy, noisy, flashy . . . it was totally fitting for a man who was into speed and comfortable with attention.

Hal got out from the driver's side and walked around

the hood. He was in a suit, a very sharp black suit with an open-collared black shirt underneath. His hair was brushed back from his face, falling in thick, gold chunks to the nape of his neck. He looked like a fantasy, sexy and powerful and mysterious.

Except his expression sure wasn't daydream material. His eyes were narrow, his lips and jaw tight.

Still, he smiled a little as he came up to her. "You wore your hair down."

"I said I would."

He lifted his hand as if to touch her, but hesitated. "You ready to go?"

"Where are you taking us?"

"I made reservations at Excel." He dropped his arm and looked away, becoming silent, unmoving.

Oh . . . hell.

"Hal, are you sure you want to do this? You're clearly a little off tonight. Frankly, so am I."

He stepped away and stared at the pavement, grinding his jaw.

"We could just do it some other time," she said, figuring he was too much of a nice guy to leave without some kind of rain check. "It's no big—"

He moved so fast she couldn't track him. One moment he was a couple of feet away from her; the next he was up against her body. He took her face in his hands and put his lips on hers. With their mouths locked, he looked her right in the eye.

There was no passion in him, just a grim intent that turned the gesture into some kind of vow.

When he let her go, she stumbled back. And fell right on her ass.

"Ah, damn, Mary, I'm sorry." He knelt down. "Are you okay?"

She nodded even though she wasn't. She felt gauche and ridiculous all sprawled out on the grass.

"You sure you're all right?"

"Yes." Ignoring the hand he offered, she got up and brushed bits of lawn off herself. Thank God her skirt was brown and the ground dry.

"Let's just go to dinner, Mary. Come on."

One big hand slid around to her nape, and he led her by the neck to the car, giving her no choice but to follow.

Although it wasn't like the concept of fighting him occurred to her. She was overwhelmed by a whole lot of things, him most among them, and she was too tired to put up any resistance. Besides, something had passed between them in that instant their mouths had met. She had no idea what it was or what it meant, but a bond was there.

Hal opened the passenger door and helped her inside the car. When he slid into the driver's seat, she looked around at the pristine interior to avoid getting caught up in his profile.

The GTO growled as he put it in first gear and they shot down her little road to the stop sign at Route 22. He looked both ways and then accelerated to the right, the sound of the engine rising and falling like breath as he shifted again and again until they were cruising.

"This is a spectacular car," she said.

"Thanks. My brother did it over for me. Tohr loves cars."

"How old is your brother?"

Hal smiled tightly. "Old enough."

"Older than you?"

"Yup."

"Are you the youngest?"

"No, but it's not like that. We're not brothers because we were born of the same female."

God, he had such a weird way of putting words together sometimes. "Were you adopted into the same family?"

He shook his head. "Are you cold?"

"Ah, no." She glanced at her hands. They were dug into her lap so deeply, her shoulders were hunched forward. Which explained why he thought she was chilly. She tried to loosen up. "I'm just fine."

She looked out the windshield. The double yellow line down the center of the road glowed in the headlights. And the forest crowded up to the edge of the asphalt. In the darkness, the tunnel illusion was hypnotic, making her feel as if Route 22 went on forever.

"How fast does this car go?" she murmured.

"Very fast."

"Show me."

She felt his eyes dart across the seat. Then he downshifted, hit the gas, and sent them into orbit.

The engine roared like a living thing, the car vibrating as the trees blurred into a black wall. They went faster and faster, but Hal remained in complete control as they hugged the turns tightly, weaving in and out of their lane.

When he started to slow, she put her hand on his hard thigh. "Don't stop."

He hesitated for only a moment. Then he reached forward and turned on the stereo. "Dream Weaver," that seventies anthem, flooded the inside of the car at ear-splitting levels. He stomped on the accelerator and the car exploded, carrying them at breakneck speed down the empty, endless road.

Mary put her window down, letting the air rush in. The blast tangled in her hair and chilled her cheeks and woke her out of the numbness she'd been in since she'd left the doctor's. She started laughing, and even though she could hear the edge of hysteria in her voice, she didn't care. She stuck her head out into the cold, screaming wind.

And let the man and the car carry her away.

Mr. X eyed his two new prime squadrons as they marched into the cabin for another meeting. The *lessers'* bodies absorbed the free space, shrinking the size of the room and satisfying him that he had enough muscle to cover the front line. He'd ordered them to come back for the usual updating reasons, but he also wanted to see in person how they'd reacted to the news that Mr. O was now in charge of them.

Mr. O was the last inside, and the man went directly to the doorway of the bedroom, leaning against the jamb casually, his arms over his chest. His eyes were sharp, but there was a reserve to him now, a reticence that was far more useful than his anger had been. It seemed as though the dangerous puppy had been brought to heel, and if the trend continued, they were both in luck. Mr. X needed a second in command.

With the losses they'd sustained of late, he had to concentrate on recruiting, and that was a full-time job. Picking the right candidates, bringing them on board, breaking them in—each step in the process required focus and dedicated resources. But while he was refilling the society's ranks, he couldn't allow the abduction and persuasion strategy he'd laid out to lose momentum. And anarchy among the slayers was not something he would tolerate.

On a lot of levels, O had good qualifications for being a right-hand man. He was committed, ruthless, efficient, clear-headed: an agent of power who motivated others by fear. If the Omega had managed to suck the rebellion out of him, he was close to perfect.

Time to get the meeting started. "Mr. O, tell the others about the properties."

The *lesser* started in on his report about the two tracts of land he'd visited during the day. Mr. X had already decided to purchase both for cash. And while those transactions were closing, he was going to order the squads to erect a persuasion center on seventy-five rural acres that were already owned by the Society. Mr. O would ultimately be in charge of the place, but because Mr. U had overseen building projects in Connecticut, he'd headline the center's construction phase.

The objectives of the assignment would include speed and suitability. The Society needed other places to work, sites that were isolated, secure, and calibrated for their work. And they needed them now.

When Mr. O fell silent, Mr. X delegated the new center's erection to him and Mr. U and then ordered the men out to the streets for the evening.

Mr. O lingered.

"Do we have some business?" Mr. X asked. "Did something else go wrong?"

Those brown eyes flared, but Mr. O didn't snap. More proof of improvement.

"I want to build some storage units in the new facility."

"For what? Our purpose is not to keep the vampires as pets."

"I expect to have more than one subject at a time, and I want to keep them for as long as I can. But I need something they can't dematerialize out of, and it has to shield them from sunshine."

"What do you have in mind?"

The solution Mr. O detailed was not only feasible, but cost-effective.

"Do it," Mr. X said, smiling.

EIGHTEEN

When Rhage pulled into the Excel parking lot, he drove right past the car attendants. Even if the GTO didn't have a finicky clutch, he wasn't about to leave his keys with someone else. Not with the kind of weapons and ammo he had in the trunk.

He picked a spot around back, one that was right next to the side door. When he flipped off the ignition, he reached for his seat belt and . . .

And did nothing with it. He just sat there, hand on the clip.

"Hal?"

He closed his eyes. God, he'd give anything just to hear her say his real name once. And he wanted . . . damn, he wanted her naked in his bed, her head on his pillow, her body between his sheets. He wanted to take her in private, just the two of them. No witnesses, no half-assed shield of his trench coat. Nothing public, no quickie hallway/bathroom action.

He wanted her nails in his back and her tongue in his mouth and her hips rocking under his until he came so hard he saw stars. Then he wanted to sleep with her in his arms afterward. And wake up and eat and make love again. And talk in the dark about things both stupid and serious—

Oh, God. He was bonding with her. The bonding thing was happening.

He'd heard with males that it could be like this. Fast. Intense. Nothing logical. Just powerful, primordial instincts taking over, one of the strongest being the urge to physically possess her and mark her in the process so that other males would know she had a mate. And would stay the fuck away from her.

He glanced over at her body. And realized he would kill any member of his sex who tried to touch her, be with her, love her.

Rhage rubbed his eyes. Yup, that whole marking urge was definitely at work.

And it wasn't his only problem. The odd hum was back in his body, egged on by the explicit images of her flashing through his head and the smell of her scent and the soft sound of her breathing.

And the rush of her blood.

He wanted to taste her . . . drink from her.

Mary turned toward him. "Hal, are you—"

His voice was like sandpaper. "I need to tell you something."

I'm a vampire. I'm a warrior. I'm a dangerous beast.

At the end of this evening, you aren't going to remember you ever met me.

And the idea of not even being a memory of yours makes me feel like I've been stabbed in the chest.

"Hal? What is it?"

Tohr's words echoed in his head. *It's safer. For her.*

"Nothing," he said, releasing the belt and getting out of the car. "It's nothing."

He went around and opened her door, holding out his hand to help her up. As she put her palm against his, he lowered his lids. Seeing her arms and legs uncoil made his muscles twitch and a soft growl come up into his throat.

And damn him, instead of stepping out of her way, he let her come up close so their bodies were almost touching. The vibration under his skin grew tighter and stronger along with his roaring lust for her. He knew he should look away because surely his irises were glowing a little. But he couldn't.

"Hal?" she said thinly. "Your eyes . . ."

He closed his lids. "Sorry. Let's go inside—"

She pulled her hand from his. "I don't think I want to have dinner."

His first impulse was to argue, but he didn't want to bully her. Besides, the less time they spent together, the less there was to erase.

Hell, he should have just scrubbed her the moment he drove up to her house.

"I'll take you home."

"No, I mean, will you walk with me a little? Through the park over there? I just don't feel like getting stuck at a table. I'm too . . . restless."

Rhage shoved the car keys into his pocket. "I'd love to."

As they meandered out onto the grass and walked beneath a canopy of colored leaves, he scanned the environs. There was nothing dangerous around, no threats he could sense. He glanced upward. A half-moon dangled in the sky.

She laughed a little. "I would never do this normally. You know, go out into the park at night. But with you? I don't worry about getting mugged."

"Good. You shouldn't." Because he would slice up anything that tried to harm her, human or vampire or undead.

"It seems wrong," she murmured. "Being outdoors in the dark, I mean. It feels a little illicit and a little scary. My mother always warned me about going places at night."

She stopped, tilted her head back, and stared upward. Slowly she extended her arm to the sky with her hand out flat. She closed one eye.

"What are you doing?" he asked.

"Holding the moon in my palm."

He bent down and followed the length of her arm with his gaze. "Yeah, you are."

As he straightened, he slid his hands around her waist

and pulled her back against his body. After a moment's stiffness, she relaxed and dropped her hand.

God, he loved her scent. So clean and fresh, with that slight hint of citrus.

"You were at the doctor's when I called today," he said.

"Yes, I was."

"What are they going to do for you?"

She broke away and started walking again. He fell into step with her, allowing her to pick the pace.

"What did they tell you, Mary?"

"We don't have to talk about all that."

"Why not?"

"You're going against type," she said lightly. "Playboys aren't supposed to handle the unattractive parts of life well."

He thought of his beast. "I'm used to unattractive, trust me."

Mary stopped again, shaking her head. "You know, something isn't right about all this."

"Good point. I should be holding your hand while we walk."

He reached out, only to have her pull away. "I'm serious, Hal. Why are you doing this? Being with me?"

"You're going to give me a complex. What's wrong with wanting to spend a little time with you?"

"You need me to spell it out? I'm an average-looking woman who's got a below-average life span. You're beautiful. Healthy. Strong—"

Telling himself he was ten kinds of stupid, he stepped in front of her and put his hands on the base of her neck. He was going to kiss her again, even though he shouldn't. And it wasn't going to be the kind he'd laid on her in front of her house.

As he lowered his head, the strange vibration in his body intensified, but he didn't stop. The hell he was going to let his body dictate to him tonight. Clamping down on the hum, he muscled the feeling around by force of will. When he managed to suppress it some, he was relieved.

And determined to get inside her, even if it was only his tongue in her mouth.

Mary stared up into Rhage's electric-blue eyes. She could swear they were blazing in the darkness, that teal light was actually coming out of them. She'd sensed a similar thing back in the parking lot.

The hair on the nape of her neck stood up.

"Don't worry about the glow," he said softly, as if he'd read her mind. "It's nothing."

"I don't understand you," she whispered.

"Don't try to."

He closed the distance between them, dipping low. His lips were soft as suede against hers, lingering, clinging. His tongue came out and stroked over her mouth.

"Open for me, Mary. Let me in."

He licked at her until she parted for him. As his tongue slid into her, the velvet thrust hit her right between the thighs, and she eased into his body, heat spearing her as her breasts met his chest. She grabbed onto his shoulders, trying to get closer to all that muscle and warmth.

She succeeded for only a moment. Abruptly, he put a space between their bodies, though he kept in contact with her lips. She wondered whether he still kissed her to hide the fact that he'd retreated. Or maybe he was just trying to cool her out a little, like she was too aggressive or something?

She turned her head to the side.

"What's wrong?" he asked. "You're into this."

"Yeah, well, not enough for the both of us."

He stopped her from stepping away by refusing to let go of her neck.

"I don't want to stop, Mary." His thumbs caressed the skin of her throat and then pressed into her jaw and angled her head back. "I want to get you hot. Hot enough so you don't feel anything but me. So you don't think of anything but what I'm doing to you. I want you liquid."

He dropped and took her mouth, going in deep, taking her over. He searched all her corners until there was no interior place he hadn't explored. Then he changed the kiss, retreating and advancing, a rhythmic penetration that got her wetter and even more ready for him.

"That's it, Mary," he said against her lips. "Let yourself go. God, I can smell your passion . . . You are *exquisite*."

His hands drifted down, going under the lapels of her coat, on to her collarbones. Good lord, she was lost to him. If he'd told her to lose her clothes, she would have stripped. If he'd told her to get on the ground and spread her legs, she would have hit the grass for him. Anything. Anything he wanted, just as long as he never stopped kissing her.

"I'm going to touch you," he said. "Not enough, not nearly enough. But a little . . ."

His fingers moved over her cashmere turtleneck, going lower and lower and—

Her body jerked as he found both of her tight nipples.

"So ready for me," he murmured, plucking them. "I wish I could take them into my mouth. I want to suckle on you, Mary. Would you let me do that?"

His palms flattened and he took the weight of her breasts.

"Would you, Mary, if we were alone? If we were in a nice warm bed? If you were naked for me? Would you let me taste these?" When she nodded, he smiled fiercely. "Yeah, you would. Where else would you like my mouth?"

He kissed her hard when she didn't answer. "*Tell me.*"

Her breath left in a wordless rush. She couldn't think, couldn't speak.

He took her hand and put it around one of his.

"Then show me, Mary," he said into her ear. "Show me where you want me to go. Lead me. Go on. Do it."

Unable to stop herself, she took his palm and put it on her neck. In a slow sweep, she brought it back to her breast. He purred his approval and kissed the side of her jaw.

"Yeah, there. We know you want me to go there. Where else?"

Mindless, out of control, she drew his hand down to her stomach. Then over to her hip.

"Good. That's good." When she hesitated, he whispered, "Don't stop, Mary. Keep going. Show me where you want me to go."

Before she lost her nerve, she put his hand between her legs. Her loose skirt gave way, letting him in, and a moan broke out of her at the feel of his palm flat against her core.

"Oh, yeah, Mary. That's right." He rubbed her and she gripped his thick biceps, her head falling back. "God, you're burning alive. Are you wet for me, Mary? I think you are. I think you're covered with honey . . ."

Needing to touch him, she shoved her hands into his jacket and onto his waist, feeling the raw, somewhat frightening power of his body. But before she could get far, he pulled her arms out and held her wrists in one hand. He clearly wasn't stopping, though. He pressed her backward with his chest, until she felt the solid trunk of a tree against her shoulder blades.

"Mary, let me make you feel good." Through her skirt, his fingers probed and found the pleasure spot. "I want to make you come. Right here, right now."

As she cried out, she realized she was on the verge of orgasm and he was utterly detached, an engineer of her lust who felt nothing himself: his breathing was even, his voice was steady, his body was unaffected.

"No," she groaned.

Hal's hand stopped the rubbing. "What?"

"No."

"Are you sure?"

"Yes."

Instantly, he backed off. And while he stood calmly in front of her, she tried to catch her breath.

His easy acquiescence hurt, but she wondered why he'd done what he had. Maybe he got off on the control. Hell, making some woman pant all over herself must be a terrific power trip. And it would explain why he wanted to be with her and not those sexy types. A not-so-attractive woman would be easier to remain distant from.

Shame constricted her chest.

"I want to go back," she said, about to start crying. "I want to go home."

He took a deep breath. "Mary—"

"If you even think of apologizing, I'm going to be sick—"

Suddenly, Hal frowned, and she started to sneeze.

God, for some reason, her nose was tingling like all get out. Something was in the air. Sweet. Like laundry detergent. Or baby powder, maybe?

Hal's hand bit into her upper arm. "Get on the ground. Right now."

"Why? What's—"

"Get on the ground." He shoved her down to her knees. "Keep your head covered."

Wheeling around, he planted himself in front of her, feet wide apart, hands up in front of his chest. From between his legs, she watched two men come out from a stand of maple trees. They were dressed in black fatigues, their pale skin and hair gleaming in the moonlight. The menace they threw off made her realize how far into the park she and Hal had wandered.

She fumbled around in her purse for her cell phone and tried to convince herself she was overreacting.

Yeah, right.

The men split apart and attacked Hal from both sides,

coming fast and low over the ground. She shouted in alarm, but Hal . . . holy Moses, did Hal know what he was doing. He lunged to the right and grabbed one of them by the arm, flipping the guy on to the ground. Before the man could get up, Hal stomped on his chest, nailing him down. The other attacker ended up in a choke hold, kicking and thrashing, gasping for air, getting nowhere fast.

Grim, deadly, Hal was in control of himself, at ease in the violence. And his cold, calm expression disturbed the hell out of her, even as she was grateful he'd saved them.

She found her phone and started dialing 911, thinking he could clearly hold the two while the police came.

She heard a sickening crack.

Mary looked up. The man who'd been in the choke hold fell to the ground, his head hanging from his neck at a totally wrong angle. He did not move.

She scrambled to her feet. "What have you done!"

Hal took a long, black-bladed knife out of somewhere and loomed over the man he'd had his boot on. The guy was scrambling across the ground to get away.

"No!" She jumped in front of Hal.

"Get back." His voice was eerie. Flat. Totally unconcerned.

She took hold of his arm. "Stop it!"

"I have to finish—"

"I'm not going to let you kill another—".

Someone grabbed her roughly by the hair and whipped her off her feet. Just as another man in black attacked Hal.

Pain shot through her head and neck and then she landed on her back, hard. The impact knocked the breath out of her, and stars burst into her vision like firecrackers. She was struggling to get air into her lungs when her arms were wrenched up and she was dragged away. Fast.

Her body banged against the ground, her teeth clapping

together. She lifted her head even though it sent needles up and down her spine. What she saw was a horrible relief. Hal was throwing yet another lifeless body onto the grass and coming after her at a dead run. His thighs ate up the distance, jacket flaring out behind him, dagger in his hand. His eyes were a screaming blue in the night, like xenon headlights on a car, and his big body was nothing but death waiting for a place to happen.

Thank God.

But then another man launched himself onto Hal's back.

As Hal fought off the guy, Mary called on her self-defense training, twisting herself until her attacker had to reposition his grip. When she felt his fingers loosen, she yanked as hard as she could. He turned and recaptured her quickly, but with a less sure hold. She pulled again, forcing him to stop and pivot around.

She cringed, ready to get hit, but hoped at least she'd allowed Hal some time to catch up.

Except there was no blow coming down at her. Instead a howl of pain erupted from the man, and her abductor fell on her, a heavy, smothering weight. Panic and terror gave her the strength to heave him off.

His body rolled over limply. Hal's dagger was through the man's left eye.

Too shocked to scream, Mary surged to her feet and took off as fast as she could go. She was sure she would be caught again, convinced she was going to die.

But then the glow from the lights of the restaurant finally came into view. When she felt the parking lot's asphalt underfoot, she wanted to weep in gratitude.

Until she saw Hal in front of her. As if he'd appeared out of nowhere.

She skidded to a halt, panting, dizzy, unable to comprehend how he'd gotten back before her. As her knees gave out, she caught herself on a random car.

"Come on, let's go," he said roughly.

In a cold rush, she remembered the snap of a man's neck. And the black blade through the attacker's eye. And Hal's calm, vicious control.

Hal was . . . death. Death in a beautiful package.

"Get away from me." She tripped over her own feet and he reached out for her. "No! Don't touch me."

"Mary—"

"Stay away from me." She backed toward the restaurant, hands raised to ward him off. For what little good that would do against him.

Hal tracked her, moving with powerful shifts of his arms and legs. "Listen to me—"

"I need . . ." She cleared her throat. "I need to call the police."

"No, you don't."

"We were attacked! And you . . . killed someone. People. You killed people. I want to call the—"

"This is private business. The cops can't protect you. I can."

She stopped, a nasty shot of truth putting who he was into sharp focus. Everything made sense. The menace he hid behind the charm. His utter lack of fear as they got jumped. His determination not to involve the police. God, the fact that he'd cracked a man's head loose with such ease, like he'd done it before.

Hal didn't want her to call 911 because he was on the other side of the law. No less a thug than the men who'd gone after them.

She grabbed under her arm to hold her purse, about to make another run for it. And realized her bag was gone.

Hal cursed, quick and hard. "You lost your purse, didn't you?" He looked around. "Listen, Mary, you need to come with me."

"The hell I do."

She made a break for the restaurant, but Hal leaped in front of her, blocking the way, taking her arms.

"I'll scream!" She eyed the parking-lot attendants. They were probably thirty yards away. "I'll scream my head off."

"You're life's in danger, but I can protect you. Trust me."

"I don't know you."

"Yes, you do."

"Oh, you're right. You're handsome, so you can't possibly be evil."

He jabbed his finger toward the park. "I saved you out there. You wouldn't be alive right now if it weren't for me."

"Fine. Thanks a hell of a lot. Now leave me alone!"

"I don't want to do this," he muttered. "I really don't."

"Do what!"

He passed his hand in front of her face.

And suddenly she couldn't remember what she was so teed off about.

NINETEEN

Standing in front of Mary, her memories at his mercy, Rhage told himself to finish the job. Just wipe himself from her like a stain.

Yeah, and how was that going to work for them?

He'd left at least one, maybe two of the *lessers* alive in the park when he'd had to go after her. If those SOBs nabbed her purse, and he could only assume they had, she was in the crosshairs. The Society was already abducting civilians who knew nothing about the Brotherhood; she'd actually been *seen* with him.

But what the hell did he do now? He couldn't leave her alone at her house because her address would be on her driver's license and it would be the first place the *lessers* would go. Taking her to a hotel wasn't an option, because there'd be no way to be sure she'd stay put. She wouldn't understand why she needed to keep away from home because she wasn't going to remember the attack.

What he wanted to do was take her back to the mansion, at least until he could figure out how to handle this shit storm. Trouble was, sooner or later someone would find out she was in his room, and that would be bad news for everyone. Even if Tohr's command to scrub her didn't stand, humans were prohibited from their world: too dangerous. The last thing the Brotherhood needed was for the race's existence and the secret war with the *lessers* to get out among Homo sapiens.

Yeah, but he was responsible for Mary's life. And rules were meant to be bent . . .

Maybe he could get Wrath to allow her in. Wrath's *shellan* was half-human and, ever since the two had gotten together, the Blind King had softened on the subject of females. And Tohr couldn't override the king. No one could.

Except, while Rhage tried to make his case, Mary needed to be kept safe.

He thought about her house. It was off the beaten path, so if the shit hit the fan he could defend her without worrying about a lot of interference from the human police. And he had plenty of weapons in his car. He could get her settled, protect her if need be, and call Wrath.

Rhage released her mind, cutting off her memories just after they'd gotten out of the car. She wouldn't even remember their kisses.

Which, all things considered, was a good thing. Damn him. He'd pushed her too far, too fast, and he'd almost cracked himself. While his mouth and hands were on her, that hum in his body had risen to a scream. Especially when she'd taken his palm and put it between her thighs.

"Hal?" Mary stared up at him in confusion. "What's going on?"

He felt god-awful as he looked into her wide eyes and finished burying the images in her mind. He'd scrubbed clean the memories of countless human females before and never thought twice about it. But with Mary, he felt like he was taking something from her. Invading her privacy. Betraying her.

He dragged a hand through his hair, grabbing onto a hunk and wanting to pull the stuff right out of his head. "So you'd rather skip dinner and go back to your place? That's fine with me. I could use some chill time."

"Good, but . . . I feel like there's something else we have to do." She looked down at herself and started brushing off grass. "Although considering what I did to this skirt as we left my house, I probably shouldn't be out in public anyway. You know, I thought I got all the lawn stuff off—Wait a minute, where's my purse?"

"Maybe you left it in the car."

"No, I—Oh, God." She began to shake uncontrollably, her breaths getting rapid, shallow. Her eyes became frantic. "Hal, I'm sorry, I . . . I need . . . Oh, hell."

It was the adrenaline racing through her system. Her mind might be calm, but her body was still flooded with fear.

"Come here," he said, taking her against his body. "Let me hold you until it passes."

As he murmured to her, he kept her hands in front so they didn't find the remaining dagger under his arm or the nine-millimeter Beretta at the small of his back. His eyes darted around, searching the shadows of the park to the right and the restaurant to the left. He was desperate to get her in the car.

"I'm so embarrassed," she said against his chest. "I haven't had a panic attack in a long time."

"You don't worry about that." When she stopped trembling, he pulled back. "Let's go."

He hurried her over to the GTO and felt better as he put the thing in gear and peeled out of the parking lot.

Mary looked all around the car.

"Shoot. My purse isn't here. I must have left it at home. I'm a forgetful mess today." She leaned back against the seat and searched her pockets. "Aha! At least I have my keys, though."

The trip out of town was fast, uneventful. As he brought the GTO to a stop in front of her house, Mary covered up a yawn and reached for the door. He put his hand on her arm.

"Let me be a gentleman and get that for you."

She smiled and dropped her eyes as if she wasn't used to men fussing over her.

Rhage got out. While he sniffed the air, he used his eyes and ears to penetrate the darkness. Nothing. A whole lot of nothing.

On his way around the back of the car, he popped the trunk, took out a large duffel bag, and paused again. Everything was quiet, including his hair-trigger senses.

As he opened Mary's door, she frowned at what was hanging off his shoulder.

He shook his head. "I don't think I'm spending the night or anything. I just noticed my trunk lock is broken and I don't want to leave this unattended. Or out in plain sight."

Goddamn, he hated lying to her. It literally turned his stomach.

Mary shrugged and walked to her front door. "Must be something important inside that thing."

Yeah, only enough firepower to level a ten-story office building. And it still didn't feel like enough to protect her.

She seemed awkward as she unlocked the front door and stepped inside. He let her roam from room to room, turning on lights and working off her nervousness, but he stuck right by her. As he followed, he visually checked the doors and windows. They were all locked. The place was secure, at least on the ground floor.

"Would you like something to eat?" she asked.

"Nah, I'm good."

"I'm not hungry either."

"What's upstairs?"

"Um . . . my bedroom."

"Will you show it to me?" He needed to go through the second story.

"Maybe later. I mean, do you really have to see it? Er . . . oh . . . hell." She stopped pacing and stared at him, hands on her hips. "I'm going to be up front with you. I've never had a man in this house. And I'm rusty at the hospitality thing."

He dropped the duffel. Even though he was battle-ready and tense as a cat, he had enough mental energy left over to get sapped out on her. The fact that another male hadn't been in her private space pleased him so much his chest sang.

"I think you're doing just fine," he murmured. He reached out and stroked her cheek with his thumb, thinking about what he wanted to do with her up in that bedroom.

Immediately his body started cranking over, that weird inner burn condensing along his spine.

He forced his hand to fall to his side. "I have to make a quick phone call. Mind if I use the upstairs for privacy?"

"Of course. I'll . . . wait here."

"It won't take long."

As he jogged up to her bedroom, he took his cell phone out of his pocket. The case of the damn thing was cracked, probably from one of the *lessers'* sidekicks, but it still dialed out. When he got Wrath's voice mail, he left a short message and prayed like hell he got a call back soon.

After doing a quick assessment of the upstairs, he came back down. Mary was on her couch, legs tucked under her.

"So what are we watching?" he asked, searching the doors and windows for pale faces.

"Why are you looking around this place like it's a back alley?"

"Sorry. Old habit."

"You must have been in one hell of a military unit."

"What do you want to watch?" He went over to the shelves where her DVDs were all lined up.

"You pick. I'm going to go change into something . . ." She flushed. "Well, to be honest, something more comfortable. And that doesn't have grass on it."

To make sure she was safe, he waited at the bottom of the stairs as she moved around her bedroom. When she started for the first floor again, he beat feet back over to the bookshelves.

One look at the movie collection and he knew he was in trouble. There were a lot of foreign titles, some deeply sincere American ones. A couple of golden oldies like *An Affair to Remember. Casa*-fucking-*blanca*.

Absolutely nothing by Sam Raimi or Roger Corman. Hadn't she heard of the *Evil Dead* series? Wait, there was a hope. He pulled a sheath out. *Nosferatu, Eine Symphonie des Grauens*. The 1922 classic German vampire movie.

"Found something you like?" she said.

"Yeah." He glanced over his shoulder.

Oh . . . man. She was dressed for love, as far as he was concerned: flannel pajama bottoms with stars and moons on them. Little white T-shirt. Floppy suede moccasins.

She tugged at the shirt's hem, trying to pull it down farther. "I thought about putting on jeans, but I'm tired, and this is what I wear to bed . . . er, to relax in. You know, nothing fancy."

"I like you in all that," he said with a low voice. "You look comfortable."

Yeah, to hell with that. She looked *edible*.

Once he had the movie up and rolling, he grabbed the duffel bag, brought it over to the couch, and sat down at the end opposite from her. He stretched out, trying to pretend for her benefit that every muscle in his body wasn't tight. Truth was, he was strung out. Between waiting for a *lesser* to break in, praying that Wrath would call at any moment, and wanting to kiss his way up the inside of her thighs, he was a living, breathing steel cable.

"You can put your feet on the coffee table, if you want," she said.

"I'm cool." He reached over and turned off the lamp to his left, hoping she'd fall asleep. At least then he could move around and keep an eye on the exterior without getting her riled up.

Fifteen minutes into the movie, she said, "I'm sorry, but I'm fading over here."

He glanced at her. Her hair was fanned over her shoulders and she'd curled up into herself. Her skin was luminous and a little flushed in the flicker of the TV, her eyelids droopy.

This was how she would look when she woke up in the morning, he thought.

"Let yourself go, Mary. I'm going to stay a little longer, though, okay?"

She tugged a soft cream throw blanket over herself. "Yes, of course. But, um, Hal—"

"Wait. Would you please call me by my . . . other name?"

"Okay, what is it?"

"Rhage."

She frowned. "Rhage?"

"Yeah."

"Ah, sure. Is that like a nickname or something?"

He closed his eyes. "Yeah."

"Well, Rhage . . . Thank you for tonight. For being so flexible, I mean."

He cursed quietly, thinking she should slap him instead of feel grateful. He'd nearly gotten her killed. She was now a target for the *lessers*. And if she knew half the things he wanted to do to her body, she'd probably lock herself in the bathroom.

"It's okay, you know," she murmured.

"What is?"

"I know you just want to be friends."

Friends?

She laughed tightly. "I mean, I don't want you to think I misinterpreted that kiss when you picked me up. I know it wasn't . . . you know. Anyway, you don't have to worry about me getting the wrong idea."

"Why do you think I'm concerned you might?"

"You're sitting on the other end of this couch stiff as a board. Like you're afraid I'm going to jump you."

157

He heard a noise outside and his eyes shot to the window on the right. But it was just a leaf blowing up against the glass.

"I didn't mean to make you feel awkward," she blurted. "I just wanted to . . . you know, reassure you."

"Mary, I don't know what to say." Because the truth would terrify her. And he'd lied to her enough already.

"Don't say anything. I probably shouldn't have brought it up. All I meant was, I'm glad you're here. As a friend. I really liked that ride in your car. And I like just hanging out. I don't need more from you, honestly. You're really good friend material."

Rhage sucked in a breath. In all his adult life, no female had ever called him a friend. Or valued his company for something other than sex.

In the Old Language, he whispered, "*I am barren of words, my female. For no sounds from my mouth are worthy of your hearing.*"

"What language is that?"

"The one I was born speaking."

She tilted her head, considering him. "It's almost French, but not quite. There's something Slavic in there. Is it Hungarian or something?"

He nodded. "Basically."

"What did you say?"

"I like being here with you, too."

She smiled and put her head down.

As soon as he knew she was out, he unzipped the duffel and double-checked that the guns inside of it were loaded. Then he walked through her house, turning off every light. When it was pitch-dark, his eyes adjusted and his senses heightened even further.

He scanned the woods behind her house. And the meadow to the right. And the big farmhouse in the distance. And the street out front.

He listened, tracking the footfalls of animals across the

grass and noting the wind as it brushed against the barn's wooden clapboards. As the temperature dropped outside, he sifted through the creaks of the house, testing, probing for a break-in. He prowled around, going from room to room, until he thought he was going to explode.

He checked his cell phone. It was on, with the ringer activated. And the thing was receiving a signal.

He cursed. Walked around some more.

The movie ended. He started it over in case she woke up and wanted to know why he was still there. Then he took another trip around the first floor.

When he was back in the living room, he rubbed his brow and felt sweat. Her house was warmer than he was used to, or maybe he was just pumped. Either way, he was hot, so he took off his jacket and put his weapons and the cell phone just inside the duffel bag.

As he rolled up his sleeves, he stood over her and measured her slow, even breaths. She was so small on that couch, smaller still with those strong, gray warrior eyes hidden behind lids and lashes. He sat down next to her and gently shifted her body so she was nestled in the crook of his arm.

Next to his brawn, she was tiny.

She stirred, lifted her head. "Rhage?"

"Go back to sleep," he whispered, urging her against his chest. "Just let me hold you. That's all I'm going to do."

He absorbed her sigh through his skin and closed his eyes as her arm went around his waist, her hand tucking into his side.

Quiet.

Everything was so quiet. Quiet in the house. Quiet out of doors.

He had a stupid impulse to wake her up and reposition her just so he could feel her ease against him once more.

Instead, he focused on her breathing, matching the draw and push of his own lungs to hers.

So . . . peaceful.

And quiet.

TWENTY

As John Matthew left Moe's Diner, where he worked as a busboy, he was worried about Mary. She'd missed her Thursday shift at the hotline, which was very unusual, and he hoped she was in tonight. As it was twelve thirty now, she had a half hour left before she took off, so he was sure to catch her. Assuming she'd showed.

Walking as fast as he could, he covered the six dirty blocks to his apartment in about ten minutes. And though the trip home was nothing special, his building was full of fun and games. When he came up to the front doorway, he heard some men arguing with the imprecision of drunks, their insults loose, colorful, and inconsistent. A woman yelled something over pounding music. The seething male response she got back was the kind he associated with folks who were armed.

John shot through the lobby and up the chipped stairs, locking himself in his studio with quick twists of his hands.

His place was small and probably five years away from being condemned. The floors were half linoleum and half carpet, and the two were trading identities. The linoleum was fraying to the point that it was developing a kind of nap, and the rug had stiffened into something close to hardwood. Windows were opaque with grime, which was actually a good thing, because it meant he didn't need shades. The shower worked and so did the basin in the bathroom, but the kitchen sink had been clogged since the day he'd moved in. He'd tried to get the thing open with some Drano, but, when that didn't work, he'd decided against getting into the pipes. He didn't want to know what had been shoved down that throat.

As he always did when he got home on Fridays, he wrenched open a window and looked across the street. The Suicide Prevention Hotline offices were glowing, but Mary wasn't at the desk she used.

John frowned. Maybe she wasn't feeling well. She'd seemed really exhausted when he'd gone to her house.

Tomorrow, he decided, he'd ride over to where she lived and check on her.

God, he was so glad he'd finally gotten the courage up to approach her. She was so nice, even nicer in person than over the phone. And the fact that she knew ASL? How was that for fate?

After shutting the window, he went over to the refrigerator and released the bungee cord that kept the door shut. Inside were four six-packs of vanilla Ensure. He took two cans out, then stretched the cord back into place. He figured his apartment was the only one in the building that wasn't infested with bugs, and it was only because he didn't keep any real food around. He just couldn't stomach the stuff.

Sitting down on his mattress, he leaned against the wall. The restaurant had been busy, and his shoulders were aching something awful.

Cautiously sipping from the first can, and hoping his belly gave him a break tonight, he picked up the newest issue of *Muscle & Fitness*. Which he'd already read twice.

He stared at the cover. The guy on the front was bulging in his tanned skin, a swollen, overstuffed package of biceps, triceps, pecs, and abs. To amplify the he-man look, he had a beautiful girl in a bright-yellow bikini wrapped around him like a ribbon.

John had been reading up on weight lifters for years and had saved for months to buy a small iron set. He worked the metal six days a week. And had nothing to show for it. No matter how hard he pumped, or how desperately he wanted to get bigger, he hadn't put on any muscle.

Part of the problem was his diet. Those Ensures were about all he could handle without getting sick, and they didn't have a ton of calories in them. The trouble wasn't just food-related, though. His genetics were a bitch. At the age of twenty-three, he was five feet, six inches tall, 102 pounds. He didn't need to shave. Had no hair on his body. Had never had an erection.

Unmanly. Weak. Worst of all, unchanging. He'd been this size and this way for the past ten years.

The sameness of his existence wore him down, exhausted him, drained him. He'd lost hope he was ever going to turn into a man, and the acceptance of reality had aged him. He felt ancient in his little body, as if his head didn't belong stuck atop the rest of him.

But he did get some relief. He loved going to sleep. In his dreams he saw himself fighting and he was strong, he was sure, he was . . . a man. At night, while his eyes were closed, he was fearsome with a dagger in his hand, a killer who did what he was so very good at for a noble reason. And he wasn't alone in his work. He had the company of other men like himself, fighters and brothers, loyal to the death.

And in his visions, he made love to women, beautiful women who made strange sounds as he entered their bodies. Sometimes there were more than one with him, and he took them hard because they wanted it like that and that was what he wanted, too. His lovers would grab onto his back, scratching at his skin as they shuddered and bucked underneath his crashing hips. With roars of triumph, he would let himself go, his body contracting and spilling into the wet heat they offered him. And after he came, in shocking acts of depravity, he drank their blood and they drank from him and the wild frenzy left white sheets red. Finally, when the needs were spent and the fury and cravings were over, he held them gently and they looked up at him with glowing, adoring eyes. Peace and harmony came and were welcomed as benedictions.

Unfortunately, he kept waking up in the morning.

In real life, he couldn't hope to defeat or defend anyone, not the way he was built. And he'd never even kissed a woman. Never had the chance. The opposite sex had two reactions to him: the older ones wanted to treat him like a child and the younger ones looked right through him. Both responses hurt, the former for underscoring his weakness, the latter for stealing any hope that he would find someone to care for.

Which was why he wanted a woman. He had this tremendous need to protect, to shelter, to guard. A calling with no conceivable outlet.

Besides, what woman would ever want him? He was so damned scrawny. His jeans hung off of his legs. His shirt pooled in the concave pit that ran between his ribs and his hips. His feet were the size of a ten-year-old boy's.

John could feel the frustration building in him, but he didn't know what he was getting upset about. Sure, he liked women. And he wanted to touch them because their skin seemed so delicate and they smelled good. But it wasn't like he'd ever been aroused, even if he woke up in the middle of one of his dreams. He was a total freak. Suspended somewhere between male and female, neither one nor the other. A hermaphrodite without the odd equipment.

One thing was for sure, though. He definitely wasn't into men. Enough of them had come after him over the years, pushing money or drugs or threats at him, trying to get him to blow them in bathrooms or cars. He'd always managed to get away, somehow.

Well, *always* until this past winter. Back in January, one had trapped him at gunpoint in the stairwell of the previous building he'd lived in.

164

After that, he'd moved and started carrying his own handgun.

He'd also called the Suicide Prevention Hotline.

That had been ten months ago, and he still couldn't stand the feel of his jeans against his skin. He'd have thrown all four pairs out if he could have afforded to. Instead, he'd burned the ones he'd had on that night and taken to wearing long johns underneath his pants, even in the summer.

So no, he didn't like men at all.

Maybe that was another reason he responded to women like he did. He knew how they felt, being a target because they had something someone more powerful wanted to take from them.

Not that he was about to bond with someone over his experience or anything. He had no intention of sharing what had happened to him in that stairwell with anybody. He couldn't imagine telling the tale.

But God, what if a woman asked whether he'd ever been with somebody? He wouldn't know how to answer that.

A heavy knock hit his door.

John sat up in a rush, reaching under his pillow for his gun. He released the safety with a flick of his finger.

The knocking came again.

Leveling the weapon at the door, he waited for a shoulder to hit the wood and splinter it.

"John?" It was a male voice, low-pitched and powerful. "John, I know you're in there. My name is Tohr. You met me two nights ago."

John frowned and then winced as his temples stung. Abruptly, like someone had uncorked a floodgate, he remembered going somewhere underground. And meeting a tall man in leather. With Mary and Bella.

As the memories hit, something stirred even deeper in him. On the level of his dreams. Something old . . .

"I've come to talk to you. Will you let me in?"

With the gun in his hand, John went to the door and opened it, keeping the chain in place. He craned his head up, way up, to meet the man's navy-blue eyes. A word came to mind, one he didn't understand.

Brother.

"You want to put the safety back on that gun, son?"

John shook his head, caught between the strange memory echo in his head and what was in front of him: a man of death in leather.

"Okay. Just watch where you point it. You don't look real comfortable handling that thing, and I don't want the inconvenience of having a hole in me." The man looked at the chain. "You going to let me in?"

From two doors down, a volley of yelling rose to a crescendo and ended with the sound of breaking glass.

"Come on, son. Little privacy's a good thing."

John reached deep into his chest and felt around his instincts for any sense of true danger. He found none, in spite of the fact that the man was big and hard and undoubtedly armed. Someone like him just had to be packing.

John slipped the chain free and stepped back, lowering the gun.

The man shut the door behind him. "You remember meeting me, right?"

John nodded, wondering why his memories had returned in such a rush. And why a splitting headache had come with them.

"And you remember what we talked about. About the training we offer?"

John flipped the weapon's safety into place. He recalled everything, and the curiosity that had struck him then came back. As well as a fierce yearning.

"So how'd you like to join up and work with us? And before you say you're not big enough, I know a lot of guys who are your size. In fact, we have a class of males coming in who are just like you."

Keeping his eyes on the stranger, John put the gun in his back pocket and went over to his bed. He grabbed a pad of paper and a Bic pen, and wrote: *I don't have $.*

When he flashed the pad, the man read the words. "You don't need to worry about that."

John scribbled, *Yeah, I do,* and turned the paper around.

"I run the place and I need some help with administrative stuff. You could work the cost off. You know anything about computers?"

John shook his head, feeling like an idiot. All he knew how to do was pick up plates and glasses and wash them. And this guy didn't need a busboy.

"Well, we got a brother who knows the damn things like the back of his hand. He'll teach you." The man smiled a little. "You'll work. You'll train. S'all good. And I've talked to my *shellan*. She'd be real happy if you stayed with us while you're in school."

John lowered his lids, growing wary. This sounded like a lifeboat in a lot of ways. But how come this guy wanted to save him?

"You want to know why I'm doing this?"

When John nodded, the man took off his coat and unbuttoned the top half of his shirt. He pulled the thing open, exposing his left pectoral.

John's eyes latched on to the circular scar that was revealed.

As he put his hand on his own chest, sweat broke out across his forehead. He had the oddest sense that something momentous was sliding into place.

"You're one of us, son. It's time you came home to your family."

John stopped breathing, a strange thought shooting through his head: *At last, I've been found.*

But then reality rushed forward, sucking the joy out of his chest.

Miracles just didn't happen to him. His good luck had

dried up before he'd even been aware he'd had any. Or maybe it was more like he'd been bypassed by fortune. Either way, this man in black leather, coming from out of nowhere, offering him an escape hatch from the hellhole he lived in, was too good to be true.

"You want more time to think?"

John shook his head and stepped back, writing, *I want to stay here*.

The man frowned when he read the words. "Listen, son, you're at a dangerous point in your life."

No shit. He'd invited this guy inside, knowing no one would come if he screamed for help. He felt around for his gun.

"Okay, take it easy. Tell you what. Can you whistle?"

John nodded.

"Here's a number where you can reach me. You whistle into the phone and I'll know it's you." The guy handed him a little card. "I'll give you a couple of days. You call if you change your mind. If you don't, don't worry about it. You won't remember a thing."

John had no idea what to make of that comment, so he just stared at the etched black numbers, getting lost in all the possibilities and improbabilities. When he glanced up again, the man was gone.

God, he hadn't even heard the door open and shut.

TWENTY-ONE

Mary shot out of sleep with a complete body spasm.

A deep-throated yell thundered through her living room, shattering the early-morning quiet. She bolted upright, but was shoved onto her side again. Then the whole sofa pitched away from the wall.

In the gray light of dawn, she saw Rhage's duffel. His suit coat.

And realized he'd jumped behind the couch.

"The drapes!" he shouted. "Shut the drapes!"

The pain in his voice cut through her confusion and sent her racing around the room. She covered every window until the only light coming in was through the kitchen's doorway.

"And that door, too . . ." His voice cracked. "The one into the other room."

She shut the thing quickly. It was now utterly dark except for the glow of the TV.

"Does your bathroom have a window in it?" he asked roughly.

"No, no, it doesn't. Rhage, what's wrong?" She started to lean over the edge of the sofa.

"Don't come near me." The words were strangled. And followed by a juicy curse.

"Are you all right?"

"Just let me . . . catch my breath. I need you to leave me alone right now."

She came around the corner of the sofa anyway. In the dimness, she could just vaguely make out the big shape of him.

"What's wrong, Rhage?"

"Nothing."

"Yeah, obviously." Damn it, she hated the tough-guy routine. "It's the sunlight, right? You're allergic to it."

He laughed harshly. "You could say that. Mary, stop. Don't come back here."

"Why not?"

"I don't want you to see me."

She reached over and clicked on the lamp nearest to her. A hissing sound shot through the room.

As her eyes adjusted, she saw that Rhage was flat on his back, one arm cradled against his chest, the other over his eyes. A nasty-looking burn had taken root on the skin exposed by the sleeves he'd rolled up. He was grimacing in pain, his lips peeled back from his—

Her blood went cold.

Fangs.

Two long canine incisors were lodged among his upper teeth.

He had fangs.

She must have gasped because he muttered, "I told you not to look."

"Jesus Christ," she whispered. "Tell me those are fake."

"They aren't."

She pinwheeled backward until she hit the wall. *Holy . . . good God.*

"What . . . are you?" she choked out.

"No sunlight. Funky choppers." He inhaled raggedly. "Take a guess."

"No . . . that isn't . . ."

He groaned and then she heard a shuffle, as if he were moving around. "Could you please shut that lamp off? My retinas got toasted and they need some time to recover."

She reached forward and clicked the switch, then snapped her hand back. Wrapping her arms around herself, she listened to the hoarse sounds he made as he breathed.

170

Time passed. He didn't say anything further. Didn't sit up and laugh and take out a fake set of teeth. Didn't tell her that he was Napoleon's best friend or John the Baptist or Elvis, like some kind of crazy lunatic.

He also didn't fly up into the air and try to bite her. Didn't turn into a bat, either.

Oh, come on, she thought. She couldn't be taking him seriously, could she?

Except he *was* different. Fundamentally unlike any man she'd ever met. What if . . .

He moaned softly. From the glow of the TV, she saw his boot poke out from behind the couch.

She couldn't make sense of what he thought he was, but she knew he was suffering now. And she wasn't going to leave him on her floor in agony if there was something she could do for him.

"How can I help you?" she said.

There was a pause. Like she'd surprised him.

"Could you bring me some ice cream? No nuts or chips if you have it. And a towel."

When she came back with a bowlful, she could hear him struggling to sit up.

"Let me come to you," she said.

He went still. "Aren't you afraid of me now?"

Considering he was either delusional or a vampire, she should be terrified.

"Would a candle be too much light?" she asked, ignoring the question. "Because I won't be able to see at all back there."

"Probably not. Mary, I won't hurt you. I promise."

She put the ice cream down, lit one of her larger votives, and rested it on the table next to the couch. In the flickering glow she took in his big body. And the arm still over his eyes. And the burns. He wasn't grimacing anymore, but his mouth was slightly open.

So she could just see the tips of his fangs.

171

"I know you won't hurt me," she murmured, while she picked up the bowl. "You've had enough chances to already."

Draping herself over the back of the sofa, she spooned up some of the ice cream and leaned down toward him.

"Here. Open wide. Häagen-Dazs vanilla."

"It's not to eat. The protein in the milk and the cold will help the burns heal."

There was no way she could reach where he'd been scalded, so she pulled the couch back farther and sat on the floor next to him. Working the ice cream into a thick soup, she used her fingers to smooth some of it over his inflamed, blistered skin. He flinched, flashing those canines, and she had a moment's pause.

He was *not* a vampire. Couldn't be.

"Yes, I really am one," he murmured.

She stopped breathing. "Can you read minds?"

"No, but I know you're staring at me, and I can imagine how I'd feel if I were you. Look, we're a different species, that's all. Nothing freaky, just . . . different."

Okay, she thought, putting more of the ice cream on his burns. *Let's try this whole thing on for size.*

Here she was with a vampire. A horror icon. A six-foot-eight, 280-pound horror icon with a set of teeth on him like a Doberman pinscher.

Could it be true? And why did she believe him when he said he wouldn't hurt her? She must be out of her mind.

Rhage groaned in relief. "It's working. Thank God."

Well, for one thing, he was too busy hurting right now to be much of a threat. It was going to take him weeks to recover from these burns.

She dipped her fingers into the bowl and carried more of the Häagen-Dazs to his arm. On her third round, she had to lean down close to make sure she was seeing right. His skin was absorbing the ice cream as if it were a salve, and he was healing. Right in front of her eyes.

"That feels so much better," he said softly. "Thank you."

He removed his arm from his forehead. Half his face and neck were brilliant red.

"Do you want me to do this part, too?" She indicated the burned area.

His uncanny teal-blue eyes opened. They were wary as he looked up at her. "Please. If you don't mind."

While he watched her, she put her fingers into the bowl and then reached out to him. Her hands shook just a little as she worked the stuff over his cheek first.

God, his lashes were thick. Thick and dark blond. And his skin was soft, though his beard had grown in some overnight. He had a great nose. Straight as an arrow. And his lips were perfect. Big enough to fit the size of his face. Dark pink. The lower one was larger.

She went back for more and covered his jaw. Then she moved down his neck, passing over the thick cords of muscle that ran from his shoulders up to the base of his skull.

When she felt something brush her shoulder, she glanced over. His fingers were stroking the ends of her hair.

Anxiety spiked. She jerked back.

Rhage dropped his hand, not surprised she rejected him.

"Sorry," he muttered, closing his eyes.

With nothing to look at, he was acutely aware of her gentle fingers as they moved over his skin. And she was so close to him, close enough that her scent was all he could smell. As the pain from the sun exposure faded, his body began to burn up in a different way.

He opened his eyes, keeping the lids low. Watching. Wanting.

When she was finished, she put the bowl aside and regarded him directly. "Let's assume that I believe you are a . . . you're different. Why didn't you bite me when you

173

had the chance? I mean, those fangs aren't just for decoration, right?"

Her body was tense, as if she were prepared to bolt at any minute, but she wasn't giving in to her fear. And she had helped him when he needed it, even though she was scared.

God, courage was a turn-on.

"I feed from females of my own species. Not humans."

Her eyes flared. "Are there a lot of you?"

"Enough. Not as many as there used to be. We're hunted for extinction."

Which reminded him: he was separated from his weapons by about six yards and a couch. He tried to get up, but the weakness in his body made his movements slow and uncoordinated.

Goddamned sun, he thought. *Suck the life right out of you.*

"What do you need?" she asked.

"My duffel. Just bring it around so it's at my feet."

She stood up and disappeared around the couch. He heard a thud and then the sound of the bag being dragged across the floor.

"Good lord, what is in here?" She came back into view. As she dropped the handles, they fell to the sides.

He hoped like hell she didn't look in there.

"Listen, Mary . . . we've got a problem." He forced his upper body off the floor, bracing his arms.

The probability of a *lesser* attacking her house now was low. Although the slayers could go out in sunlight, they worked at night and needed to trance-out to replenish their strength. Most of the time they were quiet during the day.

But he hadn't heard back from Wrath. And evening would come eventually.

Mary stared down at him, her expression grave. "Do you need to be underground? Because we can get you into the old grain cellar. The door to it is through the kitchen, but I could hang quilts over the sliders—Shoot, there are skylights. Maybe we could cover you in something. You'd probably be safer down there."

Rhage let his head fall back so that all he saw was the ceiling.

Here was this human female, who wasn't half his weight, who was ill, who'd just found out she had a vampire in her house—and she was worried about protecting him.

"Rhage?" She came over and knelt beside him. "I can help get you down—"

Before he could think, he took her hand, pressed his lips to her palm, and then put it on his heart.

Her fear swirled in the air, the sharp, smoky smell mixing with her delicious natural scent. But she didn't pull away this time, and the fight-or-flight cocktail didn't last long.

"You don't need to worry," she said softly. "I won't let anyone get to you today. You're safe."

Ah, hell. She was melting him. She really was.

He cleared his throat. "Thanks. But it's you I'm worried about. Mary, last night we were attacked in the park. You lost your purse, and I have to assume my enemies got it."

Tension shot down her arm, traveled through her palm, and hit him in his chest. As her anxiety spiked, he wished there was some way of bearing the fear for her, taking it into himself.

She shook her head. "I don't remember any attack."

"I hid your memories."

"What do you mean, 'hid'?"

He reached into her mind and released the events of the night before.

Mary gasped and put her hands to her head, blinking in rapid succession. He knew he had to explain quickly. It wasn't going to take her long to process everything and jump to the conclusion that he was a killer worth running from.

175

"Mary, I needed to get you home so I could protect you while I waited for word from my brothers." Which still hadn't come through, goddamn it. "Those men who attacked us, they aren't human, and they're very good at what they do."

She settled onto the floor with no grace, as if her knees had given out. Her eyes were wide and sightless while she shook her head.

"You killed two of them," she said in a dead voice. "You snapped the neck of one. And the other you . . ."

Rhage cursed. "I'm sorry that I got you tangled up in all this. I'm sorry that you're in danger now. And I'm sorry I stripped your memories—"

She pegged him with hard eyes. "Don't do that again."

He wished he could make her that promise. "I won't unless I have to in order to save you. You know a lot about me now, and that puts you at risk."

"Have you taken any other memories from me?"

"We met at the training center. You came with John and Bella."

"How long ago?"

"Couple days. I can give you those back, as well."

"Wait a minute." She frowned. "Why didn't you just make me forget all about you before now? You know, take everything."

As if she would have preferred that.

"I was going to. Last night. After dinner."

She looked away. "And you didn't because of what happened in the park?"

"And because . . ." God, just how far did he want to go with this? Did he really want her to know how much he was feeling her? No, he thought. She was looking totally shell-shocked. Now was hardly the time to come clean with the happy news that a male vampire had bonded with her. "Because it's an invasion of your privacy."

In the silence that followed, he could see her working

over the events, the implications, the reality of the situation. And then her body let off the sweet scent of arousal. She was remembering how he'd kissed her.

Abruptly, she winced and frowned. And the fragrance was cut off.

"Ah, Mary, in the park, when I was keeping away from you while we—"

She held her hand up, stopping him. "All I want to talk about is what we do now."

Her gray eyes met his and didn't waver. She was, he realized, ready for anything.

"God . . . you're amazing, Mary."

Her brows lifted. "Why?"

"You're handling all this shit really well. Especially the part about what I am."

She tucked a piece of hair behind her ears and studied his face. "You know something? It's not that big a surprise. Well, it is, but . . . I knew you were different from the moment I first saw you. I didn't know you were a . . . Do you call yourselves vampires?"

He nodded.

"Vampire," she said, as if trying the word out. "You haven't hurt me or scared me. Well, not really. And . . . you know, I've been clinically dead at least twice. Once when I went into cardiac arrest while they were giving me a bone-marrow transplant. Once when I came down with pneumonia and my lungs filled up with fluid. I, ah, I'm not sure where I went or why I came back, but there was something on the other side. Not heaven with the clouds and the angels and all that jazz. Just a white light. I didn't know what it was the first time. The second, I just went right into it. I don't know why I came back—"

She flushed and stopped talking, as if embarrassed by what she'd revealed.

"You have been to the Fade," he murmured, awed.

"The Fade?"

He nodded. "At least, that's what we call it."

She shook her head, clearly unwilling to go further with the subject. "Anyway, there's a lot we don't understand about this world. That vampires exist? It's just one more thing."

When he didn't say anything for a while, she glanced at him. "Why are you looking at me like that?"

"You are a *wahlker*," he said, feeling as if he should stand up and bow to her, as was custom.

"A *wahlker?*"

"Someone who has been to the other side and returned. Where I come from, that is a title of distinction."

A cell phone's bleating turned both of their heads. The sound was coming from inside the duffel.

"Could you hand me that bag?" he asked.

She leaned over and tried to lift it. Couldn't. "Why don't I just give you the phone?"

"No." He struggled to his knees. "Just let me—"

"Rhage, I'll get it—"

"*Mary, stop,*" he commanded. "I don't want you going in there."

She recoiled from the thing, as if it were carrying snakes.

With a lurch he put his hand inside. As soon as he found the phone, he cocked it and put it up to his ear.

"Yeah?" he barked, while partially zipping the duffel shut.

"Are you okay?" Tohr said. "And where the hell are you?"

"I'm fine. Just not at home."

"No shit. When you didn't meet Butch down at the gym, and he couldn't find you in the main house, he got worried and called me. Do you need a pickup?"

"No. I'm cool where I am."

"And where's that?"

"I called Wrath last night and he didn't get back to me. He around?"

178

"He and Beth went down to his place in the city for some private time. Now where are you?" When there was no quick answer, the brother's voice dropped lower. "Rhage, what the hell's going on?"

"Just tell Wrath I'm looking for him."

Tohr cursed. "Are you sure you don't need a pickup? I can send a couple of the *doggen* out with a lead-lined body bag."

"Nah, I'm good." He wasn't going anywhere without Mary. "Later, man."

"Rhage—"

He hung up and the phone rang again immediately. After checking caller ID, he let Tohr go into voice mail. He was putting the thing down next to him on the floor when his stomach let out a grumble.

"Would you like me to get you something to eat?" Mary asked.

He looked at her for a moment, stunned. And then had to remind himself she didn't know the intimacy she was offering. Still, the idea that she would honor him with food she had prepared with her own hands left him breathless.

"Close your eyes for me," he said.

She stiffened. But she lowered her lids.

He leaned forward and pressed his lips softly to hers.

Those gray eyes popped wide open, but he pulled back before she could.

"I would love it if you would feed me. Thank you."

TWENTY-TWO

As the sun came up, O riffled through the building sketches that covered U's kitchen table. He spun one around.

"This is what I want. How fast can we get it up?"

"Quick. Site's out in the middle of nowhere, and the facility's not going to be hooked to any municipal utilities, so there's no need for a building permit. Putting together the wall supports and throwing some exterior clapboards on a fifteen-hundred-square-foot space won't take long. Installing the storage facilities for the captives shouldn't be a problem. As for the shower, we can divert the nearby stream easily and install a pump to provide running water. Supplies like hardware and tools are all generic and I've kept the board lengths standard size to reduce the amount of cutting. Gas-powered generator on site will provide electricity for the saws and nail guns. It'll also give us light if we want it. We'll keep that long term."

"Give me the number of days."

"With a crew of five guys, I can have a roof over your head in forty-eight hours. Provided I can work them into the ground and the supplies come in on time."

"I'm going to hold you to two days, then."

"I'll start getting what we need from Home Depot and Lowe's this morning. I'll split the supply orders between the two. And we're going to need a small bulldozer, one of those Toro Dingos with the interchangeable bucket and hoe setup. I know where we can rent one."

"Good. This is all good."

O leaned back to stretch his arms and idly parted the

drapes. U's house was an anonymous split-level deep in soccer-mom territory. This was the part of Caldwell with streets named Elmwood and Spruce Knoll and Pine Notch, where kids rode their bikes on the sidewalks and dinner was on the table at six every night.

All the happy-happy, joy-joy made O's skin crawl. He wanted to torch the houses. Put salt on the lawns. Chop the trees down. Level the place until it couldn't resurface. The impulse went so deep it surprised him. He had no problem with destruction of property, but he was a killer, not a vandal. He couldn't figure out why he gave a shit.

"I want to use your truck," U was saying. "I'm going to rent a trailer to hitch on. Between the two, I'll be able to take delivery on the boards and roofing supplies in batches. No reason for the Home Depot folks to know where we are."

"And the stuff for the storage units?"

"I know exactly what you're looking for and where to find it."

An electronic beeping sounded.

"What the hell's that?" O asked.

"Reminder for the nine-A.M. check-in." U took out a BlackBerry, his blunt fingers flying over the little keyboard. "You want me to e-mail your status for you?"

"Yeah." O focused on U. The *lesser* had been in the society for 175 years. He was pale as paper. Calm and sharp as a tack. Not as aggressive as some, but steady.

"You're an asset, U."

U cocked a smile and looked up from the BlackBerry. "I know. And I like to be used. Speaking of which, who are you going to give me for a crew?"

"We're going to use both prime squadrons."

"You're taking all of us off-line for two nights?"

"And days. We'll sleep in shifts at the site."

"Fine." U looked back down at the thing in his hand,

fingering a little wheel on the right side of it. "Oh . . . shit. Mr. X is not going to like this."

O narrowed his eyes. "Oh, yeah?"

"It's a blast e-mail to the Beta squadrons. I'm still on the list, I guess."

"And?"

"A bunch of Betas were hunting last night and ran into one of the Brotherhood in the park. Of the five of them, three are unaccounted for. Get this, the warrior was with a human female."

"Sometimes they have sex with them."

"Yeah. Lucky bastards."

Mary stood over the stove thinking of the way Rhage had just looked at her. She couldn't figure out why offering to cook him breakfast was such a big deal, but he'd acted as if she'd given him a tremendous gift.

She flipped the omelet over and headed for the refrigerator. Taking out a plastic container of cut fruit, she spooned all there was into a bowl. It didn't look like enough, so she grabbed a banana and sliced it on top.

As she put the knife down, she touched her lips. There had been nothing sexual about the kiss he'd given her behind the couch; it had been all about gratitude. And the mouth-on-mouth action in the park had been deeper, but the distance on his side was the same. The passion had been one-sided. Hers.

Did vampires even sleep with humans? Maybe that was why he held back, instead of it being some kind of power play.

Except what about the hostess at TGI Friday's? He'd definitely sized that woman up, and not because he'd wanted to buy her a dress. So clearly his kind had no problem being with another species. What he had no interest in was being with her.

Friends. Just friends.

When the omelet was finished and the toast buttered, she rolled a fork up in a napkin, tucked the twist under her elbow, and took the plate and the bowl into the living room. She quickly shut the door behind her and turned to the couch.

Whoa.

Rhage had taken his shirt off and was leaning back against the wall, inspecting his burns. In the glow of candlelight, she got a serious look at his heavy shoulders, his powerful arms, his chest. His stomach. The skin over all that muscle he was carrying was golden, hairless.

Trying to keep it together, she put what she was carrying on the floor next to him and sat down a few feet over. To stop herself from staring at his body, she glanced at his face. He was looking down at the food, not moving, not speaking.

"I wasn't sure what you liked," she said.

His eyes flipped up to hers and he shifted so he was facing her. The frontal view was even more spectacular than the profile. His shoulders were broad enough to fill the space between the couch and the wall. And the star-shaped scar over his left pectoral was sexy as hell, like some kind of brand on his skin.

After a good beat or two of him just staring at her, she reached for the plate. "I'll get you something else—"

His hand shot out and gripped her wrist. He stroked her skin with his thumb. "I love it."

"You haven't tasted the—"

"You made it. That's enough." He picked the fork out of the napkin, the muscles and tendons in his forearm working. "Mary?"

"Hm?"

"I would feed you now." As he spoke, his stomach let out a howl.

"That's okay. I'll get something for myself . . . Ah, why are you frowning like that?"

He rubbed his eyebrows, as if ironing out his expression. "Sorry. You couldn't know."

"Know what?"

"Where I come from, when a male offers to feed a female from his hand, it is a way of showing respect. Respect and . . . affection."

"But you're hungry."

He brought the plate a little closer and tore off a corner of the toast. Then he cut a perfect square out of the omelet and placed it on top.

"Mary, eat from my hand. Take from me."

He leaned forward, extending his long arm. His teal eyes were hypnotic, calling her, pulling her forward, opening her mouth. As she put her lips around the food she had cooked for him, he growled in approval. And after she swallowed, he came toward her again, another piece of toast suspended between his fingertips.

"Shouldn't you have something?" she said.

"Not until you are full."

"What if I eat it all?"

"Nothing would please me more than to know you are well fed."

Friends, she told herself. *Just friends*.

"Mary, eat for me." His insistence had her opening her mouth again. His eyes stayed on her lips after she'd closed them.

Jesus. This didn't feel like friends.

As she chewed, Rhage picked through the bowl of fruit with his fingertip. He finally chose a slice of cantaloupe and held it out to her. She took the piece whole, a little juice escaping down the side of her mouth. She reached up with the back of her hand, but he stopped her, lifting the napkin, brushing it over her skin.

"I'm finished."

"No, you're not. I can feel your hunger." This time half a strawberry came toward her. "Open for me, Mary."

He fed her choice morsels, watching her with a primordial satisfaction that was unlike anything she'd seen before.

When she couldn't take another bite, he made quick work of what was left, and the moment he was done she picked up the plate and headed to the kitchen. She made him another omelet, filled a bowl full of cereal, and gave him the last of her bananas.

His smile was radiant as she laid it all out in front of him. "How you honor me with this."

As he ate in that methodical, tidy way of his, she closed her eyes and let her head fall back against the wall. She was getting tired more and more easily and felt a stab of cold terror because now she knew why. God, she dreaded finding out what the doctors were going to do to her after all the tests were in.

When she opened her eyes, Rhage's face was right in front of hers.

She jerked back, banging against the wall. "I, ah, I didn't even hear you move."

Crouched on all fours like an animal about to spring, he had one arm on either side of her legs, his massive shoulders bunched up from bearing the weight of his torso. This close, he was huge. And showing a lot of skin. And smelling really good, like dark spices.

"Mary, I would thank you, if you would let me."

"How?" she croaked.

He tilted his head to the side and put his lips on hers. As she gasped, his tongue penetrated her mouth and stroked her own. When he shifted back to assess her reaction, his eyes glowed with the promise of ecstasy, the kind that would boil her bone marrow.

She cleared her throat. "You're . . . welcome."

"I would do that again, Mary. Will you let me?"

"A simple thank-you is fine. Really, I—"

His lips cut her off and then his tongue took over again, invading, taking, caressing. As heat roared in her body,

Mary gave up the fight and savored the mad lust, the pounding in her chest, the aching at her breasts and between her legs.

Oh, God. It had been so long. And it had never been like this.

Rhage let out a low purr, as if he'd sensed her arousal. She felt his tongue retract, and then he took her lower lip between his—

Fangs. Those were fangs nipping at her flesh.

Fear threaded through her passion and thickened it, adding a dangerous edge that opened her even further. She put her hands on his arms. God, he was so hard, so strong. He'd be so heavy on top of her.

"Will you let me lie with you?" he asked.

Mary closed her eyes, imagining them going beyond the kissing to a place where they'd be naked together. She hadn't been with a man since well before her illness. And a lot about her body had changed since then.

She also didn't know where his desire to be with her was coming from. Friends didn't have sex. Not in her book, anyway.

She shook her head. "I'm not sure—"

Rhage's mouth fit over hers again briefly. "I just want to lie down next to you. Okay?"

Literal translation . . . right. Except as she stared at him, she couldn't ignore the differences between them. She was breathless. He was calm. She was dizzy. He was clear-sighted.

She was hot. He was . . . not.

Abruptly Rhage sat back against the wall and pulled the blanket that hung off the couch into his lap. She wondered for a split second if he was hiding an erection.

Yeah, right. More likely he was cold because he was half-naked.

"Did you suddenly remember what I am?" he asked.

"Excuse me?"

"Is that what turned you off?"

She remembered those fangs of his on her lip. The idea that he was a vampire turned her on. "No."

"Then why did you shut down? Mary?" His eyes bored into hers. "Mary, will you tell me what's going on?"

His confusion as he stared at her was appalling. Did he think she wouldn't mind being a pity fuck?

"Rhage, I appreciate the lengths you're willing to go to in the name of friendship, but don't do me any favors, okay?"

"You like what I do to you. I can feel it. I can smell it."

"For chrissakes, do you get off on making me feel ashamed of myself? Because I'll tell you, having a man get me all hot and bothered while he might as well be reading a newspaper doesn't feel good on my end. God . . . you're really sick, you know that?"

That neon gaze narrowed in offense. "You think I don't want you."

"Oh, I'm sorry. I guess I've missed all that lust on your side. Yeah, you're *really* hot for me."

She couldn't believe how fast he moved. One minute he was sitting back against the wall, looking at her. The next he had her down on the floor, underneath him. His thigh shoved her legs apart and then his hips drove into her core. What came against her was a thick, hard length.

His hand tangled in her hair and pulled, arching her up against him. He dropped his mouth to her ear.

"You feel that, Mary?" He rubbed his arousal in tight circles, stroking her, making her bloom for him. "You feel me? What does this mean?"

She gasped for air. She was so wet now, her body ready for him to drive deep into her.

"Tell me what it means, Mary." When she didn't answer, he sucked her neck until it stung and then took her earlobe between his teeth. Little punishments. "I want you to say it. So I know you're clear on how I feel."

His free hand dipped under her butt, tucked her closer, and then his erection pushed into her, hitting the right place. She could feel the head of him probing through his pants and her pajama bottoms.

"*Say it, Mary.*"

He surged forward again and she groaned. "You want me."

"And let's just make sure you remember that, shall we?"

He released her hair and took her lips with a raw edge. He was all over her, inside her mouth, on top of her body, his heat and his male smell and his tremendous erection promising her one hell of a wild, erotic ride.

But then he rolled off of her and went back to where he'd been against the wall. Just like that, he was under control again. His breathing even. His body still.

She struggled to sit up, trying to remember how to use her arms and legs.

"I'm not a man, Mary, even though parts of me look like one. What you just had is nothing compared to what I want to do to you. I want my head between your legs so I can lick you until you scream my name. Then I want to mount you like an animal and look into your eyes as I come inside of you. And after that? I want to take you every way there is. I want to do you from behind. I want to screw you standing up, against the wall. I want you to sit on my hips and ride me until I can't breathe." His stare was level, brutal in its honesty. "Except none of that's going to happen. If I felt you less, it would be different, easier. But you do something weird to my body, so totally controlled is the only way I can be with you. Otherwise I'm liable to lose it, and the last thing I want to do is scare the hell out of you. Or worse, hurt you."

Visions swam in her head, visions of everything he had described, and her body wept anew for him. He took a deep breath and growled softly, like he'd caught the scent of her sex and relished it.

"Oh, Mary. Will you let me pleasure you? Will you let me take that sweet arousal of yours where it wants to go?"

She wanted to say yes, but the logistics of what he was suggesting hit her hard: getting naked, in front of him, in the candlelight. No one but doctors and nurses knew what had been left behind on her body after the disease had retreated. And she couldn't help thinking of those sexy women she'd seen come on to him.

"I'm not what you're used to," she said softly. "I'm not . . . beautiful." He frowned, but she shook her head. "Trust me on this one."

Rhage prowled over to her, those shoulders rolling like a lion's. "Let me show you how beautiful you are. Nicely. Slowly. Nothing rough. I'll be a perfect gentleman, I promise."

His lips parted and she caught a glance of the tips of his fangs. Then his mouth was on hers and, God, he was fantastic, all drugging sweeps of lips and tongue. With a moan, she wound her arms around his neck, digging her fingers into his scalp.

As he laid her down on the floor, she braced herself for his weight. Instead he stretched out next to her and smoothed her hair back.

"Slowly," he murmured. "Gently."

He kissed her again, and it was a while before his long fingers went to the bottom of her T-shirt. As he pushed the thing up, she tried to concentrate on what he was doing to her mouth, forcing herself not to think about what he was revealing. But when he tugged the fabric over her head, cool air hit her breasts. She brought her hands up to cover them and closed her eyes, praying it was dark enough so he couldn't see much of her.

A fingertip brushed the base of her neck, where her tracheotomy scar was. Then it lingered on the puckered spots on her chest where catheters had been plugged in.

He pulled down the waistband of her pajama bottoms until all the punch holes in her stomach from the feeding tubes were revealed. Then he found the insertion site for her bone-marrow transplant on her hip.

She couldn't stand it any longer. She sat up and grabbed for the shirt to shield herself.

"Oh, no, Mary. Don't stop this." He captured her hands and kissed them. Then he tugged at the shirt. "Won't you let me look at you?"

She turned her head away as he took her cover from her. Her bare breasts rose and fell as his eyes took her in.

Then Rhage kissed each and every scar.

She trembled no matter how much she tried to hold still. Her body had been pumped full of poison. Left with holes and scars and rough spots. Rendered infertile. And here was this beautiful man worshiping it as if everything she had borne was worthy of reverence.

When he looked up and smiled at her, she burst into tears. The sobs came out hard as punches, tearing at her chest and throat, squeezing her ribs. She covered her face with her hands, wishing she had the strength to go into another room.

While she cried, Rhage held her against his chest, cradling her, rocking her back and forth. She had no idea how long it took before she wore herself out, but eventually the weeping slowed and she became aware that he was talking to her. The syllables and cadence were completely unfamiliar and the words indecipherable. But the tone . . . the tone was lovely.

And his kindness was a temptation she shrank from.

She could not rely on him for comfort, not even in this moment. Her life depended on her keeping it together, and there was a slippery slope to tears. If she started crying now, she wasn't going to stop in the days and weeks ahead. God knew, the hard inner core of her had been the only thing that had gotten her through the last time she'd been sick. If she lost that resolve, she had no power whatsoever against the disease.

Mary wiped her eyes.

Not again, she thought. She would not lose it in front of him again.

Clearing her throat, she tried to smile. "So. How's that for a buzz kill?"

He said something in the other language and then shook his head and switched into English. "You cry all you want."

"I don't want to cry." She looked at his bare chest.

No, what she wanted right now was to have sex with him. With the weeping jag finished, her body was responding to his again. And given that he'd seen the worst of her scars and didn't seem turned off, she felt more comfortable.

"Any chance you still want to kiss me after all that?" she asked.

"Yes."

Without allowing herself to think, she grabbed onto his shoulders and pulled him down to her mouth. He held back for a moment, as if surprised by her strength, but then he kissed her deep and long, as if he understood what she needed from him. In a matter of moments he had her totally naked, pajama bottoms gone, socks gone, panties tossed aside.

He stroked her from head to thigh with his hands, and she moved with him, surging, arching, feeling the bare skin of his chest against her breasts and stomach while the smooth fabric of his expensive pants rubbed like body oil over her legs. She was aching and light-headed as he nuzzled her neck and nibbled on her collarbone, working his way down to her breasts. She lifted her head and watched as his tongue came out and ran a circle around one nipple before he took it into his mouth. As he suckled her, his hand slid up her inner thigh.

And then he was touching her core. She heaved under him, breath shooting out of her lungs in a rush.

He groaned, his chest vibrating against hers as he made the sound.

"Sweet Mary, you're just as I imagined. Soft . . . drenched." His voice was rough, hard, giving her an idea how much control he was using to keep himself in lockdown. "Open your legs wider for me. A little more. That's it, Mary. That's so . . . oh, *yeah*."

He slipped a finger and then two inside of her.

It had been a long time, but her body knew where it was headed. Panting, holding onto his shoulders with her nails, Mary watched him lick her breast as he moved his hand in and out of her body, his thumb rubbing in just the right place on the downstroke. In a flash of lightning she exploded, the force of the release pitching her headlong into a void where only pulsing and white heat existed.

When she came back down, Rhage's heavy-lidded eyes were grave, his face tight and dark. He was like a total stranger, utterly removed from her.

She reached for the throw blanket to cover up with, figuring the shirt wouldn't do but half the job. The movement made her aware that his fingers still penetrated her.

"You are so beautiful," he said gruffly.

The B-word made her feel even more uncomfortable. "Let me up."

"Mary—"

"This is just too awkward." She struggled, and the shifting of her body only made her feel more of him.

"Mary, look at me."

She glared at him, frustrated.

In slow motion, he withdrew his hand from between her legs and brought the two glistening fingers to his mouth. His lips parted, and in a savoring draw he sucked off her slick passion. When he swallowed, he closed his glowing eyes.

"You're unbelievably beautiful."

Her breath froze. And then redoubled as he moved down her body, putting his hands on the inside of her thighs. She tensed as he tried to open her legs.

"Don't stop me, Mary." He kissed her navel and then her hip, spreading her wide. "I need more of you in my mouth, down my throat."

"Rhage, I—Oh, *God*."

His tongue was a warm stroke right up her center, reeking havoc on her nervous system. He lifted his head and looked at her. And then he dropped back down and licked her again.

"You kill me," he said, breath brushing where she ached. He rubbed his face on her, his beard growth a soft rasp as he bathed in her core.

She closed her eyes, feeling like she was going to fly apart.

Rhage nuzzled her and then captured her hot flesh with his lips, sucking, then tugging, now flicking with his tongue. As she arched up off the floor, one of his hands went to the small of her back, and the other landed on her lower belly. He held her in place as he worked her, keeping her body from jerking away from his mouth as she thrashed.

"Look at me, Mary. Look at what I'm doing."

When she did, she caught a glimpse of his pink tongue licking free from the top of her cleft and that was that. The release shattered her, but he just kept going. There seemed to be no end to his focus or his technique.

Finally she reached out to him, needing that thick length of his to fill her up. He resisted easily and then did something sinful with his fangs. As she came apart again, he watched her orgasm, his brilliant teal-blue eyes staring up from between her legs, casting shadows, they were so bright. After it was over, she said his name as a hoarse question.

In a fluid motion he got to his feet and backed away from her. When he turned around, her breath came out in a hiss.

A magnificent, multicolored tattoo covered his entire back. The design was that of a dragon, a fearsome creature with five-clawed limbs and a twisting, powerful body. From its resting place, the beast stared out, as if it were actually seeing through its white eyes. And while Rhage paced around, the thing moved with the undulations of muscles and skin, shifting, seething.

Like it wanted out, she thought.

Feeling a draft, Mary pulled the blanket around her body. When she looked up, Rhage was way across the room.

And still, that tattoo stared at her.

TWENTY-THREE

Rhage stalked around the living room, trying to work off the burn. It had been hard enough to keep his body in check before he'd put his mouth on her. Now that his tongue knew her taste, his spine was on fire, the burn spreading out to every muscle he had. His skin tingled all over, itching so badly he wanted to take sandpaper to it.

As he rubbed his arms, his hands shook uncontrollably.

God, he had to get away from the scent of her sex. The sight of her. The knowledge that he could take her right now because she'd let him.

"Mary, I have to be alone for a little while." He glanced at the bathroom door. "I'm going to go in there. If anyone comes to the house or you hear anything unusual, I want you to get me immediately. But I won't be long."

He didn't look at her as he closed the door.

In the mirror over the sink, his pupils glowed white in the darkness.

Oh, Jesus, he couldn't let himself change. If the beast got loose . . .

Terror for Mary's safety sent his heart on a sprint that only made the situation worse.

Fuck. What was he going to do? And why was this happening? Why—

Stop it. Just stop the thinking. Stop the panic. Get your internal engine back into idle. Then you can worry all you want.

He put the toilet lid down and sat on it, resting his hands on his knees. He forced his muscles to relax then focused on his lungs. Drawing in breath through his nose and exhaling out his mouth, he concentrated on keeping his respiration good and slow.

195

In and out with the breath. In and out with the breath.

The world receded until all sounds and sights and smells were shut out and there was only his breath.

Only his breath.

Only his breath.

Only his . . .

When he'd calmed down, he opened his eyes and lifted his hands. The trembling was gone. And a quick check in the mirror showed that his pupils were black again. He propped his arms on the sink and sagged into them.

Ever since he'd been cursed, sex had been a predictable tool that helped him deal with the beast. When he took a female, he'd become stimulated enough to make it to the release he needed, but the arousal never rose to the level where the beast was triggered. Not by a long shot.

With Mary, though, all bets were off. He didn't think he could control himself enough to enter her, much less make it to orgasm. That damn vibration she called out of him shot his sex drive straight into danger land.

He took a deep breath. The only saving grace appeared to be that he could get himself back under wraps quickly. If he got away from her, if he marshaled his nervous system, he was able to beat the feeling down to a manageable intensity. *Thank God.*

Rhage used the toilet, then washed his face in the sink and dried off with a hand towel. When he opened the door, he braced himself. He had a feeling that, when he saw Mary again, the feeling would return a little.

It did.

She was sitting on the couch dressed in khakis and a fleece. The candlelight amplified the anxiety in her face.

"Hey," he said.

"Are you okay?"

"Yeah." He rubbed his jaw. "Sorry about that. Sometimes I need a minute."

Her eyes widened.

"What?" he asked.

"It's almost six. You've been in there for nearly eight hours."

Rhage cursed. So much for a quick fix. "I didn't know I was gone for that long."

"I, ah, I checked in on you once or twice. I was worried . . . Anyway, someone called for you. Roth?"

"Wrath?"

"That's the name. Your phone kept ringing and ringing. Eventually I answered it." She looked down at her hands. "Are you sure you're okay?"

"I am now."

She took a deep breath and let it out. The exhale did nothing to ease the set of her shoulders.

"Mary, I . . ." Damn it, what exactly could he tell her that wasn't going to make things harder for her?

"It's okay. Whatever happened, it's okay."

He came over to the couch and sat down next to her. "Listen, Mary, I want you to come with me tonight. I want to take you somewhere that I know you'll be safe. The *lessers*, those things in the park, are probably gunning for you, and they'll look here first. You're a target now because you were with me."

"Where would we go?"

"I want you to stay with me." Assuming Wrath let them in the door. "It's too dangerous for you here, and if the slayers are going to come for you, it's going to be soon. We're talking tonight. Come with me for a few days until we figure out what to do."

Longer-term solutions evaded him at the moment, but he would find them. She'd become his responsibility when he got her mixed up in his world, and he wasn't going to leave her undefended.

"Trust me on this. Just a couple days."

*   *   *

Mary packed a bag, thinking she was crazy. Heading to God knew where. With a vampire.

But the thing about Rhage was, she had faith in him. He was too honest to lie and too smart to underestimate the threat. Besides, her appointments with the specialists didn't start up until Wednesday afternoon. And she'd taken the week off from work as well as been discharged from the hotline. There was nothing she would miss.

When she came back down to the living room, he turned toward her, swinging the duffel over one shoulder. She eyed his black suit jacket, seeing bulges in it she hadn't thought were significant before.

"Are you armed?" she asked.

He nodded.

"With what?" When he just looked at her, Mary shook her head. "You're right. Probably better that I don't know. Let's go."

They drove in silence down Route 22 into the dead zone between Caldwell's rural edges and the beginnings of the next large town. This was hilly, woodland country with nothing but long stretches of forest between the occasional rotting double-wide at the side of the road. There were no streetlights, few cars, and a lot of deer.

About twenty minutes after they'd left her house, he turned off onto a cramped one-laner that took them on a gradual ascent. She scanned what the headlights revealed, but couldn't discern where they were. Oddly, there didn't seem to be any identifying features to the forest or the road. In fact, the landscape had a fuzzy quality to it, a buffering that she couldn't explain and couldn't override no matter how much she blinked.

From out of nowhere a set of black iron gates appeared.

As Mary jumped in her seat, Rhage hit a garage door opener, and the heavy gates split in half, allowing them just enough space to squeeze through. Immediately they confronted another set. He put down his window and punched a code into an intercom. A pleasant voice welcomed him and he looked up and to the left, nodding to a security camera.

The second pair of gates parted and Rhage accelerated up a long, ascending drive. When they rounded a corner, a twenty-foot-tall masonry wall materialized in the same conjured-up manner of the first gateway. After going under an archway and passing through yet another set of barricades, they came into a courtyard with a fountain in the middle.

To the right, there was a four-story mansion made of gray stone, the kind of place you'd see in promos for horror films: Gothic, gloomy, oppressive, with more shadows than a person felt safe being around. Across the way, there was a small, one-story house with the same Wes Craven feel.

Six cars, mostly of expensive European flavors, were parked in an orderly fashion. Rhage plugged the GTO into a spot between an Escalade and a Mercedes.

Mary got out and craned her neck up at the mansion. She felt as though she were being watched, and she was. From the roof, gargoyles stared down at her, and so did security cameras.

Rhage came over, her overnight bag in his hand. His mouth was tight, his eyes intense.

"I'm going to take care of you. You know that, right?" As she nodded, he smiled a little. "It's going to be fine, but I want you to stick close by me. I don't want us separated. That clear? You stay with me no matter what happens."

Reassurance coupled with a command, she thought. This was not going to be fine.

They walked up to a pair of weathered bronze doors and he opened one side. After they'd stepped into a windowless vestibule, the great panel clamped shut with a reverberation that came up through her shoes. Directly ahead there was another massive set of doors, these made of wood and carved with symbols. Rhage punched a code into a keypad and there was the shifting sound of a lock coming free. He took her arm firmly and opened the second door into a vast foyer.

Mary gasped. How . . . *magical!*

The lobby was a rainbow of color, as unexpected as a garden blooming in a cave. Green malachite columns alternated with ones made of claret marble, the lengths rising up from a multi-hued mosaic floor. The walls were brilliant yellow and hung with gold-framed mirrors and crystal-strung sconces. The ceiling, three stories up, was a masterpiece of artwork and gold leafing, the scenes depicting heroes and horses and angels. And up ahead, centered among all the grandeur, was a broad staircase that ascended to a balconied second floor.

It was Russian-tsar beautiful . . . but the sounds of the place were not exactly formal and elegant. From the room on the left, hard-core rap music pumped and deep male voices carried. Pool balls cracked into each other. Someone yelled, "Go long, cop!"

A football sailed into the foyer and a muscular man came shooting out after it. He leaped up and just had his hands on the thing when an even bigger guy with a lion's mane of hair slammed into him. The two of them went down to the floor in a tangle of arms and legs, sliding hard into the wall.

"I got you good, cop."

"But you don't have the ball yet, vampire."

Grunts, laughter, and juicy curses carried up to that ornate ceiling as the men fought for the football, flipping each other over, sitting on each other's chests. Two more huge guys in black leather jogged out to check on the action. And then a little old man dressed in tails emerged from the right, carrying a bouquet of fresh flowers in a crystal vase. The butler stepped around the wrestling match with an indulgent smile.

Then everything went silent as they all noticed her at once.

Rhage shuffled her behind his body.

"Son of a bitch," someone said.

One of the men came at Rhage like a tank. His dark hair was clipped into a military brush cut, and Mary had the oddest sense she'd seen him before.

"What the *hell* are you doing?"

Rhage spread his stance, dropped her bag, and brought his hands up to chest level. "Where's Wrath?"

"I asked you a question," the other guy snapped. "What are you doing, bringing her here?"

"I need Wrath."

"I told you to get rid of her. Or do you expect one of us to do your job?"

Rhage met the man chin-to-chin. "Careful, Tohr. Don't make me hurt you."

Mary glanced behind her. The door to the vestibule was still open. And right now waiting in the car while Rhage sorted things out seemed like a really good idea. Stick-together rule notwithstanding.

As she backed away, she kept her eyes on him. Until she bumped against something hard.

She wheeled around. Looked up. And lost her voice.

What was blocking her escape had a scarred face, black eyes, and an aura of stone-cold anger.

Before she could bolt in fear, he took her arm and spun her away from the door.

"Don't even think about running." Flashing long fangs, he measured her body. "Funny, you're not his usual type. But you're alive and pants-pissing terrified. So you'll do fine for me."

Mary screamed.

Every head in the foyer turned, Rhage lunged for her, pulling her away, bringing her tight against his body. He spoke harshly, in the language she didn't understand.

The scarred man narrowed his eyes. "Easy there, Hollywood. Just keeping your little plaything in the house. You going to share her or be selfish like you usually are?"

Rhage looked as if he were about to lash out when a woman's voice cut him off.

"Oh, for God's sake, boys! You're scaring her."

Mary glanced around Rhage's chest and saw a woman coming down the stairway. She looked completely normal: long black hair, blue jeans, white turtleneck. A black cat was purring like a sewing machine in her arms. As she marched through the thicket of men, they all got out of her way.

"Rhage, we're glad you made it home safely. And Wrath is coming down in a minute." She pointed to the room the men had come out of. "The rest of you head back in there. Go on, now. If you're going to crack some balls, do it on the pool table. Dinner's in a half hour. Butch, take the football with you, okay?"

She shooed them from the foyer like they weren't hard-nosed badasses. The only guy who stayed was the one with the brush cut.

He was calmer now as he looked at Rhage. "This is going to have repercussions, my brother."

Rhage's face hardened and they broke into their secret language.

The black-haired woman came up to Mary, all the while stroking the cat's throat. "Don't worry. Everything's going to be okay. I'm Beth, by the way. And this is Boo."

Mary took a deep breath, instinctively trusting this lone feminine outpost in what was a jungle of testosterone.

"Mary. Mary Luce."

Beth offered her the petting hand and smiled.

More fangs.

Mary felt the floor underneath her shift.

"I think she's going over," Beth shouted while reaching forward. "Rhage!"

Strong arms came around her waist as her knees buckled.

The last thing she heard before blacking out was Rhage saying, "I'm taking her up to my room."

As Rhage laid Mary out on his bed, he willed on a soft light. Oh, God, what had he done, bringing her to the compound?

When she stirred and opened her eyes, he said, "You're safe here."

"Yeah, right."

"I'll make it safe for you, how about that?"

"Now I believe you." She smiled a little. "Sorry about going over like I did. I'm not usually a fainter."

"It's perfectly understandable. Look, I have to go meet with my brothers. You see that steel lock on the door? I'm the only one who has a key, so you'll be secure here."

"Those guys were not happy to see me."

"That's their problem." He brushed her hair back, tucking it behind both her ears. He wanted to kiss her, but stood up instead.

She looked so right in his big bed, nestled in the mountain of pillows he insisted on sleeping with. He wanted her there tomorrow and the day after and . . .

This wasn't a mistake, he thought. This was right where she belonged.

"Rhage, why are you doing all this for me? I mean, you don't really owe me anything, and you hardly know me."

Because you're mine, he thought.

Keeping that little ditty to himself, he bent down and stroked her cheek with his forefinger. "This won't take long."

"Rhage—"

"Just let me take care of you. And don't worry about a thing."

He shut the door behind him and turned the lock

before going down the hall. The brothers were waiting at the head of the stairs, Wrath at the front of the group. The king looked grim, black eyebrows buried behind his sunglasses.

"Where do you want to do this?" Rhage asked.

"My study."

After they'd filed into the formal room, Wrath went behind the desk and sat down. Tohr followed him, standing behind him and to his right. Phury and Z settled against a silk-covered wall. Vishous sat in one of the wing chairs next to the fireplace and lit up a hand-rolled.

Wrath shook his head. "Rhage, man, we got serious problems here. You violated a direct order. Twice. Then you drag a human into this house, which you know is forbidden—"

"She's in danger—"

Wrath slammed his fist into the desk, making the whole thing jump off the floor. "You *really* don't want to interrupt me right now."

Rhage worked his molars, grinding, biting. He forced the words of respect he usually offered freely. "I meant no offense, my lord."

"As I was saying, you disobeyed Tohr, and compounded the offense by showing up with a human. What the hell are you thinking? I mean, shit, you're not an idiot, in spite of how you're behaving. She's from the other world, so she's rank exposure for us. And you have to know her memories are both long term and traumatic by now. She is permanently compromised."

Rhage felt a growl condense in his chest and he just couldn't suck it back. The sound permeated the room like an odor. "She will not be killed over this."

"Yeah, see, that's not your call. You made it mine when you brought her onto our turf."

Rhage bared his fangs. "Then I'll leave. I'll leave with her."

Wrath's brows popped up over his wraparounds. "Now's not the time for threats, my brother."

"*Threats?* I'm dead fucking serious!" He calmed himself down by rubbing his face and trying to breathe. "Look, last night the two of us were jumped by multiple *lessers*. She got jacked and I left at least one of those slayers alive while trying to save her. She lost her purse in the process, and if any of those *lessers* survived, you know they've picked up the damn thing. Even if I wipe her memories clean, her house is not secure and I'm not going to let her be taken out by the Society. If she and I can't stay here, and the only way I can protect her is by disappearing with her, then that's what I'm going to do."

Wrath frowned. "You realize you're choosing a female over the Brotherhood."

Rhage exhaled. *Jesus.* He hadn't expected the situation to come down to that. But he guessed it had.

Unable to stay in place, he went over to one of the windows that ran from floor to ceiling. Looking outside, he saw the terraced gardens, the swimming pool, the vast rolling lawn. But he didn't focus on the manicured landscape. What he saw was the protection the compound offered.

Security lights illuminated the vista. Cameras mounted in trees recorded every passing moment. Motion sensors monitored each colorful leaf that fell to the ground. And if anyone tried to surmount that wall, they'd do a meet-and-greet with 240 volts of good night, Gracie.

This was the safest environment for Mary. Bar none.

"She's not just any female to me," he murmured. "I would have her as my *shellan*, if I could."

Someone cursed while several others inhaled sharply.

"You don't even know her," Tohr pointed out. "And she's a *human*."

"So."

Wrath's voice was low, insistent. "Rhage, man, don't

205

pull out of the Brotherhood over this. We need you. The race needs you."

"Then it looks like she's staying here, doesn't it." When Wrath muttered something vile, Rhage turned to him. "If Beth were in danger, would you let anything stand in your way of protecting her? Even the Brotherhood?"

Wrath rose from the chair and came around the desk in a full stalk. He stopped when they were chest-to-chest.

"My Beth has nothing to do with the choices you've made or the situation you've put all of us in. Contact with humans is to be limited and on their territory only, you know that. And no one lives in this house except brothers and their *shellans*, if they have them."

"What about Butch?"

"He's the sole exception. And he's only allowed because V dreams of him."

"But Mary won't be here forever."

"How you figure that? You think the Society's going to give up? You think humans will suddenly become tolerant as a race? Get real."

Rhage dropped his voice, but not his eyes. "She's sick, Wrath. She's got cancer. I want to take care of her, and not just because of this *lesser* nightmare."

There was a long silence.

"Shit, you've bonded with her." Wrath put a hand through his long hair. "For God's sake . . . You just met her, my brother."

"And how long did it take you to mark Beth as your own? Twenty-four hours? Oh, right, you waited two days. Yeah, good thing you gave it some time."

Wrath let out a short laugh. "You gotta keep bringing my *shellan* into it, don't you?"

"Look, my lord, Mary is . . . different to me. I'm not going to pretend I understand why. All I know is, she's a pounding in my chest that I can't ignore . . . hell, that I don't *want* to ignore. So the idea of leaving her at the mercy of the Society is simply not an option. When it comes to her, every protective instinct I have goes into overdrive and I can't push that shit aside. Even for the Brotherhood."

Rhage fell silent and minutes passed. Hours. Or maybe it was just a couple of heartbeats.

"If I allow her to stay here," Wrath said, "it's only because you see her as your mate and only if she can keep her yap shut. And we still have to deal with the fact that you violated those orders from Tohr. I can't let that go. I've got to bring it to the Scribe Virgin."

Rhage sagged in relief. "I'll accept any repercussions."

"So be it." Wrath went back to the desk and sat down. "We've got some other things to talk about, my brothers. Tohr, you're up."

Tohrment came forward.

"Bad news. We heard from a civilian family. Male, ten years out of his transition, disappeared last night from the downtown area. I've sent a blast e-mail to the community informing everyone that they should use extra caution when going out and that anyone who's missing needs to be reported to us immediately. Also, Butch and I have been talking. The cop's got a good head on his shoulders. Any of you have a problem if I bring him in on a little of our business?" When there were a number of shaking heads, Tohr focused on Rhage. "Now tell us what happened last night in the park."

After Rhage left, and when she felt steady enough to stand, Mary slid off the bed and checked the door. It was locked and solid, so she felt fairly safe. When she saw a light switch to the left, she hit it, illuminating the room.

Holy . . . house of Windsor.

Silk drapery hung from the windows in swaths of red and gold. Satin and velvet adorned a huge antique Jacobean bed, the posts of which must have been made out of whole

207

oak trunks. There was an Aubusson rug on the floor, oil paintings on the walls—

Good lord, was that *Madonna and Child* really a Rubens?

But it wasn't all Sotheby's stuff. There was a plasma-screen TV, enough stereo equipment to carry off a Super Bowl half-time show, a NASA-worthy computer. And an Xbox on the floor.

She wandered over to the bookshelves, where leather-bound volumes in foreign languages stood straight and proud. She scanned the titles with appreciation until she ran into a collection of DVDs.

Oh, the humanity.

The *Austin Powers* boxed set. *Aliens* and *Alien. Jaws.* All three *Naked Guns. Godzilla. Godzilla. Godzilla . . .* wait, the rest of this whole shelf was *Godzilla.* She went one lower. *Friday the 13th, Halloween, Nightmare on Elm Street.* Well, at least he hadn't bothered with the sequels to those. *Caddy-shack.* The *Evil Dead* boxed set.

It was a wonder Rhage hadn't blinded himself with all that pop culture.

Mary went into the bathroom and flipped on the lights. A Jacuzzi the size of her living room was set into the marble floor.

Now that's a true thing of beauty, she thought.

She heard the door open and was relieved when Rhage called her name.

"I'm in here checking out your tub." She walked back to the bedroom. "What happened?"

"Everything's cool."

You sure about that? she wanted to ask. Because he was tense and preoccupied as he went into a walk-in closet.

"Don't worry, you can stay here."

"But . . . ?"

"No buts."

"Rhage, what's going on?"

"I need to go out with my brothers tonight." He came

back without his suit coat on and led her over to the bed, pulling her down next to him as he sat. "The *doggen*, our servants, know you're here. They're incredibly loyal and friendly, nothing to be scared of. Fritz, who runs this house, will be bringing you up some food in a little bit. If you need anything, just ask him. I'll be back at dawn."

"Am I going to be locked in here until then?"

He shook his head and stood up.

"You're free to move around the house. No one will touch you." He took a piece of paper out of a leather box and wrote on it. "Here's my cell number. You call me if you need me and I can be back in a moment."

"You got a transporter hiding somewhere around here?"

Rhage looked at her and disappeared.

Not as in *left-the-room-really-fast* disappeared. But *poof!* disappeared.

Mary leaped off the bed, holding in a shout of alarm with her hand.

Rhage's arms came around her from behind. "In a moment."

She grabbed on to his wrists, squeezing the bones to make sure she wasn't hallucinating.

"That's a hell of trick." Her voice was thin. "What else do you have under your hat?"

"I can turn things on and off." The room plunged into darkness. "I can light candles." Two of them flared on his dresser. "And I'm handy with locks and stuff."

She heard the latch on the door click back and forth, and then the closet opened and shut.

"Oh, and I can do something really great with my tongue and a cherry stem."

He dropped a kiss on the side of her neck and headed into the bathroom. The door shut and she heard the shower come on.

Mary stayed frozen in place, her mind skipping like a needle on an LP record. Eyeing the DVD collection, she decided there was something to be said for escapism. Especially when a person had had too much weirdness, too many reorientations to reality, too much . . . everything.

When Rhage came out a while later, shaved, smelling of soap, a towel around his hips, she was propped up on the bed, *Austin Powers Goldmember* on the TV.

"Hey, this is a classic." He smiled and watched the screen.

She forgot all about the movie as she looked at those wide shoulders, the muscles of his arms, the towel following the form of his ass. And the tattoo. That twisting, fierce creature with the white eyes.

"'*Twins, Basil, twins,*'" Rhage said with perfect timing and intonation.

He winked at her and went into the closet.

Against her better instincts, she followed after him, and leaned on one of the jambs, trying to look casual. Rhage's back was to her as he pulled on a pair of black leather pants, commando. The tattoo moved with him as he did up the fly.

A soft sigh escaped her mouth. *What a man. Vampire. Whatever.*

He glanced over his shoulder. "You okay?"

Actually, she was feeling hot all over.

"Mary?"

"I'm fine and dandy." Dropping her eyes, she took consuming interest in the collection of shoes lined up on the floor. "Actually I'm going to self-medicate with your movie collection until I'm in a culture coma."

As he bent down to put his socks on, her eyes latched back onto his skin. All that bare, smooth, golden—

"About the sleeping arrangements," he said. "I'll just crash on the floor."

But she wanted to be in that big bed with him, she thought.

"Don't be silly, Rhage. We're both adults. And that thing is wide enough to sleep six."

He hesitated. "All right. I promise not to snore."

And how about not keeping your hands to yourself, either?

He pulled on a black short-sleeved shirt and pushed his feet into a pair of shitkickers. Then he paused, eyeing a floor-to-ceiling metal cabinet that was set into the closet wall.

"Mary, why don't you go back outside? I need a minute. Okay?"

She flushed and turned away. "Sorry, I didn't mean to invade your privacy—"

He took her hand. "It's not that. You just might not like what you see next."

As if there was much left that could shock her after today?

"Go ahead," she murmured. "Do . . . whatever."

Rhage stroked her wrist with his thumb then opened the metal cabinet. He took out an empty black leather chest holster and put it on across his shoulders, securing it under his pecs. A wide belt was next, like the kind cops wore, but, as with the holster, there was nothing in it.

He looked at her. And then brought out the weapons. Two long, black-bladed daggers, which he sheathed at his chest, handles down. A shiny handgun that he checked for bullets with fast, sure movements before anchoring it at his hip. Flashing martial-arts stars and matte-black ammunition clips that he tucked into the belt. Another, smaller knife he hid somewhere.

He took his black leather trench coat off a hanger and swung it on, patting the pockets. He pulled out another handgun from the weapons cabinet and assessed it quickly before burying it in the leather folds. He put a few more throwing stars in the coat's pockets. Added another dagger.

When he faced her, she backed away.

211

"Mary, don't look at me like I'm a stranger. It's still me under all this."

She didn't stop until she hit the bed. "You are a stranger," she whispered.

His face tightened and his voice grew flat. "I'll be back before dawn."

He left without any hesitation.

Mary didn't know how long she sat and stared at the carpet. But when she looked up, she went over and grabbed the phone.

TWENTY-FOUR

Bella popped open her oven, took a peek at dinner, and gave up the fight.

What a mess.

She grabbed a pair of pot holders and extracted the meat loaf. The poor thing had cowered away from the sides of the pan, blackened on top, and developed drying cracks. It was inedible, better suited to the construction supply trade than to a dinner plate. A few dozen more of these and some mortar and she'd have that wall she wanted around her terrace.

As she shut the oven door with her hip, she could have sworn the high-end Viking stove was glaring at her. The animosity was mutual. When her brother had done over the farmhouse for her, he'd gotten her the best of everything, because that was the only way Rehvenge did things. The fact that she'd preferred the old-fashioned kitchen and the squeaky doors and the gentle aging of the place hadn't mattered. And God help her if she'd kicked up a fuss about the security measures. The only way Rehvenge had permitted her to move out was if he made her home fireproof, bulletproof, and impregnable as a museum.

Ah, the joys of having a bossy brother with a lockdown mentality.

She picked up the pan and was headed for the French doors to the backyard when the phone rang.

As she answered, she hoped it wasn't Rehvenge. "Hello?"

There was a pause. "Bella?"

"Mary! I called you earlier today. Hold on a sec, I've got to feed the raccoons." She put the phone on the table, shot out to the yard, dumped the load and headed back in. When the pan was in the sink, she picked up the receiver. "How are you?"

"Bella, I need to know something." The human's voice was strained.

"Anything, Mary. What's wrong?"

"Are you . . . one of them?"

Bella sank down into a chair at her kitchen table. "You mean, am I different from you?"

"Uh-huh."

Bella glanced over at her fish tank. Everything always looked so calm in there, she thought.

"Yes, Mary. Yes, I am different."

There was a rush of breath on the line. "Oh, thank God."

"Somehow, I didn't think knowing that would be a relief."

"It is. I . . . I really have to talk to someone. I'm so confused."

"Confused about . . ." *Wait a minute.* Why were they even having this conversation? "Mary, how do you know about us?"

"Rhage told me. Well, showed me, too."

"You mean he hasn't wiped . . . You remember him?"

"I'm staying with him."

"You're *what?*"

"Here. At the house. With a bunch of men, vampires . . . God, that word . . ." The female cleared her throat. "I'm here with about five other guys just like him."

Bella put her hand over her mouth. No one stayed with the Brotherhood. No one even knew where they lived. And this female was a *human.*

"Mary, how did you . . . how did this happen?"

When the story was all out, Bella was stunned.

"Hello? Bella?"

"Sorry, I . . . Are you okay?"

214

"I think so. I'm all right now, at least. Listen, I have to know. Why did you put the two of us together? Rhage and me?"

"He saw you and he . . . liked you. He promised me he wouldn't hurt you, which was the only reason I agreed to set you up on that date."

"When did he see me?"

"The night we took John to the training center. Or don't you remember that?"

"No, I don't, but Rhage told me I'd gone there. Is John . . . a vampire?"

"Yes, he is. His change is coming, which is why I got involved. He'll die unless one of our kind is with him when the transition hits. He needs a female to drink from."

"So that night, when you met him, you knew."

"I did." Bella chose her words carefully. "Mary, is the warrior treating you well? Is he . . . gentle with you?"

"He's taking care of me. Protecting me. I have no idea why, though."

Bella sighed, thinking she knew. Given the warrior's fixation on the human, he had probably bonded with her.

"But I'll be home soon," the female said. "Just a couple of days."

Bella wasn't so sure about that. Mary was so much deeper in their world than she realized.

The smell of gas fumes was nasty, O thought as he maneuvered the Toro Dingo around in the dark.

"That's good. We're good to go," U called out.

O shut the thing off and surveyed the area he'd carved from the forest. Flat, about forty-by-forty-feet square, it was the layout of the persuasion building plus room for them to work.

U stepped into the leveled area and addressed the assembled *lessers*. "Let's start getting the walls up. I want three sides raised. Leave one open." U motioned impatiently with his hand. "Come on. Move it."

The men picked up frames made out of eight-foot-long two-by-fours and carried the things around.

The sound of an approaching vehicle stopped everyone, though the lack of headlights suggested it was another *lesser*. With their superior night vision, Society members were able to dance around in the dark as if it were high noon; whoever was behind that wheel dodging trees had the same acuity.

When Mr. X got out of the minivan, O went over.

"Sensei," O said, bowing. He knew the bastard appreciated the respect and somehow pissing off the guy just wasn't as fun as it used to be.

"Mr. O, it looks like you're making progress."

"Let me show you what we're doing."

They had to shout over the clapping of hammerheads, but there was no reason to worry about any of the noise. They were smack-dab in the middle of a seventy-five-acre plot of land about thirty minutes from Caldwell's downtown area. To the west of the property was a swamp that served as one of the Hudson River's flood zones. Covering the north and east was Big Notch Mountain, a pile of state-owned rock that climbers didn't favor because of its rattlesnake dens, and that tourists found all-around unappealing. The only point of exposure was from the south, but the rednecks who lived in the scattered, decaying farmhouses didn't seem like the type to wander.

"This looks good," Mr. X said. "Now where are you putting in the storage facilities?"

"Here." O stood over a section of ground. "We'll have the supplies in the morning. We should be ready to receive visitors in a day."

"You've done pretty well, son."

Goddamn it, O hated the *son* shit. He really did.

"Thank you, sensei," he said.

216

"Now walk me to my car." When they were a distance away from the work, Mr. X said, "Tell me something. Do you have much contact with the Betas?"

O made sure their eye contact didn't waver. "Not really."

"Have you seen any of them lately?"

Christ, where was the *Fore-lesser* going with this? "No."

"Not any time last night?"

"No, like I said, I don't hang with the Betas." O frowned. He knew that, if he demanded an explanation, he'd just look defensive, but fuck it. "What's this about?"

"Those Betas we lost in the park last night had shown some promise. I'd hate to think you were slaughtering your competition."

"A brother—"

"Yes, a member of the Brotherhood attacked them. Right. Funny, though, the brothers always make sure they stab their kills so the bodies disintegrate. But last night, those Betas were left for dead. And hurt badly enough so they couldn't really respond to questions when they were found by their backup squad. So no one knows what happened."

"I wasn't in that park and you know it."

"Do I?"

"For chrissakes—"

"Watch your mouth. And watch yourself." Mr. X's pale eyes narrowed into slits. "You know who I'll call if I need to pull your choke chain again. Now get back to work. I'll see you and the other primes at first light for your check-in."

"I thought that's why we had e-mail," O said through gritted teeth.

"It's in person from now on for you and your team."

When the minivan drove off, O stared into the night, listening to the cracking sounds of construction work. He should have been seething with anger. Instead he was just . . . tired.

God, he had no enthusiasm left for this job of his. And he couldn't even get worked up over Mr. X's bullshit.

The thrill was gone.

Mary glanced at the digital clock: 1:56. Dawn was still hours and hours away, and sleep was out of the question. All she pictured when she closed her eyes were those weapons hanging off Rhage's body.

She rolled over onto her back. The idea of not seeing him ever again was so disturbing, she refused to look into the feelings too closely. She just accepted them, bore them badly, and hoped for some relief.

God, she wished she could go back to when he'd left. She would have hugged him hard. And given him a stiff lecture about staying safe even though she knew nothing about fighting and he was, hopefully, a master at it. She just wanted him safe—

Suddenly the door was unlocked. As it swung open, Rhage's blond hair gleamed in the light from the hall.

Mary shot off the bed, crossed the room at a dead run, and threw herself at him.

"Whoa, what the . . ." His arm went around her and picked her up, keeping her with him as he came through the door and shut it. When he released her, she slid down his body. "You all right?"

As her feet hit the floor, she came back to reality.

"Mary?"

"Ah, yeah . . . yes, I'm okay." She stepped to the side. Looked around. Blushed like all hell. "I'm just . . . yeah, I'm just going to go back to bed now."

"Hold up, female." Rhage took off his trench coat, the chest holster, and the belt. "Get back over here. I like the way you welcome me home."

He opened his arms wide and she went into them, holding on hard, feeling him breathe. His body was so warm and he smelled wonderful, like fresh air and good clean sweat.

"I didn't expect you to be up," he murmured, running his hand up and down her spine.

"Couldn't sleep."

"I told you, you're safe here, Mary." His fingers found the base of her neck and massaged deeply. "Damn, you're tense. You sure you're okay?"

"I'm fine. Really."

He stopped the rubbing. "Do you ever answer that question truthfully?"

"I just did." *Sort of.*

His hand resumed the stroking. "Will you promise me something?"

"What?"

"Will you let me know when you're not okay?" His voice became teasing. "I mean, I know you're tough, so I won't hold my breath for it or anything. You won't have to worry about killing me over this."

She laughed. "I promise."

He tilted her chin up with his finger, eyes grave. "I'm going to keep you to that." Then he dropped a kiss to her cheek. "Listen, I was going to head down to the kitchen and grab something to eat. You want to come with me? The house is quiet. The other brothers are still out."

"Sure. Let me change."

"Just put on one of my fleeces." He went over to the dresser and took out something soft, black, and the size of a tarp. "I like the idea of you wearing my clothes."

As he helped her into it, his smile was a very masculine expression of satisfaction. And possessiveness.

And damned if it didn't suit his face to a tee.

By the time they finished eating and were back upstairs in his room, Rhage was having trouble concentrating. The hum was roaring in full force, worse than ever before.

And he was totally aroused, his body so hot he felt like his blood was going to dry out in his veins.

As Mary went over to the bed and settled in, he took a quick shower and wondered if he shouldn't give his erection a release before he came back out. The damn thing was hard, stiff, aching like a bitch, and the water rushing down his body made him think of Mary's hands on his skin. He palmed himself and remembered the feel of her moving against his mouth as he pleasured her soft secrets. He lasted, like, less than a minute.

When it was over, the empty orgasm just juiced him up more. It was like his body knew the real thing was out in the bedroom and had no intention of being diverted.

Cursing, he stepped out and toweled off, then headed for his closet. With a prayer for Fritz's attention to detail, he hunted around until he found—*thank you, God*—a set of pajamas he'd never put on before. He shrugged into them and then threw on the matching robe for good measure.

Rhage grimaced, feeling like he was wearing half the damn closet. But that was the point.

"Is the room too warm for you?" he asked, as he willed a candle to light and turned off the lamp.

"It's perfect."

Personally, he thought he was in the flipping tropics. And the temperature jacked higher as he approached the bed and sat on the opposite side from her.

"Listen, Mary, in about an hour, at four forty-five, you're going to hear the shutters closing for the day. They slide down on tracks over the windows. It's not that loud, but I don't want you to be startled."

"Thanks."

Rhage lay down on top of the comforter and crossed his feet at the ankles. Everything irritated him, the hot room, the PJs, the robe. Now he knew what presents felt like, all trussed up in paper and ribbons: itchy.

"Do you normally wear all that to bed?" she asked.

"Absolutely."

"Then why's the tag still on that robe?"

"In case I want another, I'll know what it is."

He turned on his side, away from her. Rolled back over so he stared at the ceiling again. A minute later, he tried his stomach.

"Rhage." Her voice was lovely in the dim quiet.

"What?"

"You sleep in the nude, right?"

"Ah, usually."

"Look, you can lose the clothes. It's not going to bother me."

"I didn't want you to feel . . . uncomfortable."

"What's making me uncomfortable is you flopping around on that side of the bed. I feel like a tossed salad over here."

He would have chuckled at her reasonable tone, but the hot pump between his legs sucked the humor right out of him.

Ah, hell, if he thought the getup he had on was going to keep him in check, he was out of his mind. He wanted her so badly that, short of chain mail, what he was or was not wearing wasn't going to make a lick of difference.

Keeping his back to her, he stood up and stripped. With some finessing, he managed to get himself under the covers without flashing her a glimpse of what the front of him was up to. That monstrous arousal was nothing she needed to know about.

He faced away from her, lying on his side.

"Can I touch it?" she asked.

His erection jerked, as if volunteering to be the "it."

"Touch what?"

"The tattoo. I'd like to . . . touch it."

God, she was so close to him, and that voice of hers— that sweet, beautiful voice—was magic. But the hum in

221

his body made him feel like he had a paint mixer in his belly.

When he stayed quiet, she murmured, "Never mind. I don't—"

"No. It's just . . ." *Shit.* He hated the distance in her tone. "Mary, it's okay. Do whatever you like."

He heard sheets brushing against sheets. Felt the mattress move a little. And then her fingertips brushed his shoulder. He kept his flinch to himself as best he could.

"Where did you get it done?" she whispered, tracing the curse's outline. "The artwork is extraordinary."

His whole body tensed as he felt precisely where she was on the beast. She was going across its left foreleg now, and he knew it because he felt the corresponding tingle in his own limb.

Rhage closed his eyes, getting trapped between the pleasure of having her hand on him and the reality that he was flirting with disaster. The vibration, the burning—it was all rising, called out of darkest, most destructive core of him.

He inhaled through his teeth as she stroked the beast's flank.

"Your skin is so smooth," she said, running her palm down his spine.

Frozen in place, unable to breathe, he prayed for self-control.

"And . . . well, anyway." She pulled back. "I think it's beautiful."

He was on top of her before he knew he'd moved. And he wasn't a gentleman. He pushed his thigh between her legs, pinned her arms over her head, and found her mouth with his own. As she arched into him, he grabbed hold of her nightgown and yanked up hard. He was going to take her. At this very moment and in his bed, just as he'd wanted to.

And she was going to be *perfect*.

Her thighs yielded to him, opening wide, and she urged him on, his name a hoarse moan leaving her lips. The sound lit off a violent shaking in him, one that dimmed his vision and sent pulses down his arms and legs. The taking of her consumed him, stripped him of whatever civilized lid there was on his instincts. He was raw, wild and . . .

On the verge of the scorching implosion that was the curse's calling card.

Terror gave him the strength he needed to leap off her and stumble across the room. He slammed into something. The wall.

"Rhage!"

Sinking down onto the floor, he put his trembling hands over his face, knowing his eyes were white. His body shook so badly his words came out in waves. "I'm out of my mind . . . This is . . . Shit, I can't . . . I need to stay away from you."

"Why? I don't want you to stop—"

He talked right over her. "I'm starved for you, Mary. I'm so damn . . . hungry, but I can't have you. I won't take . . . you."

"Rhage," she snapped, as if trying to get through to him. "Why not?"

"You don't want me. Trust me, you really don't want me like that."

"The hell I don't."

He wasn't about to tell her he was a beast waiting to happen. So he chose to disgust her rather than scare her. "I've had eight different females this week alone."

There was a long pause. "Good . . . God."

"I don't want to lie to you. Ever. So let me be very clear. I've had a lot of anonymous sex. I've been with so many females, none of whom I've cared about. And I don't want you to ever think I'd use you like that."

Now that his pupils felt as though they were black again, he looked over at her.

"Tell me you practice safe sex," she muttered.

"When the females ask me to, I do."

Her eyes flared. "And when they don't?"

"I could no more get the common cold from one of them than I could HIV or hep C or any STD. And I'm not a carrier of those diseases, either. Human viruses don't affect us."

She pulled the sheets up around her shoulders. "How do you know you're not getting them pregnant? Or can't humans and vampires . . ."

"Half-breeds are rare, but it does happen. And it's obvious to me when the females are fertile. I can smell it. If they are, or are close, I don't have sex with them, even using protection. My children, when I have them, will be born in safety in my world. And I will love their mother."

Mary's eyes skipped away, becoming fixed, haunted. He looked up to see what she was staring at. It was the *Madonna and Child* painting over the dresser.

"I'm glad you told me," she finally said. "But why does it have to be with strangers? Why can you be with someone you . . . Actually, don't answer that. It's none of my business."

"I'd rather be with you, Mary. Not being inside of you is . . . torture. I want you so badly I can't stand it." He blew out his breath. "But can you honestly tell me that you want me now? Although . . . hell, even if you did, there's still something else. The way you go to my head, it's like I told you before. I'm scared of losing control. You affect me differently than other females do."

There was another long silence. She broke it.

"Tell me again that you're miserable we're not sleeping together," she said dryly.

"I am utterly miserable. Achy. Hard all the time. Distracted and pissed off."

"Good." She laughed a little. "Boy, I'm a bitch, aren't I?"

"Not at all."

The room grew quiet. Eventually he lay down and curled onto his side, resting his head on his arm.

She sighed. "I don't expect you to sleep on the floor now."

"It's better this way."

"For chrissakes, Rhage, get up here."

His voice dropped to a low growl. "If I come back to that bed, there's no way I'm not going for that sweet spot between your legs. And it wouldn't be just my hands and my tongue this time. It would be right back to where we were. My body on top of yours, every thick inch of me desperate to get into you."

As he caught the luscious scent of her arousal, the air between them surged with sex. And inside his body, he turned back into a live wire.

"Mary, I'd better go. I'll come back after you're asleep."

He left before she could utter another word. As the door shut behind him, he sagged against the wall in the corridor. Being out of the room helped. It was harder to catch her scent that way.

He heard a laugh and looked over to see Phury sauntering down the corridor.

"You look strung out, Hollywood. As well as really goddamned naked."

Rhage covered himself with his hands. "I don't know how you can take it."

The brother stopped, swirling the mug of hot cider he carried. "Take what?"

"The celibacy."

"Don't tell me your female won't have you?"

"That's not the problem."

"So why you out in this hall standing at full attention?"

"I, ah, don't want to hurt her."

Phury looked taken aback. "You're a big one, but you've never injured a female. At least not that I've known."

"No, it's just . . . I want her so badly, I'm . . . I'm juiced, man."

Phury's yellow eyes narrowed. "You talking about your beast?"

Rhage looked away. "Yeah."

The whistle that came out of the brother was grim. "Well . . . hell, you'd better take care of yourself. You want to pay her respect, that's fine. But you keep yourself on the level or you're *really* going to hurt her, you feel me? Find a fight, find some other females if you have to, but you make sure you're calm. And if you need some red smoke, you come to me. I'll give you some of my O-Zs, no problem."

Rhage took a deep breath. "I'll pass on the smokes right now. But can I borrow some sweats and a pair of Nikes? I'm going to try to run myself into exhaustion."

Phury clapped him on the back. "Come on, my brother. I'm more than happy to cover your ass."

TWENTY-FIVE

As the afternoon's light waned through the forest, O backed the Toro up, avoiding the pile of earth he'd created with it.

"You ready for the pipes?" U yelled out.

"Yeah. Drop one down. Let's see how it fits."

A composite-metal corrugated sewer pipe about three feet in diameter and seven feet long was lowered into the hole so it stood on its end. The thing fit perfectly.

"Let's get the other two in there," O said.

Twenty minutes later the three pipe sections were lined up. Using the Dingo, O pushed the dirt in while two other *lessers* held the pipes in place.

"Looking good," U said, walking around. "Looking damn good. But how do we get the civilians in and out?"

"Harness system." O shut off the Dingo and went over to peer inside one of the pipes. "You can buy them for rock climbing at Dick's Sporting Goods. We're strong enough to lift the civilians even if they're deadweight, and they'll be drugged, in pain, or exhausted, so they won't fight much."

"This was a great idea," U murmured. "But how do we cap them?"

"The lids will be metal mesh with a weight on the center." O glanced up, seeing blue sky. "How long do you think until the roof's on?"

"We'll get the last wall up right now. Then all we have to do is erect the rafters and drop in the skylights. The shingling won't take long, and the clapboards are already on the three walls we have now. I'll move the tools in here, get a table, and we're rolling tomorrow night."

"We'll have the shades for the skylights by then?"

"Yeah. And they're retractable so you'll be able to open and lower them."

Man, those things were going to be handy. A little sunlight was the best maid a *lesser* could have. She comes in, flashes through the space, and *presto!*, no more vampire debris.

O nodded to his truck. "I'll take the Toro back to the rental place. You need anything from town?"

"Nope. We're good."

On the way into Caldwell, with the piece of machinery in the bed of the F-150, O should have been in a good mood. The building was going well. His squadron was accepting his leadership. Mr. X hadn't brought up the Betas again. But instead he just felt . . . dead. And wasn't that ironic as hell for someone who hadn't been alive for three years?

He'd been like this once before.

Back in Sioux City, before he'd become a *lesser*, he'd hated his life. He'd squeaked through high school, and there'd been no money to send him to even a community college, so his career options had been limited. Working as a bouncer had called into service his size and mean streak, but it was only moderately amusing: the drunks didn't tend to fight back, and coldcocking the unconscious was no more engaging than beating a cow.

The only good thing had been meeting Jennifer. She'd saved him from the mindless tedium, and he'd loved her for it. She was drama, excitement, and unpredictability in the flat landscape of life. And whenever he'd go into one of his rages, she'd hit him right back, even though she was smaller and bled easier than he did. He'd never figured out whether she threw her punches because she was too dumb to know he'd always win in the end or if it was because she was so used to being beaten by her father. Either way, stupidity or habit, he took everything she could give him and then pounded her into the ground. Tending to her afterward, when his fire was out, had given him the most tender moments of his life.

But like all good things, she had come to an end. God, he missed her. She'd been the only one who understood how love and hate beat side by side in the chambers of his heart, the only one who could handle both at the same time. Thinking of her long, dark hair and her lean body, he missed her so much he could almost feel her beside him.

As he came into Caldwell proper, he thought of the prostitute he'd bought the other morning. She'd ended up giving him what he'd needed after all, though she'd had to trade her life to do it. And while he drove along now, he scanned the sidewalks, looking for another release. Unfortunately, brunettes were harder to come by than blondes in the skin trade. Maybe he could buy a wig and tell the whores to put it on.

O thought about the number of people he'd taken out. The first person he'd killed had been in self-defense. The second had been a mistake. The third had been in cold blood. So by the time he'd come to the East Coast, running from the law, he'd known a little about death.

Back then, with Jennifer just gone, the pain in his chest had been a living thing, a mad dog that needed to stretch its legs before it destroyed him. Falling into the Society had been a miracle. It had saved him from tortured rootlessness, giving him a focus and a purpose and an outlet for the agony.

But now, somehow, all those benefits were gone and he felt empty. Just as he had five years ago in Sioux City, right before he'd run into Jennifer.

Well, almost the same, he thought, pulling up to the rental place.

Back then, he'd still been alive.

* * *

"Are you out of the tub?"

Mary laughed, put the phone to her other ear, and burrowed deeper into the pillows. It was sometime after four o'clock.

"Yes, Rhage."

She couldn't remember when she'd had a more luxurious day. Sleeping in. Food delivered with books and magazines. The Jacuzzi.

It was like being at a spa. Well, a spa where the phone rang all the time. She wouldn't count how many times he'd called her.

"Did Fritz bring you what I asked?"

"How did he find fresh strawberries like that in October?"

"We have our ways."

"And the flowers are beautiful." She eyed the bouquet full of roses and foxglove and delphinium and tulips. Spring and summer in a crystal vase. "Thank you."

"I'm glad you like them. I wish I could have gone out and chosen them myself. I would have enjoyed finding you only the most perfect ones. I wanted them to be bright and smell good."

"Mission accomplished."

Male voices sounded in the background. Rhage's voice dimmed. "Hey, cop, mind if I use your bedroom? I need some privacy."

The response was muffled and then she heard a door shut.

"Hi," Rhage said in a husky drawl. "Are you in bed?"

Her body stirred, heating up. "Yes."

"I miss you."

She opened her mouth. Nothing came out.

"You still there, Mary?" When she sighed, he said, "That doesn't sound good. Am I getting too real for you?"

I've had eight different females this week alone.

Oh, God. She did not want to fall for him. Just could not let herself.

"Mary?"

"Just don't . . . say things like that to me."

"It's how I feel."

She didn't respond. What could she say? That she felt the same way? That she missed him even though she'd talked to him once every hour throughout the day? It was true, but not something she was happy about. He was too damned beautiful . . . and hell, he could put Wilt Chamberlain in the shade when it came to a list of lovers. So even if she were perfectly healthy, he was a recipe for disaster. Add to the situation what she was facing healthwise?

Getting emotionally attached to him was downright absurd.

As the silence stretched between them, he cursed. "We have a lot of business to take care of tonight. I don't know when I'll be back, but you know where to find me if you need me."

As the phone connection was cut off, she felt just awful. And she knew the lectures about keeping distant were not really working.

TWENTY-SIX

Rhage stomped his shitkicker into the ground and looked around the forest. Nothing. No sounds or smells of *lessers*. No evidence anyone had been through this quiet woodland spot for years. It had been the same for the other plots of land they'd visited.

"What the hell are we doing out here?" he muttered.

He knew the damn answer. Tohr had run across a *lesser* the night before on an isolated stretch of Route 22. The slayer had taken off into the forest on a dirtbike, but had lost a handy little piece of paper in the process: a list of large land parcels that were for sale on Caldwell's fringes.

Today, Butch and V had performed a search on all properties sold in the last twelve months in the city and surrounding burgs. About fifty sales of rural stretches of land had popped up. Rhage and V had visited five of them so far, and the twins were doing the same, covering others. Meanwhile, Butch was at the Pit, compiling the field reports, making a map, and looking for a pattern. It was going to take a couple of nights to get through all of the parcels, because patrols still had to be performed. And Mary's house had to be monitored.

Rhage paced around the woods, hoping some of the shadows would turn out to be *lessers*. He was beginning to hate tree branches. Goddamned teases as they blew in the wind.

"Where are those bastards?"

"Easy, Hollywood." V smoothed his goatee and tugged at his Sox hat. "Man, you're stoked tonight."

Stoked didn't cover it. He was nearly jumping out of his skin. He'd hoped staying away from Mary during the day would help, and he'd banked on finding a fight this evening. Had also counted on the exhaustion of sleep deprivation taking him down, too.

Yeah, well, no such luck on all fronts. He wanted Mary with an increasing desperation that no longer seemed tied to proximity. They hadn't found any *lessers*. And coming up on forty-eight hours of no shut-eye was only making him more aggressive.

Worse, it was now three A.M. He was running out of time for the battle release he so desperately needed. *Damn it—*

"*Rhage.*" V waved his gloved hand in the air. "You with me here at all, my brother?"

"Sorry, what?" He rubbed his eyes. His face. His biceps. His skin itched so badly he felt like he was wearing an ant suit.

"You are seriously out of it."

"Nah, I'm cool—"

"Then why're you working your arms like that?"

Rhage dropped his hands. Only to start massaging his thighs.

"We've got to get you to One Eye," V said softly. "You're losing it. You need to have some sex."

"Fuck that."

"Phury told me how he found you out in the hall."

"You guys are a bunch of old maids, for real."

"If you won't do your female, and you can't find a fight, what's your alternative?"

"It's not supposed to be like this." He moved his head around, trying to loosen his shoulders and neck. "This isn't how it works. I just changed. It's not supposed to come out again—"

"Supposed to in one hand, shit in the other, see what you get the most of. You're in a bad space, my brother. And you know what you have to do to get out of it, true?"

*　　*　　*

When Mary heard the door open, she came awake with a groggy disorientation. Shoot, she had another night fever.

"Rhage?" she mumbled.

"Yeah, it's me."

His voice sounded like hell, she thought. And he'd left the door to the room open, so he probably wasn't staying for long. Maybe he was still angry at her from that last phone call.

From inside the closet, she heard the shifting of metal and some fabric flapping, as if he were pulling on a fresh shirt. When he came out, he went right back for the hallway, his trench coat billowing behind him. The idea that he would leave without saying good-bye was somehow shocking.

As he gripped the doorknob, he paused. Light from the hall fell on his bright hair and his broad shoulders. His face was in profile, in darkness.

"Where are you going?" she asked as she sat up.

There was a long silence. "Out."

Why did he seem so apologetic? she wondered. She didn't need a babysitter. If he had business to attend to . . .

Oh . . . right. Women. He was going out after women.

Her chest cavity turned into a cold, damp pit, especially as she looked at the bouquet of flowers he'd given her. God, the idea of him touching someone else like she knew he could made her want to retch.

"Mary . . . I'm sorry."

She cleared her throat. "Don't be. There's nothing going on between us, so I don't expect you to change your habits for me."

"It's not a habit."

"Oh, right. Sorry. Addiction."

There was a long silence. "Mary, I . . . if there were another way—"

"To do what?" She swept her hand back and forth. "Don't answer that."

"Mary—"

"Don't, Rhage. It's none of my business. Just go."

"My cell phone will be on if you—"

"Yeah. I'm *really* going to call."

He stared at her for a heartbeat. And then his black shadow disappeared through the door.

TWENTY-SEVEN

John Matthew walked home from Moe's, trailing the three-thirty A.M. police patrol. He dreaded the hours until dawn. Sitting in his apartment was going to feel like being in a cage, but it was much too late for him to be out and about on the street. Still . . . God, he was so restless he could taste the agitation in his mouth. And the fact that there was no one he could talk to made him ache.

He really needed some advice. Ever since Tohrment had left him, he'd been scrambled in his head, debating whether or not he'd done the right thing. He kept telling himself he had, but the second-guessing wouldn't stop.

He wished he could find Mary. He'd gone to her house the night before, only to find it dark and locked up. And she hadn't been going to the hotline. It was as if she'd disappeared, and worrying about her was one more reason he was twitchy.

As he approached his building, he saw a truck parked in front. The bed was full of boxes, like someone was moving in.

What a weird time of night to do that, he thought, eyeing the load.

As he saw that there was no one around to stand guard, he hoped the owner came back soon. Otherwise, their stuff was going to get disappeared.

John went into his building and up the stairs, ignoring the cigarette butts and the empty beer cans and the crumpled potato-chip bags. When he stepped off onto the second floor, he squinted. Something was spilled all over the corridor. Deep red . . .

Blood.

Backing up into the stairwell, he stared at his door. There was a sunburst in the center of it, as if someone had had their head . . . But then he saw the broken dark green bottle. Red wine. It was just red wine. The drunken couple who lived next door had taken another fight out into the hall.

His shoulders eased.

"'Scuse me," someone said from above him.

He moved aside and looked up.

John's body seized.

The big man standing over him was dressed in black camouflage pants and a leather jacket. His hair and skin were utterly white, and his pale eyes had an eerie shine to them.

Evil. Undead.

Enemy.

This was his enemy.

"Some kind of mess you got on this floor," the guy said before narrowing his gaze on John. "Something wrong?"

John fiercely shook his head and dropped his eyes. His first instinct was to run to his apartment, but he didn't want the guy knowing where he lived.

There was a deep chuckle. "You look a little pale there, buddy."

John took off, shooting down the stairs and out into the street. He raced to the corner, took a left, and kept going. He ran and ran, until he couldn't go any farther because he'd lost his breath. Squeezing himself into the juncture between a brick building and a Dumpster, he panted.

In his dreams, he fought pale men. Pale men in black clothes whose eyes were soulless.

My enemy.

He was shaking so badly he could barely get his hand into his pocket. Taking out a quarter, he gripped the thing so tightly it dug into his palm. When he had his breath back, he leaned out and peered up and down the alley. There was no one around, no sounds of heavy feet hitting the asphalt.

His enemy hadn't recognized him.

John left the Dumpster's sanctuary and walked quickly to the far corner.

The dented pay phone was covered with graffiti, but he knew it worked because he called Mary from it a lot. He put the quarter in the slot and punched out the number Tohrment had given him.

After one ring, voice mail kicked in with a robotic recitation of the numbers he'd dialed.

John waited for the beep. And whistled.

TWENTY-EIGHT

It was right before dawn when Mary heard male voices out in the hall. As the door opened, her heart skipped in her chest. Rhage filled the frame as another guy spoke.

"Man, that was one hell of a fight as we left the bar. You were a *demon* out there."

"I know," Rhage muttered.

"You're incredible, Hollywood, and not just with the hand-to-hand. That female you—"

"Later, Phury."

The door shut and the closet light came on. By the sound of clicks and metallic shifting, he was disarming. When he came out, he took a shuddering breath.

Mary faked being asleep as his footsteps hesitated by the foot of the bed and then headed for the bathroom. When she heard the shower come on, she imagined everything he was washing off of himself: sex. Fighting.

Especially the sex.

She covered her face with her hands. Today she would go home. She would pack her things and walk out the door. He couldn't make her stay; she wasn't his responsibility just because he said so.

The water shut off.

The silence sucked all the air from the room, and she grew out of breath while holding herself in place. Gasping, suffocating . . . she threw the covers back and bolted for the door. Her hands latched onto the knob and fought to free the lock, jerking, pulling, until her hair whipped around.

"Mary," Rhage said from right behind her.

She jumped and wrestled harder with the door.

"Let me out. I have to get out . . . I can't stay here in this room with you. I can't be here . . . with you." She felt his hands come down on her shoulders. "*Don't touch me.*"

She careened around the room until she bounced into the far corner and realized there was nowhere to go and no way to get out. He was in front of the door, and she had a feeling he was keeping the locks in place.

Trapped, she linked her arms over her chest and propped herself up against the wall to keep standing. She didn't know what she would do if he touched her again.

Rhage didn't even try.

He sat on the bed, a towel around his hips, his hair damp. He dragged a hand down his face, across his jaw. He looked like hell, but his body was still the most beautiful thing she'd ever seen. She pictured the hands of other women grabbing on to those powerful shoulders, just as she had. She saw him pleasuring other bodies as he had hers.

She was torn between wanting to thank God she hadn't slept with him, and being pissed off that, after all the women he'd done, he refused to have sex with her.

"How many?" she demanded, the words so hoarse they barely carried. "And tell me, was it good for you? I don't have to ask whether they liked it. I know how talented you are."

"Sweet . . . Mary," he whispered. "If you'd let me hold you, I would. God, I would kill just to hold you right now."

"You are *never* coming near me again. Now how many were there? Two? Four? A six-pack?"

"Do you really want the details?" His voice was soft, sad to the point of cracking. Abruptly his head dropped down and hung loosely from his neck. For all appearances, he looked like a ruined man. "I can't . . . I'm not going out like that again. I'll find another way."

"Another way to get off?" she snapped. "You sure as hell won't be sleeping with me, so are you thinking about using your hand, maybe?"

He took a deep breath. "That design. On my back? It's part of me."

"Whatever. I'm leaving here today."

His head twisted toward her. "No, you aren't."

"Yes, I am."

"I'll give you this room. You won't have to see me. But you aren't going anywhere."

"How are you going to keep me from leaving? Lock me in here?"

"If that's what it takes, yeah."

She recoiled. "You can't be serious."

"When's your next doctor's appointment?"

"That is none of your business."

"When?"

The hard anger in his voice cooled her temper down a little. "Ah . . . Wednesday."

"I'll make sure you get to that."

She stared at him. "Why are you doing this to me?"

His shoulders rose and fell. "Because I love you."

"Excuse me?"

"I love you."

Mary's control evaporated under a blast of fury so great she was rendered speechless. He *loved* her? He didn't *know* her. And he'd been with another . . . Her outrage boiled over as she pictured him having sex with someone else.

Suddenly Rhage sprang off the bed and came at her, as if he felt her emotions and was energized by them.

"I know you're angry, scared, hurting. Take it out on me, Mary." He grabbed her waist to keep her from running, but didn't stop her from trying to shove him away. "Use me to bear your pain. Let me feel it in my skin. Hit me if you have to, Mary."

Damn her to hell, she was tempted to. Lashing out

241

seemed like the only recourse for the kind of power surging through her body.

But she was not an animal. "*No.* Now let go of me!"

He took her wrist and she struggled against the hold, throwing her whole body into the fight until her shoulder felt like it was going to pop. Rhage stilled her easily and flipped her hand around so her rigid, curled fingertips faced him.

"Use me, Mary. Let me bear this for you." With a flash of movement, he raked his chest with her nails and then clamped his palms on either side of her face.

"Make me bleed for you . . ." His mouth stroked against hers. "Let your anger go."

God help her, she bit him. Right on his lower lip. She just sank her teeth into his flesh.

As something sinfully delicious hit her tongue, Rhage moaned with approval and pressed his body against hers. A buzz, like she'd had too much chocolate, hummed through her.

Mary cried out.

Horrified by what she'd done, scared of what she might do next, she fought to get away, but he held her in place, kissing her, telling her he loved her over and over again. The hard, hot length of his arousal pushed into her belly through the towel, and he rubbed himself against her, his body a sinuous, pumping promise of the sex she didn't want, but needed until her insides were cramping.

She wanted him . . . even though she knew he'd fucked other women. Tonight.

"Oh, God . . . no . . ." She jerked her head to the side, but he caught her chin, bringing her back to center.

"Yes, Mary . . ." He kissed her frantically, tongue in her mouth. "I love you."

Something inside of her snapped and she hurled him away, ducking out of his hold.

But instead of running for the door, she stared at him mercilessly.

Four scratches streaked down his chest. His lower lip was cut. He was panting, flushed.

She reached out and ripped the towel from his body.

Rhage was shockingly aroused, his erection straining, enormous.

And in the breathless moment between them, she despised all his smooth, perfectly hairless skin, his tight muscles, his fallen-angel beauty. Most of all, she loathed the proud length of him, that sexual tool he used so much.

And still, she wanted him.

If she'd been in her right mind, she would have backed away from Rhage. She would have locked herself in the bathroom. Hell, she would have been intimidated by the sheer size of him. But she was pissed off and out of control. She seized his hard flesh with one hand and took his balls in her other, both overflowing her palms. His head snapped backward, the cords in his neck straining, breath exploding from his mouth.

His voice vibrated, filled the room. "Do whatever it takes. Oh, God, I love you."

She led him to the bed roughly, letting go only so she could force him back on the mattress. He fell on the messy covers, his arms and legs splaying out as if he were giving himself to her with no reservations, no restrictions.

"Why now?" she asked bitterly. "Why are you willing to do me now? Or is this not about sex at all and only because you want me to draw more blood?"

"I'm dying to make love with you. And I can be with you at this moment because I'm level. I'm . . . spent."

Oh, now there was a lovely thought.

She shook her head, but he cut her off. "You want me. So take the pleasure. Don't think, just take your pleasure from me."

Crazed with lust and anger and frustration, Mary yanked

her nightgown up around her hips and straddled his thighs. But once she was on top of him, looking down into his face, she hesitated. Was she really going to do this? Take him? Use him for nothing more than getting off and getting back at him for something he had every right to do?

She started to move off of him.

In a quick surge, Rhage's legs shot up under her, toppling her onto his chest. As she fell on him, his arms wrapped around her.

"You know what you want to do, Mary," he said into her ear. "Don't stop. Take what you need from me. Use me."

Mary closed her eyes, turned off her brain, and let her body go.

Reaching between his thighs, she held him up and sat on him hard.

They both shouted as she took all of him, right to the pubic bone.

He was a tremendous presence in her body, stretching her until she thought she might tear. She breathed deeply and didn't move, her thighs straining as the inside of her struggled to adjust to him.

"You're so tight." Rhage groaned. His lips stripped free of his teeth, his fangs flashing. "Oh . . . God, I feel you all over my body. *Mary*."

His chest heaved and his abdomen clenched so hard the muscles threw shadows. As his hands squeezed her knees, his eyes dilated until there was hardly any blue left to them at all. And then his pupils flashed white.

Rhage's face contorted with some kind of panic. But then he shook his head as if to clear it and assumed an expression of concentration. Slowly the centers of his eyes turned back to black, as if he'd willed them so.

Mary stopped focusing on him and started thinking about herself.

Not caring about anything except where their bodies met, she planted her hands on his shoulders and pulled up from him. The friction was electric, and the burst of pleasure she felt helped her accept him more easily. She slid down on his erection and came forward and then repeated the motions over and over again. Her rhythm was a slow glide, each descent stretching her, each rise coating him with her body's silky response.

With increasing dominance she rode him, taking what she wanted, the thickness and the heat and the length of him creating a wild, twisting knot of energy deep in her core. She opened her eyes and looked down at him.

Rhage was a picture of male ecstasy. A fine shine of sweat covered his broad chest and shoulders. His head was kicked back, his chin high, his blond hair falling on the pillow, his lips parted. He was watching her through lowered lids, eyes lingering on her face and her breasts and where they were joined.

As if he were utterly enthralled by her.

She squeezed her eyes closed and pushed his adoration from her mind. It was either that or lose touch with the orgasm she was so close to because the sight of him made her want to weep.

It didn't take long for her to explode. With a shattering blast, the release swept through her, robbing her of sight and hearing, of breath and heartbeat, until all she could do was collapse onto him.

As her breathing slowed, she became aware that he was stroking her back gently and whispering soft words to her.

In the aftermath she was ashamed, and tears stung her eyes.

No matter who else he'd been with tonight, he didn't deserve to be used, and that was exactly what she'd done. She'd been angry when it all started, and then she'd shut him out right before she came by refusing to look at him. She'd treated him like a sex toy.

"I'm sorry, Rhage. I'm . . . sorry . . ."

She moved to get off his hips and realized he was still thick inside of her. He hadn't even finished.

Oh, God, this was bad. The whole thing was bad.

Rhage's hands clamped on her thighs. "Don't ever regret that we were together."

She stared into his eyes. "I feel like I just violated you."

"I was more than willing. Mary, it's all right. Come here, let me kiss you."

"How can you stand to have me near you?"

"The only thing I can't handle is your leaving."

He took her wrists and urged her down to his mouth. As their lips met, he slid his arms all the way around her, holding her close. The change in position made her acutely aware that he was full to bursting, so hard she could feel the involuntary twitches of his arousal.

He rocked his hips gently against her, sweeping her hair back from her face with his big palms. "I won't be able to withstand the burn for much longer. You take me so high, I'm licking the ceiling right now. But for as long as I'm able, as long as I can stay in control, I want to love your body with mine. However it starts. However it ends."

He moved his hips up and down, pulling out, sliding in. She felt herself melting all around him. The pleasure was deep, endless. Terrifying.

"Did you kiss them tonight?" she asked roughly. "The women?"

"No, I didn't kiss the female, I never do. And I hated it. I'm not doing it again, Mary. I'll find another way to keep myself from getting out of hand while you're in my life. I don't want anyone but you."

She let him roll her over. As he settled on top of her, the warm, heavy weight of him pressed into the cradle of her body where he was lodged. He kissed her tenderly, licking at her with his tongue, cherishing her with his lips. He was so gentle, though he was immense inside of her and his body housed the kind of strength that could snap her in half.

"I won't finish this if you don't want me to," he whispered into her neck. "I'll pull out right now."

She brought her hands up his back, feeling the shifting muscles and the expansion and compression of his ribs as he breathed. She inhaled deeply and caught a lovely, erotic scent. Dark, spicy, lush. Between her legs she felt an answering rush of wetness, as if the fragrance were a touch or a kiss.

"What is that wonderful smell?"

"Me," he murmured against her mouth. "It's what happens when a male bonds. I can't help it. If you let me keep going, it will be all over your skin, your hair. Inside of you, too."

With that, he thrust deeply. She arched up to the pleasure, letting the heat flow throughout her body.

"I can't go through tonight again," she moaned, more to herself than to him.

Falling completely still, he took her hand and placed it on his heart. "Never again, Mary. I swear on my honor."

His eyes were grave, the vow as good a one as she would get from any living thing. But the relief she felt at his pledge was trouble.

"I will not fall in love with you," she said. "I can't let myself. I won't."

"That's all right. I'll love you enough for the both of us." He surged inside of her, filling her depths.

"You don't know me." She nipped at his shoulder and then sucked on his collarbone. The taste of his skin made her tongue sing, that special scent condensing in her mouth.

"Yeah, I do." He pulled back, his eyes regarding her

with an animal's conviction and clarity. "I know you kept me safe when the sun was out and I was defenseless against it. I know you cared for me even though you were afraid. I know you fed me from your kitchen. I know you are a warrior, a survivor, a *wahlker*. And I know your voice is the loveliest sound my ears have ever heard." He kissed her softly. "I know all about you, and everything I see is beautiful. Everything I see is mine."

"I'm not yours," she whispered.

The rejection didn't faze him. "Fine. If I can't have you, then you do the taking. Have all of me, part of me, a small piece, whatever you want. Just please, have something."

She reached up to his face, stroking the perfect planes and angles of his cheeks and jawline.

"Don't you fear pain?" she asked.

"No. But I'll tell you what scares the hell out of me. Losing you." He looked at her lips. "Now do you want me to pull out? Because I will."

"No. Stay." Mary kept her eyes open and brought his mouth to hers, slipping her tongue inside of him.

He trembled and started to move in a steady rhythm, penetrating and retreating, each time the thick head of him teetering on breaking their connection.

"You feel . . . so perfect," he said, punctuating the words with his strokes. "I was made to . . . be inside of you."

The luscious scent coming from his body intensified as his pumping did, until all she could feel was him, all she could smell was him, all she could taste was him.

She called out his name as she climaxed, and she felt him go over the edge with her, his body shuddering into hers, his release as powerful as his thrusts had been, his orgasm pouring into her.

When he was still, he rolled them over so they were

on their sides. He gathered her close, so close she could hear the great beating heart in his chest.

She shut her eyes and slept with an exhaustion to rival death.

TWENTY-NINE

That evening, as the sun fell and the shutters rose up from the windows, Mary decided she could get used to being pampered by Rhage. What she couldn't handle was any more food. She put her fingers on his wrist, stopping the forkload of mashed potatoes coming at her.

"No, I'm stuffed," she said as she lay back against the pillows. "My stomach's about to burst."

With a smile, he picked up the tray of dishes and put it on the bedside table, then sat down next to her again. He'd been gone for most of the day, working, she assumed, and she'd been grateful for the sleep she'd gotten. Her exhaustion was getting worse by the day, and she could feel herself sliding into sickness. Her body felt as if it were struggling to maintain its regular processes, little aches and pains cropping up all over. And the bruises were back: black and blue marks were blooming under her skin at an alarming rate. Rhage had been horrified when he'd seen them, convinced he'd hurt her during sex. It had taken a lot of talking to get him to realize they weren't his fault.

Mary focused on Rhage, not wanting to think about the illness, or the doctor's appointment that was coming soon. God, he didn't look any better than she felt, although he was keyed up, not grinding to a halt. The poor man couldn't settle down. As he sat beside her on the bed, he was rubbing his thighs with his palms, looking like he had a case of poison ivy or the chicken pox. She was about to ask him what was wrong when he spoke up.

"Mary, will you let me do something for you?"

Even though sex should be the last thing on her mind,

she eyed the biceps that stretched his black shirt. "Do I get to pick what it is?"

A soft growl came out of him. "You shouldn't look at me like that."

"Why not?"

"Because I want to mount you when you do."

"Don't fight the feeling."

Like the strike of dual matches, his pupils flashed white. It was the oddest thing. One moment they were black. The next, pale light was shining out of them.

"Why does that happen?" she asked.

His shoulders thickened as he bore down on his legs and braced himself. Abruptly he stood up and paced around. She could sense an energy coming off of him, out of him.

"Rhage?"

"You don't need to worry about it."

"That hard tone in your voice tells me maybe I should."

He smiled at her and shook his head. "No. You don't. About the favor. Our race has a physician, Havers. Will you let me give him access to your medical files? Maybe our science can help you."

Mary frowned. A vampire doctor. Talk about exploring your alternative therapies.

Yeah, but what exactly did she have to lose?

"Okay. Except I don't know how to get copies—"

"My brother, V, is a computer god. He can hack into anything, and most of your stuff should be online. All I need are names and places. Dates, too, if you have them."

When he grabbed paper and a pen, she told him where she had been treated as well as the names of her doctors. After he'd written it all down, he stared at the piece of paper.

"What?" she asked.

"There are so many." His eyes lifted to hers. "How bad was it, Mary?"

Her first impulse was to tell him the truth: that she'd had two rounds of chemo and a bone-marrow transplant and had just squeaked by. But then she thought about the night before, when her emotions had gotten so out of control. She was a box of dynamite right now and her disease was the best fuse around. The last thing she needed was to get tripped again, because Christ knew nothing good had come of the last two times she'd lost it. The first she'd cried all over him. The second she'd . . . Well, biting his lip had been the least of it.

Shrugging, lying, hating herself, she murmured, "It was okay. I was just glad when it was over."

His eyes narrowed.

Just as someone pounded on the door.

Rhage's stare didn't waver, in spite of the urgent sound. "Someday you're going to learn to trust me."

"I do trust you."

"Bullshit. And here's a quick tip. I hate being lied to."

The heavy knocking started up again.

Rhage went over and opened the door, ready to tell whoever it was to screw off. He had a feeling he and Mary were about to get into an argument, and he wanted to get the thing over with.

Tohr was on the other side. Looking like he'd been hit with a stun gun.

"What the hell happened to you?" Rhage asked while stepping into the hall. He shut the door partway.

Tohr sniffed the air drifting out of the bedroom. "Jesus. You've marked her, haven't you?"

"You got a problem with that?"

"No, it makes this all easier in a way. The Scribe Virgin has spoken."

"Tell me."

"You should be with the rest of the brothers to hear—"

"Fuck that. I want to know now, Tohr."

When the brother finished speaking in the Old Language, Rhage took a deep breath. "Give me ten minutes."

Tohr nodded. "We're in Wrath's study."

Rhage went back into his room and shut the door. "Listen, Mary, I've got some business with my brothers. I might not be back tonight."

She stiffened and her eyes dropped away from his face.

"Mary, it's not females, I swear to you. Just promise me you'll be here when I get back." As she hesitated, he went over and stroked her cheek. "You said you don't have a doctor's appointment until Wednesday. What's another night? You could spend more time in the tub. You told me how much you like that."

She smiled a little. "You are a manipulator."

"I like to think of myself more as an outcome engineer."

"If I stay one more day, you're just going to try to talk me into another and another . . ."

He bent down and kissed her hard, wishing he had more time, wanting to be with her, inside of her, before he left. But hell, even if he'd had hours to spare, he wouldn't be able to do that. The tingling and the hum in him was about to vibrate his body into midair.

"I love you," he said. Then he pulled back, took off his watch, and put the Rolex in her hand. "Keep this for me."

He went over to the closet and shed his clothes. Way in the back, behind another two pairs of pajamas he was never going to use, he found his ceremonial black robe. He drew the heavy silk on over his naked skin and belted it with a thick strip of braided leather.

When he came out, Mary said, "You look like you're going to a monastery."

"Tell me you will be here when I come back."

After a moment, she nodded.

He pulled the robe's hood into place. "Good. That's good."

"Rhage, what's going on?"

"Just wait for me. Please, wait for me." As he got to the door, he took one last look at her in his bed.

This was their first good-bye that had teeth, their first separation where, when they were reunited, he'd feel the awful distance of time and experience. He knew tonight was going to be hard to get through. He just hoped that, when he came out on the other side, the aftermath of the punishment didn't linger too long. And that she was still with him.

"I'll see you later, Mary," he said as he shut her in his room.

When he walked into Wrath's study, he closed the double doors behind himself. All the brothers were there, and no one was talking. The scent of unease permeated the room, smelling like rubbing alcohol.

Wrath came forward from behind the desk, looking as rigid as Tohr had. From behind his wraparound sunglasses, the king's stare was piercing, something felt, though not seen.

"Brother."

Rhage bowed his head. "My lord."

"You wear that robe as if you want to stay with us."

"Of course I do."

Wrath nodded once. "Here is the pronouncement, then. The Scribe Virgin has determined that you offended the Brotherhood in both defying Tohr's orders and by bringing a human onto our turf. I'll be honest with you, Rhage, she wants to override my decision about Mary. She wants the human out."

"You know where that leads."

"I told her you were prepared to walk."

"That probably cheered her up." Rhage smirked. "She's been trying to get rid of me for years."

"Well, it's your choice now, brother. If you want to remain with us, and if the human is to continue to be sheltered within these walls, the Scribe Virgin has demanded that you offer a *rythe*."

The ritualistic way of assuaging offense was a logical punishment. When a *rythe* was tendered and accepted, the offender allowed the object of his insult free use of a weapon against him without putting up a defense. The offended could choose anything from a knife to a set of brass knuckles to a gun, provided the wound inflicted was not mortal.

"I so offer the *rythe*," Rhage said.

"It must be one to each of us."

There was a collective groan in the room. Someone muttered, "*Fuck*."

"I so offer them."

"Be it as you wish, brother."

"But"—Rhage hardened his voice—"I offer them only on the understanding that, if the ritual is observed, Mary stays for however long I want."

"That was my agreement with the Scribe Virgin. And you should know she came around only after I told her you wanted to take the human as your *shellan*. I think Her Holiness was shocked you could even consider that kind of commitment." Wrath looked over his shoulder. "Tohrment is to choose the weapon that all of us will use."

"The tri-whip," Tohr said in a low voice.

Oh, shit. This was going to hurt.

There were more mutters.

"So be it," Wrath said.

"Except what about the beast?" Rhage asked. "It can come out when I'm in pain."

"The Scribe Virgin will be there. She said she has a way of keeping it at bay."

But of course she would. She'd cooked the damn thing up in the first place.

"We're going to do this tonight, right?" Rhage glanced around the room. "I mean, there's no reason to wait."

"We'll go to the Tomb now."

"Good. Let's get it over with."

Zsadist was the first to leave as the group got to their feet and worked out logistics in quiet tones. Tohr needed a robe, did someone have an extra one? Phury announced he'd bring the weapon. V offered the Escalade to take them all down together.

The latter was good thinking. They were going to need something to get him home in after the *rythe* was over.

"My brothers?" he said.

They all stopped talking, stopped moving. He looked at each one, noting the grim casts to their faces. They hated this, and he understood perfectly. Hurting any one of them would have been unbearable for him. It was much better to be on the receiving end.

"I have one request, my brothers. Don't bring me back here, okay? When it's over, take me somewhere else. I don't want Mary to see me like that."

Vishous spoke up. "You can stay at the Pit. Butch and I will take care of you."

Rhage smiled. "Twice in less than a week. You two could hire out as nursemaids after this."

V clapped him on the shoulder and then left. Tohr followed, doing the same. Phury gave him a hug as he passed by.

Wrath paused on his way out.

When the king remained silent, Rhage squeezed the male's bicep. "I know, my lord. I'd feel the same way if I were you. But I'm tough. I can take it."

Wrath reached into the hood and took Rhage's face into his palms, tilting it down. He kissed Rhage's forehead and held the contact between them, a pledge of respect from the king to his warrior, a reaffirmation of their bond.

"I'm glad you're staying with us," Wrath said softly. "I would have hated to lose you."

About fifteen minutes later, they reconvened down in the courtyard by the Escalade. The brothers were all barefoot and wearing black robes. With the hoods up, it was hard to tell who was who, except for Phury. His prosthetic foot showed, and he had a bulging duffel bag slung over his shoulder. No doubt he'd thrown bandages and rolling tape into the thing as well as the weapon.

Everyone was silent as V drove them behind the house and into the mountain's thick beard of pines and hemlocks. The road was a single dirt lane, crowded by the evergreen trees.

As they shot along, Rhage couldn't stand the tense silence a minute longer.

"Oh, for God's sake, my brothers. You're not going to kill me. Could we lighten up a little?"

No one would look at him.

"V, put on some Luda or Fifty, will ya? All this quiet is boring."

Phury's laugh came out of the robe on the right. "Only you could try to turn this into a party."

"Well, hell, you've all wanted to nail me a good one for some shit I've popped, right? This is your lucky day." He clapped Phury on the thigh. "I mean, come on, my brother, I've ridden you for years about the no females. And Wrath a couple months ago I needled you until you stabbed a wall. V, just the other day you threatened to use that hand of yours on me. Remember? When I told you what I thought about that goatee monstrosity?"

V chuckled. "I had to do something to shut you up. Every damn time I've run into you since I grew it, you ask me if I've French-kissed a tailpipe."

"And I'm still convinced you're doing my GTO, you bastard."

That got the ball rolling. Rhage stories started flying around until the voices were so loud, no one could hear anyone else.

As his brothers blew off steam, Rhage settled back against the seat, looking out into the night. He hoped like hell the Scribe Virgin knew what she was doing, because if his beast got loose in the Tomb, his brothers were in deep shit. And they just might have to kill him after all.

He frowned and looked around. He located Wrath behind him. Could tell who it was because the king's black diamond ring was on the male's middle finger.

Rhage arched back and whispered, "My lord, I beg of a favor."

Wrath leaned forward, his voice deep and even. "What do you need?"

"If I don't . . . make it through this, for whatever reason, I beg of you to watch over Mary."

The hood nodded. In the Old Language, the king said, *"As you wish, so I am sworn. I shall look upon her as I would my own blooded sister and caretake her as I would any female of mine own family."*

Rhage exhaled. "That is good. That is . . . good."

Soon enough, V parked the Escalade in a small clearing. They got out and stood around, listening, looking, sensing.

All things considered it was a nice evening, and this was a serene place to be. The breeze winding its way through the countless branches and trunks of the forest carried a pleasing smell of earth and pine. Overhead, a fat moon glowed through milky clouds.

When Wrath gave the signal, they walked a hundred yards over to a cave set into the mountain. The place looked like absolutely nothing special, even when you walked inside. You had to know what you were looking for to find the little seam in the wall in the back. If triggered correctly, a slab of stone slid open.

As they filed inside the cave's inner belly, the wedge of rock closed behind them with a whisper. Torches mounted on the walls flickered gold as their flames breathed into the air, puffing and hissing.

The walk into the earth was a slow, easy descent on a rock floor that was cold beneath the feet. When they got to the bottom they disrobed, and a pair of cast-iron doors opened. The hall ahead was about fifty feet long and twenty feet high and covered with shelves.

On these racks, thousands of ceramic jars of various sizes and shapes reflected light. Each container held the heart of a *lesser*, the organ the Omega removed during the Society's induction ceremony. During a *lesser*'s existence as a slayer, the jar was his only real personal possession, and, if possible, the Brotherhood collected them after a kill.

At the end of the hall, there was another set of double doors. These were already open.

The Brotherhood's sanctum sanctorum had been carved out of bedrock and veneered in black marble back in the early 1700s when the first migration from Europe had come across the ocean. The room was good-sized and had a ceiling of white stalactites that hung down like daggers. Massive candles, as thick as a male's arm and as long as his leg, were plugged into black iron stations, their flames nearly as luminous as those of the torches.

Down in front there was a raised platform, accessed by a series of shallow steps. The altar on top was made out of a slab of limestone that had been brought over from the Old Country, its great weight propped up horizontally by two rough-cut stone lintels. In the center of the thing was a skull.

Behind the altar, a flat wall was etched with the names of every brother there had ever been, back to the very first one whose cranium was on the altar. The inscriptions ran in panels that covered every inch of the surface, save for an unmarked stretch in the middle. This smooth portion was about six feet wide and ran the whole vertical of the marble expanse. In the midst of it, about five feet up from the floor, two thick pegs jutted out, positioned so a male could grip them and hold himself in place.

The air smelled so very familiar: damp earth and beeswax candles.

"Greetings, Brotherhood."

They all turned to the female voice.

The Scribe Virgin was a tiny figure in the far corner, her black robes hovering above the floor. Nothing of her was visible, not even her face, but from underneath the draping black folds, light spilled out like water falling.

She floated toward them, stopping in front of Wrath. "Warrior."

He bowed low. "Scribe Virgin."

She greeted each one in turn, saving Rhage for last. "Rhage, son of Tohrture."

"Scribe Virgin." He inclined his head.

"How fare you?"

"I am well." Or he would be, as soon as this was over.

"And you have been busy, have you not? Continuing to set new precedents, as is your affection. Pity they are not in laudable directions." She laughed with an edge. "Somehow, it is no surprise we ended up here with you. You are aware, are you not, that this is the first *rythe* ever to be exchanged within the Brotherhood?"

Not exactly, he thought. Tohr had turned down one offered by Wrath back in July.

But it wasn't like he was going to point that out to her.

"Warrior, are you prepared to accept what you have offered?"

"I am." He chose his next words very carefully, because you didn't pose a question to the Scribe Virgin. Not unless you wanted to eat your own ass. "I would beg of you that I do not hurt my brothers."

Her voice grew hard. "You are perilously close to inquiry."

"I mean no offense."

That low, soft chuckle came again.

Man, he bet she was enjoying the hell out this. She'd never liked him, although it wasn't as if he could blame her. He'd given her antipathy plenty of reasons to breed.

"You mean no offense, warrior?" The robes moved as if she were shaking her head. "On the contrary, you never hesitate to offend to get what you wish, and that has always been your problem. It is also why we have been brought here together this night." She turned away. "You have the weapon?"

Phury put down the duffel, unzipped it, and took out the tri-whip. The two-foot-long handle was made of wood and covered with brown leather that had been darkened by the sweat of many hands. Out of the rod's tip, three lengths of blackened steel chain swung in the air. At the end of each of them there was a spiked dangler, like a pinecone with barbs.

The tri-whip was an ancient, vicious weapon, but Tohr had chosen wisely. In order for the ritual to be considered successful, the brothers could spare Rhage nothing either in the type of weapon they used or the way they put it to his skin. To give leniency would be to demean the integrity of the tradition, the regret he was offering, and the chance for a true cleansing.

"So be it," she said. "Proceed to the wall, Rhage, son of Tohrture."

He went forward, climbing the stairs two at a time. As he passed the altar, he gazed at the sacred skull, watching firelight lick over the eye sockets and the long fangs. Positioning himself against the black marble, he gripped the stone pegs and felt cold smoothness on his back.

The Scribe Virgin drifted up to him and lifted her arm. Her sleeve fell back, and a glow bright as a welder's arc was revealed, the stinging light vaguely shaped like a hand. A low-level electrical hum went through him, and he felt something shift inside his torso, as if his internal organs had been rearranged.

"You may begin the ritual."

The brothers lined up, their naked bodies gleaming with strength, their faces drawn into deep grooves. Wrath took the tri-whip from Phury and came forward first. As he moved, the weapon's links chimed with the sweetness of a bird's call.

"Brother," the king said softly.

"My lord."

Rhage stared into those sunglasses as Wrath started swinging the whip in a wide circle to build momentum. A droning sound started low and crescendoed until the weapon came forward, slicing through the air. The chains hit Rhage's chest and then the barbs clawed into him, grabbing the air out of his lungs. As he bore down on the pegs, he kept his head up while his vision dimmed and then returned.

Tohr was next, his blow knocking the wind out of Rhage so that his knees sagged before they accepted his weight again. Vishous and Phury followed.

Each time, he met the pained eyes of his brothers in hopes of easing their anguish, but, as Phury turned away, Rhage could no longer support his head. He let it fall on his shoulder and so caught sight of the blood running down his chest, over his thighs, and onto his feet. A pool was forming on the floor, reflecting the light of the candles, and staring at the red mess made him woozy. Determined to remain standing, he cocked his elbows so it was his joints and bones, not his muscles, that kept him in place.

When there was a lull, he became dimly aware of some kind of argument. He blinked several times before his eyes were clear enough to see.

Phury was holding out the whip and Zsadist was backing away from the thing in what seemed a lot like terror. Z's fisted hands were held up high and his nipple rings flashed in the firelight as he breathed far too heavily. The brother was the color of fog, his skin gray and unnaturally shiny.

Phury spoke gently and tried to take Zsadist's arm. Z pivoted wildly, but Phury stayed with him. As they moved in a grim dance, the whip marks covering Z's back shifted with his muscles.

This approach was going nowhere, Rhage thought. Zsadist was closing in on full panic, like a cornered animal. There had to be some other way to reach him.

Rhage took a deep breath and opened his mouth. Nothing came out. He tried again.

"Zsadist . . ." His reedy voice brought all eyes to the altar. "Finish it, Z . . . Can't . . . can't hold myself up much longer."

"No—"

Phury cut Zsadist off. "You have to—"

"No! Get the *fuck* away from me."

Z bolted for the door, but the Scribe Virgin got there first, forcing him to spin out to a stop so he didn't run her over. Trapped in front of the diminutive figure, his legs trembled and his shoulders shook. She talked to him quietly, the words not carrying far enough for Rhage to decipher through his haze of pain.

Finally the Scribe Virgin motioned to Phury, who brought the weapon over to her. When she had it, she reached out, took Z's hand, and placed the leather-bound grip on his palm. She pointed to the altar and Zsadist dropped his head. A moment later he came up front with a lurching stride.

When Rhage looked at the brother, he almost suggested someone else do the deed for Z. Those black eyes were cracked open so wide, there was white all around the irises.

And Zsadist kept swallowing, his throat working like it was keeping a scream down in his chest.

"S'okay, my brother," Rhage murmured. "But you need to finish. *Now.*"

Z panted and swayed, sweat rolling into his eyes and down the scar on his face.

"Do it."

"Brother," Z whispered, lifting the whip over his shoulder.

He didn't swing it for momentum, probably couldn't have coordinated his arm that well at this point. But he was strong, and the weapon sang as it traveled through the air. The chains and danglers streaked across Rhage's stomach in a blaze of needles.

Rhage's knees gave out and he tried to catch himself with his arms, only to find that they too refused to hold him. He fell to his knees, palms landing in his own blood.

But at least it was over. He took long breaths, determined not to pass out.

Abruptly a rushing sound cut through the sanctuary, something like metal against metal. He didn't think much about it. He was busy talking to his stomach, trying to convince it that dry heaves were in fact not a really good plan.

When he was ready, he crawled on his hands and knees around the altar, taking a breather before he tackled the steps. As he glanced ahead, he saw that the brothers had lined up again. Rhage rubbed his eyes at what was before him, getting blood on his face.

This was not part of the ritual, he thought.

Each one of the brothers had a black dagger in his right hand. Wrath started the chant and the others carried it until their voices were loud shouts reverberating around the sanctorum. The buildup didn't stop until they were almost screaming, and then their voices cut off abruptly.

As a unit, they slashed their daggers across their upper chests.

Zsadist's cut was the deepest.

THIRTY

Mary was downstairs in the billiard room, talking to Fritz about the history of the house, when the *doggen*'s ears picked up a sound she hadn't heard.

"That would be the sires returning."

She went to one of the windows just as a pair of head-lights swung around the courtyard.

The Escalade came to a stop, its doors opened, and the men got out. With the hoods on their robes down, she recognized them from the first night she'd come to the mansion. The guy with the goatee and the tattoos at one of his temples. The man with the spectacular hair. The scarred terror and the military officer. The only one she hadn't seen before was a man with long black hair and sunglasses.

God, their expressions were bleak. Maybe someone had been hurt.

She searched for Rhage, trying not to panic.

The group milled around and condensed at the back of the SUV just as someone came out of the gatehouse and held the door open. Mary recognized the guy between the jambs as the one who'd caught the football in the foyer.

With all of the big male bodies crowded in a tight circle at the rear of the Escalade, it was hard to tell what they were doing. But it seemed like some kind of heavy weight was being shifted among them . . .

A blond head of hair caught the light.

Rhage. Unconscious. And his body was being carried toward that open door.

Mary was out of the mansion before she realized she was running.

"Rhage! Stop! Wait!" Cold air streaked into her lungs. "Rhage!"

At the sound of her voice, he jerked and threw a limp hand out to her. The men stopped. A couple of them cursed.

"Rhage!" She ground to a halt, kicking up pebbles. "What . . . oh . . . *lord*."

There was blood on his face, and his eyes were unfocused from pain.

"Rhage . . ."

His mouth opened. Worked soundlessly.

One of the men said, "Shit, we might as well take him to his room now."

"Of course you'll take him there! Was he hurt fighting?"

No one answered her. They just changed direction and muscled Rhage through the mansion's vestibule, across the foyer and up the stairs. After they'd laid him on his bed, the guy with the goatee and tattoos on his face smoothed Rhage's hair back.

"Brother, maybe we could bring you something for the pain?"

Rhage's voice was garbled. "Nothing. Better this way. You know rules. Mary . . . where's Mary?"

She went to the bedside and took his slack hand. As she pressed her lips to his knuckles, she realized the robe was in perfect condition, with no rips or tears. Which meant he hadn't had the thing on when he'd been hurt. And someone had put it back on him.

With a horrible intuition, she reached for the braided leather tie around his waist. She loosened it and pulled the edges of the robe open. From his collarbones to his hips he was covered with white bandages. And blood had welled through, a bright, shocking red.

Afraid to look, needing to know, she gently untaped one corner and lifted.

"Dear *God*." She swayed and one of the brothers caught her. "How did this happen?"

267

When the group remained silent, she pushed whoever was holding her up away and looked at them all. They were unmoving, staring at Rhage . . .

And in as much pain as he was. *Sweet Jesus, they couldn't have . . .*

The goateed one met her eyes.

They did.

"You did this," she hissed. "You did this to him!"

"Yes," said the one with the sunglasses. "And it's none of your business."

"You *bastards*."

Rhage made a sound and then cleared his throat. "Leave us."

"We'll be back to check on you, Hollywood," said the guy with long multicolored hair. "Do you need anything?"

"Other than a skin graft?" Rhage smiled a little and then winced as he shifted on the bed.

While the men went out the door, she glared at their strong backs. Those *goddamned . . . animals*.

"Mary?" Rhage murmured. *"Mary."*

She tried to pull it together. Getting all worked up over those thugs wasn't going to help Rhage right now.

She looked down at him, choked back her fury, and said, "Will you let me call that doctor you talked about? What was his name?"

"No."

She wanted to tell him to lose the tough-guy-bearing-pain-nobly crap. But she knew he'd fight her, and an argument was the last thing he needed.

"Do you want the robe off or on?" she asked.

"Off. If you can stand the sight of me."

"Don't worry about that."

She untied the leather belt and peeled the black silk off him, wanting to scream as he rolled back and forth to help her while grunting in pain. When they were finished getting the thing out from under him, blood seeped down his side.

That beautiful duvet was going to be ruined, she thought, not giving a shit.

"You've lost a lot of blood." She rolled up the heavy robe.

"I know." He closed his eyes, head sinking into the pillow. His naked body was going through a series of flickering seizures, the trembling in his thighs, stomach, and pectorals making the mattress jiggle.

She dumped the robe in the tub and came back. "Did they clean you before they dressed the wounds?"

"I don't know."

"I probably should check at some point."

"Give me an hour. By then the bleeding will stop." He took a deep breath and grimaced. "Mary . . . they had to."

"What?" She leaned down.

"They had to do this. I don't . . ." Another breath was followed by a groan. "Don't be angry with them."

Screw. That.

"Mary," he said strongly, his dull eyes focusing on her. "I gave them no choice."

"What did you do?"

"It's over. And you are not to be angry with them." His stare fuzzed out again.

As far as she was concerned, she could be anything the hell she wanted at those bastards.

"Mary?"

"Don't worry." She stroked his cheek, wishing she could wash the blood off of his face. When he flinched at the light contact, she pulled back. "Won't you please let me get you something?"

"Just talk to me. Read to me . . ."

There were a few contemporary books on the shelves next to his DVD wasteland, and she went over to the hardcovers. She grabbed a Harry Potter, the second one, and pulled a chair up next to the bed. It was hard to concentrate at first because she kept measuring his respiration, but eventually she found a rhythm and so did he. His breathing slowed and the spasms stopped.

When he was asleep, she closed the book. His forehead was wrinkled, his lips pale and tight. She hated that the pain was with him even in the rest he'd found.

Mary felt the years peel away.

She saw her mother's yellow bedroom. Smelled disinfectant. Heard labored, desperate breaths.

Here she was again, she thought. Another bedside. Another's suffering. Helpless.

She looked around the room, eyes landing on the *Madonna and Child* over the dresser. In this context the painting was art, not icon, part of a museum-quality collection and used only as decoration.

So she didn't have to hate the damn thing. And she wasn't scared of it, either.

The Madonna statue in her mother's room had been different. Mary had despised it, and the instant Cissy Luce's body had left the house, that piece of plaster had been in the garage. Mary hadn't had the heart to break it, but she'd wanted to.

The next morning she'd taken the thing to Our Lady and dropped it off. Same with the crucifix. As she'd driven out of the church's parking lot, the triumph she'd felt, the veritable *fuck you* to God, had been heady, the only good feeling that came to her for a long time. The rush hadn't lasted, though. When she'd returned to the house, all she'd seen was the shadow on the wall where the cross had been and the dust-free spot on the floor where the statue had stood.

Two years later, to the very day she'd dropped those objects of devotion off, she'd been diagnosed with leukemia.

Logically she knew she wasn't cursed because she'd dumped the things. There were 365 days to hit on the calendar, and like a ball on a roulette wheel, the announcement of her disease had had to land on one of them. In her heart, though, she sometimes believed otherwise. Which made her hate God even more.

Hell . . . He didn't have time to spare a miracle for her mother, who'd been faithful. But He went out of His way to punish a sinner like her. *Go figure.*

"You ease me," Rhage said.

Her eyes snapped to his. She cleared her head by taking his hand. "How are you?"

"Better. Your voice soothes me."

It had been the same with her mother, she thought. Her mother had liked the sound of her talking, too.

"You want something to drink?" she asked.

"What were you thinking about just now?"

"Nothing."

He closed his eyes.

"Would you like me to wash you?" she said.

When he shrugged, she went to the bathroom and came back with a warm, damp washcloth and a dry bath towel. She cleaned his face and gently worked around the edges of the bandages.

"I'm going to take these off, okay?"

He nodded and she carefully peeled the tape from his skin. She pulled the gauze and padding back.

Mary shuddered, bile rising up into her mouth.

He'd been whipped. It was the only explanation for the marks.

"Oh . . . Rhage." Tears clouded her eyes, but she didn't allow them to fall. "I'm just going to change the dressing. This is too . . . tender to wash yet. Do you have—"

"Bathroom. Floor-to-ceiling cupboard to the right of the mirror."

Standing in front of the cabinet, she was daunted by

the supplies he kept on hand. Surgical kits. Plaster for broken bones. Bandages of all kinds. Tape. She took what she thought she'd need and went back to him. Ripping open sterile packs of twelve-inch gauze pads, she laid them on his chest and stomach and figured she'd just let them sit there. There was no way she could lift his torso off the mattress to wrap him up, and taping them all together would involve too much fiddling around.

As she patted down the lower left section of bandages, Rhage jerked. She glanced at him. "Did I hurt you?"

"Funny question."

"I'm sorry?"

His eyes flipped open, his stare hard. "You don't even know, do you?"

Clearly not. "Rhage, what do you need?"

"For you to talk to me."

"Okay. Let me finish here."

As soon as she was done, she opened up the book. He cursed.

Confused, she reached for his hand. "I don't know what you want."

"It's not that tough to figure out." His voice was weak but indignant. "Christ, Mary, can you at least once let me in?"

There was a knock across the room. They both glared at the sound.

"I'll be right back," she said.

When she opened the door, the man with the goatee was on the other side. He had a silver tray weighed down with food balanced on one hand.

"I'm Vishous, by the way. Is he awake?"

"Hey, V," Rhage said.

Vishous walked right past her and put the meal on the dresser. As he headed for the bed, she wished she were as big as he was so she could keep him out of the room.

The guy propped his hip on the side of the mattress. "How you doing, Hollywood?"

"I'm okay."

"Pain fading yet?"

"Yeah."

"So you're healing up good."

"Can't happen fast enough for me." Rhage closed his eyes in exhaustion.

Vishous stared down at him for a moment, lips drawn thin. "I'll come back later, my brother. All right?"

"Thanks, man."

The guy turned around and met her eyes, which couldn't have been easy. At the moment, she was wishing he had a taste of the pain he'd inflicted. And she knew the desire for vengeance was showing in her face.

"Tough cookie, aren't you?" Vishous murmured.

"If he's your *brother*, why did you hurt him?"

"Mary, don't," Rhage cut in hoarsely. "I told you—"

"*You told me nothing.*" She squeezed her eyes shut. It was not fair to yell at him when he was flat on his back with a chest that looked like a grid map.

"Maybe we should just let it all out," Vishous said.

Mary crossed her arms over her chest. "Now there's an idea. Why don't you tell me the whole damn thing? Help me understand why you did this to him."

Rhage spoke up. "Mary, I don't want you to—"

"*So tell me.* If you don't want me to hate them, then explain this to me."

Vishous looked over to the bed, and Rhage must have nodded or shrugged, because the man said, "He betrayed the Brotherhood to be with you. He had to make amends if he wanted to stay with us and keep you here."

Mary stopped breathing. This was all for her? Because of her?

Oh, God. He'd allowed himself to be whipped raw for her . . .

273

I'll make it safe for you, how about that?

She had absolutely no context for this kind of sacrifice. For the pain he was enduring for her. For what had been done to him by people who supposedly cared for him.

"I can't . . . I feel a little light-headed. Will you excuse . . ."

She backed away, hoping to stumble into the bathroom, but Rhage struggled up on the bed, as if he were going to come after her.

"No, you stay there, Rhage." She went back to him, sitting down in the chair and stroking his hair. "Stay where you are. Shh . . . Easy, big man."

When he'd relaxed a little, she looked at Vishous. "I don't understand any of this."

"Why would you?"

The vampire's eyes were steady on hers, the silver depths somehow frightening. She focused on the tattoo that bled out onto his face for a moment and then glanced at Rhage. She brushed his hair with her fingertips and murmured until he slid back into sleep.

"Did it hurt you to do this to him?" she demanded softly, knowing Vishous hadn't left. "Tell me it hurt you."

She heard a whispering of cloth. When she glanced over her shoulder, Vishous had taken off his shirt. On his muscular chest there was a fresh wound, a slice, as if a blade had cut into his skin.

"It killed each one of us."

"Good."

The vampire smiled rather fiercely. "You understand us better than you think. And that food is not just for him when he wants it. I brought it for you, too."

Yeah, well, she didn't want anything from them. "Thank you. I'll see that he eats."

Vishous paused on his way out. "Have you told him about your name?"

274

Her head snapped around. "What?"

"Rhage. Does he know?"

Shivers crept up the back of her neck. "Obviously he knows my name."

"No, the *why* of it. You might tell him." Vishous frowned. "And no, I didn't find out on the Internet. How could I?"

Good lord, that had been exactly what was going through her . . . "Do you read minds?"

"When I want to and sometimes when I have no choice." Vishous left, shutting the door quietly.

Rhage tried to roll over onto his side and woke up with a moan. "Mary?"

"I'm right here." She placed his hand between both of hers.

"What's the matter?" As he looked at her, his teal-blue eyes were more alert than they had been. "Mary, please. Just once, tell me what's on your mind."

She hesitated. "Why didn't you just leave me behind? All this . . . wouldn't have happened."

"There is nothing I would not bear for your safety, for your life."

She shook her head. "I don't understand how you can feel so much for me."

"Yeah, you know what?" He smiled a little. "You've got to shelve this whole understanding thing."

"It's better than going on faith," she whispered, reaching up and running a hand through his blond waves. "Go back to sleep, big man. Every time you do, you seem to wake up miles ahead in the healing process."

"I'd rather look at you." But he shut his eyes. "I love it when you play with my hair."

He craned his neck, tilting away from her so she could reach more of it.

Even his ears were beautiful, she thought.

Rhage's chest rose and fell in a great sigh. After a while,

she leaned back in the chair and kicked her legs out, propping her feet on one of the bed's massive supports.

As the hours passed, the brothers stopped by to check on him and introduce themselves. Phury, the one with the great head of hair, came in with some warm cider, which she actually took. Wrath, the guy who wore dark sunglasses, and Beth, the woman whom she'd passed out in front of, also visited. Butch, the football catcher, came by, and so did Tohrment, who had that short brush cut.

Rhage slept a lot, but kept waking up whenever he tried to shift over onto his side. He would look at her as he moved around, as if taking strength from the sight of her, and she brought him water, stroked his face, fed him. They didn't say much. The touching was enough.

Her eyelids were getting low, and she'd let her head fall back when there was another soft knocking. Probably Fritz with more food.

She stretched and went to the door.

"Come on in," she said while she opened it.

The man with the scarred face was standing in the hall. As he stood stock-still, light fell on the sharp lines of him, drawing out his deep-set eyes, the skull under his supershort hair, that jagged scar, his hard jawline. He was wearing a loose turtleneck and pants that hung low on his hips. Both were black.

She immediately moved closer to the bed to protect Rhage, even though it was stupid to think she could fend off something as big as the vampire in the doorway.

Silence stretched out. She told herself he was probably just checking in as the others had and didn't want to hurt his brother again. Except . . . he looked tight all over, his wide stance suggesting he might spring forward at any moment. And weirding her out even more was the fact that the vampire didn't meet her stare, and he didn't seem to be looking at Rhage, either. The guy's cold, black gaze was ungrounded.

"Would you like to come in and see him?" she asked finally.

Those eyes shifted to hers.

Obsidian, she thought. They were like obsidian. Glossy. Bottomless. Soulless.

She backed up farther and grabbed Rhage's hand. The vampire in the doorway smirked.

"You're looking a little ferocious there, female. You think I'm here to take another hunk out of him?" The voice was low, smooth. Resonant, really. And as detached and unrevealing as his pupils.

"Are you going to hurt him?"

"Silly question."

"Why's that?"

"You won't believe my answer, so you shouldn't ask."

There was more silence, and she measured him in the quiet. It dawned on her that maybe he wasn't just aggressive. He was also awkward.

Maybe.

She kissed Rhage's hand and forced herself to step away. "I was going to take a shower. Will you sit with him while I'm gone?"

The vampire blinked as if she'd surprised him. "You gonna feel comfortable getting naked in that bathroom with me around?"

Not really.

She shrugged. "It's your choice. But I'm sure if he wakes up, he'd rather see you than be alone."

"You're going to turn the lights out on me then?"

"Are you coming or going?" When he didn't reply, she said, "Tonight must have been hell for you."

His distorted upper lip jerked into a snarl. "You're the only one who's ever assumed I don't get off hurting people. Are you the Mother Teresa type? All into seeing the good in big, wounded things or some shit?"

"You didn't volunteer for that scar on your face, did

you? And I'm willing to bet you've got more below your jawline. So like I said, tonight must have been hell."

His eyes narrowed into slits, and a cold gust blew through the room, as if he'd pushed the air at her. "Careful, female. Courage can be dangerous."

She walked right up to him. "You know what? The whole shower thing is mostly a lie. I was trying to let you have some alone time with him, because it's obvious you're feeling bad or you wouldn't be standing in that doorway looking so damned torn. Take the offer or leave, but either way, I'd appreciate it if you don't try to scare me."

At this point, she didn't care if he lashed out at her. Then again, she was running on nervous energy and the buzz that came with exhaustion, so she probably wasn't thinking clearly.

"So what's it going to be?" she demanded.

The vampire stepped inside and shut the door, the room growing colder with him in it. His menace was a tangible thing, and it reached out, brushing over her body like hands. As the lock slid into place with a click, she became afraid.

"I'm not trying," he said in a satin drawl.

"What?" she choked out.

"To scare you. You *are* scared." He smiled. His fangs were very long, longer than Rhage's. "I can smell your fear, female. Like wet paint, it tingles in the nose."

As Mary backed away, he came forward, tracking her.

"Hmm . . . and I like your scent. Liked it from the moment I first met you."

She moved faster, putting out her hand, hoping to feel the bed at any moment. Instead she got tangled in some of the heavy drapes by a window.

The scarred vampire cornered her. He didn't carry as much muscle on his bones as Rhage did, but there was no doubt he was lethal. His cold eyes told her all she needed to know about his ability to kill.

With a curse, Mary put her head down and surrendered. She could do nothing if he hurt her, and neither could Rhage in his condition. Damn it, she hated being helpless, but sometimes that was where life put you.

The vampire leaned down to her and she cringed.

He breathed in deeply and his exhale was a long sigh.

"Take your shower, female. I had no desire to hurt him earlier in the night, and nothing's changed. And I've got no interest in pulling a nasty on you, either. If anything happened to you, he'd be in greater agony than he's in now."

She sagged as he turned away, and she caught his wince as he looked at Rhage.

"What is your name?" she murmured.

He cocked an eyebrow at her and then went back to staring at his brother. "I'm the evil one, in case you haven't figured it out."

"I wanted your name, not your calling."

"Being a bastard's more of a compulsion, really. And it's Zsadist. I am Zsadist."

"Well . . . it's nice to meet you, Zsadist."

"So polite," he mocked.

"Okay, how about this. Thank you for not killing him or me just now. That real enough for you?"

Zsadist glanced over his shoulder. His eyelids were like window blinds, allowing only slits of cold night to shine through. And with his skull-trimmed hair and that scar, he was the personification of violence: aggression, and pain anthropomorphized. Except as he looked at her through the candlelight, the slightest hint of warmth came through his face. It was so subtle she couldn't define quite how she knew it was there.

"You," he said softly, "are extraordinary." Before she could say anything further, he held up his hand. "Go. Now. Leave me with my brother."

Without another word, Mary went into the bathroom.

She stayed in the shower for so long her fingers wrinkled and the steam in the air grew thick as cream. When she got out, she dressed in the same clothes she'd had on, because she'd neglected to bring new ones in with her. She opened the door to the bedroom quietly.

Zsadist was sitting on the bed, his broad shoulders caved in, his arms wrapped around his waist. Bent over Rhage's sleeping body, he was curled down as close as possible without their actually touching. As he rocked himself back and forth, there was a faint, lilting song in the air.

The vampire was chanting, his voice rising and falling, skipping octaves, soaring high, falling low. Beautiful. Utterly beautiful. And Rhage was relaxed, resting peacefully in a way he hadn't before.

She quickly crossed the room and went out in the hall, leaving the men alone.

THIRTY-ONE

Rhage came awake sometime the following afternoon.

The first thing he did was reach out blindly for Mary, but he stopped himself, not wanting the burn to kick in. He didn't feel strong enough to fight it.

Opening his eyes, he turned his head. She was there beside him in the bed, asleep on her stomach.

God, once again she'd taken care of him when he'd needed it. She'd been unflinching. Strong. Willing to face off against his brothers.

Love filled his heart, swelling it so much his breath stopped.

He put his hand to his chest and felt the bandages she'd put on him. Working carefully, he removed them one by one. The wounds looked good. They'd closed and no longer hurt. By tomorrow they would be nothing more than pink streaks, and, the day after, they would be gone.

He thought about the stress his body had been under lately. The change. The surges around Mary. The sun exposure. The whipping. He was going to need to drink soon, and he wanted to do it before the hunger kicked in.

Feeding was something he was scrupulous about. Most of the brothers stretched out the hunger for as long as they could stand it, just because they didn't want to bother with the intimacy. He knew better than that. The last thing he needed was the beast with a case of bloodlust—

Wait a minute.

Rhage took a deep breath. There was the most amazing . . . emptiness in him. No background buzzing. No itchy drive. No burning. And this was even though he was lying right next to Mary.

It was . . . only him in his body. Just himself. The Scribe Virgin's curse was gone.

But of course, he thought. She'd taken it from him temporarily so he could make it through the *rythe* without changing. And she was obviously giving him a respite so he could heal, too. He wondered how much longer the reprieve was going to last.

Rhage exhaled slowly, air easing out of his nose. As he sank into his skin, he reveled in the perfection of peace. The heavenly silence. The great roaring absence.

It had been a century.

Good God, he wanted to cry.

In case he did and Mary woke up, he put his hands over his eyes.

Did other people know how lucky they were to find moments like this? Moments of resounding quiet? He hadn't appreciated them before the curse, hadn't even noticed. Hell, if he'd been blessed with one, he'd probably just rolled over to go back to sleep.

"How are you feeling? Can I get you anything?"

At the sound of Mary's voice, he braced himself for a blast of energy. Nothing like that came. All he felt was a warm glow in his chest. Love unfettered with the chaos of his curse.

He rubbed his face and looked at her. Adored her so intensely in the quiet darkness that he was afraid of her.

"I need to be with you, Mary. Right now. I have to be inside of you."

"Then kiss me."

He pulled her body against him. She was wearing only a T-shirt, and he slid his hands underneath, spanning her lower back. He was already hard for her, ready to take her, but with nothing to fight down, stroking her was an exquisite pleasure.

"I need to love you," he said, throwing all the sheets and blankets from the bed. He wanted to see every part of her, touch every inch of her, and he didn't want anything in the way.

He pulled the shirt up and over her head and then willed candles to light around the room. She was resplendent in the golden glow, her head turned to the side as she looked up at him with her gray eyes. Her breasts were tight at the tips already, the swells creamy white under her pink nipples. Her stomach was flat, a little too flat, he thought, worrying about her. But her hips were perfect and so were her sleek legs.

And the juncture below her navel, that sweetest piece . . .

"My Mary," he whispered, thinking about all the places he wanted to go on her.

As he straddled her legs, his sex jutted straight out of his body, heavy, proud, demanding. But before he could lean down to her skin, her hands found his length, and he shuddered, sweat breaking out all over him. Watching her touch him, he let himself go for just a moment, giving free rein to the purity of his desire, the uncontaminated ecstasy.

When she sat up, he didn't know where she was going. "Mary?"

Her lips parted and she took him into her mouth.

Rhage gasped and fell back on his arms. "Oh, my . . . God."

With all the other females he'd had since the curse, he hadn't let any of them go down on him. He hadn't wanted it, hadn't liked them touching him above the waist, much less below it.

But this was Mary.

The suction and the warmth of her mouth, but most of all the knowledge that it was her, stole his strength, putting him at her mercy. Her eyes stared up at him, watching him as he swam in the pleasure she gave him. When he sank back against the mattress, collapsing, she crawled up his thighs, advancing. He cradled her head in his hands, arching into her mouth as she found a rhythm.

Right before he went over the edge, he shifted his hips away, not wanting to release yet.

"Come here," he said, pulling her up his stomach and chest, rolling her onto her back. "I'm going to be in you when I finish."

Kissing her, he put his hand on the column of her neck and swept down the center of her, stopping over her heart. It was beating fast, and he dropped down, pressing his lips to her sternum and then moving to her breast. He suckled her as he slid his arm around under her shoulder blades and lifted her closer to his mouth.

She made an incredible noise deep in her throat, a breathless gasp that brought his head up just so he could look at her face. Her eyes were closed, her teeth clenched. He kissed a path down to her navel, where he lingered and licked before moving to her hip. Urging her onto her stomach, he parted her legs and cupped her core with his palm. The silky wetness that coated his hand had him shaking as he kissed her hip and her lower back.

Slipping a finger into her, he bared his fangs and ran them up her spinal cord.

Mary moaned, her body curving to meet his teeth.

He stopped at her shoulder. Nudged her hair out of the way. And growled as he looked at her neck.

When she tensed, he whispered, "Don't be scared, Mary. I won't hurt you."

"I'm not afraid." She shifted her hips and clenched her wet heat around his hand.

Rhage hissed as lust ripped through him. He began to pant, but took comfort. There was no vibration, no god-awful hum. Just her and him. Together. Making love.

Though he did hunger for something else from her.

"Mary, forgive me."

"For what?"

"I want to . . . drink from you," he said into her ear.

She trembled, but he felt a warm rush where he penetrated her and knew the shakes were from pleasure.

"You really want to . . . do that?" she said.

"God, yes." His mouth closed on the side of her throat. He sucked her skin, dying to do so much more. "I would love to be at your vein."

"I've wondered what it would feel like." Her voice was husky, thrilling. Good lord, was she going to let him? "Does it hurt?"

"Only a little in the beginning, but then it's like . . . sex. You'd feel my pleasure as I took you into me. And I would be very careful. So very gentle."

"I know you would."

An erotic surge pounded through him and his fangs unsheathed. He could imagine sinking them into her neck. The sucking. The swallowing. The taste. And then there would be the communion of her doing the same to him. He would feed her well, let her take as much as she wanted—

Her doing the same?

Rhage pulled back. What the *hell* was he thinking? She was a human, for chrissakes. She didn't feed.

He put his forehead down on her shoulder. And remembered that not only was she a human; she was ill. He licked his lips, trying to persuade his fangs to retract.

"Rhage? Are you going to . . . you know."

"I think it's safer not to."

"Honestly, I'm not scared of it."

"Oh, Mary, I know. You aren't afraid of anything." And her courage was part of the reason he'd bonded with her. "But I'd rather love your body than take something it can't afford to give me."

In a quick series of moves he rose above her, pulled her hips off the mattress, and entered her from behind, sliding deep. Heat roared through him as she arched under his invasion, and he ran one of his arms between her breasts, holding on to her upper body. With his hand, he twisted her chin around so he could kiss her.

Her breath was hot and desperate in his mouth as he slowly extracted himself from her core. The surge back in made them both groan. She was so incredibly tight, squeezing him hard as a vise. He got in a couple more controlled thrusts and then his hips took over, moving of their own volition until he couldn't keep contact with her lips anymore. His body pounded into hers, and he shifted his hands to her waist as he held on.

Her chest dropped down to the bed and her face turned to the side. Her lips were parted, her eyes closed. He let go of her torso and planted his fists in the mattress on either side of her shoulders. She was so small underneath him, dwarfed by the thickness of his forearms, but she took all of him, from tip to base, over and over again until he was lost.

From out of nowhere he felt a wonderful stinging in his hand. He looked down and saw that she'd curled around one of his arms and closed her mouth on the base of his thumb, biting.

"Harder, Mary," he said hoarsely. "Oh, *yeah*. Bite . . . hard."

The little burst of pain as her teeth sank into him shot his pleasure through the roof, taking him to the very verge of coming.

Except he didn't want it to end.

He pulled out and quickly turned her over. As she landed on her back, her legs flopped to the sides as if she didn't have the strength to hold them up. The sight of her open to him, glistening for him, swollen from him, nearly had him releasing all over her thighs. He dropped his head and kissed where he had been, tasting a little of himself, a little of that marking scent he was leaving all over her body.

She cried out wildly as she climaxed. And before her pulses faded, he shot up over her and plunged back inside.

She called his name, nails scoring his back.

He let himself go over the edge while looking into her wide, dazed eyes. With nothing to hold back, he came over and over again, pumping his flow into her. The orgasm kept going and he rode the waves that overtook him. The ecstasy seemed to have no end, and there was no stopping it.

Not that he would have if he'd had the power to.

Mary held on to Rhage as he shuddered once more, his body seizing, his breath coming out of him in a rush. He groaned deep in his chest, and she felt him jerk and release again inside of her.

It was a shattering kind of intimacy, she so calm, he in the throes of some kind of multiple orgasming. With her concentration undiminished by passion, she felt every small thing in his body as well as each heavy thrust. She knew exactly when another release was coming for him, could feel the trembling in his belly and thighs. It was happening now, his breath catching, his pecs and shoulders going tight along with his hips as he surged again.

He lifted his head this time, lips peeling off his fangs, eyes squeezed shut. His body contracted, all his muscles tensing, and then she felt the movement deep inside of her.

His eyes opened. They were glazed over.

"I'm sorry, Mary." Another spasm overtook him, and he did his best to talk through it. "Never . . . happened . . . before. Can't stop. *God damn*."

He let out a guttural sound, a mixture of apology and ecstasy.

She smiled at him and ran her hands up his smooth back, feeling those thick muscles grab bone as his lower body drove into her again. She was saturated between her legs and deliciously hot from all the heat pouring off of him. That wonderful smell of his bond for her was thick in the air, the dark fragrance surrounding her.

He heaved himself up on his arms, making as though he were going to pull out.

"Where are you going?" She wrapped her legs around his hips.

"Crushing . . . you." His breath sucked in again on a hiss.

"I'm perfectly fine."

"Oh, Mary . . . I . . ." He arched again, chest coming forward, head falling back, neck straining, shoulders bulging. Good lord, he was gorgeous.

Abruptly he sagged, his body going completely limp on top of her. His deadweight was immense, more than she could bear and still breathe. Fortunately, he rolled away and tucked her against him. His heart thundered in his chest, and she listened as it slowed.

"Did I hurt you?" he asked roughly.

"Not at all."

He kissed her and withdrew, lurching into the bathroom. He came back with a towel, which he gently eased between her legs.

"Do you want me to start the shower?" he said. "I've, ah, kind of made a mess of you."

"Hardly. And no, I just want to lie here."

"I can't explain why that happened." He frowned as he pulled the covers and blankets back on the bed and over them both. "Although . . . well, maybe I do know."

"Whatever the reason, you're incredible." She pressed her lips to his jawline. "Absolutely incredible."

They lay together quietly for a while.

"Listen, Mary, my body's been through a lot lately."

"It sure has."

"I'm going to need to . . . take care of myself."

Something in his tone of voice was off, and she looked up at him. He was staring at the ceiling.

A chill shot through her. "How so?"

"I'm going to need to feed. From a female. Of my species."

"Oh." She thought of how his fangs had felt traveling up her spine. And remembered the shiver of anticipation when he'd nuzzled her neck. Shades of his night out had her pulling back. She couldn't go through that again. Waiting in his bed, knowing that he was with another woman.

He took her hands in his. "Mary, I have to feed now so I can stay in control. And I want you to be with me when I do it. If it's too difficult for you to watch, at least you can be in the same room. I don't want there to be a question in your mind about what happens between myself and the female."

"Who will you"—she cleared her throat—"drink from?"

"I've thought about that. I don't want it to be with anyone I've had."

So that should narrow the pool down to what, five women? Maybe six?

She shook her head, feeling like a bitch.

"I'm going to call on one of the Chosen."

Tell me they are toothless hags, she thought. "What are they?"

"Primarily they serve the Scribe Virgin, our deity, but for a while they serviced unmated members of the Brotherhood for blood. In modern times we haven't used them like that, but I'm going to contact them, see if something can be arranged."

"When?"

"As soon as possible. Perhaps tomorrow night."

"I'll be gone by then." As his expression went dark,

she didn't give him a chance to speak. "It's time for me to go."

"The hell it is."

"Rhage, be realistic. Do you honestly expect me to just stay here with you forever?"

"That's what I want. So, yes."

"Has it occurred to you I miss my house, my things, my—"

"I'll have them moved here. Everything."

She shook her head. "I need to go home."

"It's not safe."

"Then we're going to have to make it safe. I'll install an alarm, learn to shoot, I don't know. But I have to get back to my life."

He closed his eyes.

"Rhage, look at me. *Look* at me." She squeezed his hand. "I have things I need to do. In my world."

His lips tightened into a slash. "Will you let me have Vishous install a security system?"

"Yes."

"And you will come stay here with me some days."

She took a deep breath. "What if I say no?"

"Then I'll come to you."

"I don't think—"

"I've told you before. Stop thinking."

His lips found hers, but, before his tongue slipped inside and stole her ability to be logical, she pushed him back.

"Rhage, you know this isn't going anywhere. This . . . whatever it is between us. It's not. It can't."

He rolled over onto his back, putting an arm behind his head. As his jaw clenched, the cords of his neck stood out.

She hated this; she really did. But it was better to get it all out. "I appreciate everything you've done for me. The sacrifice to keep me safe—"

"Why did you get so upset the night I went out?"

"Excuse me?"

"Why did you care that I'd been with someone else? Or did you just feel like a little rough sex and needed to hide behind a reason for it?" His eyes shifted to hers. The blue was neon sharp, nearly too bright to look into. "Listen, the next time you want some hard grind, all you've got to do is ask. I can play it like that."

Oh, God. This anger was not what she'd wanted. "Rhage—"

"You know, I really got into it. I liked that domination shit you threw out. Liked the sadistic part, too. Tasting my blood on your lips after you bit my mouth? Huge turn-on."

The cold tone of voice was awful. His flat, glowing eyes were worse.

"I'm sorry," she said. "But—"

"In fact, I'm getting hard right now, just thinking about it. Kind of surprising, considering how I spent the last twenty minutes."

"What exactly do you think the future holds for us?"

"We'll never know, will we. But you'll stick around until nightfall, right? If only because you need me to take you home. So let me see if I can get myself tuned up again. I'd hate to waste your time." He reached under the covers. "Damn, you're good. I'm hard as a baseball bat."

"Do you know what the next six months are going to be like for me?"

"No, and I'm not going to know, am I? So how about some sex. Since that's all you want from me, and because I'm enough of a pathetic loser to take you any way I can get you, I guess I'd better hop to it."

"Rhage!" she shouted, trying to get his attention.

"Mary!" he mocked. "I'm sorry, am I talking too much? You'd rather have my mouth doing something else, right?

You want it on yours? No, your breasts. Wait, lower. Yeah, you like it lower, don't you. And I know just how to do you right."

She put her head in her hands. "I don't want to leave you like this. Fighting."

"But that's not going to slow you down, is it? Not you, not superstrong Mary. No, you're just going to go out into the world—"

"*To be sick*, Rhage! I'm leaving you to go be sick, okay? I'm going to the *doctor's* tomorrow. There isn't some huge party waiting for me when I get home."

He stared at her. "Do you think I am so unworthy that I cannot attend to you?"

"What?"

"Will you not let me attend to you in your illness?"

She thought about how hard it had been for her to see him in pain and not be able to make the hurt go away.

"Why would you want to do that?" she whispered.

Rhage's mouth went lax, as if she'd struck him.

He shot out of bed. "Yeah, fuck you, Mary."

He jabbed his legs into a pair of leather pants and snapped a shirt from the dresser.

"Get yourself packed, sweetheart. You won't have to put up with a stray dog anymore." He pushed his arms through the shirt's sleeves and pulled it over his head. "I'll get V to hardwire your house ASAP. It shouldn't take him long, and, until he's done, you can sleep somewhere else. One of the *doggen* will show you to your new room."

She leaped off the mattress, but, before she could reach him, he pegged her with a hard look, stopping her dead.

"You know, Mary, I deserve this. I really do. I've done the same thing to so many, just walked away without giving a shit." He opened the door. "Although the females I screwed were lucky. At least they never remembered me.

292

And man, I'd kill to forget about you right now, I really would."

He didn't slam the door on the way out. Just shut it firmly.

THIRTY-TWO

O leaned over the civilian male and tightened the vise. He'd abducted the vampire in the alley next to Screamer's downtown, and so far the newly erected persuasion center was working perfectly. He was also making headway with the captive. Turned out the guy had a tangential connection to the Brotherhood.

Under normal circumstances, O should have been as close to a hard-on as he could get. Instead, as he watched the vampire's cold shakes and glassy, lolling eyes, he saw himself with the Omega. Under that heavy body. Powerless. Out of control. In pain.

The memories clogged his lungs with siltlike dread until he had to look away. As the vampire moaned, O felt like a pussy.

Christ, he had to get his shit together.

O cleared his throat. Sucked some air in. "And, ah . . . just how well does your sister know the Brotherhood?"

"She . . . has sex . . . with them."

"Where?"

"Don't know."

"You're going to have to do better than that." O hit the pressure some more.

The civilian yelled and his wild eyes bounced around the center's dim interior. He was getting close to passing out again, so O loosened the clamp.

"Where does she meet them?"

"Caith goes to all the bars." The male coughed weakly. "Zero Sum. Screamer's. She went to One Eye the other night."

"One Eye?" Odd. That was out in the sticks.

294

"Can I please go home now? My parents are going to be—"

"I'm sure they are worried. And they should be." O shook his head. "But I can't let you go. Not yet."

Not at all, but the vampire didn't need to know that.

O reapplied the vise grip. "Now tell me, what was your sister's name again?"

"Caith."

"And which of the brothers does she fuck?"

"Know for sure . . . the one with the goatee. Vishous. She likes the blond warrior . . . but he's not into her."

The blond brother with the beast? "When did she see the blond last?"

A tumble of sounds came out.

"What was that? I couldn't hear you."

The male struggled to speak, but suddenly his body seized up and his mouth gaped as if he were suffocating.

"Oh, come on," O muttered. "It doesn't hurt that badly."

Shit, this vise action was just kindergarten stuff; they weren't even close to anything lethal yet. Still, ten minutes later the vampire was dead, and O was standing over the body wondering what the hell had happened.

The door to the persuasion center opened and U strode in. "How we doing tonight?"

"This civilian kicked it, but damned if I know why. I was just getting started."

O disengaged the vise from the vampire's hand and tossed the thing where the other tools were. As he stared at the lifeless bag of skin on the table, he found himself suddenly, shockingly queasy.

"If you broke a bone, maybe he threw a clot."

"What . . . huh? Oh, yeah. But wait, from just his finger? A thigh bone, I could believe, but I was working his hand."

"Doesn't matter. One can get sprung from anywhere. If it works its way to the lungs and gets lodged? Game over."

"He was gasping for breath."

"Probably what happened."

"Bad timing, too. His sister is fucking the brothers, but I didn't get much out of him."

"Home address?"

"No. The idiot had his wallet stolen right before I found him. He was drunk and got mugged in an alley. He did name some places, though. The usual clubs downtown, but also that hick bar, One Eye."

U frowned as he took out his gun and checked the chamber. "You sure he wasn't just talking to get you to stop? One Eye's not far from here, and those bastard brothers are city dwellers, aren't they? I mean, that's where we find them."

"That's where they *let* us find them. God only knows where they live." O shook his head at the body. "Damn it, he said something right before he died. I didn't understand the words."

"That language of theirs is a bitch. Wish we had a translator."

"No kidding."

U looked around. "So how's the place working for you?"

Whatever, O thought.

"Perfect," he said. "I had him in one of the holes for a while, waiting for him to come around. The halter system works just fine." O flipped the vampire's arm up onto its chest and tapped the stainless-steel slab the body was on. "And this table is a godsend. The drain holes, the restraints."

"Yeah, I thought you'd like that. Stole it from a morgue."

"Nice."

U walked over to the fireproof closet they used to store ammunition. "Mind if I take a few rounds?"

"That's what they're there for."

U took out a palm-sized cardboard box marked

REMINGTON. As he refilled his clips, he said, "So I heard that Mr. X put you in charge of this place."

"He gave me the key, yeah."

"Good. It'll be run right."

Of course, there had been a condition to the privilege. Mr. X had required that O move in, but the relocation did make some sense. If they were going to be keeping vampires over a period of days, someone had to monitor the captives.

O propped his hip against the table. "Mr. X is going to announce a new orientation of the Primes. Within each squadron we'll be pairing up, and I get to pick first. I want you."

U smiled as he closed the box of bullets. "I was a trapper up in Canada, did you know that? Back in the eighteen twenties. I like being in the field. Catching things."

O nodded, thinking that, before he'd lost his drive, he and U would have made a hell of a pair.

"So is it true about you and X?" U asked.

"Is what true?"

"That you met with the Omega recently?" When O's eyes flickered at the name, U caught the reaction and, thank God, misread it. "Holy shit, you did see him. Are you going to be X's second in command? Is that where all this is leading?"

O swallowed in spite of the nauseating whirl in his gut. "You'll have to ask sensei."

"Yeah, sure. I'm *really* gonna do that. Don't know why you have to keep it a secret, though."

As O didn't know any more than the other *lesser* did, he had no choice.

Jesus. A little while ago, the idea of being second *Forelesser* would have elated him.

U headed for the door. "So when and where do you want me?"

"Here. Now."

"What do you have in mind?"

"We're going back downtown. I wanted to call the others in for a lesson tonight, but I seem to have lost my textbook."

U inclined his head. "Let's head for the library, then. And get us another."

Rhage prayed for an outlet as he stalked the bar alleys downtown. In the cold rain he was a twitchy mess, anger and agony seething in his chest. Vishous had given up trying to talk to him two hours ago.

As they emerged on Trade Street once again, they paused next to the front door of Screamer's. An impatient, shivering crowd was waiting to get into the club, and there were four civilian males mixed in with the humans.

"So I'll try one last time, Hollywood." V lit a hand-rolled and repositioned his Sox cap. "What's up with all this quiet? You're not still hurting from last night, are you?"

"Nah, I'm good to go."

Rhage squinted into a dark corner of the alley.

Yeah, bullshit he was fine. His night vision was shot to hell, its acuity way off no matter how much he blinked. And his ears weren't working as well as they should, either. Normally he could hear sounds from almost a mile away, but now he was concentrating just to catch the chatter from the club's wait line.

Sure, he was upset at what had happened with Mary; getting shut out by the female you love will do that to a male. But these changes were physiological, not tied to emotional, crybaby crap.

And he knew what the problem was. The beast was not with him tonight.

It should have been a relief. Getting rid of the damn thing even temporarily was a blessing beyond measure.

Except evidently he'd come to rely on the creature's flinchy instincts. God, the idea that he had a kind of symbiotic relationship with his curse was a flipping surprise, and so was the vulnerability he was now sporting. It wasn't that he doubted his hand-to-hand skills or his flash and slash with a dagger. It was more like his beast gave him information about his environment that he was used to relying on. Plus the ugly-ass thing was a terrific trump card. If all else failed, it would lay waste to their enemies.

"Well, what do you know," V said, nodding to the right.

A pair of *lessers* were coming down Trade Street, their white hair gleaming in the headlights of a passing car. Like puppets on the same string, their heads turned in unison toward him and Vishous. The two slowed. Stopped.

V dropped the cigarette, crushing it with his shitkicker. "A lot of damned witnesses for a fight."

The Society members seemed to realize this as well, making no move to attack. In the standoff, the odd etiquette in the war between the Brotherhood and the *lessers* played out. Discretion among Homo sapiens was critical to retaining the secrecy of both sides. The last thing any of them needed was to get into it with a throng of people watching.

While the brothers and the *lessers* glared at one another, the humans in their midst had no idea what was going on. The civilian vampires in the wait line, however, knew what was doing. They shuffled around in place, clearly thinking of running. Rhage pegged them with a hard look and slowly shook his head. The best place for those boys was in public, and he prayed like hell they got the message.

But of course, the four of them took off.

Those damn *lessers* smiled. And then sprinted after their prey like a couple of track-and-field stars.

Rhage and Vishous flipped into high gear, tearing off at a dead run.

Foolishly, the civilians headed down an alley. Maybe they were hoping to dematerialize. Maybe they were just scared stupid. Either way, they drastically increased the likelihood of their deaths. Back here, there were no humans around on account of the icy rain, and with no streetlights and no windows in the buildings, there was nothing to prevent the *lessers* from doing their job out in the open.

Rhage and V ran even harder, shitkickers pounding through puddles, spraying dirty water everywhere. As they closed the distance on the slayers, it looked as if they were going to take them down before the civilians were caught.

Rhage was about to grab the *lesser* on the right when a black truck cut into the alley up ahead, skidding on the wet asphalt and then finding traction. The thing slowed down just as the *lessers* caught one of the civilians. With a messy flip, the two slayers tossed the male into the back and then wheeled around, ready to fight.

"I get the truck," Rhage shouted.

V took the slayers on as Rhage sprinted forward. The truck had slowed for the pickup, and its tires were spinning out, giving him an extra second or two. But just as he came up to the F-150, it took off again, shooting past him. With an awesome surge, he launched himself into the air, catching the lip of the bed just in the nick of time.

But his grip slipped on the wet metal. He was scrambling to get a better hold when the rear window slid open and a gun muzzle came out. He ducked, expecting to hear the sharp crack of a bullet discharging. Instead the civilian, who was trying to jump out, jerked and grabbed his shoulder. The male looked around in confusion and then fell in slow motion back into the bed.

The truck ripped free of Rhage's fingers, and he twisted as he fell, landing faceup. As he bounced and skidded on the pavement, his leather coat saved him from getting shredded.

He leaped to his feet and watched the truck round a distant street corner. Cursing like a son of a bitch, he didn't stick around to mourn the failure, but ran back to V. The fight was on and it was a good one, the slayers confident in their skills, far from their recruitments. V was holding his own, his dagger out and doing a number on the slayers.

Rhage fell upon the first *lesser* he got to, pissed off at losing the civilian to that truck, rank mad at the world because of Mary. He beat the holy hell out of the bastard with his fist, cracking bones, breaking through skin. Black blood kicked up into his own face, getting into his eyes. He didn't stop until V peeled him off and shoved him back against the alley wall.

"What the fuck are you doing!" Rhage had half a mind to go at V because the brother was blocking his access to the slayer.

V fisted the lapels of the trench coat and gave Rhage a good slam, as if trying to get him to focus. "The *lesser*'s not moving. Look at me, my brother. He's on the ground and he's staying there."

"I don't care!" He fought to get free, but V held him in place. Barely.

"Rhage? Come on, talk to me. What's going on? Where are you, brother?"

"I just need to kill it . . . I need . . ." From out of nowhere, hysteria crept into his voice. "For what they do to . . . The civilians can't fight back . . . I need to kill . . ." He was cracking up, but couldn't seem to stop the fracturing. "Oh, God, Mary, they want her . . . they're going to take her like they took that civilian, V. Ah, shit, my brother . . . What am I going to do to save her?"

"Shh. Easy there, Hollywood. Let's just cool out."

V clamped a hand on Rhage's neck and smoothed his thumb back and forth over Rhage's jugular. The hypnotic stroking brought him down first by inches, then by yards.

"Better?" V asked. "Yeah, better."

Rhage took a deep breath and walked around for a minute. Then he went back to the *lesser's* body. He riffled through the pockets, finding a wallet, some cash, a gun.

Oh, this was good.

"Look what I got," he muttered. "Say hello to Mr. BlackBerry."

He tossed the device to V, who whistled under his breath. "Nice."

Rhage unsheathed one of his daggers and buried the black blade in the slayer's chest. With a pop and flash, the thing disintegrated, but he didn't feel like he'd done enough. He still wanted to roar and weep at the same time.

He and V did a quick patrol of the neighborhood. All was quiet. With any luck, the other three civilians had taken their asses home and were right now shivering from adrenaline overload in safety.

"I want those *lessers'* jars," Rhage said. "You get anything off the one you took out?"

V waved a wallet. "Driver's license says One Ninety-five LaCrosse Street. What's in yours?"

Rhage went through it. "Nothing. No license. Why the hell did he carry—Huh. Now this is interesting."

The three-by-five index card had been neatly folded in half. On the inside was an address not far from where they were.

"Let's check this out before we head over to LaCrosse."

THIRTY-THREE

Mary packed up her overnight bag under Fritz's watchful eye. The butler was dying to help, shuffling from side to side, aching to do what he clearly felt was his job.

"I'm ready," she said finally, even though she wasn't.

Fritz smiled now that he had a purpose and led her around the balcony to a room that faced the gardens behind the mansion. She had to give him credit: he was incredibly discreet. If he thought it was odd that she was moving out of Rhage's room, he didn't show it, and he treated her with the same courtesy he always had.

When she was by herself, she thought about her options. She wanted to go home, but she wasn't stupid. Those things in the park had been deadly, and as badly as she needed her space, she wasn't about to get killed over a bid for independence. Besides, how long could it take to install a security system? Maybe that Vishous guy was working on it right now.

She thought about her appointment at the doctor's tomorrow afternoon. Rhage had told her he'd let her go to it and, even though he'd been pissed off as he'd left, she knew he wouldn't prevent her from going to the hospital. Fritz was probably going to take her, she thought. When he'd given her the house tour, he'd explained that he could go out in the daylight.

Mary glanced at her bag. As she was considering leaving for good, she knew she couldn't walk away while being at such raw odds with Rhage. Maybe the night out would calm him down. She was certainly feeling more rational now herself.

She opened the bedroom's door wide enough so she

could hear when he came home. And then she sat on the bed and waited.

It didn't take her long to get wobbly anxious, so she picked up the phone. When Bella answered, it was a relief to hear her friend's voice. They talked about nothing special for a little while. Then, when she felt up to it, she said she was coming home as soon as a security system was installed in her house. She was thankful Bella didn't press for details.

After a while, there was a long pause between them. "Ah, Mary, may I ask you something?"

"Sure."

"Have you seen any of the other warriors?"

"Some, yes. But I don't know if I've run into all of them."

"Have you met the one who is . . . whose face is scarred?"

"That's Zsadist. His name is Zsadist."

"Oh. Ah, is he . . ."

"What?"

"Well, I've heard things about him. He has a dangerous reputation."

"Yeah, I can imagine. But you know, I'm not sure he's all bad. Why do you ask?"

"Oh, no reason. Really."

At one A.M., John Matthew left Moe's and headed for home. Tohrment hadn't come. Maybe the man wasn't going to come. Maybe the chance to get away with him was lost.

Walking along in the cold night, John was frantic, his need to leave his building approaching evacuation levels. The fear was so bad, it was coming out in his dreams. He'd taken a nap before work, and his nightmares had been terrifying, filled with visions of white-haired men coming after him, and catching him, and taking him somewhere dark and underground.

As he approached the door to his studio, he had his key in hand and he didn't dawdle. He shot inside and closed himself in, locking everything: the two dead bolts, the chain. He wished he had one of those door poles that plugged into the floor.

He knew he should eat, but he didn't have the energy to deal with the Ensure so he sat on his bed, hoping his flagging strength would magically rebound. He was going to need it. Tomorrow he had to go out and start looking for a new place to live. It was time to save himself.

But God, he wished he'd gone with Tohrment when he'd had the—

A knock sounded on the door. John looked up, hope and fear twisting into a rope in his chest.

"Son? It's me, Tohrment. Open up."

John rushed across the room, tore the locks back, and nearly threw himself at the man.

Tohrment's brows came down over his navy-blue eyes. "What's the matter, John? You got trouble?"

He wasn't sure how much to say about the pale man he'd met in the stairwell, and, in the end, decided to keep quiet. He wasn't going to risk Tohrment's changing his mind because the kid he was thinking of taking in was a paranoid psycho.

"Son?"

John went for his pad and pen while Tohrment shut the door.

I'm glad you came. Thank you.

Tohrment read the words. "Yeah, I would have gotten here sooner, but last night I had . . . business I needed to attend to. So have you thought about—"

John nodded and scribbled quickly. *I want to come with you.*

Tohrment smiled a little. "That's good, son. That's a good choice."

John took a deep breath, beyond relieved.

"Here's what we're going to do. I'm going to come back tomorrow night and pick you up. I can't take you home now because I'm out in the field until dawn."

John swallowed fresh panic. *But come on*, he told himself. What was one more day?

Two hours before dawn, Rhage and Vishous went to the Tomb's entrance. Rhage waited in the woods while V took inside the jar they'd found at the *lesser*'s place on LaCrosse.

The other address had proven to be an abandoned torture center. In the stuffy basement of the low-rent two-story, they'd found dust-covered instruments as well as a table and restraints. The place was a horrifying testimony to the Society's change in strategy from fighting the brothers to snatching and hurting civilians. Both he and Vishous had been choked with vengeance as they'd left.

On the way back to the compound, they'd stopped at Mary's so V could scope the rooms and figure out what he'd need to wire the place up good and tight. Being there had been hell. Seeing her things. Remembering the first night he'd gone to find her. He hadn't been able to look at the couch at all because it reminded him of what he'd done to her body on the floor behind it.

All that felt like a lifetime ago.

Rhage cursed and resumed scanning the forest around the cave's mouth. When V came out, the two of them dematerialized to the main house's courtyard.

"Hey, Hollywood, Butch and I are going to One Eye for a nightcap. You want to come?"

Rhage looked up at the dark windows of his bedroom.

Even though a trip to One Eye left him cold, he knew he shouldn't be alone. With the way he was feeling, he was liable to go find Mary and make an ass out of himself by begging. Which would just be wasted humiliation. She'd made it clear where they stood, and she wasn't the kind of female who was open to persuasion. Besides, he was through playing the lovesick idiot.

For the most part.

"Yeah. I'll hang with you boys."

V's eyes flared as if he'd made the offer to be polite and hadn't expected a yes. "Okay. Good deal. We're leaving in fifteen. I need a shower."

"Me, too." He wanted to get the *lesser* blood off him.

As he walked through the mansion's vestibule and into the foyer, Fritz came out of the dining room.

The butler bowed deeply. "Good evening, sire. Your guest is here."

"Guest?"

"The Chosen's Directrix. She indicated you had called upon her."

Shit. He'd forgotten he'd put the request in, and it wasn't like he needed their services anymore. If Mary wasn't in his life, he didn't require any special feeding arrangements. He was free to go suck and fuck whoever he wanted. *Oh, joy.*

God, the idea of being with anyone but Mary made him shrivel in his pants.

"Sire? Are you receiving?"

He was about to say no, but then figured that was not a smooth move. Considering his past history with the Scribe Virgin, it wasn't wise to offend her special class of females.

"Tell her I'll be with her in a few minutes."

He jogged upstairs to his room, turned the shower on to warm up, and then called V. The brother didn't seem surprised he was bailing on the trip to the bar.

Too bad it wasn't for the reason Vishous obviously assumed.

Mary came awake because she heard talk drifting up from the foyer. It was Rhage's voice. She'd recognize that deep rumble anywhere.

Slipping from the bed, she went to the gap she'd left in the door.

Rhage was coming up the stairs. His hair was damp, as if he'd just taken a shower, and he was dressed in a loose black shirt and baggy black pants. She was about to step into the hall when she saw he was not alone. The woman with him was tall and had a long blond braid of hair down her back. She was dressed in a filmy white gown, and together they looked like some kind of Goth wedding pair, he in all that black, she draped in that gossamer fabric. When they got to the head of the stairs, the woman paused, as if she didn't know which way to turn. Rhage put his hand under her elbow and looked down at her solicitously, as if she were so fragile, she might crack a bone just getting to the second floor.

Mary watched them go into his room. The door shut behind them.

She went back over to the bed and got in it. Images came crashing down on her head. Rhage all over her body with his mouth and his hands. Rhage thanking her for feeding him. Rhage looking at her while he told her he loved her.

Yeah, he loved her all right. So much so that he was doing another woman across the hall.

The instant the thought streaked through her mind, she knew she was being unreasonable. She'd pushed him away. He'd taken the hint. She had no right to blame him for having sex with someone else.

She'd gotten exactly what she'd asked for.

He was letting her go.

THIRTY-FOUR

The following evening, just before nightfall, Rhage went to the gym as a matter of public service. When he finished with the weights, he got on the treadmill and started running. The first five miles flew by. By mile six, he'd polished off his water. When mile nine arrived, the ass-kicking started.

He increased the incline and fell back into his stride. His thighs were screaming, clenching, burning. His lungs were on fire. His feet and knees were aching.

Grabbing the shirt he'd taken off and hung on the console, he used the thing to wipe the sweat out of his eyes. He figured he was dehydrated as shit by now, but he wasn't getting off for water. He had every intention of going until he fell over.

To keep up the bruising pace, he lost himself in the music pounding through the speakers. Marilyn Manson, Nine Inch Nails, Nirvana. The stuff was loud enough to drown out the hum of the treadmill, the songs screeching through the weight room, vile, aggressive, deranged. Same as his frame of mind.

When the sound got cut off, he didn't bother looking around. He figured the stereo had kicked it or someone wanted to talk to him, and he wasn't interested in dealing with either.

Tohr stepped in front of the machine. The brother's expression had Rhage off the belt and punching the STOP release.

"What." He was breathing hard and did another scrub job on his face with the shirt.

"She's gone. Mary. She's gone."

Rhage froze with the wet wad under his chin. "What do you mean, gone?"

"Fritz waited for her in front of the hospital for three hours during her appointment. When he went inside, the clinic she hit was closed. He drove to her house. When she wasn't there, he went back and searched the whole medical center."

Temples pounding from fear instead of exertion, Rhage bit out, "Any signs of forced entry or violence at her house?"

"No."

"Was her car in the garage?"

"Yes."

"When did he last see her?"

"It was three o'clock when she went to the appointment. FYI, Fritz called you repeatedly, but kept getting voice mail on your cell."

Rhage looked at his watch. It was just after six. Assuming sixty minutes or so for the doctor's appointment, she'd been missing for two hours.

He found it hard to imagine that the *lessers* could have picked her up off the street. A far more likely scenario was that she went home and the slayers found her there. But, with no sign of a struggle at her house, there was a chance she wasn't hurt.

Or maybe that was just blind hope talking.

Rhage leaped off the machine. "I need to get armed."

Tohr shoved a bottle of water into his hand. "Drink this now. Phury's bringing your gear. Meet him in the locker room."

Rhage took off at a jog.

"The Brotherhood will help you find her," Tohr called out.

Bella came upstairs at the break of night, throwing open the door to her kitchen with triumph. Now that the days

310

were getting shorter, she had so much more time to be out and about. It was only six o'clock, but it was pitch-black. Lovely.

She was debating whether to have toast or fire up some pancakes when she saw lights on at the far edge of the meadow. Someone was in Mary's house. Probably the warriors installing the security system.

Which meant that if she went over she might be able to see that scarred male again.

Zsadist had been on her mind since she'd met him, to the point where her diary entries were filled with specu-lations about the male. He was just so . . . raw. And after having been cosseted for years by her brother, she was dying to get out and experience something wild.

And God knew, Zsadist's brute sexuality fit that bill.

She put on a coat and traded her slippers for a pair of running shoes. Jogging through the field grass, she slowed down as she approached Mary's backyard. The last thing she needed was to run into a *lesser*—

"Mary! What are you doing here?"

The human seemed dazed as she looked up from the lounge chair she was lying on. Even though it was cold, she was wearing only a sweater and jeans.

"Oh . . . hey, there. How are you?"

Bella sank down on her haunches beside the female. "Has Vishous finished?"

"With what?" Mary moved stiffly as she sat up. "Oh, the alarm. I don't think so. Or at least, no one's mentioned anything to me, and it all looks the same inside."

"How long have you been out here?"

"Not long." She rubbed her arms, then blew into her hands. "I was just watching the sunset."

Bella glanced at the house, dread stirring. "Is Rhage picking you up soon?"

"Rhage isn't coming for me."

"Then one of the *doggen?*"

Mary winced as she got to her feet. "Jeez, it's really cold."

As she walked into her home like a zombie, Bella followed. "Mary, ah . . . you really shouldn't stay here by yourself."

"I know. I figured I was safe because it was daylight."

"Did Rhage or one of the brothers tell you that *lessers* couldn't be out in the sun? Because I'm not sure, but I think they can be."

Mary shrugged. "They haven't bothered me so far, but I'm not stupid. I'm heading to a hotel. I just have to pack a few things."

Except instead of going upstairs, she wandered around the first floor of her house with an odd kind of dislocation.

She was in some kind of shock, Bella thought. But whatever the problem was, the two of them *really* needed to get the hell out of here.

"Mary, why don't you come have dinner with me?" She eyed the back door. "And, you know, you could stay with me until Vishous finishes up here. My brother had my place all wired and everything. It even has an underground escape route. I'm very safe there, and it's far enough away so that, if the *lessers* come looking for you, they won't assume you're with me."

She got ready for an argument, lining up counterpoints in her head.

"Okay, thanks," Mary said. "Give me a minute."

The female went upstairs and Bella paced around, wishing she had a weapon and knew how to use it.

When the human came down with a canvas tote bag five minutes later, Bella took a deep breath.

"How about a coat?" she said, when Mary went for the door without one.

"Yes. A coat." Mary dropped the bag, walked over to a closet, and drew on a red parka.

As they crossed the meadow together, Bella tried to rush their pace.

"Moon's almost full," Mary said as they rustled through the grass.

"Yes, it is."

"Listen, when we get to your place, I don't want you calling Rhage or anything. He and I . . . we've gone our separate ways. So don't bother him about me."

Bella swallowed her surprise. "Doesn't he know you're gone?"

"No. And he'll find out on his own. Okay?"

Bella agreed only to keep Mary's feet moving. "Can I ask you one thing, though?"

"Of course."

"Did he break it off or did you?"

Mary walked along in silence for a moment. "I did."

"Um, did you, by any chance . . . Were the two of you intimate?"

"Did we have sex?" Mary shifted the L.L. Bean bag to her other hand. "Yes, we did."

"When you made love, did you notice a kind of fragrance coming from his skin? Something like dark spices and—"

"Why are you asking me this?"

"I'm sorry. I don't mean to pry."

They were almost at the farmhouse when Mary murmured, "It was the most beautiful thing I've ever smelled."

Bella kept her curse to herself. No matter what Mary thought, the blond warrior would be coming for her. A bonded male did not let his mate go. Ever. And that was based on her experience with civilians.

She could only guess what a warrior would do if his female took off.

Rhage walked through each room in Mary's house. In her bath upstairs, he found the cabinet under the sink open.

Lined up inside there were extra toiletries, like bars of soap, tubes of toothpaste, deodorant. There were gaps in the neat rows, as if she'd taken some.

She was staying somewhere else, he thought, glancing out the window. If it was a hotel he was probably screwed, because she'd be smart enough to register under a different name. Maybe he could try her work—

He focused on the farmhouse way across the meadow. Lights twinkled inside.

Would she have gone to Bella's?

Rhage went downstairs and locked up. A split second later he materialized on Bella's front porch and pounded on the door. When Bella answered, the female just stepped aside as if she'd expected him.

"She's upstairs."

"Where?"

"Front bedroom."

Rhage took the stairs two at a time. Only one door was closed, and he didn't knock, just opened it wide. Light from the hall spilled into the room.

Mary was sound asleep on an enormous brass bed, wearing a sweater and a pair of blue jeans he recognized. A patchwork quilt had been pulled over her legs, and she was half on her stomach, half on her side. She looked utterly exhausted.

His first instinct was to take her into his arms.

He stayed right where he was.

"Mary." He kept his voice impersonal. "Mary. Wake up."

Her eyelashes fluttered, but then she only sighed and moved her head a little.

"Mary."

Oh, for fuck's sake.

He went over to the bed and bounced on the mattress with his hands. That got her attention. She shot up, eyes petrified until she saw him.

And then she just looked confused.

"What are you doing here?" She pushed her hair out of her face.

"Yeah, maybe you want to answer that first?"

"I'm not at home."

"No, you aren't. You're not where you need to be, either."

She settled back against the pillows, and he became acutely aware of the dark circles under her eyes, the pale line of her lips . . . and the fact that she wasn't fighting with him.

Don't ask, he told himself.

Ah, hell. "What happened this afternoon?"

"I just needed some time alone."

"I'm not talking about how you ditched Fritz. We'll get to that later. I want to know about the doc's."

"Oh, yeah. That."

He stared at her while she fiddled with the edge of the quilt. As she stayed silent, he wanted to scream. Throw things. Burn something down.

"Well?" he forced out.

"It wasn't that I thought you were unworthy."

What the hell was she talking about? Oh, yeah, that lovely little attending-her-when-she-was-ill conversation. Man, she was in full avoidance mode.

"How bad is it, Mary? And don't even think about lying to me."

Her eyes met his. "They want me to start chemo next week."

Rhage exhaled slowly. Well, if that didn't just peel the skin right off him.

He sat on the far edge of the bed and shut the door with his mind. "Will it work?"

"I think so. My doctor and I are going to meet again in a couple of days after she talks to some of her colleagues. The biggest question is how much more of the treatment I can handle, so they took blood to check my liver and kidneys. I told them I'll take as much as they can give me."

He rubbed his face with his palm. "Jesus Christ."

"I watched my mother die," she said softly. "It was awful. Seeing her lose her faculties and be in such pain. By the end she didn't look like herself, she didn't act like herself. She was gone except for the body that refused to quit its basic functions. I'm not saying that's where I'm headed, but it's going to be rough."

Goddamn, his chest hurt. "And you don't want me going through that?"

"No, I don't. I don't want that for either of us. I'd rather you remember me the way I am now. And I'd rather remember us the way we've been. I'm going to need some happy places to go."

"I want to be there for you."

"And I don't need that. I'm not going to have the energy to put up a front. And pain . . . pain makes people change."

It sure the hell did. He felt like he'd aged about a century since he'd met her.

"Oh, Rhage . . ." When her voice wavered, she cleared it sharply. And he despised her for needing to be in control. "I'm going to . . . miss you."

He glanced at her over his shoulder. He knew if he tried to hold her she'd bolt from the room, so he grabbed on to the edge of the mattress. And squeezed.

"What am I doing?" She laughed awkwardly. "I'm sorry to burden you with all this. I know you've moved on and everything."

"Moved on?" he ground out. "How you figure that?"

"The woman last night. Anyway—"

"What female?"

When she shook her head, he lost his temper. "God *damn* you, can you just answer my question without a fucking fight? Consider it a pity throw, a novelty. I'm leaving in a

316

few minutes anyway, so you won't have to worry about doing it again."

As her shoulders sagged he felt like hell for yelling at her. But before he could apologize, she said, "I'm talking about the woman you took to bed last night. I . . . I waited for you. I wanted to tell you I was sorry . . . I saw you go into your room with her. Look, I didn't bring this up to guilt you or something."

No, of course not. She didn't want anything from him. Not his love. Not his support. Not his guilt. Not even the sex.

He shook his head, his voice going flat. He was so tired of explaining himself to her, but he did it out of reflex. "That was the Directrix of the Chosen. We were talking about my feeding, Mary. I wasn't having sex with her."

He looked down at the floor. Then let go of the bed and put his head in his hands.

There was a silence. "I'm sorry, Rhage."

"Yeah. So am I."

He heard a hiccupping noise and shuffled his fingers so he could see her face through a hole. But she wasn't crying. No, not Mary. She was too strong for that.

He wasn't, though. He had tears in his eyes.

Rhage cleared his throat and blinked a lot. When he glanced over at her again, she was staring at him with a tenderness and sorrow that made him violent.

Oh, great. Now she was pitying him because he was all sloppy and shit. Man, if he didn't love her as much as he did, he would have hated her at this moment.

He stood up. And made damn sure his voice was as tough as she was when he spoke. "That alarm system in your house will be wired to us. If it gets triggered, I'll"— he corrected himself—"one of us will come running. Vishous will contact you here when it's up and rolling."

As the silence stretched, he shrugged. "So . . . bye."

He walked out the door and did not allow himself to look back.

When he got downstairs, he found Bella in the living room. The instant the female saw his face, her eyes popped wide. Clearly he looked as god-awful as he felt.

"Thanks," he said, though he wasn't sure what he was thanking her for. "And just so you know, the Brotherhood is going to do drive-bys on your house. Even after she leaves."

"That's very kind of you."

He nodded and didn't dawdle. At this point it was all he could do to get himself out the door without splitting wide-open and howling like a baby.

As he walked away from the house and down the lawn a little, he had no idea what to do or where to go. He probably should call Tohr, find out where the other brothers were, link up with them.

Instead he stopped dead in his tracks. Ahead, the moon was rising just above the tree line, and it was full, a fat, luminescent disk in the cold, cloudless night. He extended his arm toward it and squeezed one eye shut. Angling his line of sight, he positioned the lunar glow in the cradle of his palm and held the apparition with care.

Dimly, he heard a pounding noise coming from inside of Bella's. Some kind of rhythmic beat.

Rhage glanced behind him as it got louder.

The front door flew open, and Mary shot out of the house, jumping off the porch, not even bothering with the steps to the ground. She ran over the frost-laden grass in her bare feet and threw herself at him, grabbing on to his neck with both arms. She held him so tightly his spine cracked.

She was sobbing. Bawling. Crying so hard her whole body was shaking.

He didn't ask any questions, just wrapped himself around her.

"I'm not okay," she said hoarsely between breaths. "Rhage . . . I'm not okay."

He closed his eyes and held on tight.

THIRTY-FIVE

O lifted the mesh cover off the sewer pipe and shined a flashlight down into the hole. The young male inside was the one they'd caught the night before with the truck. The thing was alive, having survived the day. The storage facility had worked beautifully.

The center's door swung open. Mr. X walked in, all pounding boots and sharp eyes. "Did it live?"

O nodded and put the mesh cover back into place. "Yeah."

"Good."

"I was just going to take him out again."

"Not right now, you don't. I want you to visit these members." Mr. X handed over a piece of paper with seven addresses on it. "E-mail check-ins are efficient, but proving somewhat unreliable. I'm getting confirmations from these Betas, but when I talk to their squadrons, I hear reports that no one has seen them in days or longer."

Instinct told O to step carefully. Mr. X all but accused him of killing Betas in the park, and now the *Fore-lesser* wanted him to go check on them?

"There a problem, Mr. O?"

"No. No, problem."

"And another thing. I have three new recruits I'm bringing on. Their initiations are taking place over the next week and a half. Do you want to come? Watching from the sidelines provides quite a show."

O shook his head. "I'd better stay focused here."

Mr. X smiled. "Worried that the Omega might get distracted by your charms?"

"The Omega is not distracted by anything."

"You're so wrong about that. He can't stop talking about you."

O knew there was a good chance Mr. X was fucking with his head, but his body didn't have the same confidence. His knees loosened and he broke out in a cold sweat.

"I'll start on the list now," he said, going for his jacket and keys.

Mr. X's eyes glinted. "You do that, son, you run right along. I'm going to play with our visitor a little."

"Whatever you like. Sensei."

"So this is home now," Mary murmured when Rhage shut the door to their bedroom.

She felt his arms come around her waist, and he pulled her back against his body. As she glanced at the clock, she realized they'd left Bella's only an hour and a half ago, but her whole life had changed.

"Yeah, this is your home. Our home."

The three boxes lined up against the wall were full of her clothes, her favorite books, some DVDs, a few photos. With Vishous, Butch, and Fritz showing up to help her, it hadn't taken long to pack up some things, get them into V's Escalade, and be driven back to the mansion. Later she and Rhage would return to finish the job. And in the morning she was going to call the law office and quit. She was also getting a real estate agent to sell the barn.

God, she'd really gone and done it. Moved in with Rhage and given up on her old life completely.

"I should unpack."

Rhage took her hands and pulled her in the direction of the bed. "I want you to rest. You look too tired to even be standing."

While she stretched out, he took off his trench coat and removed his dagger holster and his gun belt. He eased down next to her, creating a dip in the mattress that sucked her right against him. All the lamps went out at once, the room plunging into ink.

"You sure you're ready for all this?" she said as her eyes adjusted to the ambient glow from the windows. "For all my . . . stuff?"

"Don't make me use the F-word again."

She laughed. "I won't. It's just—"

"Mary, I love you. I'm more than ready for all your stuff."

She put her hand on his face and they were quiet for a time, just breathing together.

She was on the verge of falling asleep when he said, "Mary, about the arrangements for me to feed. While we were at your house, I called on the Chosen. Now that you're back with me, I'll need to use them."

She stiffened. But hell, if she was going to be with a vampire, and he couldn't live off her blood, they were going to have to deal with the problem somehow.

"When will you do it?"

"A female is supposed to be coming tonight, and, as I said before, I'd like you to be with me. If you'd be comfortable with that."

What would it look like? she wondered. Would he hold the woman in his arms and drink from her neck? God, even if he didn't have sex with her, Mary wasn't sure she could watch that.

He kissed her hand. "Trust me. It'll be better this way."

"If I don't, ah, if I can't handle it—"

"I won't force you to watch. It's just . . . there's an unavoidable intimacy to it, and I think you and I will both be more comfortable if you were there. That way you know exactly what's involved. There's nothing hidden or shady about it."

She nodded. "All right."

He took a deep breath. "It's a fact of life I can't change."

Mary ran her hand down his chest. "You know, even though it's a little frightening, I wish it were me."

"Oh, Mary, so do I."

John checked his watch. Tohrment was coming for him in five minutes, so it was time to head downstairs. He grabbed his suitcase with both hands and headed for the door. He prayed he wouldn't meet the pale man on the way or while he waited, but he wanted to meet Tohrment outside. It felt more equal, somehow.

When he got out to the curb, he looked up at the two windows he'd stared out of for so many hours. He was leaving the mattress and the barbell set behind, as well as his security deposit and last month's rent for breaking his lease. He was going to have to pop back inside for his bike after Tohrment came, but other than that, he was free of the place.

He looked down the street, wondering which direction the man would come from. And what kind of car he drove. And where he lived. And who he was married to.

Shivering in the cold, John rechecked his watch. Nine o'clock on the dot.

A single light flared down to the right. He was pretty sure Tohrment wouldn't use a motorcycle to pick him up. But the fantasy of roaring off into the night was a good one.

As the Harley growled by, he looked across the street at the Suicide Prevention Hotline's offices. Mary had missed her Friday- and Saturday-night shifts as well, and he truly hoped she was just taking a vacation. As soon as he was settled, he would go see her again and make sure she was okay.

Except . . . wow, he had no clue where he was going. He was assuming he'd stay in the area, but who knew? Maybe he was going far away. Just imagine that, getting out of Caldwell. God, he'd like to make a fresh start.

And he could always find a way to get to Mary, even if he had to take a bus.

Two more cars and a truck went by.

It had been so easy to pull out of his pathetic existence. No one at Moe's cared that he was leaving without notice because busboys were a dime a dozen. And it went without saying that nobody in his building would miss him. Likewise, his address book was clean as a whistle, no friends, no family to call.

Actually, he didn't even have an address book. And how lame was that?

John glanced down at himself, thinking how pitiful he must look. His sneakers were so dirty, the white parts had turned gray. His clothes were clean, but the jeans were two years old, and the button-down shirt, the best one he had, looked like a Goodwill reject. He didn't even have a jacket because his parka had been stolen last week from Moe's and he was going to have to save up before he could buy another one.

He wished he looked better.

Headlights swung quickly around the corner off Trade Street and then flashed upward, as if the car's driver were stomping on the accelerator. Which was not good. In this neighborhood, anyone barrel-assing along was usually running from the cops or something worse.

John stepped behind a dented mailbox, trying to get real inconspicuous, but the black Range Rover skidded to a stop in front of him. Darkened windows. Serious chrome rims. And G-Unit was banging inside, the rap music thumping loud enough to be heard around the block.

John grabbed his suitcase and headed for his building. Even if he ran into the pale man, it would be safer inside the lobby than anywhere near the drug dealer who sported that Rover. He was hustling for the door when the music fell silent.

"You ready, son?"

John turned at the sound of Tohrment's voice. The man was coming around the hood of the car, and in the shadows he was all menace, a hulking figure that sane folks ran from.

"Son? You good to go?"

As Tohrment stepped into the weak light of a streetlamp, John's eyes latched onto the man's face. God, he'd forgotten how frightening the guy looked with that military-cut hair and that hard jaw.

Maybe this was a bad idea, John thought. A choice made out of fear of one thing that only got him deeper into another kind of trouble. He didn't even know where he was going. And kids like him could end up in the river after they got into a car like that. With a man like this.

As if he sensed John's indecision, Tohrment leaned back against the Rover and crossed his feet at the ankles.

"I don't want you to feel forced, son. But I'll tell you, my *shellan*'s cooked up a good meal, and I'm hungry. Maybe you come, you eat with us, you see the house. You can check us out. And we can even leave your stuff here. How's that sound?"

The voice was quiet, even. Nonthreatening. But would the guy really pull out the badass if he wanted to get John in the car?

A cell phone went off. Tohrment reached inside his leather jacket and flipped it open.

"Yeah. Hey, no, I'm right here with him." A small smile broke the line of the man's lips. "We're thinking it over. Yeah, I'll tell him. Uh-huh. Okay. I will. Yeah, I'll do that, too. Wellsie, I . . . I know. Look, I didn't mean to leave it out—I won't do it again. I promise. No . . . Yes, I really . . . Uh-huh. I'm sorry, *leelan*."

It was the wife, John thought. And she was giving this tough guy a tongue-lashing. And the man was taking it.

"Okay. I love you. Bye." Tohrment flipped the phone closed and put it in his pocket. When he focused on John again, he clearly respected his wife enough not to roll his eyes and make some macho, shithead comment about pesky women. "Wellsie says she's really looking forward to meeting you. She's hoping you'll stay with us."

Well . . . okay, then.

Listening to his instincts, which told him Tohrment represented safety regardless of what he looked like, John humped his luggage over to the car.

"This all you have?"

John flushed and nodded.

"You got nothing to be embarrassed about, son," Tohrment said softly. "Not when you're with me."

The man reached out and took the suitcase like it weighed nothing, swinging it casually into the backseat.

As Tohrment went to the driver's side, John realized he'd forgotten the bike. He tapped on the Rover's hood to get the man's attention; then he pointed to the building and held up his index finger.

"You need a minute?"

John nodded and shot upstairs to his apartment. He had his bike, and was leaving the keys on the counter, when he paused and looked around. The reality of getting away from the studio made him recognize the squalor of the place. But still, it had been his for a short while, the best he could afford with what little he had. On impulse, he took a pen out of his back pocket, opened one of the flimsy cabinets, and wrote his name and the date on the wall inside.

Then he led his bike out into the hall, shut the door, and moved quickly down the stairwell.

THIRTY-SIX

"Mary? Mary, wake up. She's here."

Mary felt her shoulder get nudged, and when she opened her eyes Rhage was staring down at her. He'd changed into some kind of white outfit, long-sleeved with loose pants.

She sat up, trying to pull it together. "Can I have a minute?"

"Absolutely."

She went into the bathroom and rinsed off her face. With cold water dripping from her chin, she stared at her reflection. Her lover was about to drink blood. In front of her.

And that wasn't even the weirdest part. She felt inadequate because what was feeding him wasn't hers.

Not about to get pulled into that mental tailspin, she picked up a towel and dried off with a good scrub. There was no time to change out of her blue jeans and sweater. And nothing else she really wanted to wear, at any rate.

As she came out, Rhage was taking off his watch.

"You want me to hold that?" she asked, remembering the last time she'd babysat the Rolex.

He walked over and pressed the heavy weight into her palm. "Kiss me."

She got up on her tiptoes as he leaned down. Their mouths met for a moment.

"Come on." He took her hand and led her out into the hall. When she looked confused, he said, "I don't want to do it in our bedroom. That's our space."

He took her around the balcony to another guest room. When he opened the door, they went inside together.

Mary smelled roses first and then saw the woman in the corner. Her lush body was draped in a white wrap-around gown, and her strawberry-blond hair was coiled up on her head. With the low, wide neckline of the dress and the chignon, her neck was as exposed as possible.

She smiled and bowed, speaking in that unfamiliar language.

"No," Rhage said. "In English. We do this in English."

"Of course, warrior." The woman's voice was high and pure, like a songbird's call. Her eyes, pale green and lovely, lingered on Rhage's face. "I am pleased to serve you."

Mary shifted, trying to quell the urge to defend her turf. *Serve him?*

"What is your name, Chosen?" Rhage asked.

"I am Layla." She bowed again. As she righted herself, her eyes traveled up Rhage's body.

"This is Mary." He put his arm around her shoulders. "She is my . . ."

"Girlfriend," Mary said sharply.

Rhage's mouth twitched. "She is my mate."

"Of course, warrior." The woman bowed again, this time toward Mary. When she lifted her face, she smiled warmly. "Mistress, it is my pleasure to serve you as well."

Fine, good, Mary thought. *Then how about dragging your skinny ass out of here and making sure your replacement is an ugly, two-toothed gorgon in a muumuu.*

"Where would you like me?" Layla asked.

Rhage glanced around the room before focusing on the luxurious canopy bed. "There."

Mary hid her wince. Oh, that was so not her first choice.

Layla went over as told, that silky dress swirling behind her. She sat down on the satin duvet, but, when she shifted her legs up, Rhage shook his head.

"No. Stay sitting."

Layla frowned, but didn't argue. She smiled again as he took a step forward.

"Come on," he said, pulling on Mary's hand.

"This is close enough."

He kissed her and went over to the woman, sinking to his knees in front of her. When her hands went to her gown as if she were going to undo it, Rhage stopped her.

"I drink from the wrist," he said. "And you are not to touch me."

Dismay played over Layla's features, widening her eyes. This time, when she inclined her head, it seemed out of shame, not deference. "I have been properly cleansed for your use. You may inspect me, should you wish."

Mary clamped a hand over her mouth. That this woman saw herself as nothing more than an object to be handled was appalling.

Rhage shook his head, clearly uncomfortable with the answer, too.

"Do you wish for another of us?" Layla said softly.

"I don't want any of this," he muttered.

"But why did you call upon the Chosen if you had no intention of availing yourself?"

"I didn't think it would be this difficult."

"Difficult?" Layla's voice deepened. "I beg your pardon, but I fail to see how I have inconvenienced you."

"It's not that, and I mean no offense. My Mary . . . she's human, and I cannot drink from her."

"So she will join us only in the pleasures of the bed. It will be my honor to administer to her there."

"Ah, yeah, that's not . . . She's not here to . . . Ah, the three of us are not going to—" Good lord, Rhage was blushing. "Mary is here because I will have no other female, but I must feed, do you understand?" Rhage cursed and got to his feet. "This isn't going to work. I don't feel right about this."

Layla's eyes flashed. "You say you must feed, but you are unable to take her vein. I am here. I am willing. It would please me to give to you what you need. Why should you feel uncomfortable? Or perhaps you want to wait longer? Until the hunger consumes you and the danger is upon your mate?"

Rhage shoved his hand into his hair. Grabbed a chunk. Pulled at it.

Layla crossed her legs, the gown splitting open to her thigh. She was a picture, sitting on that lush bed, so proper and yet so incredibly sexual.

"Have the traditions faded from your mind, warrior? I know it has been a long time, but how can you feel unsettled about my attending you? It is one of my duties, and I find great honor in it." Layla shook her head. "Or shall I say, I used to. *We* used to. The Chosen have suffered these centuries. None of the Brotherhood call upon us anymore, we are unwanted, unused. When you finally reached out, we were so pleased."

"I'm sorry." Rhage glanced at Mary. "But I cannot—"

"It is her that you worry about most, is it not?" Layla murmured. "You worry what she will think if she sees you at my wrist."

"She is not used to our ways."

The woman held her hand out. "Mistress, come sit with me so he can look upon you while he drinks, so he can feel your touch and smell you, so that you will be a part of this. Otherwise he will refuse me, and then where will the two of you be?" When there was only silence and Mary stayed put, the woman motioned impatiently. "Surely you realize he will not drink otherwise. You must do this for him."

"So this is it," Tohrment said as he parked the Rover in front of a sleek, modern house.

They were in a section of town John was unfamiliar with, where the houses were set back from the street and far away from each other. There were lots of black iron gates and rolling lawns, and the trees weren't just maples and oaks, but fancy kinds, the names of which he didn't know.

John closed his eyes, wishing he weren't wearing a shirt that had a missing button. Maybe if he kept his arm around his stomach, Tohrment's wife wouldn't notice.

God . . . what if they had kids? Who'd make fun of him . . .

Do you have children? John signed without thinking.

"What's that, son?"

John fumbled in his pockets for some folded-up sheets of paper. When he found his Bic, he wrote quickly and turned the paper around.

Tohrment went very still and looked up at his house, that hard face tensing as if he were afraid of what was inside.

"We might have a child. In a little over a year. My Wellsie's pregnant, but our females have a very difficult time in childbirth." Tohrment shook his head, lips growing tight. "As you get older, you'll learn to fear pregnancy. It's a goddamn *shellan* robber. Frankly, I'd rather have no kids than lose her." The man cleared his throat. "Anyway, let's head in. We'll eat, and then I'll take you on a full tour of the training center."

Tohrment hit the garage door opener and got out. While John tugged the suitcase from the backseat, the man took the ten-speed out of the rear. They walked into the garage and Tohrment flipped on the lights.

"I'm going to leave your bike here against the wall, okay?"

John nodded and looked around. There was a Volvo station wagon and . . . a 1960s-era Corvette Sting Ray convertible.

John could only stare.

Tohrment laughed softly. "Why don't you go over and say hello to her?"

John dropped his suitcase and walked up to the Vette

in a daze of love. He reached out, wanting to stroke the smooth metal, but then took his hand back.

"No, touch her. She likes the attention."

Oh, the car was beautiful. A shiny, metallic ice blue. And the top was down so he could see inside. The white seats were gorgeous. The steering wheel gleamed. The dashboard was all dials. He was willing to bet it sounded like thunder when the engine was started. Probably smelled like fresh oil when you put the heater on.

He glanced up at Tohrment, thinking his eyes were going pop. He wished he could talk, just to tell the man how special the car was.

"Yeah, she's a looker, isn't she? Restored her myself. I'm about to put her up on blocks for the winter, but maybe we'll take her to the center tonight, how about that? It's chilly, but we can pile on the coats."

John beamed. And kept on grinning as the man's heavy arm came around his thin shoulders.

"Let's feed you, son."

Tohrment picked up the suitcase and they headed for the door John's bike was next to. As they walked into the house, the smell of Mexican food wafted, spicy and rich.

John's nose was thrilled. His stomach rolled. Holy hell, he wasn't going to be able to eat any of that kind of stuff. What if Tohrment's wife got upset . . . ?

A stunning redhead stepped into their paths. She was easily six feet tall, had skin as fine as white china, and was wearing a loose yellow dress. Her hair was just incredible, a flowing river of waves falling from the crown of her head way down her back.

John put an arm around his middle, hiding the buttonhole.

"How's my *hellren?*" the woman said, lifting her mouth for Tohrment's kiss.

"I'm good, *leelan*. Wellsie, this is John Matthew. John, this is my *shellan*."

"Welcome, John." She offered her hand. "I'm so happy you'll be staying with us."

John shook her palm and quickly put his arm back in place.

"Come on, boys. Dinner's ready."

The kitchen was all cherry cupboards, granite countertops, and glossy black appliances. A round glass-and-iron table set with three places was in a windowed alcove. Everything looked brand new.

"You two go sit," Wellsie said. "I'll bring the food."

He looked to the sink. It was white porcelain with a graceful brass faucet rising up high.

"You want to wash your hands?" she said. "Go right ahead."

There was a bar of soap in a little dish, and he was careful to clean everywhere, even under his fingernails. After he and Tohrment sat down, Wellsie came over with plates and bowls heaping with food. Enchiladas. Quesadillas. She went back for more.

"Now, that's what I'm talking about," Tohrment said as he served himself, piling his plate high. "Wellsie, this looks fantastic."

John eyed the display. There was nothing he could stomach on the table. Maybe he could just tell them he ate earlier . . .

Wellsie put a bowl down in front of him. It was filled with white rice that had some kind of pale sauce on it. The aroma was delicate, but appealing.

"This will ease your stomach. It's got ginger in it," she said. "And the sauce is high in fat, which will help you put on some weight. For your dessert, I've made banana pudding. It goes down easy and has lots of calories in it."

John stared at the food. She knew. She knew exactly what he couldn't eat. And what he could.

The bowl in front of him got blurry. He blinked quickly. Then frantically.

Squeezing his mouth shut, he tightened his hands in his lap until his knuckles cracked. He was *not* going to cry like a child. He refused to disgrace himself like that.

Wellsie's voice was quiet. "Tohr? You want to give us a minute?"

There was the sound of a chair moving back, and then John felt a solid hand on his shoulder. The weight lifted and heavy footfalls sounded out of the room.

"You can let go now. He's gone."

John closed his eyes and sagged, tears rolling down his cheeks.

Wellsie pulled a chair over to him. With slow, sweeping motions, she rubbed his back.

He felt so blessed that Tohrment had come and found him just in the nick of time. That this house he was going to stay in was so nice and clean. That Wellsie had made him something special, something his stomach could tolerate.

That they'd both let him have his pride.

John felt himself get pulled to one side and then he was being hugged. Rocked.

Parched, he soaked up the kindness.

A little later he lifted his head and felt a napkin get put in his hand. He wiped his face, threw his shoulders back, and looked at Wellsie.

She smiled. "Better?"

He nodded.

"I'm going to go get Tohr, okay?"

John nodded again and picked up a fork. When he tried the rice, he moaned. It didn't have much of a taste, but when it hit his stomach, instead of spasms he felt a wonderful loosening in his gut. It was as if the stuff had been specifically calibrated for what his digestive system needed.

He couldn't bear to look up as Tohrment and Wellsie

sat back down, and he was relieved when they started talking about normal stuff. Errands. Friends. Plans.

He finished all the rice and looked over at the stove, wondering if there was more. Before he could ask, Wellsie took his bowl and brought it back refilled. He ate three servings. And some of the banana pudding. By the time he put his spoon down, he realized it was the first time in his life he'd ever been full.

He took a deep breath, leaned back in the chair, and closed his eyes, listening to the deep tones of Tohrment's voice and Wellsie's dulcet replies.

It was like a lullaby, he thought. Especially as they slipped into a language he didn't recognize.

"John?" Tohrment said.

He tried to sit up, but was so sleepy all he could do was open his eyes.

"How about I take you to your room so you can crash. We'll go to the center in a couple of days, okay? Give you a little time to adjust."

John nodded, thinking he didn't feel up to much more than a really good night's sleep.

Still, he carried his dish to the sink, rinsed it out, and put it in the dishwasher. When he went back to the table to help clear, Wellsie shook her head.

"No, I'll take care of this. You go with Tohr."

John got out his pen and paper. When he was finished writing, he turned the words to face Wellsie.

She laughed. "You are very welcome. And yes, I'll show you how to make it."

John nodded. And then narrowed his eyes.

Wellsie was smiling so widely that he saw some of her teeth. Two in the front were very long.

She closed her lips, as if catching herself. "Just go to sleep, John, and don't worry about anything. There'll be plenty of time to think tomorrow."

He looked over at Tohrment, whose face was remote.

And that was when he knew. Knew without being told. He'd always been aware that he was different, and finally he was going to know why: these two lovely people were going to tell him what he was.

John thought of his dreams. Of the biting and the blood.

He had a feeling they weren't his imagination.

They were his memories.

THIRTY-SEVEN

Mary stared at the Chosen's outstretched hand and then looked at Rhage. His face was grim, his body tense.

"Will you not help him?" Layla asked.

Taking a deep breath, Mary went forward and placed her palm against the one extended toward her.

Layla tugged her down and smiled a little. "I know you are nervous, but worry not, it will be over quickly. Then I will go and it will just be you and him. You can hold each other and banish me from your thoughts."

"How can you stand to be . . . used like this?" Mary said.

Layla frowned. "I am providing what is needed, not being used. And how can I not give to the Brotherhood? They protect us so that we may live. They give us our daughters so that our traditions may continue . . . or at least, they used to. Of late our numbers dwindle, because the brothers no longer come to us. We are in desperate need of children, but by law we may breed only with members of the Brotherhood." She glanced up at Rhage. "That is why I was selected tonight. I am close to my needing, and we had hoped that you would take me."

"I will not lie with you," Rhage said softly.

"I know. And still I will serve you."

Mary closed her eyes, imagining the kind of child Rhage could give a woman. As her hand found her flat stomach, she tried to picture growing swollen and heavy. The joy would be overwhelming; she was quite sure. Because the pain of knowing that would never happen was tremendous.

"So, warrior, what will you do? Will you take what

I am pleased to give? Or will you run the risk of hurting your mate?"

As Rhage hesitated, Mary realized the only solution they had was right in front of him. He needed to do this.

"Drink," she commanded him.

He met her eyes. "Mary?"

"I want you to feed. Now."

"Are you sure?"

"Yes."

There was a heartbeat of frozen silence. Then he dropped to the floor in front of Layla again. As he leaned forward, the woman lifted her sleeve and laid her arm down on her thigh. The veins on the inside of her wrist were pale blue underneath white skin.

Rhage reached for Mary's hand as he opened his mouth. His fangs elongated, growing three times as long as usual. With a slight hissing sound, he bent down and put his mouth on Layla. The woman jerked and then relaxed.

Rhage's thumb stroked over Mary's wrist, his hand warm against hers. She couldn't see exactly what he was doing, but the subtle movement of his head suggested sucking. When he squeezed her palm, she returned the gesture weakly. The whole experience was too foreign, and he was right: there was a shocking intimacy to it.

"Stroke him," Layla whispered. "He's about to stop, and it's too soon. He hasn't taken enough."

Numbly, Mary reached out and put her free hand on his head. "It's all right. I'm fine."

When Rhage made a movement to sit back, as if he knew she was lying, she thought of everything he was willing to go through for her, everything he'd *been* through for her.

Mary held his head in place, pushing down. "Take your time. Really, everything's okay."

As she squeezed his palm, his shoulders eased up and he moved closer to her, shifting his body around. She parted her legs so that he could settle between them, his chest resting on her thigh, his broad back dwarfing her. She ran her hand through his blond hair, its thick, smooth waves sinking in between her fingers.

And all of a sudden, the whole thing wasn't that weird.

Even though she could feel the pulls he was taking on Layla's vein, Rhage's body against her own was familiar, and the rubbing on her wrist told her he was thinking of her while he was feeding. She looked over at Layla. The woman was watching him, but the concentration on her face was clinical.

Mary remembered what he'd said about the drinking: that if he bit her, she would feel his pleasure. Clearly there was none being exchanged between him and the Chosen. Both of their bodies were still, calm. Not in the throes of any kind of passion.

Layla's eyes shifted up and she smiled. "He's doing well. Just another minute or so."

Then it was done. Rhage lifted his head slightly and turned to Mary's body, easing into the cradle of her hips, putting his arms around her. He rested his face on her thigh and, though she couldn't see his expression, his muscles were slack, his breathing deep and even.

She glanced at Layla's wrist. There were two puncture wounds and a red blush, only a little trickle of blood.

"He'll need a little time to collect himself," Layla said as she licked herself and then rolled down her sleeve. She got to her feet.

Mary rubbed Rhage's back while looking at the woman. "Thank you."

"You are so very welcome."

"Will you come again when he needs you?"

"The two of you would want me? Me, specifically?"

Mary steeled herself against the woman's thrill. "Yes, I, ah, I think we would."

Layla absolutely glowed, her eyes alive with happiness.

"Mistress, it would be my honor." She bowed. "He knows how to summon me. Call upon me at any time."

The woman left the room with a spring in her step.

As the door shut, Mary bent down and kissed Rhage's shoulder. He stirred. Lifted his head a little. Then he rubbed his mouth with his palm, as if he didn't want her to see any blood that might be on him.

When he looked up at her, his eyelids were low, his bright-teal gaze a little fuzzy.

"Hi," she said, stroking his hair back.

He smiled that special smile of his, the one that made him look like an angel. "Hi."

She touched his lower lip with her thumb. "Did she taste good?" When he hesitated, she said, "Be honest with me."

"She did. But I would rather it have been you, and I thought of you the entire time. I imagined it was you."

Mary leaned down and licked his mouth. As his eyes flared in surprise, she slid her tongue inside of him and caught a hint of the lingering flavor, a sweet red wine.

"Good," she murmured against his lips. "I want you to think of me when you do that."

He put his hands on the sides of her neck, his thumbs right over her veins. "Always."

His mouth found hers and she grabbed onto his shoulders, urging him closer. As he pulled up the bottom of her sweater, she lifted her arms so he could get it off her and then let herself fall back on the bed. He took off her pants and her panties and then did away with his own clothes.

He loomed over her, picking her up with one arm and putting her farther back on the bed. His thigh came between her legs and then his body pressed hers into the mattress, that heavy arousal running up the very center of her. She undulated against him, stroking herself, stroking him.

His mouth moved urgently as they kissed, but he entered her slowly, parting her gently, stretching her, joining them together. He was thick and hard and heavenly and he moved languidly, deeply. That delicious dark scent came out of his skin, saturating her.

"I will have no other," he said against her throat. "I will take none but you."

Mary wrapped her legs around his hips, trying to have him so far inside that he could stay with her forever.

John followed Tohrment through the house. There were a lot of rooms, and all the furniture and decorations were really nice, really old. He paused by a painting of a mountain scene. A little brass nameplate on the gilt frame read Frederic Church. He wondered who that was and decided the guy was awfully good at what he did.

Down at the end of a hallway, Tohrment opened a door and turned on a light. "I put your suitcase in here already."

John walked inside. The walls and ceiling were painted dark blue and there was a big bed with a sleek headboard and lots of fat pillows. There was also a desk and a bureau. And a set of sliding glass doors that opened onto a terrace.

"Bathroom's through here." Tohrment turned on another light.

John put his head in and saw a whole lot of dark-blue marble. The shower was glassed in and . . . wow, there were four heads for the water to come out.

"If you need anything Wellsie is here, and I'll be back around four A.M. We go downstairs about that time every night. If you need us during the day, just pick up any phone and dial pound one. We'd be happy to see you anytime. Oh, and we have two *doggen*, or staff, who help out around here, Sal and Regine. Both of them know you're with us now. They show up around five-ish. If you need to go out, just ask them to take you."

John went over to the bed and touched a pillowcase. It was so soft, he could barely feel it.

"You're going to be fine here, son. It might take some getting used to, but you're going to be fine."

John looked across the room. Shoring up his courage, he walked over to Tohrment and opened his mouth. Then he pointed up to the man.

"You sure you want to do this now?" Tohrment murmured.

When John nodded, Tohrment slowly parted his lips. And bared a set of fangs.

Oh . . . man. Oh . . .

John swallowed and put his fingers to his own mouth.

"Yeah, you're going to get them, too. Sometime in the next couple of years." Tohrment crossed the room and sat on the bed, plugging his elbows into his knees. "We go through the change around age twenty-five. After that you're going to need to drink to survive. And I'm not talking about milk, son."

John cocked his eyebrows, wondering from whom.

"We'll find you a female to get you through the change, and I'll tell you what to expect. It's no party, but, once you have it behind you, you'll be so strong, you'll think it was all worth it."

John's eyes flared as he measured Tohrment. Abruptly he spread his hands apart horizontally and lengthwise, then put his thumb to his own chest.

"Yeah, you'll be my size, too."

John mouthed the words *get out*.

"Really. That's why the transition is a bitch. Your body goes through a big change in a period of hours. Afterward you're going to have to relearn things, how to walk, how to move." Tohr looked down at himself. "These bodies of ours are hard to control at first."

John absently rubbed his chest, where the circular scar was. Tohrment's eyes tracked the movement.

"I have to be honest with you, son. There's a lot we don't know about you. For one thing, there's no telling how much of us is in your blood. And we have no clue what line you descend from. As for that scar, I can't explain it. You say you've had the thing all your life, and I believe you, but that marking is given, not something we're born with."

John took out his paper and wrote, *Everyone has it?*

"No. Just my brothers and me. That's why Bella brought you to us."

Who are you? John wrote.

"The Black Dagger Brotherhood. We're warriors, son. We fight to keep the race alive, and that's what we're going to train you to do. The other males in your class will become soldiers, but you, with that marking, you may end up being one of us. I don't know." Tohrment rubbed the back of his neck. "Sometime soon I'm going to take you to meet Wrath. He's the boss in charge, our king. I'd also like to have you checked out by our doctor, Havers. He might be able to get a read on your bloodline. Would that be cool with you?"

John nodded.

"I'm glad we found you, John. If we hadn't you'd have died, because there would have been no one to give you what you needed."

John went over and sat down next to Tohrment.

"You got anything you want to ask me?"

John nodded, but couldn't marshal his thoughts into any coherent pattern.

"Tell you what, you think on it tonight. We'll talk more tomorrow."

John was dimly aware that his head was nodding in response. Tohrment got up and walked to the door.

From out of nowhere a bullet of panic ricocheted through John's chest. The idea of being alone seemed terrifying, even though he was in a pretty house, with kind people, in a very safe area. He just felt . . . so very small.

Tohrment's shitkickers came into his line of sight.

"Hey, John, maybe I'll hang for a while in here with you. You like that? We can channel surf."

Thank you, he signed without thinking. *I feel a little weird.*

"I'll take that as a yes." Tohrment propped himself up on the pillows, grabbed the remote, and turned on the TV. "Vishous, one of my brothers, wired this house. I think we get about seven hundred stations on this thing. What do you like to watch?"

John shrugged and shuffled back against the headboard.

Tohrment clicked around until he found *Terminator 2*. "You like?"

John whistled softly through his teeth and nodded.

"Yeah, me, too. This is a classic, and Linda Hamilton is hot."

THIRTY-EIGHT

Rhage slept late, very late, and what woke him up was bad news. The restlessness, the awful itch, was alive inside of him again. The Scribe Virgin's reprieve was over. The beast was back.

He opened his eyes and saw Mary's hair on his pillow. And the curve of her neck. And her naked back.

He broke out in a sweat, an erection popping up quick as a heartbeat.

He thought of the way they had come together after the feeding. And then again when they'd returned to their room. He'd reached for her twice more during the day, feeling bad about making the demands because he'd been all over her so much. Still, each time she'd smiled up at him and welcomed him inside, even though she must have been exhausted and probably a little sore.

And he wanted her again right now, but with a pounding need that was different than he'd felt before. This hunger was savage, as if he'd never had her at all or hadn't seen her for months. As he fought the urge, his hands curled up on themselves, fingers tingling, skin tightening. He was completely strung out, the very bones in him vibrating.

He got out of bed and headed for the shower. By the time he came back, he'd regained some control, but then he saw that Mary had kicked the covers off of herself. She was gloriously naked as she lay on her stomach, her beautiful ass a temptation that ate at him.

"Can I get you something from the kitchen?" he asked hoarsely.

"Sleep," she murmured, turning over onto her back. Her pink-tipped breasts tightened as the air hit them.

Oh, sweet Jesus . . . Wait, something was off here. Her face was flushed like she had windburn, and her legs were sawing on top of the mattress.

He went over and put his hand on her forehead. She was hot and dry.

"Mary, I think you have a fever."

"Low-level. Not unusual."

Fear put a chill on his craving to take her. "You want me to get you some aspirin?"

"Just need to sleep through it."

"Do you want me to stay with you?"

She opened her eyes. He hated the dull look in them. "No, this happens. Honestly, I'm all right. I just need to sleep it off."

Rhage stayed with her awhile longer and then pulled on some black nylon warm-ups and a T-shirt. Before he left, he stared at her. He could barely stand her having a slight fever. What the hell was it going to be like when she got really sick?

Havers. He hadn't heard back from Havers yet, and the doctor should have had access to her files for long enough. Rhage picked up his cell phone and went out in the hall.

The conversation with the doctor didn't last long, because there was nothing the male could do for her. As vampires did not get cancer, he hadn't focused on the disease and neither had any of his colleagues.

Rhage was about to hang up when the other male said, "Forgive me, sire, as I do not wish to pry. But have you . . . are you aware of how extensive her treatments were?"

"I know there were a lot of them."

"Do you realize how intense they were, though? If the leukemia has returned, her options may well be limited—"

"Thanks for looking at her records. I appreciate it."

346

Like he needed confirmation of how serious the situation was?

"Wait . . . Please know that I am here to help in any way I can. Even though I cannot be of aid with regard to the chemotherapy, we have the drug formularies for a lot of the pain medications and various other things she was on before. I can help ease her and watch over her, even though she will receive her treatments in a human hospital. You must call me."

"I will. And . . . thanks, Havers."

After he hung up, he went to Wrath's study, but the room was empty so he turned to go downstairs. Maybe Wrath and Beth were grabbing something to eat.

From out of thin air, a wall of leather topped with a head of long black hair materialized in front of him. Wrath's sunglasses were silver wraparounds today.

"Looking for me?" the king said.

"Hey. Yeah. Mary's moved in. Permanently."

"So I heard. Fritz said she brought some stuff with her."

"Uh-huh. Listen, do you mind if I have a little shindig here tonight? I want Mary to see her friend Bella, and I was thinking the Brotherhood could play nice. You know, suit up and all. Maybe Wellsie could come, too. Mary has me, but she needs to be around some other folks. I don't want her feeling like she's isolated."

"Damn good idea. Beth wanted us to go to the city tonight, but—"

"Don't change your plans. This is just real casual."

"Well, my *shellan* was looking forward to getting away. She kind of likes having me to herself. And I, ah, I really like it when she has me that way, you feel me?"

Rhage smiled a little as Wrath's body released a blast of heat. "Yeah. I do."

There was a pause. The king said, "My brother, is there something else?"

"Ah, yeah. Mary's going to be very ill soon. I'll go out nightly with the brothers for as long as I can, but when things get hard—"

"Of course. You do what you have to do."

"Thanks, man."

Wrath shook his head. "You know something—you're a male of worth. You really are."

"Yeah, well, just keep it to yourself. I've got a reputation as an egocentric asshole to protect."

"Tohr, I could see doing this. Phury, absolutely. Maybe V."

Rhage frowned. "You make it sound like it's a sacrifice, for chrissakes. I love her."

"That is the sacrifice. You love her even though you know she's leaving unto the Fade."

"She's not *going* anywhere." Rhage bit down on his molars. "She'll be fine. It'll be rough, but she *will* be fine."

"Forgive me." Wrath bowed his head. "Of course she will."

Rhage looked down. He didn't know what to do with the apology because he only had experience in offering them. And besides, anytime he thought about Mary dying, he felt like he had a blowtorch in his chest cavity.

"Later, my lord," he said, wanting to leave before he disgraced himself by becoming emotional.

Except as he glanced up, it was into Wrath's eyes for the very first time. The king never took his sunglasses off. Ever.

Rhage stopped breathing, focusing on the iridescent, silver-green irises staring back at him. There were no pupils really, just two little dots of black. And the warmth in those blind, glowing circles was shocking.

"You make me proud to call you brother," Wrath said.

Rhage felt heavy arms come around him as he was pulled against a solid chest. He tensed, but then let himself hang on to Wrath's massive shoulders.

348

"Wrath?"

"Yeah?"

Rhage opened his mouth to speak, but lost his voice.

Wrath replied into the silence, "We are all going to be there for you. So you're going to ask for help when you need it. And if the time comes, she will be afforded a full Fade ceremony, as the *shellan* of a warrior deserves."

Rhage squeezed his eyes shut. "Thank you . . . my lord."

Later that night Mary stood in their bathroom, brushing her hair out and blowing it dry. When she was finished, she looked at herself in the mirror and smoothed down the brunette waves. They were soft under her fingers, and in this light the color did have a little gold and red in it.

She refused to think of going bald again. Just put the thought right out of her mind. God knew, there'd be time to dwell on it when it actually happened.

"You're still as beautiful as you were yesterday," Rhage said as he got out of the shower. While he toweled off, he came up behind her and blew her reflection a kiss.

She smiled. "Thank you so much for inviting Bella and John over. She's become such a good friend, and I've been worried about him."

"I don't want you to lose touch with people just because you're here. Besides, the Brotherhood needs to play civilized every once in a while. It's good for us."

"You know, Tohrment and Wellsie are so kind to take John in."

"They're the best, those two."

As Rhage left the bath, the eyes of his tattoo stared out at her. The effect was eerie, she thought, but not exactly unpleasant. It was kind of like being watched by a guard dog who really wanted you to pet him.

She went over and sat on the edge of the bed. "Hey, I'm sorry if I kept you awake this morning. I toss and turn a lot when the fevers come."

Rhage came out of the closet, zipping up a pair of black pants. "You didn't bother me at all. But can we do anything about them?"

"Not really. I'll go into another bedroom if it bothers you." She laughed at the look he gave her. "Okay, I won't be doing that."

"About Havers. I was hoping there'd be something we could do for you."

"Don't worry. And I appreciate your trying."

"When are you going to see your oncologist again?"

"Soon, but no more talking about that, okay? Tonight, it's all about life. I feel good, and I'm not wasting one damned minute of it."

Rhage's mouth lifted at the corners, his eyes glowing with approval, respect.

And she'd thought for even a moment about shutting him out? *Idiot*.

She smiled back at him, looking forward to the end of the evening, when they could be alone together. In the dark. With nothing between them.

When he disappeared into the closet, she went after him, thinking they had a few minutes before the party began so maybe they could get a headstart. While he stared at the dress shirts that were lined up on hangers, she put her hand on his back, right on the beast's shoulder.

Rhage flinched and stepped away.

"Are you hurt?" she asked.

As she circled around him, he kept turning away, the two of them trading places a couple of times.

"Rhage—"

"We need to hurry or we're going to be late." His voice was a little hoarse, his pecs twitching.

"What's wrong with your back?"

He peeled a shirt off a hanger and pulled it on, buttoning the thing quickly. "Back's fine."

Rhage gave her a peck on the cheek and quickly

squeaked by her. Out in the bedroom he opened the door that led into the hall and then picked up his watch from the dresser and put the thing on his wrist. His fingers trembled as he did up the clasp.

Just as she was going to ask him what was wrong, Phury appeared in the doorway.

"Hey, my brother, Mary," the man said with a smile. "You want to go down together?"

Mary hid her frustration. And decided if there had to be an interruption, she couldn't think of a better-looking one. Phury's glorious, multicolored hair was fanned out around his broad shoulders, and he was dressed to kill. In the proverbial sense. His suit was blue-black and subtly pin-striped, and his pale-pink shirt showed off his thick throat and ridiculously good coloring. His loafers were slick as hell, his French cuffs were anchored with heavy gold links, and he was sporting a diamond pinkie ring.

The brother was total *GQ* material. And Bella and he would look really good together, she thought.

"Tell me, Phury, have you met Bella yet?"

The guy fiddled with the handkerchief in his breast pocket, even though the thing wasn't out of place. "Yeah, I met her. The night you and the boy came to the center."

"She's coming this evening."

"I, ah, I know."

"And she's not seeing anyone right now."

Boy, that blush really did it, she thought. Phury was adorable.

"He's not interested," Rhage said while clipping a handgun to the small of his back.

Mary shot her man a dirty look, which he missed as he pulled on his jacket.

"But you're single, too," she said to Phury. "Aren't you?"

"Oh, he's single, all right."

"Rhage, how about you let him answer? So Phury, if

351

both of you are free, why don't you ask her to have dinner sometime?"

Phury smoothed his lapels, blushing even more. "Yeah, I don't know about that."

"She's really fabulous—"

Rhage shook his head and ushered her out into the hall. "Leave it alone, Mary. Come on."

Halfway down the stairs, she pulled Rhage to a stop. As Phury got ahead of them, she whispered, "Give it a break, will you? Bella and he might enjoy each other."

"The only thing Bella would get out of Phury is conversation."

"What the—"

"He doesn't do females."

"He's gay?"

"No, but don't push Bella on him, okay? It isn't fair to either one of them."

Mary's eyes shot to Phury, who'd just stepped onto the foyer's mosaic floor. Even with his slight limp, he had the swagger of a man who had all of his parts in working order. But maybe that was just an illusion. Maybe he'd been injured while fighting.

"Is he, you know, impotent?"

"Not as far as I know. He's celibate."

God, what a waste, she thought, eyeing the way the man moved.

"So he's in some kind of religious order?"

"No."

"Then why?"

"With Phury, all roads lead back to his twin, Zsadist. And yes, I know they don't look alike." Rhage gave her a little nudge and she started down the stairs again.

"Why does Phury limp?"

"He has a prosthesis. He lost half his left leg."

"Good lord, how?"

"He shot it off."

Mary stopped. "*What?* Did it happen by mistake?"

"Nope, on purpose. Mary, come on, we can finish this later." He took her hand and pulled her forward.

Bella stepped through the mansion's vestibule with the *doggen* who'd driven her to the compound. As she looked around, she was stunned. Her family owned a grand house, but it was nothing like this. This was . . . royal living. Which she supposed made sense, because the Blind King and his queen made their residence here.

"Welcome, Bella," a deep male voice said.

She turned and saw the brother with the multicolored hair, the one who had interrupted her and Zsadist that night at the training center.

"I'm Phury. We met before. At the gym."

"Warrior," she said, bowing fully. It was hard not to be in awe of the brothers, especially one like this. So big. So . . . Was that hair for real?

"We're glad you could come." He smiled at her, his yellow eyes warm. "Here, let me help you with your coat."

When it was off, she looped the thing over her arm. "I can't believe I'm here, to tell you the truth. Mary! Hi!"

The two of them embraced and then they talked with Phury. Before long Bella was completely comfortable around the warrior. There was just something so calm and trustworthy about him, and those eyes were a knockout. They were honest-to-God yellow.

Attractive as he was, though, she was looking for the scarred brother. While keeping up with the conversation, she discreetly scanned the vast, colorful foyer. Zsadist was nowhere around. Maybe he was skipping the party. He didn't seem like the social type; that was for sure.

As Mary left to be with Rhage, Bella was determined not to feel let down. For God's sake, she had no business chasing after the likes of Zsadist, anyway.

"So, Phury," she said. "May I . . . I know this is rude,

but I just have to touch your hair." She reached up before he could say no and captured some of the blond and red waves, rubbing the thick lengths in her hand. "How gorgeous. The colors are amazing. And . . . oh, it smells so good. What kind of shampoo do you use?"

She looked into his eyes, expecting him to make some kind of light comment. Instead he was frozen stiff. Wasn't even blinking as he stared down at her.

And she suddenly realized that Rhage was staring at her from a doorway with an expression of shock on his face. And so was another warrior with a goatee. And a large human male. And . . .

Well, the party had kind of ground to a halt, hadn't it?

She dropped her hand and whispered, "I'm so sorry. I just did something horribly improper, didn't I?"

Phury snapped out of whatever trance he'd been in. "No. It's all right."

"Then why is everyone looking at me?"

"They're not used to seeing me with . . . that is, no females . . . ah . . ." Phury took her hand and gave it a squeeze. "Bella, you didn't do anything wrong. Seriously. And don't worry about my brothers, okay? They're just jealous because they want you touching their hair."

But something was still seriously off with him, and she wasn't surprised when he excused himself a moment later.

A *doggen* stepped in front of her. "Forgive me, madam, I should have taken your coat earlier."

"Oh, thank you."

After she dropped it into the male's hands, she realized the party had migrated into what looked like a billiard room. She was about to head over when she felt a cold draft coming from somewhere behind her. Had the front doors blown open?

She turned around.

Zsadist was in a dim corner by the vestibule, staring

at her from the shadows. He was dressed in the same kind of black turtleneck and loose black pants he'd worn the last time she'd seen him, and just as before, his night eyes were feral. Sexual.

Oh, yes, she thought as she flushed. This was why she had come. She'd had to see this male again.

Taking a deep breath, she went up to him.

"Hello." When he said nothing, she forced a little smile. "Lovely evening, isn't it?"

"Did you like the feel of my twin?"

That was his *twin?* How could the two of them . . . Well, there was a resemblance. If she imagined Zsadist's scar gone and his hair grown out.

"I asked you a question, female. Did his hair feel good to you?" Black eyes traveled down her body, tracing the lines of the silk blouse and the tight skirt she wore. When they returned to her face, they lingered on her mouth. "You gonna answer me, female?"

"Bella," she murmured automatically. "Please call me Bella."

Zsadist's stare grew hooded. "Do you think my brother's beautiful?"

"Ah . . . he's handsome, yes."

"Handsome. Yeah, that's the word. Tell me something, do you want him badly enough to lie with me?"

Heat bloomed in her, a fire lit by the words he spoke and the way he stared at her with sex in his eyes. But then she realized what he'd said.

"I'm sorry, I don't understand—"

"My twin's celibate from his tongue to his toes. So I'm afraid I'm the closest you'll ever get to Phury." He made a clucking sound. "But I'm a poor substitute, aren't I?"

Bella put her hand up to her neck, drowning in images of being under Zsadist's body while he moved inside of her. What would that be like? To be taken by him? The reckless part of her was desperate to know.

Oh, God. Just thinking about it made her shake.

Zsadist laughed coolly.

"Have I shocked you? Sorry. Just trying to help you out of your rock and hard place. Wanting something you can't have must be a bitch." His eyes latched on to her throat. "Myself, I've never had that problem."

As she swallowed, he tracked the movement. "Problem?" she whispered.

"What I want, I take."

Yes, she thought. *You certainly do, don't you.*

In a burning rush, she imagined him looking down at her while their bodies were merged, his face inches from her own. The fantasy had her lifting her arm. She wanted to run her fingertip down that scar until it got to his mouth. Just to know the feel of him.

With a quick jerk to the side, Zsadist dodged the contact, eyes flaring as if she'd shocked him. The expression was buried fast.

In a flat, cold voice he said, "Careful there, female. I bite."

"Will you ever say my name?"

"How about a drink, Bella?" Phury interjected. He took her elbow. "The bar's over here in the billiard room."

"Yeah, take her away," Zsadist drawled. "You're such a good hero, brother. Always saving somebody. And you should know, she thinks you're handsome."

Phury's face tightened, but he said nothing as he led her across the foyer.

When she looked back, Zsadist was gone.

Phury gave her arm a tug to get her attention. "You need to stay away from him." When she didn't respond, the warrior pulled her into a corner and gripped her shoulders. "My twin's not broken. He's ruined. Do you understand the difference? With broken, maybe you can fix things. Ruined? All you can do is wait to bury him."

Her mouth opened slightly. "That's so . . . callous."

"That's reality. If he dies before I do, it will kill me. But that doesn't change what he is."

She pointedly separated herself from the male. "I'll keep that in mind. Thanks."

"Bella—"

"You were going to get me a drink?"

THIRTY-NINE

O parallel-parked in front of the towering apartment building. The monolithic eyesore was one of Caldwell's high-rise, luxe setups, an attempt by some developers to turn the riverbank around. C's apartment was on the twenty-sixth floor facing the water.

Pretentious. Seriously pretentious.

Most *lessers* lived in shitholes because the Society believed in putting its money where its war was. C got away with the flashy style because he could afford it. He'd been a trustafarian before he'd joined in the seventies, and he'd somehow kept his money. The guy was an unusual combination: a dilettante with serial-killer tendencies.

As it was after ten there was no doorman, and picking the electronic lock on the lobby door was the work of a moment. O took the steel-and-glass elevator to the twenty-seventh floor and walked down one flight of stairs, more out of habit than necessity. There was no reason to think anyone would give a crap who he was or where he was going. Besides, the building was a ghost town this time of night, the Euro-trash residents out doing Ecstasy and coke at Zero Sum downtown.

He knocked on C's door.

This was the fifth address he'd visited on Mr. X's list of unaccounted-for members and the first of tonight's forays. The evening before, he'd had good success. One of the slayers had been out of state, having decided on his own to help out a buddy in D.C. Two of the AWOLs, who were roommates, had been injured from getting into a fight with each other; they were healing up and would be back online within a couple of days. The final *lesser* had been a perfectly healthy SOB who'd just been watching the tube and lying around. Well, perfectly healthy, that was, until he'd sustained an unfortunate accident as O was leaving. It would be a good week before he was up and running again, but the visit had certainly clarified his priorities.

Funny how a couple of cracked kneecaps could do that to a guy.

O knocked again on C's door and then picked the lock. When he opened the door, he recoiled. *Oh, shit.* The place smelled bad. Like rotting garbage.

He headed for the kitchen.

No, that wasn't trash. That was C.

The *lesser* was facedown on the floor, a dried pool of black blood around him. Within reach of his hand, there were some bandages and a needle and thread, as if he'd tried to fix himself up. Next to the first-aid stuff was his BlackBerry and the keypad was covered with his blood. A woman's purse, also stained, sat on the other side of him.

O rolled C over. The slayer's neck had been slashed, a good deep cut. And given the way the skin had been cauterized, the slice had been made by one of the Brotherhood's nasty black daggers. Man, whatever they had in that metal was like battery acid on a *lesser* wound.

C's throat was working, kicking out guttural sounds, proving that you could in fact be a little bit dead. When he brought up his hand, there was a knife in it. A few shallow cuts marked his shirt, as if he'd tried to stab himself in the chest but had lacked the strength to get the job done.

"You're in bad shape, my man," O said, taking the blade away. He sat back on his heels, watching the guy flail around in slow motion. Lying on his back like that, arms and legs moving uselessly, he was like a june bug about to give up the ghost.

O glanced at the purse.

"You taking up an alternative lifestyle, C?" He picked the thing up and went through the contents. Bottle of medicine. Tissues. Tampon. Cell phone.

Hello, wallet.

He took out the driver's license. Brown hair. Gray eyes. Impossible to tell whether the female was a vampire or a human. Address was out Route 22 in the sticks.

"Tell me if I get this right," O said. "You and one of those brothers went head-to-head. The warrior had a female with him. You escaped after being knifed and took this purse so you could finish the job on the male's lady friend. Trouble was, your wounds were too severe and you've been lying here ever since you got home. How'm I doing?"

O tossed the wallet into the bag and looked down at the man. C's eyes were rolling around, loose marbles in his deflating bag of a head.

"You know, C, if it were up to me, I'd just leave you here. I don't know if you're aware of this, but when we poof it out of existence, we go back to the Omega. Believe me, what you're going to find on the other side with him is going to make the way you feel now seem like a fucking vacation." O looked around. "Unfortunately, you're stinking up the place. Some human's going to come in, and then we've got us a problem."

O picked up the knife, gripping the handle hard. As he lifted it above his shoulder, C's relief brought all those body struggles to a standstill.

"You really shouldn't feel better about this," O said softly.

He sank the blade into the *lesser*'s chest. There was a flash of light and a popping sound. And C was gone.

O picked up the purse and headed out.

* * *

Mary walked over to Rhage, keeping her hand behind her back while she waited for the right moment. He was in the middle of a game of pool, he and Butch beating the tar out of V and Phury.

As she watched them play, she decided she really liked the brothers. Even Zsadist, with all his brooding. They were so good to her, treating her with a kind of respect and reverence she wasn't sure what she'd done to deserve.

Rhage winked at her as he leaned over the table and lined up his stick.

"It's the way you care for him," someone said in her ear.

She jerked in her shoes. Vishous was right behind her.

"What are you talking about?"

"That's why we adore you. And before you tell me to quit reading your mind, I didn't mean to catch the thought. It was just too loud to tune out." The vampire took a swallow from a squat glass of vodka. "But that's why we accept you. When you treat him well, you honor each one of us."

Rhage looked up and frowned. As soon as he took his shot, he came around the table to her and pointedly nudged V out of the way with his body.

Vishous laughed. "Relax, Hollywood. She's only got eyes for you."

Rhage grunted and tucked her into his side. "You just remember that and your arms and legs will stay right where they are."

"You know, you were never the possessive type before."

"That's because I never had something I wanted to keep. You're up at the table, my brother."

As V put his drink down and got serious about the game, Mary stuck her hand out. From her fingertips, a cherry dangled.

"I want to see your other trick," she said. "You told

me you could do something great with your tongue and a cherry stem."

He laughed. "Come on—"

"What? No trick?"

His smile was slow. "You just watch my mouth go to work, female."

Looking at her from under hooded lids, Rhage bent down to her hand. His tongue came out and captured the cherry, pulling it between his lips. He chewed and then shook his head as he swallowed.

"Not quite there," he murmured.

"What?"

"Your secrets are so much sweeter."

Flushing, she covered her eyes with her hand.

Oh, sure. Now he wants to get sexy, she thought.

As she took a deep breath, she caught the erotic, dark fragrance he threw off whenever he wanted to be inside her. She lifted her hand and peeked at him.

He was staring at her with total absorption. And the centers of his eyes were as white and gleaming as fresh snow.

Mary stopped breathing.

Something else is in there, she thought. There was . . . something else looking through his stare at her.

Phury came up, smiling. "Go get a room, Hollywood, if you're going to be like this. The rest of us don't need to be reminded of all you have."

He clapped his palm on Rhage's shoulder.

Rhage wheeled around and snapped at his brother's hand with his teeth. The sound of his jaws clamping shut was loud enough to suck the conversation out of the room.

Phury leaped back, yanking his arm away. "Jesus Christ, Rhage! What's your—*Shit*. Your eyes, man. They've turned."

Rhage paled and then stumbled away, squinting and

blinking. "I'm sorry. Hell, Phury, I didn't even know I was—"

All around the room, the men put down whatever was in their hands and came at him, circling him.

"How close are you to the change?" Phury asked.

"Clear the females out," someone commanded. "Get them upstairs."

As the sound of people leaving filled the air, Vishous squeezed Mary's arm. "Come with me."

"No." She struggled. "Stop it. I want to stay with him."

Rhage glanced over at her, and immediately that odd, fixated look came back. Then his white eyes shifted to Vishous. Rhage's lips pared off his teeth and he growled, loud as a lion.

"V, man, let go of her. *Right now*," Phury said.

Vishous dropped his hold, but whispered to her, "You need to get out of here."

Screw that, she thought.

"Rhage?" she said softly. "Rhage, what's going on?"

He shook his head and broke their eye contact, backing himself up against the marble fireplace. Sweat gleamed on his face as he grabbed on to the stone, and he strained as if he were trying to lift the whole damn mantelpiece off the wall.

Time slowed to a crawl as he battled with himself, chest pumping, arms and legs trembling. It was a long while before he sagged and the tension left his body. Whatever the fight had been, he'd won. But not by much.

As he looked up, his eyes were back to normal, but he was pasty as hell.

"I'm sorry, my brothers," he mumbled. Then he glanced at her and opened his mouth. Instead of speaking, he hung his head as if ashamed.

Mary walked through the barrier of male bodies and put her hands on his face.

As he gasped in surprise, she kissed him on the mouth. "Let's see the cherry thing. Come on."

The men standing around them were stunned; she could feel it in their stares. Rhage was shaken, too. But when she just looked at him pointedly, he started chewing, working the stem over with his teeth.

She glanced back at the warriors. "He's fine. We're fine. Go back to doing whatever, okay? He needs a minute, and all you guys staring at him like this isn't helping."

Phury laughed a little and walked over to the pool table. "You know, she's fabulous."

V picked up his cue and his glass. "Yeah. True."

As the party resumed, and Bella and Wellsie came back, Mary stroked Rhage's face and neck. He seemed to have trouble looking her in the eye.

"Are you okay?" she said softly.

"I'm so sorry—"

"Cut out the sorry bit. Whatever that is, you can't help it, right?"

He nodded.

"So there's no sorry."

She wanted to know what had just happened, but not here, not now. Sometimes, pretending to be normal was the very best antidote to weirdness. Fake-it-until-you-make-it was more than psychobabble bullshit.

"Mary, I don't want you to fear me."

For a moment, she watched his mouth and jaw work the stem.

"I'm not afraid. V and Phury might have been in a little trouble, but you wouldn't have hurt me. No way. I'm not sure how I know that, I just do."

He took a deep breath. "God, I love you. I really, really love you."

And then he smiled.

She laughed in a loud crack that brought every head in the room around.

The cherry stem was tied neatly around one of his fangs.

FORTY

Bella was staring, and it had to stop.

Except she couldn't help herself. Zsadist was the only thing she could see.

Not that he was really involved in the party. Except for when that episode with Rhage had happened, Zsadist stayed away from them all. He talked to no one. Drank nothing. Ate nothing. He was a statue over by one of the long windows, and the stillness in him was fascinating. He didn't even seem to be breathing. Only his eyes moved.

And always to get away from hers.

Bella gave them both a break by heading over for some more wine. The billiard room was a dark, luxurious space, covered in forest-green silk wallpaper and festooned with black-and-gold satin drapes. Over in the corner where the bar was set up, the shadows were even thicker, and she took shelter in them.

Maybe she could be more discreet if she watched him from here.

Over the past few days she'd asked around and heard every Zsadist story there was. The rumors were down-right gruesome, especially the ones about him and females. People said he killed her sex for sport, but it was hard not to wonder how much of that was lore. A male who looked as dangerous as he did, people were bound to talk. Her brother was the same way. She'd heard whispers about Rehvenge for years, and God knew, all of them were false.

There was just no way all the chatter about Zsadist was accurate. For heaven's sake, folks maintained he lived off the blood of human prostitutes. That wasn't even physiologically possible, not unless he drank every other night. And even then, how could he be as strong as he was with that weak sustenance?

Bella turned from the bar and scanned the room. Zsadist was gone.

She glanced out into the foyer. She hadn't even seen him leave. Perhaps he'd dematerialized—

"Looking for me?"

She jumped and twisted her head around. Zsadist was right behind her, rubbing a Granny Smith apple on his shirt. As he lifted it to his mouth, he eyed her throat.

"Zsadist . . ."

"You know, for a female of the aristocracy, you're pretty damn rude." He bared his fangs and bit through the bright-green flesh with a crack. "Didn't your mother ever tell you it's not polite to stare?"

She watched him chew, his jaw working in circles. God, just looking at his lips made her breathless. "I don't mean to offend you."

"Well, you are. And I think you're upsetting my dear twin while you're at it."

"What?"

Zsadist's eyes lingered on her face, then drifted over her hair. He took another hunk out of the apple. "Phury likes you. I think he might even be attracted to you, which is a first, at least since I've known him. He doesn't get distracted by females."

Funny, she hadn't gotten that vibe at all. Then again, she'd been focused on Zsadist.

"I don't think Phury's—"

"He keeps watching you. While you're looking at me, he's staring at you. And it's not because he's worried about you. His eyes are on your body, female." Zsadist tilted his head to the side. "You know, maybe I was wrong. Maybe you are the one who'll shake him out of his celibacy. Shit, you're beautiful enough, and he ain't dead."

She flushed. "Zsadist, you should know that I, ah, I find you—"

"Revolting, right? Kind of like a good car accident." He bit off some more apple. "I can understand the fascination, but you need to be taking those eyes elsewhere. Look at Phury from now on, we clear?"

"I want to look at you. I like to look at you."

His eyes narrowed. "No, you don't."

"Yes. I do."

"No one likes to look at me. Not even I do."

"You're not ugly, Zsadist."

He laughed, deliberately running a fingertip down his scar. "Now, there's a ringing endorsement. As well as a blatant fucking lie."

"I find you mesmerizing. I can't get you out of my mind. I want to be with you."

Zsadist frowned, falling still. "Be with me exactly how?"

"You know. Be with you." She blushed a brilliant red, but figured she had nothing to lose. "I want to . . . lie with you."

Zsadist backed up so fast he hit the bar. And as the liquor bottles rattled, she knew for certain the stories about him were false. This was no female-killer. If anything, he seemed petrified by the thought that she was sexually attracted to him.

She opened her mouth, but he cut her off.

"You stay away from me, female," he said, pitching the half-eaten apple into the trash. "If you don't, there's no telling what I might do to defend myself."

"From what? I'm no threat to you."

"No, but I can goddamn guarantee I'm hazardous to your health. There's a very good reason why people stay away from me."

He walked out of the room.

Bella looked at all the people around the pool table. Everyone was focused on the game. Which was perfect.

She didn't want any of them to talk her out of what she was about to do.

She put her glass of wine down and slipped from the billiard room. As she came into the lobby, Zsadist was going upstairs. After giving him some time to get ahead of her, she took the steps quickly, moving silently up to the second floor. When she got to the top, she caught sight of the heel of his shitkicker disappearing around a corner. She jogged swiftly over the carpet, keeping a distance as he headed down a corridor that led away from the balcony and the foyer below.

Zsadist paused. She ducked behind a marble sculpture.

When she leaned out, he was gone. She walked to where she'd seen him and found a door slightly ajar. She stuck her head in. The room was pitch-dark, the light from the hall making little headway into the blackness. And it was freezing cold, as if the heat wasn't just off for the night, but hadn't been turned on since summer's warmth had faded.

Her eyes adjusted. There was a broad, sumptuous bed, dripping with heavy crimson velvet. The other furniture was equally lavish, although there was something odd in the corner on the floor. A pallet of blankets. And a skull.

Bella was yanked inside by the arm.

The door slammed shut and the room plunged into total darkness. Quick as a gasp, she was spun around and pushed face-first into the wall. Candles flared.

"What the *fuck* are you doing here?"

She tried to catch her breath, but with Zsadist's forearm pressed into the middle of her back, she couldn't squeeze much air into her lungs.

"I, ah, I . . . thought we could talk."

"Really. Is that what you want to do up here? Talk."

"Yes, I thought—"

His hand clamped on the back of her neck. "I don't

talk with females who are dumb enough to come after me. But I'll show you what I am willing to do to them."

His put a thick arm around her stomach, popped her hips out from the wall, and pushed her head down. Off balance, she braced herself by holding on to a piece of molding.

His arousal came against her core. Breath exploded out of her lungs.

As heat licked between her legs, his chest brushed her back. He pulled her blouse out from her skirt and slipped his hand onto her belly, spanning it with his long fingers and wide palm.

"A female like you should be with another aristocrat. Or are the scars and the reputation part of my appeal?" When she didn't answer, because she was breathless, he muttered, "Yeah, of course that's it."

In one swift movement he shoved her bra up and captured her breast. Caught in an onslaught of raw lust, she hissed and jerked. He laughed a little.

"Too fast?" He took her nipple between his fingers and rolled it, pleasure and pain combining. She cried out. "This too rough for you? I'll try to control myself better, but, you know, I'm a savage. Which is why you want this, right?"

But it wasn't too fast or too rough. God help her, she liked it. She wanted it hard and now, and she wanted it with him. She wanted to break the rules, wanted the danger and thrill, wanted the wild heat and the power of him. And she was so ready, especially as he pushed her skirt over her hips. All he had to do was move her thong over and he could sink in deep.

Except she wanted to see him when he penetrated her. And she wanted to touch his body, too. She started to stand up, but he kept her down, leaning on her neck, holding her in place.

"Sorry, I'm a one-trick pony. I only do it this way."

She struggled, dying to kiss him. "Zsadist—"

"It's a little late to have second thoughts." His voice was a sensuous growl in her ear. "For some reason, I want to fuck you. Badly. So do us both a favor and grit your teeth. I won't take long."

His hand left her breast, shot between her legs, and found her core.

Zsadist froze.

Instinctively she moved her hips, rubbing herself against his fingers, feeling a wonderful friction—

He leaped back. "Get out of here."

Disorientated, fiercely aroused, she swayed as she righted herself. "What?"

Zsadist went over to the door, threw it open and stared at the floor. When she didn't move, he roared, "Get out!"

"Why—"

"God, you make me *sick*."

Bella felt all the blood leave her face. She pulled her skirt down and fumbled with the blouse and bra. Then she bolted out of the room.

Zsadist slammed the door shut and ran for the bathroom. Popping the toilet seat, he bent over and threw up the apple he'd eaten.

As he hit the flusher, he sank to the floor, shaky and queased out. He tried taking some deep breaths, but all he could smell was Bella. Her lovely, inexplicable arousal was on his fingers. He whipped off his turtleneck and wrapped it around his hand, needing to dim the scent.

God, the satin perfection of her. The gorgeous fragrance of her passion. All that luscious rain.

No female had been wet for him for a hundred years. Not since his time as a blood slave. And back then . . . he hadn't wanted it, had learned to fear that very arousal.

He tried to focus his mind on the present, tried to keep himself in his bathroom, but the past sucked him down . . .

He was back in the cell, shackled, his body not his own. He felt the Mistress's hands, smelled the salve she had to put on him before she could get the erection she needed. And then she was riding him, pumping until she got off. After that, the biting and the drinking assaulted him as she fed from his veins.

It all came back. The rapes. The humiliation. The decades of abuse until he lost any conception of time, until he was nothing, all but dead except for the incessant beating of his heart and the rote suck and push of his lungs.

He heard a weird sound. Realized he was moaning.

Oh . . . Bella.

He wiped his forehead on his biceps. Bella. God, she made him so ashamed of his scars and his ugliness, his ruined appearance and his black, nasty nature.

At the party she'd effortlessly talked to his brothers and the females, smiling, laughing. She had a charm and an easiness about her that spoke of the comfortable life she'd led. She'd probably never known a mean word or an unkind deed. She'd certainly never shown cruelty or harshness to another. She was a female of worth, not at all like the trashy, angry humans he'd been drinking from.

He hadn't believed her when she'd told him she wanted to lie with him, but she had. That was what all her silky wetness had meant. Females could lie about a lot of things, but not that. Never that.

Zsadist shuddered. When he'd had her bent over and was touching her breasts, he'd planned on stopping in spite of what he'd said. He'd figured he'd scare her into leaving him alone, overwhelm her a little before sending her along her way.

Except she actually had wanted him.

He replayed what it had been like to dive in between her thighs. She'd been so . . . soft. So incredibly warm and smooth and slick. The first he had touched who had been like that for him. He'd had no idea what to do, but then from out of his confusion, the Mistress had come back to him. He'd seen her face and felt her body on top of his.

The Mistress had always been turned on when she'd come to him, and she'd taken great pains to make sure he knew it, though she'd never made him touch her with his hands. She'd been smart. After everything she'd done to him, if he'd been able to get at her, he'd have torn her apart like a rabid animal, and they'd both known it. The caged danger he'd represented had thrilled her.

He thought of Bella's attraction to him. It was based on the same thing, wasn't it? Power-trip sex. The shackled savage used for pleasure.

Or in Bella's case, the dangerous male used for adventure.

His stomach heaved again and he lurched over the toilet.

"I thought you were just being cruel," Bella said from behind him. "I didn't know I actually made you sick."

Fuck. He hadn't locked the door.

It had never dawned on him she'd come back.

Bella wrapped her arms around herself. Of all the things she could have dreamed up, this pushed the fiction envelope. Zsadist was sprawled half-naked in front of a toilet, his shirt wrapped around his hand, the dry heaves making him twitch.

While he cursed, she stared at his body. *Dear lord, his back*. The broad expanse was streaked with scars, evidence of a past whipping that, like his face, had somehow not healed smoothly. Although how that had happened she couldn't guess.

"Why are you in my room again?" he asked, voice echoing around the porcelain rim.

"I, ah, I wanted to yell at you."

"Mind if I finish throwing up first?" Water rushed and gurgled as he flushed.

"Are you okay?"

"Yeah, this is just loads of fun."

She came into the bathroom and had a brief impression that it was very clean, very white, and totally impersonal.

In the blink of an eye, Zsadist was up on his feet and facing her.

She swallowed a gasp.

Though clearly powerful, his muscles stood out in stark relief, the individual fibers striated and visible. For a warrior, for any male, he was thin, too thin. Frankly he was close to starving. And he was scarred on the front, though only in two places; over his left pectoral and on his right shoulder. Both his nipples were pierced, silver hoops with little balls catching the light as he breathed in and out.

But none of that was what stunned her. The thick black bands tattooed around his neck and wrists were the shocker.

"Why do you bear the markings of a blood slave?" she whispered.

"Do the math."

"But that's . . ."

"Not supposed to happen to someone like me?"

"Well, yes. You are a warrior. A noble."

"Fate is a cruel bitch."

Her heart opened wide for him, and everything she'd thought about him changed. He was no longer a thrill, but a male she wanted to ease. Comfort. Hold. On impulse, she took a step toward him.

His black eyes narrowed. "You really don't want to come near me, female. Especially not now."

She didn't listen. As she closed the distance between them, he backed away until he got caught in the corner between the glass shower door and the wall.

"What the hell are you doing?"

She didn't answer, because she wasn't sure.

"Back off," he snapped. He opened his mouth, his fangs elongating to the size of a tiger's.

374

That gave her some pause. "But maybe I can—"

"Save me or some shit? Oh, right. In your fantasy, this is the part where I'm supposed to be transfixed by your eyes. Give my beastly self up into the arms of a virgin."

"I'm not a virgin."

"Well, good for you."

She reached out her hand, wanting to put it on his chest. Right over his heart.

He shrank from her, flattening himself against the marble. As sweat broke out all over him, he craned his neck away and his face squeezed into a wince. His chest pumped up and down, nipple rings flashing silver.

His voice thinned out until it was barely a sound. "Don't touch me. I can't . . . I can't stand to be touched, okay? It hurts."

Bella stopped.

"Why?" she said softly. "Why does it—"

"Just get the fuck out of here, *please*." He could barely get the words out. "I'm about to destroy something. And I don't want it to be you."

"You won't hurt me."

He closed his eyes. "Goddamn. What is it with you refined types? Are you bred to get off on torturing people?"

"Good lord, no. I just want to help you."

"*Liar,*" he spat, eyes popping open. "You're such a liar. You don't want to help me, you want to poke the rattlesnake with a stick just to see what it does."

"That's not true. At least . . . not now."

His gaze went cold, soulless. And his voice lost all intonation. "You want me? Fine. You can fucking have me."

Zsadist lunged at her. He took her down to the floor, rolled her over onto her stomach, and dragged her hands behind her back. The marble was cold against her face as his knees jack-knifed her legs apart. There was a ripping sound. Her thong.

She went numb. Her thoughts couldn't keep up with

the pace of his actions, and neither could her emotions. But her body knew what it wanted. Angry or not, she would take him in.

The weight of him left her briefly, and she heard the sound of a zipper. Then he was lying on her with nothing between his tremendous erection and her core. But he didn't thrust. He just panted as he froze in place, his breath a loud rush in her ear, so loud . . . Was he sobbing?

His head dropped down onto her nape. Then he rolled off her, covering her up as he left her body. Lying on his back, he put his arms across his face.

"Oh, God," he moaned, ". . . Bella."

She wanted to reach out to him, but he was so tense she didn't dare. With an uneasy lurch she got to her feet and stared down at him. Zsadist's pants were around his thighs, his sex no longer erect.

Jesus, his body was in rough shape. His stomach was hollow. His hip bones jutted out of his skin. He must indeed only drink from humans, she thought. And not eat much at all.

She focused on the tattooed bands covering his wrist and neck. And the scars.

Ruined. Not broken.

Although she was ashamed to admit it now, the darkness in him had been the largest part of his allure. It was such an anomaly, a contrast to what she'd known from life. It had made him dangerous. Exciting. Sexy. But that was a fantasy. This was real.

He suffered. And there was nothing sexy or thrilling about that.

She picked up a towel and went over to him, laying it gently across his exposed flesh. He jumped and then clutched it to himself. As he looked up at her, the whites of his eyes were bloodshot, but he wasn't crying. Maybe she'd been mistaken about the sobbing.

"Please . . . leave me," he said.

"I wish—"

"Go. Now. No wishing, no hoping. No nothing. Just leave. And don't ever come near me again. Swear it. *Swear it.*"

"I . . . I promise."

Bella hurried out through his bedroom. When she was down the hall far enough, she paused and finger-combed her hair, trying to smooth it down. She could feel the thong up around her waist and left it there. She had no place to put the thing if she took it off.

Downstairs the party was still in full swing, and she felt out of place, drained. She went over to Mary, said her goodbyes, and looked around for a *doggen* to take her home.

But then Zsadist came into the room. He'd changed into white nylon workout clothes and had a black bag in his hand. Without looking at her at all, he walked up behind Phury, who was a couple feet away.

When Phury turned around and saw the bag, he recoiled.

"No, Z. I don't want—"

"Either you do it, brother, or I'll find someone else who will."

Zsadist held out the bag.

Phury stared at it. When he took the thing, his hand shook.

The two of them left together.

FORTY-ONE

Mary put the empty platter down next to the sink and handed Rhage a tray so they could gather empties together. Now that the party was over, everyone was helping clean up.

As they went out into the foyer, she said, "I'm so glad Wellsie and Tohr have taken John in. And I would have loved to see him tonight, but I'm happy to know he's in good hands."

"Tohr told me the poor kid can't get out of bed, he's so exhausted. All he's been doing is sleeping and eating. Hey, by the way, I think you're right. Phury kind of digs Bella. He spent a lot of time looking her over. I've never seen him do that before."

"But after what you said about—"

As they passed the grand staircase, a hidden door underneath it opened.

Zsadist came out. His face was battered, his workout shirt shredded. There was blood on him.

"Oh, shit," Rhage muttered.

The brother passed them, glassy black eyes not tracking. His small smile of satisfaction seemed totally out of context, like he'd had a good meal or maybe some sex instead of getting the holy hell beaten out of him. He went upstairs slowly, one leg not bending right.

"I had better go clean up Phury." Rhage gave the tray to Mary and kissed her lightly. "I might be a while."

"Why would Phury . . . Oh . . . God."

"Only because he was forced to. That's the only reason, Mary."

"Well . . . take as long as you need."

But before he reached the passageway, Phury came out wearing exercise gear. He looked as spent as Zsadist was, except he didn't have a mark on him. No, that wasn't right. His knuckles were bruised and cracked. And there were smudges of blood on his chest.

"Hey, man," Rhage said.

Phury looked around and seemed startled to find himself where he was.

Rhage stepped in front of him. "My brother?"

Shell-shocked eyes focused. "Hey."

"You want to go upstairs? Hang out a little?"

"Oh, yeah, no. I'm fine." His eyes skipped to Mary. Glanced away. "I, ah, I'm fine. Yeah. Really. Party's ended, I guess?"

Rhage took the bag. Phury's pale-pink shirt was sticking out of it, caught in the zipper.

"Come on, let's go up together."

"You should stay with your female."

"She understands. We go together, my brother."

Phury's shoulders sank into his torso. "Yeah, okay. Yeah, I don't . . . I'd rather not be by myself right now."

When Rhage finally got back to his and Mary's room he knew she'd be asleep, so he closed the door silently.

There was a candle burning on the nightstand, and in the glow he saw that the bed was a mess. Mary had pushed the comforter off and scattered the pillows around. She was lying on her back, a lovely cream nightgown twisted around her waist, riding up on her thighs.

He'd never seen the silk before, knew that she'd worn it because she'd wanted tonight to be special. The sight of her cranked him up, and even though the vibration made him burn, he knelt by her side of the bed. He needed to be close to her.

He didn't know how Phury kept going, especially on nights like this. The brother's one and only love had wanted to bleed, had demanded pain and punishment. So Phury had done what he'd been asked to do, accepting the transfer of misery. Z was no doubt sleeping it off. Phury would be rattling around in his own skin for days.

He was such a good male, loyal, strong, devoted to Z. But working off the guilt over all that had happened to Zsadist was killing him.

God, how could anyone deal with beating the one they loved because that was what the person wanted?

"You smell good," Mary murmured, curling onto her side and looking at him. "Like a Starbucks."

"It's the red smoke. Phury lit up something fierce, but I don't blame him." Rhage took her hand and frowned. "You have another fever."

"It just broke. I feel much better." She kissed his wrist. "How's Phury?"

"A mess."

"Does Zsadist make him do that a lot?"

"No. I don't know what set it off tonight."

"I'm so sorry for both of them. But mostly for Phury."

He smiled at her, loving her for the way she cared about his brothers.

Mary sat up slowly, shifting her legs around so they hung off the bed. Her nightgown had a lace bodice, and through the pattern he could see her breasts. His thighs tightened and he closed his eyes.

It was hell. Wanting to be with her. Being scared of what his body would do. And he wasn't even thinking just about sex. He needed to hold her.

Her hands rose to his face. When her thumb brushed over his mouth, his lips opened of their own accord, a subversive invitation she accepted. She bent down and kissed him, her tongue penetrating, taking what he knew he should not be offering.

"Hmm. You taste good."

He'd smoked some with Phury, knowing he was coming

back to her, hoping that the relaxant might take him down a little. He couldn't handle a repeat of what had happened in the billiard room.

"I want you, Rhage." She shifted, opening her legs, pulling his body against her.

Swirling energy condensed along his spine and radiated outward, punching into his hands and feet, making his nails sing with pain and his hair tingle.

He leaned back. "Listen, Mary . . ."

She smiled and swept the nightgown over her head, tossing it so the thing fell to the floor in a swirl. Her naked skin in the candlelight tangled him up. He couldn't move.

"Love me, Rhage." She took his hands and put them to her breasts. Even as he told himself not to touch her, he cupped the swells, thumbs smoothing over her nipples. She arched her back. "Oh, yes. Like that."

He went for her neck, licking up her vein. He wanted to drink from her so badly, especially as she held his head in place as if that was what she wanted, too. It wasn't that he needed to feed. He wanted her in his body, in his blood. He wanted to be sustained by her, live off of her. He wished she could do the same with him.

She wrapped her arms around his shoulders and pulled back, trying to take him down on the mattress. God help him, he let her. She was under him now, smelling of the arousal she had for him.

Rhage closed his eyes. He couldn't deny her. He couldn't stop the rush inside of him. Trapped between the two, he kissed her and prayed.

Something wasn't right, Mary thought.

Rhage was staying out of reach. When she wanted to take his shirt off, he didn't let her get to the buttons. When she tried to touch his erection, he moved his hips away. Even as he suckled her breasts and swept his hand between her legs, it was as if he were making love to her from a distance.

"Rhage . . ." Her voice broke as she felt his lips on her navel. "Rhage, what's wrong?"

His big hands parted her legs wide, his mouth going to the inside of her thigh. He nipped at her, his fangs teasing, never hurting.

"Rhage, stop for a minute . . ."

He put his mouth on her sex, pulling her between his lips, sucking, moving back and forth, savoring. She bowed off the bed at the sight of his blond head dipped low, his bunched shoulders under her knees, her legs so pale and thin against the massive backdrop of him.

She was going to be totally lost in another second.

Grabbing a hunk of his hair, she yanked him away from her.

His teal-blue eyes shimmered with sexual power as he breathed through open, glossy lips. Deliberately he took the lower one between his teeth and sucked on it. Then his tongue did a long, slow lick of the upper one.

She closed her eyes, swelling, melting.

"What's the problem?" she croaked.

"Wasn't aware there was one." He brushed her core with his knuckles, rubbing sensitive skin. "You don't like this?"

"Of course I do."

His thumb started going in circles. "So let me get back to what I was doing."

Before he could drop his head and put that tongue on her again, she clamped her legs shut around his hand as best she could.

"Why can't I touch you?" she asked.

"We are touching." He moved his fingers. "I'm right here."

Oh, God, could she get any hotter? "No, you're not."
She tried to withdraw from him and sit up, but his

382

free arm shot out. His palm landed on her chest, pushing her back down onto the bed.

"I'm not finished," he said in a deep rumble.

"I want to touch your body."

His gaze flared brightly. But then just like that, the glow was gone and a quick emotion passed over his face. Fear? She couldn't tell, because he lowered his head. He kissed the top of her thigh, nuzzling her with his cheek, his jaw, his mouth.

"There's nothing like your heat, your taste, your softness. Let me pleasure you, Mary."

The words gave her a chill. She'd heard them before. Back in the beginning.

His lips moved to the inside of her leg, closer to home.

"*No.* Stop it, Rhage." He did. "One-sided isn't sexy to me. I don't want you servicing me. I want to be *with* you."

His mouth tightened, and he got off the bed with a sharp surge. Was he going to leave her?

But he just knelt on the floor, arms braced on the mattress, head hanging off his shoulders. Collecting himself.

She stretched out her leg, touching his forearm with her foot.

"Don't tell me you're going to say no," she murmured.

He looked up at her. From the low position of his head, his eyes were mere slits in his face, spitting out brilliant beams of neon blue.

Arching her body, she shifted her leg, giving him a little flash of what she knew he wanted so badly.

She held her breath.

In one mighty, fluid movement, Rhage sprang up from the floor and leaped on top of her, landing between her thighs. He undid his pants and—

Oh, thank you, God.

She came immediately, clenching on to all that hardness

in waves. When the thundering receded, she felt him shaking above her, inside of her. She was about to tell him to let go of his self-control when she realized restraint wasn't the problem. He was having some kind of mini-seizure, every muscle in his body spasming.

"Rhage?" She looked up into his face.

His eyes were glowing white.

In an attempt to calm him, she ran her hands up his back, only to feel something on his skin. A raised pattern. Lines, almost.

"Rhage, there's something on your—"

He vaulted off her and went straight for the door.

"Rhage?" She grabbed the nightgown and threw it on as she went after him.

Out in the hall he paused to put his pants back together, and Mary nearly screamed. The tattoo was alive. The thing had lifted up from his back, the design throwing shadows.

And it moved even though he was still. The great dragon seethed as it stared right at her, the head and eyes trained on her as its body undulated.

Looking for a way out.

"Rhage!"

He took off like a bullet, going down to the foyer and disappearing through the hidden door under the stairs.

Rhage didn't stop running until he was well inside the training facility. When he got to the locker room, he punched open the doors and went to the communal shower. Turning on one of the showerheads, he slid down the tile and sat under a spray of cold water.

It was all so terribly clear. The vibrations. The humming. Always around Mary, especially if she was aroused.

God, he didn't know why he hadn't figured it out before. Maybe he'd just wanted to avoid the truth.

Being with Mary was different because . . . he wasn't the only one who wanted to make love to her.

The beast wanted her, too.

The beast wanted out so it could take her.

FORTY-TWO

When Bella got home she couldn't settle down. After writing for an hour in her diary, she changed into some jeans and a sweatshirt and put her parka on. Outside, flurries were falling in a disorganized rush, swirling in eddies of cold air.

Zipping up the parka, she walked into the taller, rougher grass of the meadow.

Zsadist. She couldn't close her eyes and not see him lying on his back in that bathroom.

Ruined. Not broken.

She stopped and watched the snow.

She'd given him her word that she wouldn't bother him, but she didn't want to keep the promise. God help her, she wanted to try again with him . . .

In the distance she noticed someone walking around Mary's house. Bella stiffened in fear, but then saw the dark hair, so she knew it wasn't a *lesser*.

Vishous was obviously working on the security-alarm installation. She waved to him and headed over.

After having talked with V at the party, she liked him tremendously. He had the kind of smarts that usually sucked the social skills right out of a vampire, but with that warrior, you had the whole package. He was sexy, all-knowing, powerful, the kind of male that made you think of having babies just to keep his DNA in the gene pool.

She wondered why he wore that black leather glove. And what the tattoos on the side of his face were about. Maybe she'd ask about those, if it seemed okay.

"I thought you wouldn't have to finish now," she

called out as she came up onto the terrace. "What with Mary—"

The dark-haired figure that stepped in front of her was not Vishous. And it was not alive.

"Jennifer?" the *lesser* said in awe.

For a split second Bella froze. Then she turned and ran, moving fast over the ground. She didn't stumble; she didn't falter. She was quick and she was sure as she crossed the meadow, even though she was terrified. If she could make it to her house, she could lock the *lesser* out. By the time he broke in through the glass, she'd be down in the basement where no one could get in. She'd call Rehvenge and take the underground tunnel to the other side of the property.

The *lesser* was behind her—she could hear the pounding of his stride and the rustle of his clothes—but he wasn't closing as they tore across the crispy, frosted grass. Training her eyes on the cheerful lights in her house, she reached down into her muscles for more speed.

The first shot of pain hit her in the thigh. The second in the middle of her back, through the parka.

Her legs slowed and her feet became flippers of enormous size. Then the distance she had to close got greater, stretched to infinity, but she kept going anyway. By the time she made it to her back door, she was weaving. Somehow she got inside, but she struggled to engage the lock with fingers that had gone boneless.

As she wheeled away and lurched for the basement, the sound of the French doors being kicked in was oddly quiet, as if it were happening somewhere far, far away.

A hand closed on her shoulder.

The fighting urge came up strong in her and she hauled off and smashed the *lesser* in the face with her closed fist. He was momentarily stunned and then he hit her back, sending her spinning to the ground. He rolled her over and hit her again, his open palm clapping on her cheekbone, kicking her head back against the floor.

She felt nothing. Not the slap, not her skull's impact. Which was good because she wasn't distracted as she bit him in the arm.

Flailing around together, they knocked into the kitchen table, scattering the chairs. She got free by grabbing one of the things and knocking him in the chest with it. Disorientated, panting, she crawled away.

Her body gave out at the foot of the basement stairs.

Lying there, she was conscious, but incapable of movement. She had a vague thought that something was dripping into her eyes. Probably her own blood, maybe some of the *lesser*'s.

Her scope of vision swung around as she was turned over.

She looked into the *lesser*'s face. Dark hair, pale-brown eyes.

Good God.

The slayer was crying as he lifted her from the floor and cradled her in his arms. The last thing she was aware of was the sight of his tears falling to her face.

She felt absolutely nothing.

O carefully lifted the female out of the cab of his truck. He wished like hell he hadn't agreed to give up his own place so he could live at the persuasion center. He would have preferred to keep her away from the other *lessers*, but then again, if she were here he'd be able to make sure she didn't escape. And if any other slayer got near her . . . well, that's what they made knives for.

As he carried the female through the door, he looked down at her face. She was so like his Jennifer. Different-colored eyes, but that heart-shaped face. The thick, dark hair. And the body—lean, perfectly proportioned.

Actually, she was more beautiful than Jennifer had been. And she hit harder, too.

He laid the female on the table and fingered the bruise on her cheek, the split lip, the marks on her throat. The fighting had been tremendous: all-out, nothing spared, no stopping until he won and held her spent body in his arms.

Staring at the vampire, he thought back to the past. He'd always been afraid he'd be the one to kill Jennifer, that some night all the hitting would cross the line. Instead he'd ended up murdering the drunk driver who'd nailed her car head-on. The bastard had been liquored up at five in the afternoon, and she'd just been coming home from work.

Taking her killer out had been easy. He'd found where the guy had lived and had waited for him to come home shit-faced. Then he'd beaten the man's head in with a tire iron and pushed him down the stairs. With the body cooling, O had driven north and east, all the way across the country.

Where he'd fallen into the Society.

A car pulled up outside. Quickly he picked up the female and carried her over to the holes. After slipping a halter around her chest, he opened the lid of one and dropped her inside.

"You got another?" U asked as he came inside.

"Yeah." O made a show of looking into the other hole, at the male Mr. X had worked on the night before. The civilian was shifting in the pipe, making little scared, mewing noises.

"So let's get to work on the fresh capture," U said.

O put his boot on the cover over the female. "This one is mine. Anyone touches her and I will skin them with my teeth."

"Her? Excellent. Sensei will be psyched."

"You say nothing to him about this. We clear?"

U frowned, then shrugged. "Sure. Whatever, man. But you know he's going to find out sooner or later. When he does, just don't think it came from me."

O could actually see U keeping the secret, and on impulse he gave the slayer the address of the converted barn he'd been breaking into. A little boon in exchange for the *lesser*'s integrity.

"The name of the female who lives there is Mary Luce. She was seen with a brother. Go get her, my man."

U nodded. "Will do, but it's close to dawn and I need to crash. I've been up for two nights too long, and I'm getting weak."

"Tomorrow then. Now leave us."

U cocked his head and glanced down at the pipe hole. "Us?"

"Get the fuck out of here, U."

U took off and O listened as the sound of the *lesser*'s car faded.

Satisfied, he look down at the mesh cover. And couldn't stop smiling.

FORTY-THREE

Rhage did not return to the main house until five in the afternoon. As he walked through the tunnel, he made no sound. He'd taken his shoes off because they'd been soggy and then forgotten where he'd left them.

He was a live wire, the burn in him a roar he couldn't get rid of no matter how exhausted he was or how much weight he lifted or how far he ran. At this point, not that he'd even consider it, he couldn't imagine that having sex with a hundred different females would bring him down.

There was no escape for him, but he had to talk to Mary. He dreaded telling her he'd been condemned a century ago and had no idea how to explain that the beast wanted to have sex with her. But she needed to know why he stayed away.

He braced himself and opened their bedroom door. She wasn't there.

He went downstairs and found Fritz in the kitchen.

"Have you seen Mary?" he asked, doing his best to keep his voice level.

"Yes, sire. She departed."

Rhage's blood went glacial. "Where was she headed?"

"She didn't say."

"Did she take anything with her? Purse? Overnight bag?"

"A book. A bagel. A parka."

Outside. Rhage hit the underground tunnel and was at the Pit in half a minute. He pounded on the door.

Vishous took his damn time answering and was sporting boxer shorts and bed head when he did. "What the—"

"Mary's out of the house. By herself. I need to find her."

V went from rubbing his eyes and looking cranked-off to being totally focused. He went to his computer, called up every exterior image he had, and found her curled up in the sun right against the mansion's front doors. Which was smart. If anything came at her, she'd be able to get into the vestibule in the work of a moment.

Rhage took a deep breath. "How do you get this thing to move in closer?"

"Hit zoom in the upper right-hand corner with the mouse."

Rhage zeroed in. She was feeding a couple of sparrows, throwing little pieces of her bagel at them. Every once in a while she'd lift her head and look around. The smile on her face was a private one, just a slight lift to her lips.

He touched the screen, brushing his fingertip against her face. "You know, you were wrong, my brother."

"Was I?"

"She is my destiny."

"Did I say she wasn't?"

Rhage looked across all the computer equipment, focusing on V's tattooed eye. "I am not her first lover. You told me my fate was a virgin. So you were wrong."

"I am never wrong."

Rhage frowned, rejecting out of hand the idea that some other female would mean more to him or would take Mary's place in his heart.

Man, fuck fate if it was going to try to make him love someone else. And to hell with V's prognostications.

"Must be nice to know it all," he muttered. "Or at least think you do."

As he turned and headed for the tunnel, his arm was gripped hard.

V's diamond eyes, usually so calm, were narrow and pissed off. "When I say I'm never wrong, I'm not on an ego trip. Seeing the future is a goddamned curse, my brother. You think I like knowing how everyone's going to die?"

Rhage recoiled and Vishous smiled coldly. "Yeah, chew on that. And then realize the only thing I don't know is the *when*, so I can't save any of you. Now, you want to tell me why I should showboat about this curse of mine?"

"Oh, God . . . my brother. I'm sorry . . ."

V blew out his breath. "S'all right. Look, how about you go get with your female? She's been thinking about you all afternoon. No offense, but I'm getting tired of hearing her voice in my head."

Mary leaned back against the great brass doors and looked up. Overhead, the sky was a brilliant expanse of blue, the air dry and crisp after the previous night's unseasonably early snowfall. Before the sun set, she wanted to walk the grounds, but the warmth coming through her parka made her lethargic. Or maybe it was just exhaustion. She hadn't been able to sleep after Rhage left their room, had spent all day long hoping he'd come back.

She had no idea what had happened last night. Wasn't even sure that she'd seen what she thought she had. For chrissakes, tattoos did not levitate off someone's skin. And they did not move. At least, not in her world.

Rhage wasn't the only reason for insomnia, though. It was time to find out what the doctors were going to do to her. The appointment with Dr. Della Croce was tomorrow, and, when it was over, she was going to know how bad the treatments were going to be.

God . . . She wanted to talk to Rhage about all that. To try to get him prepared.

As the sun dipped below the tree line, a chill sank into her. Standing up, she stretched and then went through the first of the doors into the vestibule. When those had closed, she showed her face to a camera and the inner set opened.

Rhage was sitting on the floor right next to the entrance. He got up slowly. "Hi. I've been waiting for you."

She smiled awkwardly, shifting her book back and forth between her hands. "I wanted to tell you where I was. But you'd left your cell phone behind when you—"

"Mary, listen, about last night—"

"Wait, before we start on that." She held up her hand. Took a deep breath. "I'm going to the hospital tomorrow. For the consultation before treatment starts."

His frown went so deep, his eyebrows met in the middle of his forehead. "Which hospital?"

"Saint Francis."

"What time?"

"In the afternoon."

"I want someone to go with you."

"A *doggen?*"

He shook his head. "Butch. The cop's good with a gun, and I don't want you unprotected. Look, can we go upstairs?"

She nodded and he took her hand, leading her up to the second floor. When they were in their bedroom, he paced incessantly while she sat on the bed.

As they talked about the doctor's appointment, it turned out preparing him was more like preparing herself. And then they were silent.

"Rhage, explain to me what happened last night." As he hesitated, she said, "Whatever it is, we'll get through it. You can tell me anything."

He stopped. Faced her. "I'm dangerous."

She frowned. "No, you aren't."

"You know what's all over my back?"

With a chill, she thought about the tattoo moving— *Hold up*, she told herself. It hadn't done that. He'd been breathing hard or something, and that was why the thing had appeared to have shifted positions.

"Mary, it's part of me. The beast. It's *inside* of me."
He rubbed his chest and then his arms. Now his thighs.
"I try to control it as best I can. But it . . . I don't want
to hurt you. I don't know what to do. Even now, being
around you, I'm . . . Christ, I'm a fucking mess."

As he held out hands that trembled, he did look totally
strung out.

"Part of the reason why I have to fight is that combat
brings me down," he said. "And it's what the females were
about. I took them because the release helped keep the
beast at bay. Except now that I can't have sex, I'm unstable.
That's why, last night, I almost lost it. Twice."

"Wait a . . . What are you talking about? You have me.
Make love with me."

"I can't let that happen anymore," he said through
gritted teeth. "I can't . . . lie with you anymore."

Stunned, she just stared at him. "You mean, you won't
be with me at all? Ever again?"

He shook his head. "Never."

"What the hell? You want me." Her eyes flicked down
to the thick bulge in his pants. "I can see you're hard. I
can smell the need you have for me."

Suddenly his eyes stopped blinking and flashed white.

"Why do your eyes change?" she whispered.

"Because it . . . comes alive."

As she fell silent, he began to breathe in a strange
rhythm. Two draws in, one long exhale. Two short gasps,
one slow blow.

She struggled to come to grips with what he was saying.
And failed, for the most part. He must mean that he had
some kind of hard-core alter ego, she thought.

"Mary, I can't . . . lie with you because . . . when I'm
with you it wants out." Two more quick breaths. "It
wants . . ."

"What, exactly?"

"It wants you." He backed away from her. "Mary, it

395

wants to . . . be inside of you. Do you understand what I'm saying? My other side wants to *take* you. I . . . I have to go now."

"Wait!" He stopped at the door. Their eyes met. "So let him have me."

Rhage's mouth dropped open. "Are you insane?"

No, she wasn't. They'd had sex with a desperation that had bordered on violence. She'd felt his hard thrusts before. If this other personality of his was tough, she figured she could handle it.

"Just let yourself go. It's all right."

Two short gasps. One long sigh. "Mary, you don't know . . . what the fuck you are saying."

She tried to make light of it. "What are you going to do? Eat me?"

When he just stared at her with those white eyes, she went cold. Jesus, maybe he had a point.

But she was definitely insane.

"We'll tie you down," she said.

He shook his head as he tripped over his feet and grabbed the doorknob. "I don't want to chance it."

"Wait! Do you know for sure what will happen?"

"No." He scratched his neck and shoulders, twitching. "Is there a possibility you'll just have the release you need?"

"Maybe."

"So we'll try it. I'll run if . . . well, if something weird happens. Rhage, let me do this for us. Besides, what's the alternative? I move out? We don't see each other? We never have sex again? I mean, come on, you're so itchy right now you're about to jump out of your skin."

Fear flooded into his face, tightening his mouth, widening his eyes. Shame followed on its heels, a terrible, gut-wrenching misery that carried her across the room to him. She took his hands, feeling them shake.

396

"I hate to see you like this, Rhage." When he started to speak, she cut him off. "Look, you know what we're dealing with here. I don't. Do what you have to do to secure yourself and we'll . . . see what happens."

He stared down at her. She wanted to press him, but had a feeling that would only push him in the opposite direction.

"Let me go talk to V," he said finally.

"Chains," Rhage repeated, while standing in the middle of the Pit's living room.

V looked over the top of his computer screen. "Like what kind?"

"The ones you'd tow a car with."

Butch came in from the kitchen, Bud in one hand, sandwich in the other. "Hey, big man. S'up?"

"I want the two of you to chain me to my bed."

"Kinky."

"So do we have something we can use, V?"

Vishous repositioned his Sox hat. "The garage. I think there are some in the garage. But, Rhage, man, what are you thinking?"

"I need to . . . be with Mary. But I don't want to go through the—" He stopped. Exhaled. "I'm afraid of changing. Too juiced."

V's pale eyes narrowed. "And you gave up the other females, didn't you?"

Rhage nodded. "I only want Mary. I couldn't even get hard for anyone else at this point."

"Ah, shit, man," Vishous said under his breath.

"Why's monogamy a bad thing?" Butch asked as he sat down and popped open the can of beer. "I mean, that's a damn fine woman you got. Mary's good people."

V shook his head. "Remember what you saw in that clearing, cop? How'd you like that anywhere near a female you loved?"

Butch put down the Bud without drinking from it. His eyes traveled over Rhage's body.

"We're going to need a shitload of steel," the human muttered.

FORTY-FOUR

O was getting nervous. The female still wasn't fully conscious, and it had been eighteen hours. Those darts had been calibrated for a male, but she should be up by now.

He worried that he'd given her a concussion.

God, this was just as it had been before. He and Jennifer would fight and, afterward, he'd get all nervous that he'd done some serious damage. While he'd cleaned her up, he'd always carefully tended her wounds, searching for broken bones and deep cuts. And as soon as he was sure she was okay, he'd made love to her even if she was still out of it. Coming while he was on top of her, on the heels of the relief of knowing he hadn't taken things too far, had always been the best kind of release.

He wished he could make love with the female he'd abducted.

O walked over to the hole she was in. He took off the mesh plate, clicked on a flashlight, and trained the beam inside. She was crumpled at the bottom, sagging against the pipe.

He wanted to take her out. Hold her. Kiss her and feel her skin against his. He wanted to come inside of her. But all *lessers* were impotent. The Omega, that bastard, was a jealous master.

O replaced the cover and prowled around, thinking about the night and day he'd spent with the Omega and the depression he'd been in since then. Funny—now that he had that female, his mind had cleared up and a new commitment energized him.

He knew it wasn't Jennifer in that hole, but the vampire

was so close to what had been taken from him, and he wasn't going to be picky. He'd accept the gift he'd been given and guard it well.

This time no one was going to take his woman from him. *No one.*

As the shutters lifted for the night, Zsadist got off his pallet and walked naked around the room he stayed in.

What had happened last night with Bella was killing him. He wanted to find her and apologize, but how was that going to go?

Sorry I jumped you like an animal. And you don't make me sick. Really.

God, he was *such* an asshole.

He closed his eyes and remembered being up against the wall by the shower while she reached out to his bare chest. Her fingers had been long and elegant, with pretty, unpolished nails at the tips. Her touch would have been light, he suspected. Light and warm.

He should have kept himself together. If he had, he would have known just once as a free male what it felt like to have a female's soft hand on his skin. As a slave he'd been touched too often, and always against his will, but freed . . .

And it wouldn't have been just any hand. It would have been Bella's.

Her palm would have landed on his chest, between his pecs, and maybe she would have stroked him a little bit. He might have liked that, if she'd gone slowly. Yeah, the more he thought about it, the more he could see himself maybe liking that—

Ah, what the hell was he going on about? The ability to tolerate intimacy of any kind had been raped out of him years ago. And anyway, he had no business entertaining fantasies of a female like Bella. He wasn't worthy even of the angry human whores he was forced to feed from.

Zsadist opened his eyes and dropped the bullshit. The kindest thing he could do for Bella, the best way to make amends, was to be sure she never saw him again, even inadvertently.

Although he would see her. Every night he would visit her house and make sure she was okay. It was a dangerous time now for civilians, and she needed to be watched over. He would just stay in the shadows while he did it.

The thought of protecting her eased him.

He couldn't trust himself to be with her. But he had absolute faith in his ability to keep her safe, no matter how many *lessers* he had to eat alive.

FORTY-FIVE

Mary paced along the second-floor balcony, just outside the bedroom door. She hadn't been able to watch Butch and V go to work with all those chains. And it was hard to know whether the two of them preparing Rhage to have sex with her was erotic as hell or downright scary.

The door opened.

Butch's eyes bounced around, not meeting hers. "He's ready."

Vishous came out lighting a hand-rolled. He took a deep drag. "We're going to hang around here in the hall. In case you need us."

Her first instinct was to tell them to go away. How creepy was it that they'd be right outside while she and Rhage were having sex? Privacy, after all, was a state of mind as well as a secluded, intimate place.

But then she thought of the amount of steel they'd gone in there with. That load of hardware hadn't been at all what she'd expected. Some rope, maybe. Handcuffs. But not the kind of stuff you'd lift an engine block off the ground with.

"Are you sure you have to wait?" she said.

They both nodded.

"Trust us on this one," Butch muttered.

Mary went into the room and closed the door. Candles were lit on either side of the bed, and Rhage was lying naked on the mattress, his arms angled up over his head, his legs spread to the point that they were stretched. Chains wrapped around his wrists and ankles and then looped about the bed's heavy oak supports.

Rhage lifted his head, teal-blue eyes piercing the dimness. "You sure about this?"

Actually, no, she wasn't. "You look uncomfortable."

"It's not bad." His head fell back. "Although I'm glad those are bedposts and not horses heading off in four different directions."

She eyed his colossal body, sprawled out for her like some kind of sexual sacrifice.

Holy . . . Moses. Was this real? Was she really going to—

Stop it, she told herself. *Don't keep him there any longer than you have to. And once this is over, and he knows everything's fine, you won't have to do it again.*

Mary kicked her shoes free, whipped her fleece and turtleneck over her head, and stripped out of her jeans.

Rhage's head rose again. As she took off her bra and her panties, his sex stirred. Lengthened. She watched him transform for her, hardening, thickening, growing. The arousal brought a flush to his face and a mist of sweat to his beautiful, hairless skin.

"Mary . . ." His pupils went white and he started to purr, gyrating his hips. The erection moved on top of his stomach, the head of it reaching his belly button and then some. With a sudden rush, his forearms shot up and pulled at the bonds. Chains rattled, shifted.

"Are you okay?" she said.

"Oh, God, Mary. I'm . . . we're hungry. We are . . . starving for you."

Shoring up her courage, she went over to the bed. She bent down and kissed him on the mouth, then she got up on the mattress. Got up on him.

As she straddled his hips, he writhed under her in waves.

Taking him into her hand, she tried to get him inside. She couldn't do it on the first try. He was too big and she wasn't ready and it hurt. She gave it another shot and grimaced.

"You aren't primed for me," Rhage said, arching as she put his blunt head against her core one more time. He made some kind of wild, humming sound.

"It'll be fine, let me just—"

"Come here." As he spoke, his voice changed. Deepened. "Kiss me, Mary."

She dropped down onto his chest and took his mouth, trying to will herself to get turned on. It didn't work.

He broke off the contact, as if sensing her lack of arousal.

"Come up higher on me." Chains stirred, the metallic sound almost a chime. "Give me your breast. Bring it to my mouth."

She shimmied up and dropped her nipple to his lips. The instant she felt a gentle sucking, her body responded. She closed her eyes, relieved as heat took hold.

Rhage seemed to recognize the change in her, because the purring sound he made grew louder, a beautiful *twrr*ing in the air. As he caressed her with his lips, his body moved in a great surge under her, his chest rising and then his neck and his head kicking back. Sweat bloomed anew on his skin, the scent of his need for her filling the air with spice.

"Mary, let me taste you." His voice was so low now that his words distorted. "Your sweetness. Between your legs. Let me taste you."

She looked down and two gleaming white orbs stared up at her. There was a hypnotic quality to them, an erotic persuasion she couldn't deny, even though she knew it wasn't just Rhage she was with.

She crawled up his body, stopping when she was at his chest. The intimacy was somehow shocking, especially with him tied down.

"Closer, Mary." Even the way he said her name was not the same. "Come closer to my mouth."

She moved above him awkwardly, trying to accommodate the position he was in. She ended up with one knee on his chest and the other over his opposite shoulder. He craned his neck and twisted his head, rising to meet her flesh, capturing her with his lips.

His moan vibrated into her core, and she planted a hand on the wall. The pleasure stole her inhibitions completely, rendering her a servant to the sex as he licked and sucked at her. As her body responded in a rush of wetness, there was a sharp sound followed by a groan as the chains were pulled tight and the bed frame's wood protested. Rhage's great arms were strained against the bonds that held him, his muscles rigid, his fingers spread wide and curled into clawlike points.

"That's it," he said between her legs. "I can feel you . . . coming."

His voice sank down and disappeared into a growl.

Her release shot through her and she fell over, sinking onto the bed, her leg dragging across his face before falling onto his neck at the ankle. As soon as her pulses faded, she looked at him. His white, unblinking eyes were wide with wonder and awe. He was utterly captivated by her as he lay there, breathing in that pattern of two beats in followed by one long release.

"Take me now, Mary." The words were deep, warped. Not Rhage's.

But she didn't feel scared or as if she were betraying him.

Whatever had come out of him, it wasn't malevolent and it wasn't entirely unfamiliar either. She'd sensed this . . . thing in him all along and knew it was nothing she needed to be frightened of. And as she met his eyes now, it was as it had been in the billiard room, a separate presence looking at her, but Rhage just the same.

She moved down him and took him inside her body, fitting him perfectly. His hips surged, and another high call came out of his throat as he began pumping. The thrusts went in and out of her, a delicious pounding slide that came up with increasing force. To keep from getting bucked off, she braced herself on all fours and tried to stay stable.

The keening sound got louder as he went wild, slapping his hips against her, trembling all over. Urgency grew and grew, building, a storm coming, about to hit. Suddenly he bowed off the mattress, the bed squealing as his arms and legs contracted. His eyelids peeled back and white light pierced the room, making it as bright as high noon. Deep inside she felt the contractions of his climax, and the sensations kicked off another orgasm for her, taking her over the edge.

She fell onto his chest when it was over, and they were both still except for the breathing, hers normal, his in that odd rhythm.

She lifted her head and stared into his face. White eyes burned as they focused on her with total adoration.

"My Mary," the voice said.

And then a low-level electrical shock flowed through her body and charged the air. Every light came on in the room, flooding the space with illumination. She gasped and glanced around, but the surge left as quickly as it came. Just like that, the energy was gone. She looked down.

Rhage's eyes were normal again, the teal color shining.

"Mary?" he said in a dazed, indistinct voice.

She had to take a few breaths before speaking. "You're back."

"And you're okay." He lifted his arms, flexed his fingers. "I didn't change."

"What do you mean, change?"

"I didn't . . . I could see you while it was with me. You were hazy, but I knew you weren't getting hurt. It's the first time I've ever remembered anything."

She didn't know what to make of that, but saw that the chains had rubbed his skin raw. "Can I let you go?"

"Yeah. Please."

Getting him undone took some time. When he was free, he massaged his wrists and ankles and watched her carefully, as if reassuring himself she was okay.

She looked around for a robe. "I'd better go tell Butch and V it's safe to leave."

"I'll do it." He went over to the bedroom door and stuck his head out.

As he spoke with the men, she looked at the tattoo on his back. She could have sworn it was smiling at her.

God, she was nuts. She really was.

She hopped up on the bed and pulled the blankets over herself.

Rhage shut the door and leaned back against it. He still looked tense, in spite of the release he'd had. "After all that . . . are you finally afraid of me?"

"No."

"Aren't you afraid of . . . it?"

She held her arms out. "Come here. I want to hold you. You look like you've got a case of the rattles."

He approached the bed slowly, as if he didn't want her to feel stalked or something. She motioned with her hands, urging him to hurry up.

Rhage lay down beside her, but didn't reach for her.

After a heartbeat she went for him, wrapping her body around his, running her hands over him. When she brushed against his side, catching the edge of the dragon's tail, Rhage flinched and shifted.

He didn't want her anywhere near the tattoo, she thought.

"Roll over," she said. "Onto your stomach."

When he shook his head, she pushed at his shoulders. It was like trying to move a grand piano.

"Roll over, damn it. Come on, Rhage."

He complied with no grace whatsoever, cursing and flopping onto his belly.

407

She ran her hand right down his spine, right over the dragon.

Rhage's muscles contracted in random order. No, not random. They were the parts of his body that corresponded to where she was touching the tattoo.

How extraordinary.

She stroked his back some more, feeling as if the ink were rising up to meet her palm like a cat.

"Are you ever going to want to be with me again?" Rhage said stiffly. He turned his face to the side so he could see her. Except he didn't look up.

She lingered on the beast's mouth, tracing the line of its lips with her fingertip. Rhage's own set parted as if he were feeling her touch.

"Why wouldn't I want to be with you?"

"That was a little weird, wasn't it?"

She laughed. "Weird? I'm sleeping in a mansion full of vampires. I've fallen in love with a—"

Mary stopped. *Oh, God.* What had just come out of her mouth?

Rhage pushed his upper body off the bed, twisting his chest around so he could look at her. "What did you just say?"

She hadn't meant for it to happen, she thought. The falling or the telling.

But she would take neither of them back.

"I'm not sure," she murmured, taking in the brute strength of his shoulders and arms. "But I think it was something along the lines of 'I love you.' Yeah, that was it. I, ah, I love you."

Now, that was lame. She could do a hell of a lot better.

Mary grabbed his face, planted a good hard one on his mouth, and looked him straight in the eye.

"I love you, Rhage. I love you something fierce."

Those heavy arms wrapped around her and he buried his head in her neck. "I didn't think you ever would."

"Am I that hardheaded?"

"No. I'm that undeserving."

Mary pulled back and glared at him. "I don't want to hear you say that again. You are the very best thing that's ever happened to me."

"Even with the beast?"

Beast? Sure, she'd sensed something else was in him. But a beast? Still, Rhage was looking so worried, she humored him.

"Yeah, even with him as well. Only can we do it without all the metal next time? I'm very confident that you won't hurt me."

"Yeah, I think we can lose the chains."

Mary urged him back into the crook of her neck and found herself focusing on the *Madonna and Child* across the room.

"You are the oddest miracle," she whispered to him, looking at the picture.

"What?" he said into her throat.

"Nothing." She kissed the top of his blond head and went back to staring at the Madonna.

FORTY-SIX

Bella took a deep breath and smelled dirt.

God, her head hurt. And her knees were killing her. They were jammed against something hard. And cold.

Her eyes flew open. Darkness. Blackness. Blindness.

She tried to lift a hand, but her elbow ran into a bumpy wall. There was another wall at her back and in front of her and to the sides. She banged around in the small space, panicking. Opening her mouth until it gaped, she found she couldn't breathe. There was no air, only the smell of damp earth, clogging . . . nose . . . she—

Screamed.

And something above her moved. Light blinded her as she looked up.

"Ready to come out?" a man's voice said softly.

It all came back: the race for her house across the meadow, the fight with the *lesser*, the blacking out.

With a quick jerk she was lifted by a chest harness from what she realized was a pipe in the ground. As she looked around in terror, she had no idea where she was. The room was not large and the walls were unfinished. There were no windows, just two skylights in the low ceiling, which were both covered with black cloth. Three bald lightbulbs hung from wires. The place smelled sweet, a combination of fresh pine boards and the *lesser*'s baby-powder scent.

When she saw a stainless-steel table and dozens of knives and hammers, she trembled so badly she started to cough.

"Don't worry about all that," the *lesser* said. "That's not for you as long as you behave."

His hands burrowed into her hair and fanned it out

over her shoulders. "You're going to take a shower now, and you're going to wash this. You're going to wash this for me."

He reached over and picked up a bundle of clothes. As he pressed them into her arms, she realized they were her own.

"If you're good, you get to put these on. But not until we get you clean." He pushed her toward an open door, just as a cell phone started to ring. "Into the shower. *Now.*"

Too disoriented and petrified to argue, she stumbled into an unfinished bathroom that had no toilet. Like a drone, she shut herself in and turned the water on with hands that shook. When she pivoted around, she saw the *lesser* had opened the door and was watching her.

He put his hand over the bottom of the cell phone. "Take off the clothes. Now."

She glanced over at the knives. Bile rose in her throat as she stripped. When she was finished, she covered herself with her hands and shivered.

The *lesser* hung up and put the phone down. "You do not hide from me. Drop your arms."

She backed up, shaking her head numbly.

"Drop them."

"Please, don't—"

He took two steps forward and slapped her across the face, sending her into the wall. Then he grabbed her.

"Look at me. *Look at me.*" His eyes glittered with excitement as she met his stare. "God, it is so good to have you back."

He put his arms around her, holding her close. The sweet smell of him overwhelmed her.

Butch was one hell of an escort, Mary thought as they departed the Saint Francis oncology suite. Wearing a black wool coat, a 1940s-style hat, and a terrific pair of aviator sunglasses, he looked like a very chic hit man.

411

Which was not deceiving. She knew he was armed to the teeth, because Rhage had inspected the man's weapons before he'd let the two of them out of the house.

"You need anything before we go back?" Butch asked when they were outside.

"No, thanks. Let's head home."

The afternoon had been grueling and inconclusive. Dr. Della Croce was still conferring with her partners and had ordered Mary to have an MRI as well as another physical. More blood had been drawn also because the team wanted to recheck a couple of liver functions.

God, she hated that she was going to have to come back tomorrow and had yet another night of not knowing to go through. As she and Butch went over to the open lot and got into the Mercedes, she was that horrible combination of wired and tired. What she really needed to do was go to bed, but she was so anxious, sleep was not in her future.

"Actually, Butch, will you take me by my house on the way home? I want to pick up some medicine I left there." Those low-dose sleeping pills were going to come in handy.

"I'd like to avoid heading over there if we could. Any chance you could pick up what you want at a CVS or something?"

"They're prescription."

He frowned. "All right. But you make it quick, and I'm coming in with you."

Fifteen minutes later they parked in her driveway. In the golden glow of the setting sun, her place looked deserted. There were leaves blown up against the front door, her chrysanthemums were half-dead, and there was a tree limb down in the yard.

She hoped whoever bought it would love the place as much as she had.

When she walked into the house, a cold gust shot

through the living room, and it turned out that the window over the kitchen sink was cracked about three inches. As she shut it, she assumed V must have left it open when he'd come over to work on the alarm system before she'd moved out. She locked the thing and then went upstairs to get the Ambien.

Before they left, she paused at the rear sliding door and looked at her backyard. The pool was covered with a patina of leaves, the surface dull. The meadow beyond was an undulation of pale grass—

Something was flashing over at Bella's house.

Her instincts flared. "Butch, do you mind if we check that out?"

"Not a chance. I need to get you home."

She slid the door back.

"Mary, it's not safe."

"And that's Bella's. There shouldn't be anything moving at her house this time of day. Come on."

"You can call her from the car."

"I'll do it from here." A moment later she hung up and headed back for the door. "No answer. I'm going over."

"The hell you are—Mary, hold up! Christ, don't make me throw you over my shoulder and carry you out of here."

"You pull something like that and I'll tell Rhage you had your hands all over me."

Butch's eyes flared. "Jesus, you're as bad a manipulator as he is."

"Not quite, but I'm learning. Now, are you coming with me or am I going it alone?"

He let out a juicy curse and palmed a gun. "I don't like this."

"Duly noted. Look, we'll just make sure she's okay. Shouldn't take more than ten minutes."

They walked through the meadow, Butch scanning the

413

field with hard eyes. As they got closer to the farmhouse, she could see Bella's back French door swinging in the wind and catching the sun's last rays.

"Stay tight with me, okay?" Butch said as they walked onto the lawn.

The door bounced open again.

"Oh, shit," he muttered.

Its brass lock had been splintered and several panes had been broken.

They stepped cautiously inside.

"Oh, my God," Mary breathed.

Chairs were strewn about the kitchen along with broken plates and mugs and a shattered lamp. Burn marks streaked the floor and so did some kind of black, inklike substance.

As she bent down to look at the oily smears, Butch said, "Don't get near that stuff. It's the blood of a *lesser*."

She closed her eyes. Those things in the park had Bella.

"Her bedroom in the basement?" he asked.

"That's what she told me."

They jogged down to the cellar and found the double doors to her room wide-open. A few of her dresser drawers had been thrown about, and it looked as if some of her clothes had been taken. Which didn't make a whole lot of sense.

Butch flipped open his cell phone as they went back up to the kitchen.

"V? We've had a break-in. Bella's." He eyed the black stains on a cracked chair. "She put up a good fight. But I think she's been taken by the *lessers*."

As Rhage pulled on a set of leathers, he pinned the cell phone between his shoulder and his ear. "Cop? Let me talk to Mary."

There was a shuffling sound and then he heard, "Hello? Rhage?"

"Hey, my female, you okay?"

"I'm fine." Her voice was shaky as hell, but what a fricking relief just to hear it.

"I'm coming for you." He grabbed his chest holster as he pushed his feet into his shitkickers. "Sun's just going down now, so I'll be right there."

He wanted her safe and at home. While he and the brothers went after those assholes.

"Rhage . . . Oh, God, Rhage, what are they going to do to her?"

"I don't know." Which was a lie. He knew exactly what they were doing to Bella. God help her. "Listen, I realize you're worried about her. But right now I need you to focus on yourself. I want you on Butch like a screw cap, understand?"

Because it was faster for Rhage to dematerialize to her than have the cop drive her home to him. But he hated her being so exposed.

As he inserted his daggers into the holster, he realized there was only silence coming over the phone. "Mary? Did you hear what I said? Think about yourself. Stay next to Butch."

"I'm right beside him."

"Good. Keep it that way. And don't worry, one way or the other we'll get Bella back. I love you." He hung up and pulled on the heavy weight of his trench coat.

As he shot out into the hall, he ran into Phury, who was in leather and fully armed.

"What the fuck is going on?" Zsadist came down the corridor. "I get this hot and bothered message from V about a female—"

"Bella's been taken by the *lessers*," Rhage said, checking his Glock.

A cold draft came out of Z like a blast. "*What did you say?*"

Rhage frowned at the brother's intensity. "Bella. Mary's friend."

"When?"

"Don't know. Butch and Mary are at her house—"

Just like that, Zsadist was gone.

Rhage and Phury were right behind him, dematerializing to Bella's. The three of them ran up the farmhouse's front steps together.

Mary was in the kitchen, right by Butch who was checking out something on the floor. Rhage thundered over and grabbed on to her, holding her against him so hard their bones met.

"I'm going to take you home," he murmured into her hair.

"Mercedes's back at her place," Butch said as he rose from the black stains he'd been looking at. He tossed a set of keys at Rhage.

Phury cursed while righting a chair. "What've we got?"

The cop shook his head. "I think they took her alive, based on this pattern of scorched streaks to the door. Her blood trail burned up when the sun hit it—"

Even before Butch stopped short and glanced at Mary, Rhage started for the door with her. The last thing she needed was to hear the god-awful details.

The cop continued, "Besides, she's no use to them dead—Zsadist? You okay, man?"

In passing, Rhage glanced over his shoulder at Z.

Z was in a shaking fury, his face twitching along the scar under his left eye. Hell, he looked as if he were going to blow up, except it was hard to believe the capture of a female would matter one way or the other to him.

Rhage paused. "Z, what's doing?"

The brother turned away as if he didn't want to be seen, then leaned closer to the window he was in front of. With a low growl, he dematerialized.

Rhage glanced outside. All he could see was Mary's barn across the field.

"Let's go," he said to her. "I want you out of here."

She nodded and he gripped her arm, leading her from the house. They said nothing as they walked quickly through the grass.

Just as they stepped onto her lawn, glass shattered with a crash.

Something—someone—was thrown out of Mary's house. Right through the slider.

As the body bounced on the terrace, Zsadist jumped through the opening, fangs bared, face contoured with aggression. He launched himself onto the *lesser*, catching the thing by the hair and lifting its torso off the ground.

"Where is she?" the brother snarled. When the thing didn't answer, Z switched his hold and bit it on the shoulder, right through its leather coat. The slayer howled in pain.

Rhage didn't stick around to watch the show. He raced Mary around the side of the house, only to run into two more *lessers*. Forcing her behind him, he protected her with his body while he went for his gun. Just as he got it into firing position, popping sounds rang out from the right of him. Bullets whizzed by his ear and pinged into the house and hit him in the arm and the thigh and . . .

He'd never been so glad to have the beast emerge. He threw himself into the vortex with a roar, embracing the change, welcoming the flash of heat and the explosion of his muscles and bones.

As a blast of energy came out of Rhage, Mary was thrown against the house, her head snapping back and banging into the clapboards. She slid to the ground, dimly aware of a huge presence taking Rhage's place.

There were sounds of more gunshots, screams, a deafening roar. Dragging herself over the ground, she hid behind a juniper bush just as someone turned the outdoor lights on.

Holy . . . Christ.

It was the tattoo come to life: a dragonlike creature covered with iridescent purple and lime-green scales. The thing had a slashing tail with barbs, long yellow claws, and a wild black mane. She couldn't see the face, but the sounds it was making were horrific.

And the beast was deadly, making quick work of the *lessers*.

She covered her head with her arms, unable to watch. She hoped like hell the beast wouldn't notice her, and that, if it did, it would remember who she was.

More roaring. Another scream. A terrible grinding crunch.

From the back of the house, she heard a rapid splatter of gunshots.

Someone yelled, "Zsadist! Stop! We need them alive!"

The fighting went on and on and probably lasted only five or ten minutes. And then there was just the sound of breathing. Two breaths in. One slow breath out.

She looked up. The beast was looming over the bush she hid behind, that steady white gaze trained on her. Its face was huge, its jaw carrying a shark's load of teeth, its mane falling over its broad forehead. Black blood ran down its chest.

"Where is she? Where's Mary?" V's voice traveled from around the corner. "Mary? Oh . . . *shit*."

The beast's head whipped around as Vishous and Zsadist pulled up short.

"I'll distract it," Zsadist said. "You get her out of the way."

The beast turned on the brothers and positioned itself in an attack stance, claws up, head forward, tail waving steadily. The muscles in its hindquarters quivered.

Zsadist kept coming as V started to close in on where she was.

The beast snarled and snapped its jaws.

Z cursed in its direction. "Yeah, what you gonna do to me that hasn't already been done?"

Mary shot to her feet. "Zsadist! Don't!"

Her voice froze everything like a tableau: Zsadist walking forward. The beast preparing to lunge. Vishous sidling up to her. All three of them looked at her for a split second. And then refocused on one another, going right back to the collision course they'd been on.

"Will you two get out of here!" she hissed. "Someone's going to get hurt. You're just pissing it off!"

"Mary, we need to get you out of its way." V's tone was that awful *let's-be-reasonable* one men pulled out at traffic accidents.

"It won't hurt me, but it's about to tear the two of you apart. Back off!"

No one was listening to her.

"God, spare me from heroes," she muttered. "Back the fuck off!"

That got their attention. The two brothers stopped moving. And the beast looked over its shoulder.

"Hey," she murmured, stepping out from behind the bush. "It's me. Mary."

The great dragon's head shook up and down like a horse's, its mane flashing black. The massive body swung a little toward her.

The beast was beautiful, she thought. Beautiful in the way a cobra was, its ugliness overshadowed by graceful, shifting movements and a predatory intelligence you had to respect.

"You are really huge, you know that?" She kept her voice low as she approached it slowly, remembering how Rhage liked her to talk to him. "And you did an excellent job keeping those *lessers* from me. Thank you."

When she was right next to the beast, the jaws opened and it called out to the sky while keeping its eyes on her. Abruptly the great head lowered, as if it were seeking her touch. She reached out, stroking smooth scales, feeling the great tensile strength in the thickness of its neck and shoulder.

"You are scary as hell up close, you really are. But you feel nice. I didn't think your skin would be so soft or warm."

Those white eyes flickered to the left and narrowed, its lips curling up into a snarl.

"Tell me someone isn't coming closer," she said without varying her tone or turning away. She kept her eyes locked on that huge face.

"Butch, hang back, man," V muttered. "She's talking him down."

The beast growled low in its throat.

"Hey, now, don't bother with them," she said. "They're not going to do anything to either one of us. Besides, haven't you had enough tonight?"

The creature heaved a great breath.

"Yeah, you're done," she murmured, stroking under the mane. Heavy muscles ran in great ropes under the skin. There was no fat, nothing but power.

It eyed the vampires once again.

"No, they're nothing you and I need to worry about. You just stand right here with me and—"

Without warning, the beast whirled around and knocked her to the ground with its tail. It leaped into the air at her house, crashing its upper body through a window.

A *lesser* was pulled out into the night, and the beast's roar of outrage was cut off as it took the slayer between its jaws.

Mary tucked into a ball, shielding herself from the tail's barbs. She covered her ears and closed her eyes, cutting off the juicy sounds and the horrible sight of the killing.

Moments later she felt her body being nudged. The beast was pushing at her with its nose.

She rolled over and looked up into its white eyes.

"I'm fine. But we're going to have to work on your table manners."

The beast purred and stretched out on the ground next to her, resting its head between its forelegs. There was a brilliant flash of light and then Rhage appeared in the same position. Covered in black blood, he shivered in the cold.

She shrugged out of her coat as the brothers ran over. Each one of the men took their jackets off and laid them down on Rhage, too.

"Mary?" he croaked.

"I'm right here. Everyone's fine. The two of you saved me."

FORTY-SEVEN

Butch wouldn't have believed it if he hadn't seen the whole thing for himself. Mary had turned that raging beast into a pet.

Jesus, that woman had some kind of way about her. And courage, too. After seeing that nasty-looking piece of work *eat* those slayers in front of her, she'd stood up in front of the damn thing and actually touched it. He wouldn't have had those kind of *cojones*.

Mary looked up from Rhage's body. "Will some of you help me get him to the car?"

Butch went right over, taking Rhage's legs while V and Zsadist each picked up an arm. They carried him around to the Mercedes and muscled the brother into the backseat.

"I can't drive him home," Mary said. "I don't know the way."

V went to the driver's-side door. "I'll take you guys. Cop, I'll be back in twenty."

"Be careful with them," Butch murmured. When he turned, Phury and Tohr were staring at him with an expectation he was used to.

Without even noticing, he slid right back into homicide detective land and took control.

"Let me tell you what I know so far." He led the two to the back of Mary's house and pointed at a pattern of black patches on the ground. "You see these burned marks in the turf? Bella was taken by the *lesser* and carried across the field from her place to here. She was bleeding, and when the sun came out her trail of blood incinerated and left this pattern on the ground. And why did he have to take her through the meadow? I think the slayer came looking for Mary and somehow ran into Bella on this piece of property. Bella tore off for her house and he had to bring her back, probably because he'd parked his car here. Follow me, boys."

He went around the side of the house and down to the street where there was a Ford Explorer parked at the curb.

"Bella was, for them, a lucky mistake, and they came back tonight to finish the job by getting Mary. I'll get V to run this car's plates." Butch eyed the sky. Light snow flurries were coming down. "With this shit falling, the integrity of the outdoor scenes is disintegrating, but I think we know what we can from the exteriors. Let me go through the SUV while you boys clean up the bodies of those *lessers*. I don't need to tell you to take anything you can off them, wallets, BlackBerrys, cell phones. Give it all to V when he comes back so he can take the stuff to the Pit. And stay out of both houses until I clear the scenes."

As the brothers got to work, Butch went through the Explorer with a fine-toothed comb. By the time he was finished, the vampires had finished poofing the *lessers*.

"SUV's clean as a whistle, but it's registered to a guy named Ustead." He handed the registration card to Phury. "Probably a false identity, but would one of you boys check out the address anyway? I'm heading back to Bella's to finish up there."

Tohr checked his watch. "We'll check this Ustead's place out, then go do our civilian sweeps. Unless you need help?"

"No, it's better if I go it alone."

The brother paused. "What about some cover, cop? Because the *lessers* might show up again. None of the ones here got away, but, when those boys don't check in, some of their buddies could come back for a look-see."

423

"I can handle myself." He took out his gun and checked it. "But I spent my clip. Can I borrow another?"

Phury held out a Beretta. "Take this and start fresh."

And Tohr wouldn't leave until Butch accepted one of his Glocks as well.

Tucking one gun into his holster and keeping the other in his hand, Butch took off across the meadow at a jog. His body was primed and pumped, and he covered the distance in no time at all, barely breaking a sweat. As he ran, his mind was sharp as the night air, churning over lists of things to follow up on and theories about where Bella might have been taken.

As he ran up to the back of the farmhouse, he caught a flash of movement inside. He flattened against the wall next to the broken French door and eased the Beretta's safety off. From inside the kitchen there was the sound of crunching glass, like popcorn on a stove. Someone was walking around. Someone big.

Butch waited until whoever it was got closer; then he jumped into the doorway, aiming the gun at chest level.

"It's just me, cop," Z muttered.

Butch swung the muzzle to the ceiling. "Christ, I could have shot you."

But Z didn't seem to care that he'd almost been plugged. He just leaned down and fished around some dish shards with his fingertip.

Butch took off his coat and rolled up his sleeves. He wasn't going to ask Zsadist to leave. There was no point in getting into an argument with him, and besides, the brother was acting totally weird, kind of like he was in a stupor. The dead calm in him was eerie as hell.

Z picked something off the floor.

"What is it?" Butch asked.

"Nothing."

"Try not to disturb the scene, okay?"

As Butch looked around, he cursed to himself. He wanted

his old partner from the force, José. He wanted his whole Homicide team. He wanted his CSI folks back in the lab.

He allowed himself a couple of seconds of black frustration and then got to work. Starting at the busted French doors, he was prepared to go through every inch of the house, even if it took him until dawn.

Mary brought out another round of Alka-Seltzer from the bathroom. Rhage was lying on their bed, breathing slowly, more than a little green around the gills.

After he drank the stuff, he looked up at her. His face tensed and his eyes grew leery, worried.

"Mary . . . I wish you hadn't seen all that."

"Shh. Just rest for a little while, okay? There's time to talk later."

She got undressed and slid in next to him. The moment she was between the sheets, he curled himself around her, his big body a living blanket.

Lying next to him, all safe and secure, made her think of Bella.

Mary's chest constricted and her eyes squeezed shut. If she believed in God at all, she would have prayed right now. Instead she just hoped as hard as she could.

Sleep came eventually. Until hours later, when Rhage let out a mighty yell.

"Mary! Mary, run!"

He began flailing around with his arms. With a lunge, she dove between them, putting herself against his chest, holding him down, talking to him. When his hands still scrambled, she captured them and put his palms to her face.

"I'm okay. I'm right here."

"Oh, thank God . . . Mary." He stroked her cheeks. "I can't see very well."

In the candlelight, she looked down into his unfocused eyes.

"How long does the recovery take?" she asked.

"Day or two." He frowned and then stretched his legs. "Actually, I'm not as stiff as I usually am. Stomach's a mess, but the aches aren't bad at all. After I change—"

He stopped, jaw going rigid. Then he loosened his hold on her as if he didn't want her to feel trapped.

"Don't worry," she murmured. "I'm not afraid of you even though I know what's in you."

"Hell, Mary . . . I didn't want you to ever see it." He shook his head. "It's just so awful. The whole thing is awful."

"I'm not so sure about that. I went right up to it, actually. The beast. I was as close as you and I are now."

Rhage's eyes shut. "Shit, Mary, you shouldn't have done that."

"Yeah, well, either I did or the creature would have eaten V and Zsadist. Literally. But don't worry, your beast and I get along just fine."

"Don't do that again."

"The hell I won't. You can't control it. The brothers can't handle it. But that thing listens to me. Like it or not, the two of you need me."

"But isn't it . . . ugly?"

"No. Not to me." She pressed a kiss to his chest. "It's fearsome and terrifying and powerful and awe-inspiring. And if anyone ever tried to get at me, that thing would wipe out a neighborhood. How could a girl not be charmed? Besides, after seeing those *lessers* in action, I'm grateful for it. I feel safe. Between you and the dragon, I don't have to worry."

When she looked up at him with a smile, Rhage was blinking rapidly.

"Oh, Rhage . . . it's okay. Don't be—"

"I thought if you knew what it looked like," he said hoarsely, "you wouldn't be able to see me anymore. All you'd remember is some horrible monster."

She kissed him and wiped a tear off his face. "It's a part of you, not all of you or all of what you are. And I love you. With it or without it."

He gathered her close and tucked her head into his neck. When he let out a deep sigh, she said, "Were you born with it?"

"No. It's a punishment."

"For what?"

"I killed a bird."

Mary glanced at him, thinking that seemed a little extreme.

Rhage smoothed her hair back. "I did a lot more than that, but killing a bird was what finally tipped the scales."

"Will you tell me?"

He paused for a long while. "When I was young, right after my transition, I was . . . uncontrollable. I had all this energy and strength and I was stupid with how I used it. Not mean, just . . . dumb. Showing off. Picking fights. And I, ah, I slept with a lot of females, females who I shouldn't have taken because they were the *shellans* of other males. I never did it to piss off their *hellrens*, but I took what they offered. I took . . . everything I was offered. I drank, I smoked opium, fell into laudanum . . . I'm glad you didn't know me then.

"That went on for twenty, thirty years. I was a disaster waiting for a coastline, and sure enough I met a female. I wanted her, but she was coy, and the more she teased me, the more I was determined to have her. It wasn't until I was inducted into the Brotherhood that she came around. Weapons turned her on. Warriors turned her on. She only wanted to be with brothers. One night I took her out into the forest and showed her my daggers and my guns. She was playing with my rifle. God, I can remember the look of it in her hands, it was one of those flintlock ones they were making in the early eighteen hundreds."

1800s? Good God, how old was he? Mary wondered.

"Anyway, it went off in her hand and I heard something hit the ground. It was a barn owl. One of those lovely white barn owls. I can still see the red stain as its blood seeped onto its feathers. When I picked up the bird and felt its light weight in my hands, I realized that carelessness was a form of cruelty. See, I'd always told myself that, because I meant no harm, anything that happened wasn't my fault. At that moment, though, I knew I was wrong. If I hadn't given the female my gun, the bird wouldn't have been shot. I was responsible even though I didn't pull the trigger."

He cleared his throat. "The owl was such an innocent thing. So fragile and small compared to me as it bled and died. I felt . . . wretched, and I was thinking about where to bury it, when the Scribe Virgin came to me. She was livid. *Livid.* She loves birds to begin with, and the barn owl is her sacred symbol, but of course the death was only part of it. She took the body from my palms and breathed life back into the bird, sending it off into the night sky. The relief when that bird flew away was tremendous. I felt as if the slate had been wiped clean. I was free, cleansed. But then the Scribe Virgin turned on me. She cursed me, and since then, anytime I get out of control, the beast comes out. In a way, it's really the perfect punishment. It's taught me to regulate my energy, my moods. It's taught me to respect the consequences of all my actions. Helped me understand the power in my body in a way I never would have otherwise."

He laughed a little. "The Scribe Virgin hates me, but she did me one hell of a favor. Anyway . . . that's the awful why of it. I killed a bird and got the beast. Simple and complicated by turns, right?"

Rhage's chest expanded as he took in a great breath. She could feel his remorse as clearly as if it were her own.

"By turns. Indeed," she murmured, stroking his shoulder.

"The good news is that in another ninety-one years or

428

so, it's over." He frowned, as if considering the prospect. "The beast will be gone."

Funny, he looked a little worried.

"You'll miss it, won't you?" she said.

"No. No, I . . . It'll be a relief. Really."

Except that frown stayed in place.

FORTY-EIGHT

Around nine the next morning, Rhage stretched in bed and was surprised to feel like himself. He'd never recovered so fast before and had a feeling it was because he hadn't fought the change. Maybe that was the trick. Just go with it.

Mary came out of the bathroom with a load of towels in her arms and headed into the closet to drop them down the chute. She looked tired, grim. Which made sense. They'd spent a lot of the morning talking about Bella, and, though he'd done his best to reassure her, they both knew the situation was bad.

And then there was another reason for her to be worried.

"I want to come to the doctor's with you today," he said.

She came back out into the room. "You're awake."

"Yeah. And I want to come with you."

As she walked over to him, she had that tight look she got whenever she was going to argue.

He jumped the gun on the most obvious objection. "Switch the appointment to late in the day. Sun goes down by five thirty now."

"Rhage—"

Anxiety made his voice hard. "Do it."

She put her hands on her hips. "I don't appreciate your pushing me around."

"Let me rephrase myself. Change the appointment, please." But he didn't ease up on his tone in the slightest. When she got the news, whatever it was, he was going to be by her side.

She reached for the phone, all the while cursing under

her breath. When she hung up, she seemed surprised. "Ah, Dr. Della Croce will see me . . . us . . . tonight at six."

"Good. And I'm sorry about being such a hard-ass. I just have to be with you when you hear. I need to be a part of this as much as I can."

She shook her head and bent down to pick a shirt up from the floor. "You are the sweetest thug I've ever known."

As he watched her body move, he felt himself harden.

Inside, the beast shifted as well, but there was a curious calm to the sensation. It was no big rush of energy, just a slow burn, as if the creature were content to share his body, not take it over. A communion, not a domination.

Probably because the thing knew that the only way to be with Mary was through Rhage's form.

She kept going around the room, tidying up. "What are you looking at?"

"You."

Sweeping her hair back, she laughed. "So your sight's returning."

"Among other things. Come here, Mary. I want to kiss you."

"Oh, sure. Make up for being a bully by plying me with your body."

"I'll use any asset I've got."

He threw the sheets and duvet off himself and swept his hand down his chest, over his stomach. Lower. Her eyes widened when he took his heavy erection in his palm. As he stroked himself, the scent of her arousal bloomed like a bouquet in the room.

"Come over here, Mary." He twisted his hips. "I'm not sure I'm doing this right. It feels so much better when you touch me."

"You are incorrigible."

"Just looking for some instruction."

"Like you need that," she muttered, taking off her sweater.

They made love in an unhurried, glorious way. But when he held her afterward, he couldn't go to sleep. Neither could she.

That night Mary tried to breathe normally as they took the elevator up to the hospital's sixth floor. Saint Francis was quieter in the evening, but still teeming with people.

The receptionist let them in and then left, pulling a cherry-red coat on as she locked the door behind her. Five minutes later Dr. Della Croce entered the waiting room.

The woman almost managed to hide her double take at Rhage. Even though he was dressed like a civilian, in slacks and a black knit turtleneck, that leather trench coat was still something to see falling from those broad shoulders.

Well, and Rhage was . . . Rhage. Unbearably beautiful.

The doctor smiled. "Ah, hi, Mary, would you come down to my office? Or will it be the two of you?"

"Both of us. This is Rhage. My—"

"Mate," he said loud and clearly.

Dr. Della Croce's eyebrows shot up, and Mary had to smile in spite of all the tension in her body.

The three of them went down the hall, past the doors of the exam rooms and the scales in the little alcoves and the computer stations. There was no small talk. No chatty, how's-the-weather, gee-the-holidays-are-coming-up-fast kind of stuff. The doctor knew Mary hated social chatter.

Something Rhage had picked up on at TGI Friday's on their first date.

God, that felt like years ago, Mary thought. And who could have foreseen they'd end up here together?

Dr. Della Croce's office was cluttered with neat piles of papers and files and books. Diplomas from Smith and Harvard hung on the wall, but the thing that Mary had

432

always found most reassuring was the line of thriving African violets on the windowsill.

She and Rhage sat down as the doctor went behind her desk.

Before the woman was in her chair, Mary said, "So what are you giving me, and how much can I handle?"

Dr. Della Croce looked up over the medical records and the pens and the binder clips and the phone on her desk.

"I spoke with my colleagues here as well as two other specialists. We've reviewed your records and the results from yesterday's—"

"I'm sure you have. Now tell me where we are."

The other woman took off her glasses and inhaled deeply. "I think you should get your affairs in order, Mary. There's nothing we can do for you."

At four thirty in the morning, Rhage left the hospital in an absolute daze. He'd never expected to go home without Mary.

She'd been admitted for a blood transfusion, and because evidently those night fevers and the exhaustion were also tied to the beginnings of pancreatitis. If things improved she'd be released the next morning, but no one was making any commitments.

The cancer was strong. Its presence had multiplied even in the short time between when she'd had her quarterly checkup a week ago and when the blood test had been taken the day before. And Dr. Della Croce and the specialists all agreed: because of the treatments Mary had already been through, they couldn't give her any more chemo. Her liver was shot and just couldn't handle the chemical load.

God. He'd been prepared for one hell of fight. And a whole lot of suffering, particularly on her part. But never death. And not so fast.

They only had a matter of months. Springtime. Maybe summer.

Rhage materialized in the courtyard of the main house and headed for the Pit. He couldn't bear to go back to his and Mary's room by himself. Not yet.

Except as he stood in front of Butch and V's door, he didn't knock. Instead he looked over his shoulder at the facade of the main house and thought of Mary feeding the birds. He pictured her there, on the steps, that lovely smile on her face, the sunshine in her hair.

Sweet Jesus. What was he going to do without her?

He thought of the strength and resolve in her eyes after he'd fed from another female in front of her. Of the way she loved him even though she'd seen the beast. Of her quiet, shattering beauty and her laugh and her gunmetal gray eyes.

Mostly he thought of her the night she'd torn out of Bella's, running out into the coldness on her bare feet, running out into his arms, telling him that she wasn't okay . . . Finally turning to him for help.

He felt something on his face.

Aw, fuck. Was he crying?

Yup.

And he didn't care that he was going soft.

He looked down at the pebbles in the driveway and was struck by the absurd thought that they were very white in the floodlights. And so was the stuccoed retaining wall that ran around the courtyard. And so was the fountain in the center that had been drained for winter—

He froze. Then his eyes peeled open.

He slowly pivoted toward the mansion, lifting his head up to the window of their room.

Purpose galvanized him and carried him into the vestibule at a dead run.

Mary lay in the hospital bed and tried to smile at Butch, who was sitting in a chair in the corner with his hat and sunglasses on. He'd come as soon as Rhage had left, to guard her and keep her safe until nightfall.

"You don't have to be social," Butch said softly, as if he knew she was struggling to be polite. "You just do your thing."

She nodded and looked out the window. The IV in her arm wasn't bad; it didn't hurt or anything. Then again, she was so numb they could have hammered nails into her veins and she probably wouldn't have felt a thing.

Holy hell. The end had finally come. The inescapable reality of dying was finally upon her. No outs this time. Nothing to be done, no battle to be waged. Death was no longer an abstract concept, but a very real, impending event.

She felt no peace. No acceptance. All she had was . . . rage.

She didn't want to go. Didn't want to leave the man she loved. Didn't want to give up the messy chaos of life.

Just stop this, she thought. *Someone . . . just stop this.*

She closed her eyes.

As everything went dark, she saw Rhage's face. And in her mind she touched his cheek with her hand and felt the warmth of his skin, the strong bones underneath. Words started marching through her head, coming from someplace she didn't recognize, going . . . nowhere, she supposed.

Don't make me go. Don't make me leave him. Please . . .

God, just let me stay here with him and love him a little longer. I promise not to waste the moments. I'll hold him and never let him go . . . God, please. Just stop this . . .

Mary started to cry as she realized she was praying, praying with everything she had, throwing her heart open, begging. As she called out to something she didn't even believe in, an odd revelation came to her in the midst of the desperation.

So this was why her mother had believed. Cissy hadn't

wanted to get off the carnival ride, hadn't wanted the carousel to stop turning, hadn't wanted to leave . . . Mary. The impending separation from love, more than the ending of life, had kept all that faith alive. It was the hope of having a little more time to love that had made her mother hold crosses, and look to the faces of statues, and cast words up into the air.

And why had those prayers focused heavenward? Well, it kind of made sense, didn't it? Even when there were no more options for the body, the heart's wishes find a way out and, as with all warmth, love rises. Besides, the will to fly was in the nature of the soul, so its home had to be up above. And gifts did come from the sky, like spring rain and summer breezes and fall sun and winter snow.

Mary opened her eyes. After blinking her vision clear, she focused on the dawn's nascent glow behind the city's nest of buildings.

Please . . . God.
Let me stay here with him.
Don't make me go away.

FORTY-NINE

Rhage raced into the house, whipping off his trench coat as he pounded through the foyer and up the stairs. Inside their room he ditched his watch and changed into a white silk shirt and pants. After grabbing a lacquered box from the top shelf of the closet, he went to the center of the bedroom and got down on his knees. He opened the box, took out a string of marble-sized black pearls, and put the necklace on.

He sat back on his heels, laid his hands palm up on his thighs, and closed his eyes.

Slowing down his breathing, he sank into the position until his bones, not his muscles, held him in place. He swept his mind clean as best he could and then waited, begging to be seen by the only thing that might save Mary.

The pearls warmed against his skin.

When he opened his eyes he was in a brilliant courtyard of white marble. The fountain here was working splendidly, the water sparkling as it went up into the air and came down into the basin. A white tree with white blossoms was in the corner, the songbirds trilling on its branches the only splashes of color in the place.

"To what do I owe this pleasure," the Scribe Virgin said from behind him. "You have surely not come about your beast. There is quite some time left on that, as I recall."

Rhage remained on his knees, his head bowed, his tongue tied. He found that he didn't know where to begin.

"Such silence," the Scribe Virgin murmured. "Unusual for you."

"I would choose my words carefully."

"Wise, warrior. Very wise. Given what you have come here for."

"You know?"

"No questions," she snapped. "Truly, I am getting tired of having to remind the Brotherhood of this. Perhaps when you return you will recall such etiquette to the others."

"My apologies."

The edge of her black robes came into his vision. "Lift your head, warrior. Look at me."

He took a deep breath and complied.

"You are in such pain," she said softly. "I can feel your burden."

"My heart bleeds."

"For this human female of yours."

He nodded. "I would ask that you save her, if it would not offend."

The Scribe Virgin turned away from him. Then she floated over the marble, taking a slow turn around the courtyard.

He had no idea what she was thinking. Or whether she was even considering what he'd requested. For all he knew she was out for a little exercise. Or about to walk away from him.

"That I would not do, warrior," she said as she read his mind. "In spite of our differences, I would not desert you in that manner. Tell me something—what if saving your female meant you would never be free of the beast? What if having her live meant you must remain in your curse until you go unto the Fade?"

"I would happily keep it within me."

"You hate it."

"I love her."

"Well, well. Clearly you do."

Hope fired in his chest. It was on the tip of his tongue

to ask if they had struck a deal, if Mary could live now. But he wasn't going to risk tipping the balance of the negotiation by pissing the Scribe Virgin off with another question.

She smoothed her way over to him. "You have changed quite a bit since we had our last private meeting in that forest. And I believe this is the first selfless thing you have ever done."

He exhaled, a sweet relief singing in his veins. "There is nothing I would not do for her, nothing I would not sacrifice."

"Fortunate for you, in a way," the Scribe Virgin murmured. "Because in addition to keeping the beast within you, I require you to give up your Mary."

Rhage jerked, convinced he hadn't heard right.

"Yes, warrior. You understand me perfectly."

A death chill went through him, stealing his breath.

"Here is what I offer you," she said. "I can take her out of the continuum of her fate, making her whole and healthy. She will grow no older, she will never be ill, she will decide when she wishes to go unto the Fade. And I will give her the choice to accept the gift. However, as I present the proposal, she will not know of you, and whether or not she consents, you and your world will be ever unknown to her. Likewise, she will not be known by any of those whom she has met, *lessers* included. You will be the only one who remembers her. And if ever you approach her, she will die. Immediately."

Rhage swayed and fell forward, catching himself with his hands. It was a long time before he could squeeze any words from his throat.

"You truly hate me."

A mild electrical shock went through him, and he realized the Scribe Virgin had touched him on the shoulder.

"No, warrior. I love you, my child. The punishment of the beast was to teach you to control yourself, to learn your limits, to focus inward."

He lifted his eyes to her, not caring what she saw in them: hatred, pain, the urge to lash out.

His voice trembled. "You are taking my life from me."

"That is the point," she said in an impossibly gentle tone. "It is yin and yang, warrior. Your life, metaphorically, for hers, in fact. Balance must be kept, sacrifices must be made if gifts are given. If I am to save the human for you, there must be a profound pledge on your part. Yin and yang."

He put his head down.

And *screamed*. Screamed until the blood rushed into his face and stung. Until his eyes watered and all but popped out of his skull. Until his voice cracked and faded into hoarseness.

When he was finished, he focused his eyes. The Scribe Virgin was kneeling in front of him, her robes spilling out all around her, a pool of black on the white marble.

"Warrior, I would spare you this if I could."

God, he almost believed that. Her voice was so hollow.

"Do it," he said roughly. "Give her the choice. I would rather she live long and happily without knowing me than die now."

"So be it."

"But I beg of you . . . let me say good-bye. One last goodbye."

The Scribe Virgin shook her head.

Pain ripped through him, slicing him until he wouldn't have been surprised to find his body bleeding.

"I beg—"

"It is now or not."

Rhage shuddered. Closed his eyes. Felt death come to him as surely as if his heart had stopped beating.

"Then it is now," he whispered.

FIFTY

Butch's first stop when he got home from the hospital was the mansion's upstairs study. He had no idea why Rhage had called and told him to leave Mary's room. His impulse had been to argue with the brother, but the sound of the guy's voice had been freaky, so he'd left it alone.

The Brotherhood was waiting in Wrath's room, all grim and focused. And they were waiting for him. As Butch stared at them all, he felt as if he were about to make a report to the department, and, after a couple months of sitting on his ass, it was good to be back on the job.

Though he was damn sorry his skills were needed.

"Where's Rhage?" Wrath asked. "Someone go get him."

Phury disappeared. When he came back he left the door open. "My man's in the shower. He'll be right with us."

Wrath looked across his desk at Butch. "So what do we know?"

"Not much, although I'm encouraged by one thing. Some of Bella's clothes were gone. She was a neat type, so I could tell it was just jeans and nightgowns, not the kind of stuff she might have taken to a dry cleaners or something. It gives me hope they might want her alive for a while." Butch heard the door shut behind him and figured Rhage had come in. "Anyway, both sites, Mary's and Bella's, were pretty clean, although I'm going to do one more sweep—"

Butch realized nobody was listening to him. He turned around.

A ghost had walked into the room. A ghost who looked a lot like Rhage.

The brother was dressed in white and had some kind of scarf wrapped around his throat. There were white binds on both his wrists, too. All his drinking points, Butch thought.

"When did she go unto the Fade?" Wrath asked.

Rhage just shook his head and went over to one of the windows. He stared out of it even though the shutters were down and he couldn't see anything.

Butch, who was floored by the death that had apparently come so fast, didn't know whether to continue or not. He glanced at Wrath, who shook his head and then got to his feet.

"Rhage? My brother? What can we do for you?"

Rhage looked over his shoulder. He stared at each one of the males in the room, ending on Wrath. "I can't go out tonight."

"Of course not. And we will stay in and mourn with you."

"No," Rhage said sharply. "Bella's out there. Find her. Don't let her . . . go."

"But is there anything we can do for you?"

"I can't . . . I find that I can't concentrate. On anything. I can't really . . ." Rhage's eyes drifted to Zsadist. "How do you live with it? All the anger. The pain. The . . ."

Z shifted uneasily and stared at the floor.

Rhage turned his back to the group.

The silence in the room stretched out.

And then with a slow, halting walk, Zsadist went over to Rhage. When he was standing next to the brother, he didn't say a word, didn't lift a hand, didn't make a sound. He just crossed his arms over his chest and leaned his shoulder into Rhage's.

Rhage jerked as if surprised. The two men looked at each other. And then both stared out the obscured window.

"Continue," Rhage commanded in a dead voice.

Wrath sat back down behind the desk. And Butch started to speak again.

By eight o'clock that night, Zsadist was finished at Bella's.

He poured the last bucket of suds out in the kitchen sink and then put the container and the mop away in the closet next to the garage door.

Her house was now clean and everything was back where it needed to be. When she came home, all she would see was a whole lot of normal.

He fingered the small chain with little diamonds in it that was at his throat. He'd found the thing on the floor the night before, and after he'd fixed the broken link he'd put it on. It barely went around his neck.

He scanned the kitchen one more time and then took the stairs down to her bedroom. He'd refolded her clothes neatly. Slid the dresser drawers back in place. Lined up her perfume bottles again on the vanity. Vacuumed.

Now he opened her closet and touched her blouses and sweaters and dresses. He leaned in and breathed deeply. He could smell her, and the scent made his chest burn.

Those fucking bastards were going to bleed for her. He was going to tear them apart with his bare hands until their black blood ran over him like a waterfall.

With vengeance throbbing in his veins, he went over to her bed and sat down. Moving slowly, as if he might crash the frame, he lay back and put his head on her pillows. There was a spiral-bound book on top of the duvet and he picked it up. Her handwriting filled the pages.

He was illiterate, so he couldn't understand the words, but they were beautifully composed, her penmanship curling into a lovely pattern over the paper.

On a random page, he caught the one word that he could read.

Zsadist.

She'd written his name. He flipped through the journal,

looking closely. She'd written his name a lot recently. He cringed as he imagined the content.

Closing the book, he returned it to the precise spot it had been in. Then he glanced to the right. There was a hair ribbon on the bed stand, as if she'd whipped the thing off before getting into bed. He picked it up and wound the black satin through his fingers.

Butch appeared at the base of the stairs.

Z shot up off the bed as if he'd been caught doing something wrong. Which, of course, he had been. He shouldn't be all over Bella's private space.

But at least Butch didn't seem any more comfortable than he was at their meeting.

"What the hell are you doing here, cop?"

"I wanted to look at the scene again. But I see you're handy with a paper towel."

Zsadist glared across the room. "Why do you care about all this? What's the abduction of one of our females to you?"

"It matters."

"In our world. Not yours."

The cop frowned. "'Scuse me, Z, but given your reputation, what's all this to *you*?"

"Just doing my job."

"Yeah, right. Then why are you marking time on her bed? Why'd you spend hours cleaning up her house? And why are you holding that ribbon so tight your knuckles are white?"

Z looked down at his hand and slowly released his grip. Then he pegged the human with a stare.

"Don't fuck with me, cop. You won't like what comes back at you."

Butch cursed. "Look, I just want to help find her, Z. I gotta . . . It means something to me, okay? I don't like women getting brutalized. I got some nasty personal history with this kind of shit."

444

Zsadist pushed the strip of satin into his pocket and circled the human, closing in on him. Butch sank into a defensive position, waiting for the attack.

Z stopped dead in front of the guy. "The *lessers* have probably killed her already, haven't they?"

"Maybe."

"Probably."

Z leaned forward and took a deep breath. He could smell no fear coming out of the human even though his big body was tense and ready to fight. This was good. The cop was going to need some balls if he really wanted to play in the Brotherhood's sandbox of hell.

"Tell me something," Z muttered. "Will you help me slaughter the *lessers* that took her? You got the stomach for that, cop? Because . . . straight up, I'm going to go crazy over this."

Butch's hazel eyes narrowed. "They take from you, they take from me."

"I'm nothing to you."

"You're wrong about that. The Brotherhood's been good to me, and I stick with my boys, you feel me?"

Z measured the male. The aura Butch threw off was all business. Down-to-the-blood business.

"I don't do gratitude," Z said.

"I know."

Z braced himself and extended his hand. He felt the need to seal the pact between them, even though he was going to hate the sensation. Luckily, though, the human's grip was gentle. Like he knew how hard the contact was for Z to handle.

"We go after them together," the cop said as they dropped their arms.

Z nodded. And the two of them headed upstairs.

FIFTY-ONE

Mary waved as the big Mercedes eased to a stop in front of the hospital. She jogged over at such a clip that Fritz was just getting out of the driver's side as she jumped into the car.

"Thanks, Fritz! Listen, I've called Rhage six times and he's not answering his cell. Is everything okay?"

"All is well. I saw your sire this afternoon."

She beamed at the *doggen*. "Good! And as it's eight o'clock, it's still early for him to have gone out."

Fritz put the car in drive and gently eased into traffic. "Is there anything you require—"

She reached across the seat, threw her arms around the little old man, and kissed him on the cheek. "Take me home fast, Fritz. Faster than you've ever gone before. Break every traffic law."

"Madam?"

"You heard me. As fast as you can!"

Fritz was all flustered from the attention, but he recovered quickly and punched the gas.

Mary put her seat belt on and then popped the visor down and looked at herself in the little lighted mirror. Her hands were shaking as she put them to her cheeks, and giggles broke out of her mouth, especially as the car careened around a corner and she was thrown against the door.

When sirens sounded, she laughed even harder.

"I beg your pardon, madam." The *doggen* glanced over at her. "But I must evade the police and this might get rather bumpy."

"Blow their doors off, Fritz."

The *doggen* flipped something and all the lights in and outside the car were extinguished. Then the Mercedes let out a roar that reminded her of that ride in the GTO with Rhage through the mountains.

Well, except they'd had headlights then.

She grabbed on to the seat-belt strap and shouted over the din of squealing tires, "Tell me you have perfect night vision or something!"

Fritz smiled at her calmly, as if they were just chatting it up in the kitchen. "Oh, yes, madam. Perfect."

With a jerk to the left he swerved around a minivan and then shot down an alley. After slamming on the brakes to avoid hitting a pedestrian, he nailed the gas pedal to the floor again as soon as he had a clear path down the narrow street. Darting out the other side, he cut off a taxi, dodged a bus. Even made an SUV the size of the *QE II* think twice before pulling out in front of him.

The old guy was an artist behind the wheel.

Okay, an artist in a Jackson Pollock kind of way, sure, but amazing nonetheless.

And then he shot into a parking spot. Right on the main drag. Just like that.

The chorus of sirens got so loud she had to yell. "Fritz, they're going to—"

Two police cars sped right by them.

"One more moment, madam."

Another cop car went flying down the street.

Fritz eased out and continued at a brisk pace.

"Nice trick, Fritz."

"With no offense to you, madam, human minds are rather easily manipulated."

As they sped along, she laughed and fidgeted and tapped her fingers on the armrest. The trip seemed to take forever.

When they got to the compound's first set of double gates, she was practically vibrating, she was so excited.

And the moment they pulled up in front of the house, she bolted from the car, not even bothering to shut the door.

"Thanks, Fritz!" she called out over her shoulder.

"You're welcome, madam!" he shouted back.

She burst through the vestibule and bounded up the grand staircase. As she took the corner at the top, going at a dead run, her purse swung out and clipped a lamp. She doubled back and righted the thing before it crashed.

She was laughing out loud as she burst into their bedroom—

Mary careened to a halt.

In the center of the room Rhage was naked and kneeling in a trance on some kind of black slab. He had white binds tied around his neck and wrists. And there was blood dripping onto the rug, though she couldn't see where it was coming from.

His face looked as if he'd aged decades since she'd seen him.

"Rhage?"

His eyes slowly opened. They were opaque, dull. He blinked at her and frowned.

"Rhage? Rhage, what's going on?"

Her voice seemed to snap him to attention.

"What are you—" He stopped. Then shook his head as if he were trying to clear a vision. "What are you doing here?"

"I'm cured! I'm a miracle!"

As she ran to him, he leaped out of the way, holding his hands up and glancing around frantically. "Get out! She'll kill you! She'll take it all back! Oh, God, get away from me!"

Mary stopped dead. "What are you talking about?"

"You took the gift, didn't you!"

"How do you . . . how do you know about that weird dream?"

"Did you take the gift!"

Jesus. Rhage had lost it completely. Shaking, naked, he was bleeding from his shins and white as limestone.

"Calm down, Rhage." Boy, this was *so* not how she'd pictured this conversation going. "I don't know about any gift. But listen to this! I fell asleep while I was getting another MRI and something happened to the machine. It exploded or something, I guess, I don't know, they said there was some flash of light. Anyway, when they took me back upstairs, they drew some blood and everything was perfect. Perfect! I'm clean! No one has any idea what happened. It's like the leukemia just disappeared and my liver fixed itself. They're calling me a medical miracle!"

Happiness poured through her. Until Rhage grabbed her hands and squeezed so hard he hurt her.

"You need to leave. Now. You can't know me. You have to go. Don't ever come back here again."

"What?"

He started pushing her out of the room, and then dragged her when she resisted.

"What are you doing? Rhage, I don't—"

"You have to go!"

"Warrior, you can stop now."

The wry female voice halted them both.

Mary looked over his shoulder. A small figure covered in black was in the corner of the room, light glowing from underneath the flowing robe.

"My dream," Mary whispered. "You were the woman in my dream."

Rhage's arms crushed her as they went around her body, and then he thrust her away from him.

"I did not go to her, Scribe Virgin. I swear, I didn't—"

"Be at ease, warrior. I know you kept the bargain." The small figure floated over to them, not walking, just moving through the room. "And all is well. You just left out one small detail about the situation, something I did not know until I approached her."

"What?"

"You failed to tell me she could no longer bear children."

Rhage looked at Mary. "I didn't know."

Mary nodded and wrapped her arms around herself. "It's true. I'm infertile. From the treatments."

The black robes shifted. "Come here, female. I will touch you now."

Mary stepped forward in a daze as a glowing hand appeared from the silk. The meeting of their palms resulted in a warm electrification.

The woman's voice was low and strong. "I regret that your ability to bring forward life has been taken from you. The joy of my creation sustains me always, and I take great sorrow that you will never hold flesh of your flesh in your arms, that you will not see your own eyes staring at you from the face of another, that you will never mix the essential nature of yourself with the male you love. What you have lost is enough of a sacrifice. To take the warrior from you as well . . . that is too much. As I told you, I give you life eternal until you decide to go unto the Fade of your own volition. And I have a feeling that choice shall be made when it is this warrior's turn to leave the earth."

Mary's hand was released. And all the joy she'd felt drained out of her. She wanted to cry.

"Oh, hell," she said. "I'm still dreaming, aren't I? This is all just a dream. I should have known . . ."

Low, feminine laughter came out of the robes. "Go to your warrior, female. Feel the warmth of his body and know this is real."

Mary turned. Rhage was staring at the figure in disbelief as well.

She stepped up to him, wrapped her arms around him, heard his heart beating in his chest.

The black figure disappeared, and Rhage started speaking in the Old Language, words falling from his mouth so fast she couldn't have understood them even if they'd been in English.

Prayers, she thought—he was praying.

When he finally stopped, he looked down at her. "Let me kiss you, Mary."

"Wait, will you please tell me what just happened? And who she is?"

"Later. I can't . . . I'm not thinking clearly right now. Actually, I'd better go lie down for a minute. I feel like I'm going to faint, and I don't want to fall on you."

She threw his heavy arm over her shoulder and grabbed him around the waist. When he leaned on her, she grunted from the weight.

As soon as Rhage was lying down flat, he tore off the white sashes at his wrists and neck. It was then that she saw that sparkles were mixed with the blood on his shins. She eyed the black slab. There were chips on it, like glass. Or diamonds? God, he'd been kneeling on them. No wonder he'd been cut raw.

"What were you doing?" she asked.

"Mourning."

"Why?"

"Later." He pulled her down on top of him and held her hard.

Feeling his body under hers, she wondered whether it was possible for miracles to actually happen. And not as in the I've-just-had-some-really-good-luck kind, but the mystical, incomprehensible variety. She thought of the doctors racing around with her blood work and her charts. Felt the shock of electricity going through her arm and into her chest as the black-robed figure had touched her.

And she thought about the desperate prayers she'd thrown to the sky.

Yes, Mary decided. Miracles did actually happen in the world.

She started laughing and crying at the same time and drank in Rhage's soothing response to the outburst.

A little later she said, "Only my mother could have believed this."

"Believed what?"

"My mother was a good Catholic. She had faith in God and salvation and eternal life." She kissed his neck. "So she would have believed in all this instantly. And she would have been convinced the mother of God had been under those black robes just now."

"Actually, that was the Scribe Virgin. Who's a lot of things, but not Jesus's mom. At least, not as far as our lexicon goes."

She lifted her head. "You know, my mother always told me I'd be saved whether I believed in God or not. She was convinced I couldn't get away from the Grace because of what she named me. She used to say that, every time someone called out for me or wrote my name or thought about me, I was protected."

"Your name?"

"Mary. She named me after the Virgin Mary."

Rhage's breath caught. And then he laughed softly.

"What's so funny?"

His eyes were a bright, shining teal blue. "Just that V . . . well, Vishous is never wrong. Oh, Mary, my beautiful virgin, will you let me love you for as long as I live? And when I go unto the Fade, will you come with me?"

"Yes." She stroked his cheek. "But does it bother you that I can't have your children?"

"Not in the slightest. I have you, that's all that matters."

"You know," she murmured, "there's always adoption. Do vampires ever adopt?"

"Just ask Tohrment and Wellsie. I can already tell they think of John as their own." Rhage smiled. "You want a

452

baby, I'll get you one. And you know, I might be okay as a dad."

"I think you'll be more than okay."

When she bent down to kiss him, he stopped her. "Ah, there's just one other thing."

"What?"

"Well, we're stuck with the beast. I kind of bargained with the Scribe Virgin—"

Mary pulled back. "You bargained?"

"I had to do something to save you."

She stared at him, stunned, and then closed her eyes. He had set the wheels in motion; he had saved her.

"Mary, I had to trade something—"

She kissed him hard. "Oh, God, I love you," she breathed.

"Even if it means you're going to have to live with the beast? Because the curse is perpetual now. Set in stone. Forever."

"I told you, that's fine with me." She smiled. "I mean, come on. He's kind of cute, in a Godzilla sort of way. And I'll look at it as a two-for-one kind of deal."

Rhage's eyes flashed white as he rolled her over and put his mouth on the side of her neck.

"I'm glad you like him," he murmured, his hands tugging up her shirt. "Because the two of us are yours. For as long as you'll have us."

"That would be eternally," she said as she let herself go.

And reveled in all the love.

Turn the page for an exclusive sneak preview of the
next thrilling instalment in the Black Dagger
Brotherhood series!

Lover Awakened

Available now from Piatkus

Twelve hours after having been rescued from the *lessers* by the Brotherhood, Bella looked around the opulent bedroom she'd been given and felt as if she had to transcribe what she was seeing. The safety she was surrounded by now seemed like another language, one she had forgotten how to speak or read.

She couldn't believe she'd really been saved. Or that she'd been brought to the Brotherhood's compound to recover.

In the corner of the room, the grandfather clock chimed. Now it was thirteen hours, she thought. Thirteen hours since the brothers had come for her and taken her from the earth back into the air.

She pulled the silk robe more tightly around her.

After God only knew how many weeks in that pipe in the ground, being free was alarming. It had been what she'd prayed for, and then given up any hope of, and she felt as though she should be rejoicing. The problem was that everything around her felt fake and insubstantial, especially given the luxury of this room: the heavy velvet drapes, the canopied bed, the museum-quality antiques should have been grounding in their stately beauty. Instead it was all papier-mâché to her.

Only one thing felt real. And she had to find him.

Bella opened the door and put her head out. The hall was empty.

Which was perfect. She didn't want to be seen.

Slipping from the room, she glided over the oriental runner, making no sound at all in her bare feet. When she got to the head of the grand staircase, she paused, trying to remember which way to go.

The corridor with the statues, she thought, remembering another trip down that hall so many, many weeks ago.

She walked quickly and then ran, clutching the lapels of the robe and holding the slit on the bottom closed over her thighs. She passed statues and doors until she remembered the right combination of the two.

As she stopped, she didn't bother to collect herself because she was uncollectible. She was loose, ungrounded, in danger of disintegration. She knocked loudly.

Through the door came a growl. "Fuck off. I've crashed."

She turned the knob and opened.

In the light from the hall, she watched as Zsadist sat up on a pallet of blankets that lay on the floor in the corner. He was naked, his muscles flexing, his nipple rings flashing silver. His fearsome face, with that scar, was full of aggression.

"I said, *fuck off*— Bella?" He covered himself with his hands. "Jesus Christ. What are you doing?"

Good question, she thought as her courage dimmed. "Can—can I stay here with you?"

He frowned as if she'd lost her mind. "What are you— No, you can't."

He grabbed something off the floor and held it in front of his hips as he stood up. She drank in the sight of him: the tattooed slave bands around his wrists and neck, the plug in his left earlobe, his black eyes, his skull-trimmed hair. His body was as starkly lean as she remembered, all striated muscles and hard-cut veins. And he threw off raw power like a scent.

To her, he was utterly beautiful.

"Bella, get out of here, okay? This is not the place for you."

She ignored the command in his eyes and his voice. Because, although her bravery was gone, desperation gave her strength. Now her voice no longer faltered.

"When I was so out of it in the car, you were behind the wheel." When he didn't respond, she said, "Yes, you were. That was you. You spoke to me. You were the one who came for me, weren't you?"

He flushed. "The Brotherhood came for you."

"But you drove me away from there. And you brought me here first. To your room." When he stayed silent, she said, "Let me stay. Please."

"Look, you need to be safe—"

"I am safe only with you. You saved me. You won't let them get me again."

"No one's getting you here. This place is wired like the goddamned Pentagon."

"Please—"

"No," he snapped. "Now get the hell out of here."

She started to shake, fear surging. "I can't be alone. Please let me stay with you. I need to . . ." She needed him specifically, but didn't think he'd respond well to that. "I need to be with someone."

Zsadist ran his hand over his head. A number of times. Then his chest expanded.

"Please," she whispered. "Don't make me go."

He cursed. "I have to put some pants on."

That was as close to a *yes* as she was going to get, she thought.

Bella stepped inside and closed the door, lowering her eyes only for a moment. When she looked up again, he'd turned away and was pulling a pair of black nylon sweats up his thighs.

His back, with its streaks of scars, flexed as he bent over. Seeing the evidence of old wounds, she was struck with the need to know exactly what he'd been through. All of it. Each and every lash. The idea that he knew what it was like to be at the mercy of someone cruel was a powerful common thread.

He'd survived. So had she. They were . . . linked.

459

Zsadist walked over to the bed and pulled the covers back. Then he stood to one side. Awkwardly.

"Get in," he told her.

As she came forward, she noticed that he wore something around his neck—

Oh, my God . . .

"My necklace. You're wearing my necklace."

She reached out to touch it against his skin, but he flinched away and removed the thing.

He dropped it in her hand. "Here. Take it back."

She looked down at the fragile gold and the little diamonds that were set every couple of inches. Diamonds by the Yard. By Tiffany. She'd worn it for years and now couldn't remember what it felt like against her throat.

Such a symbol of the normal life she'd led, she thought. And an opportunity to get back to herself.

She put it into the pocket of the robe, hiding it.

"Have you eaten?" he asked.

She moved a little closer to him. She wanted to throw her arms around him, but he wasn't looking at her. He was staring at the floor.

"Yes, Phury brought me food."

A flicker of expression passed over Zsadist's face. But it was gone so fast she couldn't read it.

"Are you in pain?" he demanded.

"Not particularly."

Please look at me, she thought.

Except he didn't, so she got into the bed. When he leaned down, she scooched over to make room for him.

All he did was pull the covers over her and then go back to the corner, to the pallet on the floor.

Bella closed her eyes for a few minutes. Then she grabbed a pillow, slid out of the bed, and went over to him.

"What are you doing?" His voice was high. Alarmed.

She dropped her pillow next to him and lay down,

easing onto the floor beside his big body. His scent was so much stronger now, smelling of evergreen and pine and distilled male power, and she sought the heat of him, inching closer until her forehead hit the back of his arm. He was so hard, like a stone wall that had been warmed by the sun.

Her body relaxed. Next to him she was able to feel the weight of her own bones, the hard floor underneath her, the currents in the room as the heat came on: his presence somehow helped her connect to the world around her again.

She pushed herself forward with her feet until she was flush against the side of him, from breast to heel.

As he trembled, she recalled that he couldn't bear to be touched, but she couldn't help herself. Not this day. Maybe tomorrow.

"I'm sorry," she whispered. "I need this from you. My body needs . . ." *You.* "Something warm."

Z shifted, moving away until he hit the wall. Then he abruptly leapt to his feet.

Oh, no. He was going to kick her out.

"Come on," he said gruffly. "We're going to the bed. I can't stand the idea of you on the floor."

THE BLACK DAGGER BROTHERHOOD: AN INSIDER'S GUIDE

Prepare to enter the dark, passionate world of the Black Dagger Brotherhood and get up close and personal with each of the Brothers. You'll find insider information on the Brotherhood and interviews with your favourite characters, including a heartbreaking conversation with Tohrment and Wellsie, conducted three weeks before she was killed by *lessers*. You'll discover deleted scenes in addition to exciting material from the J. R. Ward message boards and the answers to questions about the series posed by readers. You'll learn what it's like for J. R. Ward to write each instalment of the series and, in a fascinating twist, you'll read an interview with the author – conducted by the Brothers themselves.

For the first time ever, you'll see a brand new, never-before-published novella about Zsadist and Bella, and witness the miracle of their daughter Nalla's birth. Also, you'll receive a sneak peek at the much-anticipated next book in the *Black Dagger Brotherhood* series, Rehvenge's story.

This is a compendium no *Black Dagger Brotherhood* fan should miss.

978-0-7499-4029-4

'The newest in Ward's ferociously popular Black Dagger Brotherhood series bears all the marks of a polished storyteller completely at home in her world . . . This fix will give Brotherhood addicts a powerful rush'
Publishers Weekly

'Loss, sacrifice, and darkness continue to be major themes as one of Ward's most damaged heroes gets his story. Sex and violence make this tale of emotional redemption unusually graphic and powerful. Ward pulls no punches and delivers an extraordinary paranormal drama'
Romantic Times